THE PIT

Also by Peter Papathanasiou

The Stoning (2021)
The Invisible (2022)

Son of Mine (Salt, 2019) – a memoir

PETER PAPATHANASIOU

THE PIT

MACLEHOSE PRESS

QUERCUS · LONDON

First published in Great Britain in 2023 by

MacLehose Press
An imprint of Quercus Editions Limited
Carmelite House
50 Victoria Embankment
London EC4Y 0DZ

An Hachette UK company

A CIP catalogue record for this book is available
from the British Library.

ISBN (HB) 978 1 52942 447 8
ISBN (TPB) 978 1 52942 448 5
ISBN (Ebook) 978 1 52942 449 2

10 9 8 7 6 5 4 3 2 1

Typeset by CC Book Production
Printed and bound in Great Britain by Clays Ltd, Elcograf S.p.A.

Papers used by MacLehose Press are from well-managed forests and other responsible sources.

For JMC, who helped inspire this story

1

Perth / Whadjuk Noongar Country, 2017

"I want to confess to a murder. I killed a man."

The voice through the phone handset sounded reedy and weak. By contrast, the words it spoke were weighty and unambiguous. There was no more serious crime or grave confession.

The admission seemed to strike Sparrow's ear with force, leaving him momentarily unstable in his ergonomic office chair. The constable who had taken the call on the station's front desk was fresh out of the academy and soon realised that it was no neighbourhood noise complaint or stolen vehicle report. He'd patched the call through to Sparrow, who had just sat down to a shot of freshly brewed coffee. Sparrow held the hot mouthful for a moment, rolling it over his tongue as the grave words settled in his brain.

"Zat right?" he said finally. "You killed a man. You're a bloody murderer."

"Yes," said the voice gently. "I'm a bloody murderer."

Sparrow paused a moment. He'd never had anyone call his phone and voluntarily confess to committing a crime – let alone a murder – with such candour. He had no reason to disbelieve the claim; some of the most vicious murderers were the calmest individuals. His superior officer, Detective Sergeant George Manolis, had said as much before he left for Greece on stress leave, leaving a newly promoted Sparrow under the command of Detective Inspector Paul Bloody Porter. Sparrow still felt like the country mouse, and there was no Manolis to lean on for advice now, or to protect him from the wrath of Porter. But Sparrow knew he needed information, specifics, and ultimately proof. He carefully put down his mug and picked up his biro and notepad.

"Right then, mate," he said casually. "Can we start with some details. First, what's your name?"

"Mr Robert Cooper," said the man without hesitation. "And who am I speaking with?"

"G'day, Robert. My name's Senior Constable Andrew Smith."

"It's nice to meet you, Andrew."

"You can call me Sparrow, everyone else does. Now, can I get your permanent home address, Robert?"

"Well, if I call you Sparrow, you can call me Bob," said the man. "And I'm sure the police can source my home address from this phone number. This is a landline telephone. Remember those?"

Sparrow smiled to himself. "You know us well," he said. "But mate, if you can just provide your address, we can then simply cross-check with our system."

Bob duly obliged. "You'll find it's actually a nursing home," he added. "But please don't hold that against me."

That figured, Sparrow thought. To him, a nursing home explained the wearied nature of the caller's voice, and also suggested advanced years. Sparrow wondered if the bloke was sick, if the confession was prompted by a terminal disease. He thought about the number of similarly heinous admissions that must come from people knocking at death's door, sinners keen to repent before their time ran out, perhaps in the hope of securing a ticket to a better place. Maybe the call to Sparrow's phone was more common than he imagined.

"Thanks, Bob," Sparrow said. "So, how old are you?"

"I'm sixty-five."

"That seems young for a nursing home . . ."

"It is a bit. Oh well."

"And are you married, got a wife, kids?"

"God no," Bob replied. "I am neither married, nor have children. I'm an eternal bachelor." He chuckled lightly.

Sparrow jotted notes. "Righto," he said, mind firmly on the case. "Now, Bob mate, can I ask for some details about the person you claim to have killed. It was another bloke, err, a male individual, you say?"

"Yes. It was a man."

"Right. And when did this occur? Earlier today, yesterday?"

Bob now snorted a much louder laugh. "Sorry, that's just funny to me," he said.

"Murder is funny, Bob?"

"No, I mean it was quite some time ago, a long time ago in fact, coming on some thirty years now, probably before you were even born. I was a young man at the time and physically capable of so much more than I am now. Did you honestly think I was calling with fresh blood on my hands?"

"I didn't think anythin'," Sparrow said swiftly. "I was just askin' a question. We cops don't often get people callin' us up three decades after a murder to confess."

"More's the pity," said Bob. "There must be hundreds of unsolved murders in this State alone. Hundreds of people walking around freely, murderers and rapists and paedophiles, taking their secrets to the grave when they should be locked away and punished for what they done."

"Well, mate, if only everyone was like you."

"Thanks, Sparrow."

"So, lemme ask – why now? Why admit to this crime today when you've clearly been one of those people you just mentioned walking around free for so long?"

Bob sighed heavily. Sparrow almost felt the breath escape the handset and materialise before his eyes.

"Mainly for the man's family, to give them closure," Bob said. "But also for the man himself, for his memory, since I knew him well."

"Knew him well? So, he was a mate?"

"You could say that, yes," Bob replied. "And lastly, and somewhat selfishly, I'm confessing for myself, to clear my conscience, for I fear that I'm not long for this world."

I knew it, Sparrow thought to himself. This fella wants to be spared an afterlife of eternal damnation in the fiery pits of Hell. But it wasn't as if Mr Robert Cooper's motivation actually mattered to the young cop. All that mattered was solving crimes, closing cases, and bringing criminals to justice. He'd had a rough time of it in the outback town of Cobb with the stoning of schoolteacher Molly Abbott and what it did to his small community. It had left him questioning his choices and doubting his motivations. But his time with Manolis and reassignment to the big smoke had changed everything. His first case had been unfortunate; a jammed firearm, Manolis's accidental killing of an innocent youth, an internal investigation. But Sparrow had been cleared of all wrongdoing and was finally on the right path. And he had every intention of taking his chance while Manolis was busy working on his suntan in Greece.

"Sorry to hear that," Sparrow replied. "So, tell me, this bloke – *this mate* – that you killed, when was it? And where, how and why?"

There was a long pause punctuated with several prolonged breaths. Sparrow could tell the sinner was composing himself.

"You've asked a lot there," Bob finally said. "And you can't even begin to imagine the willpower that it took me to call you today, the number of times I had to work myself up, pick up the receiver, dial, put it down again, rehearse what I was going to say. And now, you've done the right thing, you've put me on the spot, asked all the right bloody questions. And I want to give you the answers, but I don't even know where to begin."

"Then begin at the beginning," said Sparrow, clicking his pen. "You said it was about thirty years ago. So that would be, what, about nineteen eighty-two . . . ?"

"Thereabouts," Bob replied. "Maybe 'eighty-one. But not far off. Does it really matter? It was a long time ago, whenever it was exactly."

"Okay, good. And yair, you're right, the exact date doesn't matter. But the location does. Where'd you kill this bloke? Was it here in the city?"

"Actually no, unfortunately not, that would make things very simple and straightforward. It was several thousand kilometres away, to the north, way up in the Kimberley."

The Kimberley was the northernmost region of Western Australia. Bordered to the west by the Indian Ocean, to the north by the Timor Sea, to the east by the Northern Territory, and to the south by two of the world's largest deserts. It was territory that was breathtakingly beautiful, seldom visited, and barely habitable. Despite growing up in the blisteringly hot outback, Sparrow had never been that far north within Australia, let alone to work a cold case murder investigation.

"That's certainly a helluva long way away," Sparrow said. "What were you doing up there?"

"I was working on the mines in the Pilbara at the time," Bob said. "I worked as a dump truck driver, and we sometimes travelled to the Kimberley for a change of scenery, to take a break from work."

"Mines, eh. Was this iron ore?"

"Yes," Bob replied. "Don't let anyone tell you that Australia rode to prosperity on the sheep's back. That may have been the case once, when we had a dignified merino ram's head adorn our shilling, but if that coin was minted today, it would be a dirty lump of iron ore."

"Sounds like you came back a rich man then," Sparrow said.

Bob exhaled. "Some men did," he said. "But I wasn't one of them."

"Whereabouts in the Kimberley did these events happen? Was it a town?"

"It wasn't a town," Bob replied. "In fact, the area was so remote, it was barely on the map."

"Right," Sparrow said, rubbing his forehead, contemplating the prospect of a harder investigation.

"But I remember the area distinctly, crystal clear in my mind's eye, as if it were only yesterday. Things like that, you don't easily forget."

Sparrow cleared his throat. "Can I ask the dead bloke's name?"

"You can, but I couldn't tell you," said Bob. "I didn't know his name, I only ever knew his nickname. Nicknames were all some blokes had back then. Those were different times."

"We still have nicknames now," Sparrow said. "But we also have real names, and we had real names then as well."

"Be that as it may, I still couldn't tell you his real name. The mine owners hardly knew them either. The region attracted all manner of scum and outlaws, men on the run from the law and from women, men who wanted to disappear. The mine owners didn't ask many questions. All they cared about was whether you could bend your back."

"And the dead bloke was a good mate of yours?"

"Well, now that I remember, he was more of an acquaintance. And I never learned his name, so I can't tell you what I don't know."

Sparrow leaned back in his chair and eyed the ceiling tiles above his head. A few had come loose and were hanging precariously.

"Mr Cooper, Bob mate, listen," Sparrow said. "You'll have to excuse all my questions but I gotta do all this to verify your story. There are heaps of people walking into cop stations across the country every day or calling us claiming this and that, only for us to investigate their stories and find out that they're complete bullshit. These people have done nothing more than waste valuable police time. I don't want to dismiss you as one of them, as a time-waster, an attention-seeker. But before I take this any further and try to allocate resources, I need some precise details so I can take you seriously."

There was a protracted pause. Sparrow expected the phone to go dead at any moment, for the fraudster to be scared away. The man, this Mr Robert Cooper, was supposedly calling from a nursing home. Sparrow reasoned that there was a distinct possibility that he might even have dementia. He thought to say that, but it would've meant nothing. In the end, he kept quiet and kept listening.

Eventually, a dry cough rattled down the phone line.

"What you say is not unexpected," said Bob. "I realise you're only doing your job, and as a man of law, you need a certain amount of evidence to please your masters, to please the court, and secure a conviction. And that's what I want too. So, tell you what – I'll give you the best evidence of all . . ."

It was a proposition. Bob offered to personally escort Sparrow to the murder scene, where he'd buried the man's body. Through exhumation and the use of forensic DNA analysis in the lab, he was confident that reliable genetic identification of the dead man's skeleton could be made and cross-checked against reports of missing persons. His family would be notified, and Bob would be willingly, and gratefully, locked away for the remainder of his natural life.

"There are just a few conditions," Bob said. "First of all, I like you, Sparrow. I feel we have an immediate rapport, and I think I have a sixth sense for people who are inherently good. So, I'd like to ask if you would accompany me to the Kimberley."

Sparrow put down his pen. What was now being discussed didn't need documentation.

"You mean, just the two of us?" he asked. "As in, off the record?"

"I mean you as the only police officer."

"But I would need to discuss this with my commanding officer, get his approval. Personally, I don't have a problem but I suspect I'll be told to take backup."

"Hmm, I'm not so sure about that, mate. I just want *you* to work this case. Don't you want to arrest the villain and be the hero?"

Of course, Sparrow did. It was a chance to make a name for himself – even if it wasn't strictly by the book, solving a murder was still solving a murder. But was this Mr Robert Cooper worth the risk? He didn't come across as a threat in any way. He wanted to do things on his terms. And being able to see things from an elderly pensioner's perspective surely showed maturity, not immaturity.

"Yair, sure," Sparrow said. "So, what do you suggest?"

"Well, I imagine you have some annual leave up your sleeve."

"Hmm, maybe. And what if I do?"

"Take it with me, work this case and I'll pay for your time."

Sparrow paused. "That doesn't seem unfair," he said.

"Excellent then," said Bob. "See how easy that was. As for the journey, there'll actually be three of us making it. You, me, and my friend."

"Wait, hold on. Who is your 'friend'?"

"My mate here in the nursing home. His name's Luke."

"What's his role in all this? Was he involved in the murder? Is he your accomplice?"

Bob laughed. "Far from it, he wasn't even born when these events happened. He'd be closer to your age than mine. Luke's just my mate here in the home. He's my only mate, and we look after each other."

Sparrow pretended to consult his calendar. Was he really going to use his leave and go through with this? What would Manolis do?

"When?" Sparrow asked. "When do you wanna travel? It's January, school holidays, middle of summer, so commercial flights are expensive and hard to come by. But we might be able to book something in the next few days and—'

"Flights?" said Bob. "Oh no, I'm afraid I can't fly. My medical condition precludes air travel."

"So, what are you suggestin'?" Sparrow asked, half-expecting the answer.

"We'll need to drive," Bob said. "That's our only option. I'll provide the vehicle. Now, given the distances involved, it'll take a few days. But we'll see some absolutely spectacular scenery on the way, that I promise you. And I can also promise it'll be the journey of a lifetime. One you'll never forget."

2

Perth / Whadjuk Noongar Country, 2017

The city's silver skyscrapers jutted up like nails hammered into the earth. Reflected white in their polished glass, the rising sun assailed Sparrow's eyes. He squinted, in need of sunglasses. Sitting in the passenger seat, he instinctively reached up to lower a sun visor that wasn't there. The odometer nudged a third digit on the dial.

"So where are we headed, dude?"

The query was impatient and came from the back seat. Bob, who was both driver and navigator, paused, distracted.

"Jesus Christ," Bob finally said. "Look at all these new roads. I used to know these streets like the back of my hand. Glorious Perth now looks more like goddamn Sydney. How does anyone get anywhere anymore?"

Even with its high roof, the Toyota Hiace van was dwarfed by hordes of four-wheel drives, mobile discotheques that made the windows rattle as they rumbled past. It felt like it could fall to pieces at any time on the freeway. Sparrow had already checked the air conditioner and found it only blew hot air and moth skeletons. The van's interior smelled musty and medicinal: bad breath, body odour and dead skin.

Sparrow had rendezvoused with the Hiace on a pre-determined street corner not far from his apartment at a pre-determined time. The hour was early, not long after dawn on a Monday, which Bob had insisted upon since it maximised driving time. He paid Sparrow in advance, a generous cash sum that both affirmed his commitment to the venture and avoided a paper trail. Porter hadn't been thrilled with Sparrow's sudden request for annual leave, but Sparrow knew the payoff would be worth it when he brought in a body and a culprit in cuffs.

On first impression, Sparrow had found Bob to be of sound mind. He appeared lucid and conversational, if a little lost. But Sparrow had to admit that all the new roadworks in Perth confused him too and that he was still finding his own way around. By contrast, Luke came across as immature and tempestuous, despite being confined to a wheelchair.

"Bob, stop fucking around!" Luke said. "I'll guide us. Just tell me where the fuck we're heading."

"Hey!" Bob said, flicking his head back. "Quit swearing while I'm at the wheel."

"Whoa! When did this become a problem, man?"

Bob took a moment to respond. "It's always been a problem," he said. "I've just never said anything before. It's worse when I'm trying to concentrate, doing a hundred on a busy highway."

Sparrow sensed a tension in the air, as if it had taken on a pre-storm stillness. But even good friends argued from time to time.

"I'm sure Bob's just trying to keep us from getting lost here," Sparrow said calmly.

"Oh yeah?" Luke said defensively. "Well, it's apparently okay for him to blaspheme, but not for me to swear."

Bob paused again. "That's different."

"So, what can I say instead?" Luke asked.

"Dunno," said Bob. "Maybe 'frig' or 'eff'. Or just not at all."

Luke went quiet for some time. "Friggin' hell," he eventually said.

"Better," said Bob.

Sparrow had packed a single bag, filled it with enough socks and jocks to last a week. Bob introduced him to Luke as his "hired carer", his "personal aide", since they would obviously need assistance to make the trip north. Bob had asked Sparrow to not reveal the purpose of their mission to Luke; another condition. Sparrow was getting suspicious but went along with the story. Now that he'd met both Bob and Luke, he didn't see either of them as any threat.

"Spare him the details," Bob had said. "He's got nothing to do with what happened thirty years ago. I feel sorry for the kid, confined to a wheelchair and forced to live in a nursing home with old people. You're young, can you imagine what that would be like? I'm his only mate in there, and just want to show him a little fun before I'm locked away. Can you at least do me that favour?"

Sparrow couldn't help but empathise with the young man's plight. He'd heard of unfortunate cases where young disabled people ended up in nursing homes because they had no-one to care for them. Bob explained that Luke had been orphaned when his parents died in a car accident. It was tempting to see Bob as benevolent and big-hearted, but Sparrow reminded himself this was supposedly a murderer he was trusting, and was doing so on his own time, so he remained apprehensive. Nonetheless, he had stashed his police firearm securely in the pocket of his combat pants and planned to keep his phone on to triangulate his geographic position, even though he imagined they would eventually be out of range.

"I think I finally know where we're going," said Bob. "Provided the ocean's still in the same place. They haven't moved *that*, have they?"

"Don't be stupid," said Luke. "The ocean's right where—'

A Western Australian police van pulled up alongside the Hiace and silenced the cabin instantly. Bob even turned the radio down. Would Sparrow somehow be recognised? It seemed unlikely. He watched Luke swallow his words. Sparrow wasn't sure what to make of it at first, but it dawned on him that his travel companions were potentially two fugitives on the lam.

"Be cool," Bob said to Luke, rolling up his window. "Nothing to fear."

The fat cop stuffed into the driver's seat kept his eyes on the road until he saw what he was looking for up ahead. His siren wailed into life and the paddy wagon roared after a swerving ute with all the muscle trimmings. Bob exhaled and rolled down his window. He shot a sideways glance at Sparrow who returned a look of reassurance. Given what was at stake, their secret was safe with him; for now.

The first rays of sun on the van's vinyl interior liberated all manner of new odours hidden deep inside the seating. Ammonia and uric acid, stale sweat and menthol, seeped into the cracks. Sparrow's eyes watered, the air packed tight around his face. He leaned sideways out the window and rode with his nose in the hot January wind.

Bob piloted the van as far west as it could go, to the coast, the western edge of the vast Australian continent. He then reefed the steering wheel hard right and headed north for the equator. They parked near the water on Scarborough Beach. Clicking open the rear door, Sparrow flicked a big red switch on the inside of the van. The hydraulic lifter fell back like a rusty drawbridge. He unfastened the wheelchair's tie-down straps. Luke's chair hummed into position and descended to the earth like a spaceship landing.

The trio were soon sitting in a café overlooking the ocean. Luke and Sparrow had the pleasure of watching, in Bob's opinion, the sweetest sight imaginable – him inhaling a Black Angus sirloin. It wasn't on the breakfast menu, but Bob's bulging wallet had insisted they prepare him one.

"The thickest bastard you've got, with all the fat, no butter or pepper sauce or garnish," was how Bob had placed his order. "And as blue as buggery."

Sparrow ordered raisin toast and coffee. Luke had blueberry pancakes and two vanilla milkshakes.

"To be honest, I could smell the sheep," Bob said, his mouth full.

"What sheep?" Luke asked. He slurped his second milkshake from a tall stainless-steel cup beaded with condensation. "That there's cow on your plate."

"No, mate." Bob swallowed. "I meant there's obviously a big ship with sheep at the port today. When it's hot and humid, you can smell their urine and faeces."

"Gross!"

"Couldn't you smell it?" Bob asked. "From the trucks ahead of us on the highway. People complain, but I always remember it as part of Fremantle's charm. You want another shake?"

Luke burped. It smelled sickly sweet. "Nah, I'm chockers."

"Me too. But I'm tempted to order another steak just because I can. How about you, Sparrow, another flat white?"

"No thanks," said Sparrow. "I'm awake enough."

Luke examined Sparrow crookedly from beneath the brim of his black baseball cap. Sparrow felt surprisingly self-conscious. He was familiar with the feeling of people sizing him up in his role as a police officer, and also as a young Aboriginal man in Australia, but he wasn't used to pretending to be something he was clearly not. He wondered if the kid was buying it. Did kids ever buy anything anymore . . .? Their whole lives were an exercise in cynicism and disillusionment.

"Bob told me you used to be a nurse," Luke said to Sparrow. "You don't look like no nurse to me. And I've seen heaps."

"What's that supposed to mean?" Sparrow said.

"Where'd you train?" Luke asked sharply.

Sparrow swallowed hard. "Where'd you reckon? At a university, a nursing degree. You need to see it?"

"Send it to my people."

"Nurses take all shapes and forms these days. Even blackfellas like me can be nurses."

Luke smiled sharp yellow teeth. "Nurse, eh. We'll see. We'll see soon enough."

Bob piped up to change the subject. "By the way, mate, I noticed you left all your artwork behind."

"Meh," Luke said. "They're just drawings. I can pick 'em up someday. Or I can do more."

Bob called for the bill. In addition to Sparrow's time, he'd said he would be paying for everything on the trip north – Sparrow's wallet wouldn't be needed. The bill was delivered by a skinny young man with more sleeve tattoos than skin and more metal in his ears than cartilage. Sparrow thanked him. He flashed an unnaturally white smile.

"In the history of all mankind, that was the best fifty-dollar steak anyone has ever eaten," Bob told his companions. He licked his lips.

Pulling out his kangaroo-leather wallet, Bob slapped two pineapples on the table. "That's our food and drinks," he said. "But what tip should I leave?"

"Ten per cent?" said Sparrow.

"Stuff that," Luke said. "Leave zero per cent. The service was crap. Our food took forever. My pancakes were overcooked. Sparrow's coffee looked like dishwater."

"It was fine," Sparrow said simply.

"Plus I reckon the bloke who served us drills for Vegemite," Luke added.

The hairs on Sparrow's neck bristled, while Bob's eyes grew large.

"Agreed," Bob said. "With almost all of that. For what they charged, it wasn't great. But they didn't have to cook my steer so early in the morning, and they still didn't complain."

Bob fished a third fifty-dollar bill from his wallet and added it to the yellow-green pile. Sparrow nodded approvingly. Luke arched his eyebrows and shook his head lightly.

"Don't be like that," Bob said. "That's good karma. Where we're heading, we'll need it."

From the promenade, the three men watched a big green tractor shuttling between land and sea. A front-end loader was replacing the dunes being washed away by the dumping waves. Another tractor pulling a sandboni raked the beach clear of hypodermic needles and beer bottles. Three British backpacker girls squealed in the water, their hair peroxide, skin orange, breasts plastic. The Indian Ocean was sable-blue and clear, with frothy white crests that sizzled on the sand. The light was crisp, clean. Razor-sharp shadows fell across the ground. Bob stretched his arms out wide, opened his palms, extended his arthritic fingers. Sparrow watched him breathe in deeply. It was as if he couldn't get enough rejuvenating sea air into his ragged old lungs.

The group made their way onto the beach. Bob bent down and slipped off his Blundstone boots and work socks. He stepped forward to feel the hot sand between his toes and taste the sticky salt on his lips. Sparrow stood uncomfortably, checking his watch, eyeing the angle of the burning-hot sun, feeling it scalding his skin. Luke didn't move. He couldn't move. He remained in his motorised wheelchair on the concrete, his gaze fixed on the water. Sparrow suddenly realised that unlike the van, the beach didn't come with an electrical hoist.

"Strewth," Bob said. "Sorry, mate. Wait a sec . . ."

Sparrow accompanied Bob as they approached two bronzed life-guards. Bob pointed back at Luke, explaining the situation.

"Is he, like, okay, mentally?" one of the guards asked.

Sparrow wanted to tell them that he still needed to properly grow up and mature, but he knew what they meant.

"Oh yes, absolutely," Bob replied. "He just can't use his legs or right arm."

"Well, I reckon it's great you can still enjoy the beach with your son," the other guard said.

The two lifeguards had biceps like Christmas hams. Together, they lifted Luke from his chair and removed his clothes, leaving only his tight black jocks in place. Sparrow and Bob stood back a metre, watching the process closely. Bob moistened his thin dry lips with a sandpaper tongue. Muscles tensing, the guards carried Luke down to the surf using a two-handed seat carry. Cradling his flabby body between them, they let Luke half float in the water in their brawny lifeboat arms. Bob sat where the surf flirted with the sand, hearing laughter above the music of the waves.

"Fucken aye!" Luke was saying.

A big wet woolly dog materialised from nowhere to shake Sparrow an impromptu shower and attempt to lick Bob's face, then disappeared just as quickly.

Sparrow considered his suspect and the situation. It felt surreal to be on the road under such circumstances. False confessions were common in criminal investigations. Some people made them to protect others, some to bolster their own reputations and earn notoriety. What did this old man stand to gain other than a clear conscience . . .? A confession on its own was insufficient for a conviction, particularly when it came to murder; proof was needed. And if Sparrow chose to arrest Bob on suspicion of murder, the old man had made it clear he'd immediately stop cooperating. What danger was Sparrow truly in . . .? He was armed and travelling with two relatively harmless individuals, a pensioner and a paraplegic. And so far, the trip had felt more like a fully paid summer holiday than a criminal investigation, and it was his choice how he spent his leave.

"That was a bloody nice thing to do," Sparrow told Bob.

"The poor kid hasn't been in the surf in years," he said. "It's the least I can do."

A tennis ball flew back and forth between two packs of teenagers wrestling in the surf. Further out, windsurfers ricocheted across the water like skipping stones.

Bob held up his fingers and felt the stretchy leathered skin on his face. Sparrow saw that he was smiling.

Back on the road, Luke had exhausted every superlative in his lexicon in describing his day at the beach.

"Those lifeguards were better than the nurses," he said. "Effing strong bastards. Bet they pull chicks like nuthin' else."

Bob glanced at him in the rear-view mirror. "I bet they do too," he smiled.

"And the water . . . Jesus, I feel great!"

"Glad you liked it," Bob said. "I did too. My sixty-five-year-old body feels like its actual age, not eighty-five. Have a good time, Sparrow?"

"Yair," he replied. "I'm originally from inland, so I didn't really grow up with the water. I can't swim but I've always found the ocean to be healing, especially for my patients." He sold the lie as best he could.

"But hey, Bob, you kept your shirt on," said Luke. "And I thought I'd finally get to see your tatts."

Bob flashed a grin. "Show 'em to you later," he said.

"So where to now, aye, me Cap'n?"

It was the second time that Luke had asked where they were going. Sparrow looked across at Bob who kept his eyes fixed on the road ahead. It seemed he had no intention of revealing the reason behind their "escape" from the nursing home. At least, not yet.

"You'll see," was all Bob said. "It's a surprise."

Their next stop was thirty minutes down the West Coast Highway, past the open dunes and giant red Dingo sign on the flour mill. They crossed the serpentine Swan River and rattled into East Fremantle. The traffic was backed up on High Street and into Fremantle proper, near the golf course as the road turned into the Leach Highway. Every car had a personalised number plate, every driver an attention-seeker. They stopped and got out when a distinctive angular lightning bolt on a black metal gate came into view. Luke's eyes lit up.

"Fuck yes!" he said.

"Language!" said Bob.

Luke pounded the armrest of his wheelchair with glee using his good arm. "Quick, roll up my sleeve," he said. "I want him to see."

Ronald "Bon" Scott's grave was marked by a modest brass plaque no larger than a paperback novel. Mementos left by his legions of fans adorned it. Guitar picks, beer bottle tops, dollar coins, empty whiskey bottles. It was a fitting visual eulogy for a man who choked on his own vomit after a night of heavy drinking in wintry South London in 1980.

With the messy parrot tattoo on his arm looking even uglier in the morning sun, Luke reached into his bumbag and retrieved a cigarette. He sparked it and eased back in his chair, inhaling a cool lungful of tar. "How awesome is that?" he said. "That's how I want my grave to look."

Sparrow stood beside him, his weight on one leg. Careful what you wish for, he thought.

"We're both massive fans," Bob explained to Sparrow.

"I figured," he replied. "I like AC/DC too."

Luke made a big O with his mouth and puffed out two perfect smoke rings.

"Those things will bloody kill ya," Bob said. "When you gonna give up?"

"Give it a rest. How long did it take you to quit?"

Bob didn't answer.

"I just stopped smoking," said Sparrow. "Cold turkey. Never felt better."

"C'mon," Bob said. "We gotta keep moving."

"Where to now?" Luke asked.

"We can't stay here in the city," Bob said. "It's too risky, there's too many people, too much traffic and noise. We need less of everything around us, we need space."

Sparrow nodded in furious agreement.

"So what do we do?" asked Luke. "Where do we go?"

"We leave," Sparrow said. "We leave town."

"Leave town . . . ?" Luke's tone suggested the idea was brand new to him.

"Nurse Sparrow is right," Bob said. "We can't stay here, that's suicide. But first, there's something we need to get a hold of . . ."

It was a quick stop at a nearby pub on Riverside Road overflowing with thirsty patrons. Luke and Sparrow stayed in the van, watching Bob operate through the window. Bob took a deep breath, ran a wet finger of saliva over both eyebrows, and entered the sweaty beer garden. There were a few targets to pick from, but he marched right up to the first group of pot-bellied men dressed in hi-vis yellow and orange. A few minutes of intense negotiations followed. In the end, Bob handed over a thick wad of notes and returned to the car with his bounty.

"Jesus Christ," Bob said. "Those gorillas wanted to haggle, and then ripped me off blind. But bugger 'em, I got the shirts. And they even got corporate logos as a bonus. Here . . ."

Bob handed out two brightly coloured shirts. Sparrow's was orange, Luke's yellow.

"What'd you say to those guys?" Sparrow asked.

"Not much," Bob replied. "Just offered to buy their work shirts. They didn't ask why I wanted them, the only issue was price. That's all anyone cares about around here – money, cash. Anyway, mission accomplished. Now we look like every other mining bastard out there. More or less."

Bob fired the engine, pointed the van north, and made the tyres squeal. They filled up on unleaded at the first servo they came across and bought three matching pairs of Aviator sunglasses. Sparrow opened the glovebox, checked the outdated street directory, and located the nearest artery out of the city. Evening came. The Hiace was soon passing through pockets of apricot street light. A strange feeling of comfort washed over Sparrow as a bright canopy of stars filled the windscreen.

"Okay, old boy," Luke said. "So, you wanna tell me where we're headin' and why?"

Bob stayed silent, his focus on the headlights and the darkening road, with only the sound of the rushing air pouring in through the cracked windows.

"Well," Luke said. "Gonna tell me?"

Nurse Sparrow looked across at Bob, whose expression remained fixed. Finally, Bob said, "We're probably driving on a highway to Hell."

And pushed his foot to the floor.

Bob

So then, young Sparrow... You've been immensely obliging so far, indulging me in my strange request to travel north. You obviously have your own interests at play – promotion, glory, and what not – and I also have mine. But the difference is that I hold all the cards. You are trusting me. And so, it seems the least I can do – the fairest thing – is to show you some of my hand and fill you in on what actually happened in the past, and what now leads us on this foolish journey to nowhere. I made this choice, to head through the red-hot guts of Western Australia, as crazy or as stupid as it was. It was certainly no Kerouac On the Road *malarkey. And I could've taken only you and gone together, just the two of us. But in the end, for better or worse, I decided to take the kid with us.*

And that's the thing – I'm only telling this story to you, not to Luke. He doesn't deserve to know the background and what I went through. But you do. You're like me, I can tell. You'll understand, I know you will. This is as much a journey for your own personal growth as it is for Luke. Except I trust you with my secrets, too.

And besides, I'm not about to tell Luke that if we succeed on our journey north, life will never be the same again.

3

Perth / Whadjuk Noongar Country, 1969

Bob

At seventeen, I had the strapping body of a full-grown man. The night I leapt from the carriage before the train had fully stopped, my big heart filled my ears with its own beat. The moon was out, full and high. It lit my way along the leafy avenues of Nedlands. The night was warm. The night was mine.

I pounded through the sleepy suburb under tall swaying eucalypts. I felt like I was flying under the radar and tried to drown out my thoughts by hitting the asphalt harder. I was running to leave my parents' world behind.

My mother was at home passed out on the couch. A devout alcoholic, she never missed an evening liturgy. My father was in bed, snoring until his pre-dawn start at the docks. It was this firm commitment to parenting that had led my parents Cliff and Norma Cooper to send their only child to the nearby Catholic boys' boarding school.

I was soon puffing and removed my white T-shirt. My chest and back were sweaty. My denim jeans felt hot and tight, and my thin sandshoes hurt. I forced large gulps of air into my lungs. Dogs barked. I ran harder, faster, further.

My schoolteachers had been moral protectors of the highest order. Flowing black robes, heavy wooden rulers they would thwack onto my nefarious left hand whenever they saw me using it to write. I had shared a room with seven other pale boys, all of whom could trace their forebears to the British Isles. In the evenings, a compulsory shower before bed. Clean body, clean mind, they said. It was only then, during that brief hour after bland meat and limp two veg, that I first caught a glimpse of my true self. I was inspired.

That true self now eased its pace to a fast walk on reaching the last street in Crawley. Just beyond, the river serpentined its way through the sleepy city. I wiped my face with my T-shirt, pulling it over my head, letting it soak the sweat on my back. I had covered the two miles in Olympic time. My destination, silent and dark, lay ahead – the park in Matilda Bay.

Sitting on the dry grass, I leaned my back against a wooden street post. I lit a cigarette to calm my breathing. The park was adjacent to the University of Western Australia, and less peopled during summer with students away. A few cars were parked by the side of the road, all appearing unoccupied. The silhouette of a possum scurried across the ground and disappeared up a tree. The last cooling gasp of the Fremantle Doctor sea breeze whistled through the leaves and rocked the yachts moored on the river, their naked masts swaying metronomically. I ran an unsteady hand through my windswept hair and flared my nostrils at the faint waft of peppermint in the air. My eyes darted left, right, left again. Not a soul. My foot tapped the ground restlessly.

Now came the hard bit.

Willing myself to stand, I dusted off my shirt and jeans and moved quickly across the grass. I stopped with my back against a long row of melaleuca bushes. Drawing hard on my cigarette, I made the end glow lava orange and let it hover. But no-one returned my signal with their own bright flare of tobacco. Just another scampering possum and the dim lemony lights of the suburbs on the southern side of the river.

I extinguished my beacon and made a mad dash for the concrete toilet block near the river's edge. I flung myself into the first stall, turned the latch, and locked the door.

My chest heaved, threatening to burst open, even if all that pounded inside was the heart of a scared bird gripped by an unfamiliar hand. A flush of heat pooling in my belly and another in my head nearly made me pass out. There was a distinct wheeze to my breathing. I reached down, felt for the cold porcelain, and sat on the bowl.

The toilet block stank of stale urine, salt and moss. It was damp and held a chill. A slab of beef wouldn't have gone off in there. The taps dripped. The walls were covered with scrawls and carvings from previous encounters. An access hole the size of a fist was cut into the wooden partition between the two stalls, blocked up with thick wads of crumpled toilet paper. It was the last place on earth I wanted to be. And yet, all I could do was smile. I had made it. Now all I needed to do was savour the anticipation. And wait.

Boarding school had changed everything. My parents hadn't allowed me home leave on weekends like the other kids. On one occasion, when all the beds in my dorm room were unoccupied, I'd turned to my feather pillow, under the covers, not long after the lights went out, all alone. At first, I didn't realise what had happened, fearing the wrath of the Brethren when I thought I'd wet myself. For a brief period around the age of ten, I quite honestly believed that babies were made after a man pissed inside a woman.

A boisterous little imp named Greg Wilson provided enlightenment. One evening, he ran around naked with the other boys after the showers, before finally sitting at the end of my bed.

"Gotta show you this . . ."

Red-faced and panting, sandy-haired Wilson started banging away with his tiny fists.

It only took him a few frantic seconds to spill his glob. Fortunately, Brother Ryan missed the spot on the floorboards when he burst in a minute later ordering, "Lights out!"

In the showers, the boys took great delight in watching fingers disappear. I thought it was more intimate than anything I'd ever experienced and loved how warm it felt under the cold shards of Catholic water.

Attachment after such episodes came to me readily. I wanted more than fingers. I wanted to hug and rub and kiss and to be kissed. But I didn't know how to say any of that, or how it would be received. So I went mute.

The Brothers preached chastity, followed by the noble transmission of life through marriage of a man and woman. "Flesh is the hinge of salvation," they told the boys. "The conjugal act between a man and a woman forms one heart and soul. It is a sign of the love between God and humanity." Meanwhile, what I had playing on loop inside my head was proclaimed a "detestable, filthy, sinful vice".

Back then, newspaper banner headlines screamed when "evil perverts" were arrested, named and publicly humiliated.

"These dirty animals, corrupting society," Cliff had said more than once.

"Yes, dear," Norma would reply calmly. "Remember your blood pressure."

A sudden noise like a snapping twig outside the toilet block made my ears prick up. For several heartbeats, I was unable to think and could only hear.

But there was just the wind, howling from the distant Indian Ocean.

A minute later, another *ka-rack*, then a tapping, a thud, a click.

I held my breath, felt a strange quickening in my blood. Swift footsteps, then the door to the second stall was slammed shut and locked. The new resident let out a light moan as they eased onto their own bowl. The entire world outside fell away and it was just the two strangers, our asynchronous breathing, the night air so thick with anticipation that I could taste it. I closed my eyes and flashed a broad grin.

I tried to picture what my neighbour might look like.

Elvis. Yes. Elvis would do nicely.

I refrained from looking through the hole and sending Elvis from the building, running into the night. There was no talking. Talk only got in the way of action. And time was of the essence, getting it over and done with as quickly as possible.

With no movement from my neighbour, I decided to start the dance.

Gently and methodically, I tapped my left foot three times in a way that was visible beneath the partition.

The wait was only a few seconds. My neighbour responded with a similar tap. I blushed. It felt like receiving a bright, beautiful smile. Slowly, I moved my left foot closer to the partition and smiled back. A second later, my neighbour moved their right foot closer. I only saw a grubby sandshoe, though pictured it as blue suede. Another three taps, returned by three more. Inch by inch, our two feet moved closer. Until we touched. A jolt of electricity surged up my left leg, bathing my entire body in a warm glow before concentrating in my groin. A brief game of footsie, two sneakers copulating clumsily.

And that was it. It was time. Any longer and we would only be wasting it.

I reached down to prepare myself through my jeans. At least I had retained my left-handedness for some things. I heard my neighbour's latch unlock, the hinges squeaking as the door swung open. It was decided – I would be the home team. I suddenly felt self-conscious, as if company was coming over and my bachelor pad needed tidying. I examined the filthy stall and rearranged the rolls of toilet paper atop the cistern into a neat pyramid. Noticing the roll already in the holder, I re-hung it in its correct overhang orientation, and gently put the toilet lid down. There. Lovely.

I swallowed one last time. I undid my belt, unbuttoned my fly, and reached forward to unlock the latch. I nudged the door ajar. It was now or never, come hold me tight . . .

The door flung open violently, almost off its hinges. With the moon behind him, the stranger's hulking frame cast a shadow that engulfed me in darkness. Only there were more shadows, growing in size and volume. They shouted over each other and pinned me to the cubicle wall, my clavicle crunching against the cold ceramic. A kick to my lower back forced me down onto my knees. Sharp spokes of pain shot down my legs. A large set of fingers took hold of my hair, pulling hard, dragging me along the slick wet floor. The toilet seat flipped up, my head was wrenched around and shoved roughly into the bowl. I struggled, arms flailing, the smell of piss and shit and grime. Flushed water forced its way into my ears and nostrils, up my nose and into my mouth, hard and metallic. I heard more shouting, echoey and muffled through water-logged ears. Turning my head to face the shadows, I felt the toilet seat slam down, and found myself unable to breathe. Darkness flooded my brain as the pressure crushed my windpipe.

4

Wheatbelt / Ballardong Noongar Country, 2017

The city limits blurred past. The Hiace was soon out on the open road, barrelling along the Great Eastern Highway, leaving in its wake a twisted mess of bloodied roadkill and shattered speed limits.

Sparrow, Bob and Luke spent their first night in a roadside motel that stank of cigarettes and pine air freshener. With no hydraulic lifter to help with manoeuvring Luke out of his wheelchair, improvisation was needed. Sparrow was lucky to find an old boat windscreen by the road-side next to an abandoned car. The windscreen doubled as a makeshift sliding board and a thick elastic occy strap acted as a rudimentary gait belt. With a little heavy lifting, the contraption worked a treat.

In the morning, Sparrow got his first taste of what it meant to be a real carer when he emptied what Luke called his "gross bag" down the toilet. Sparrow had to turn his head to save his nose – Luke's diet needed an overhaul, with a focus on fibre. Sparrow then sterilised the prosthesis with a cotton ball and what droplets of Jack Daniels remained in the bottom of the bottle that Bob and Luke had polished off before bed.

"Thanks, mate," Luke said gently. "I know that's pretty disgusting."

"It is what it is," Sparrow lied. "And it's nothin' I haven't dealt with before."

Luke gave him a lopsided smile.

They checked out of their room and set off. The road was baking asphalt. Mighty grain silos and soaring salmon gums now dotted the landscape beneath a cobalt-blue sky. Cockatoos screeched from the highest branches, their feathers the colour of sifted flour. The Wheatbelt region was the State's giant breadbasket: grains, lamb and mutton, oranges, honey. And now, Sparrow was behind the wheel.

Luke looked bored, his eyes half-closed. He let his travel companions know as much. He rabbited on about all his problems, his prejudices, all about "terrorists and poofters and sluts". Sparrow tried to ignore the comments about "no-good blackfellas", which Luke voiced without apology, as if Sparrow were somehow invisible. He'd heard them his whole life but they still stung.

Paraplegic or not, Sparrow thought the kid came across as nasty. Every kilometre, he questioned what the hell he was doing on the trip. He wanted to say something, wanted to do something. Suggest to Bob that they dump him at the next roadhouse, keep on driving . . . ? But he couldn't; it was too late, he was already on board with the plan. He needed Bob to make sure they got to wherever they were going, and Bob couldn't do it alone.

"C'mon, guys," Luke said. "Let's pick up a hitchhiker!"

After an hour of one-way conversation, Luke's outlook and thirst for adventure had worn away Sparrow's nerves. 'I don't think that's a good idea," he said.

"He's right," said Bob. "What if they turn out to be a serial killer?"

"As if," Luke said.

"They're out there, you know," Sparrow said. "In the desert. Haven't you seen the news or the movies?"

"Pfft. Movies are fake, and so is most of the news. C'mon man, make it the next bastard we come across."

Sparrow kept quiet and pushed down on the accelerator. He knew where Luke was going with this. His insistence on a hitchhiker was part thrill-seeking and part survival instinct. Did he truly trust Bob and Nurse Sparrow? Another traveller likely meant another witness;

safety in numbers, just in case. But to Sparrow, it just ramped up the risk. Bob had told Sparrow that Luke had been willing to do almost anything to escape the nursing home with him. Even still, Luke wasn't stupid.

"And besides," Luke added, "you brought your gun, right, Bob?"

Sparrow glanced over at Bob with blazing eyes. Bob looked relaxed, gave his poker face. Was this self-proclaimed murderer packing his own heat . . .? The tension went up a notch.

Bob reached nonchalantly for the radio. After a few seconds tweaking the analogue dial, a news bulletin emerged from the ether of ghostly voices. The newsreader was touting it as a red-letter day for the State's economy following announcements from its two biggest miners. One was reporting an annual profit of twenty-three billion dollars, or "the same size as the economy of the oil sheikdom of Bahrain". The other had just shipped its symbolic one-billionth tonne of iron ore to Chinese steel mills.

"Hallelujah," Bob said dryly.

"Bloody oath," Luke said. "We talk in billions now, not millions. We're rich, bitch."

In other news, a cyclone was forming off the northwest coast, south of Indonesia, and fast heading east. It was tracking in a favourable environment for development in a low northerly wind shear, and intensifying as it approached landfall. The Bureau of Meteorology had named her Gina.

"Graves are always prepared during the wet season up north," Bob said. "The ground's softer, easier to dig."

His voice betrayed zero emotion. In his rear-view mirror, Sparrow watched Luke's pupils dart from side to side. Fresh sweat stung his eyes, causing him to wince. He rubbed and blinked the pain away.

Sparrow broke his own sweat when the next news story came on the radio. He eased off the accelerator and turned up the volume. A report of two missing persons, both last seen "at Leafy Gums Aged Care Facility at approximately twenty-two hundred hours on Sunday the eighth of January".

"Mr Robert Cooper is a sixty-five-year-old white male," said the constable. "He is described as having short greying hair and is approximately six feet tall, eighty kilos. He was last seen wearing a check shirt and tan trousers. He has a distinct buffalo hump on his upper back and a prominent scar on his left cheek."

Bob subconsciously scratched his cheek. His hair was more salt than pepper.

"The other is Mr Lukas Harper, a thirty-two-year-old white male," the constable continued.

"Awesome." Luke smiled contentedly. "I'm famous."

"He is described as having medium-length black hair, a black goatee beard, and is confined to a motorised wheelchair. He was last seen wearing a black T-shirt, jeans, and black baseball cap."

Luke examined his clothing, identical to the description. "Wow," he said. "They're good."

"We'll all change into our mining shirts when we're a bit further north," Bob said. "We'll fit right in."

Sparrow nodded in agreement.

"Their departure coincided with the disappearance of a wheel-chair-accessible yellow Toyota van," the constable said. "We are appealing to the public. If anyone sees these two individuals or their vehicle or has any information, we urge you to contact your local police or Crime Stoppers. The circumstances of the escape indicate that the older man may have planned it for some time, and we fear for the younger man's welfare."

Bob snapped his hand forward and killed the broadcast.

Luke went quiet. After driving in silence for some time, he asked, "What does that mean?"

Bob waited a moment before finally saying, "Huh?"

"I said what does that mean?"

"What does what mean?"

"The last thing the cop said. About our escape."

"Oh that. S'nothing. They're probably referring to the stacks of prescription drugs that I took for us. To be on the safe side."

Sparrow sucked on his teeth. He kept driving, eyes front, hands at ten and two.

"Hey, nurse, what do you think about all this?" Luke asked.

Sparrow glanced at his rear-view mirror. "I think prescription meds are a very wise idea," he said with a light smile. "Otherwise, it's got nuthin' to do with me."

Sitting at the confluence of two rivers, Northam was the next township. Sparrow counted at least five churches on the way in. He parked the van outside a large Christian bookshop and walked along the street until they found the first takeaway. It was deserted. The chalked order board was faded, indecipherable, and the shiny fryer devoid of golden battered goodness. A rusty fan whirred in the corner, circulating hot air.

"At least they're open," Bob said. "Let's sit."

They took the table nearest the door. Sparrow dragged his chair across the grimy linoleum floor. The groan summoned the proprietor, a short sphere of a woman with thinning hair and two teeth. Her blood-red T-shirt bore the white-lettered slogan: "Send back the boats".

"Three of your biggest, juiciest hamburgers, thanks," Bob said.

"Righto, love," she whistled through her fangs. "Three Gut Busters cummin' up!" and she waddled off to the kitchen.

A man walking a mangy hound without a leash strolled past the shop window. He wore the same red sloganed T-shirt as the proprietor.

"Cool shirts," said Luke. "I want one."

"Really?" Sparrow asked.

"Yeah. They look cool."

Three towering hamburgers piled high with salad, egg, bacon, beetroot and pineapple and oozing with grease and tomato sauce were swiftly delivered to the table. Staring at them gave Sparrow altitude sickness.

The woman stood back. "Where you folks from?" she asked.

"Perth," Bob replied.

"Passin' through, eh?"

"Day trip," Bob said. "We'll head back tonight. This is my son and his mate."

Sparrow nodded a polite "g'day". Luke stayed focused on his hamburger, which was falling apart in his hand. He scooped up each fallen storey and swallowed it like he was eating from a banana leaf.

"My son was just telling me how much he likes your T-shirt," Bob said.

The woman's laugh was full-bellied. Her undulating stomach and generous breasts competed for what little space was left under her shirt.

"Nice, ain't they?" she said, admiring her bosoms. "Ol' Jack up the road, his nephew runs a printing shop in Perth. Jack's idea. His nephew made 'em for last month's town meeting."

"Meeting?" Sparrow asked.

"Yip. About the new detention centre they're gonna build. Immigration department, whopping great monstrosity. Gonna cram it full of reffos, just like the boats what brought 'em over."

She laughed again. Bob forced a smile. Sparrow's chest tightened as his memories stirred.

"Bloody towel heads! What if they escaped, ran riot through town?" the woman continued. "We already got enough trouble 'ere with them young kids of ours drinkin' and fightin' and lootin'."

Sparrow chewed his next bite slowly, buying himself time to consider his response. Shovelling in his own greasy layer, Luke's priorities remained firmly on the task at hand.

"And what happens if the guv'mint then sez they can stay?" The woman flapped her arms. "Do these abber jabbers just move into town, start takin' our jobs? You'd get no burgers then, boys. Only goat meat and roast camel and whatever other rat vermin they bloody eat. And their women would walk round all covered up like black ghosts, looking like letter boxes. What are they hidin', eh?"

There was a long pause. "You know," Bob finally said, "these are some really delicious hamburgers."

The woman smiled warmly through a gummy mouth. "Best in the

State!" she said. "Oh, it's so nice to see a family out for the day. There should be more of it. Tell you what – how's about I fry youse boys up some fresh potato scallops? On the house."

She returned behind the counter, where her deep fryer was soon bubbling away like a witch's cauldron.

Sparrow looked back at Luke, whose goatee beard was now peppered with flecks of egg and lettuce.

"Nice lady," Luke said through oily, glistening lips.

By late afternoon, gangs of kangaroos had started lining the highway on suicide watch. The Hiace was driving commando; that was, without the security of a roo bar. Sparrow was tired from steering all day and relieved to make it to their next port before dusk. It was a guesthouse attached to a Benedictine monastery in New Norcia, the only monastic town in Australia. The monastery was known to open its doors to all guests and travellers. There was an affordable price for the double room and meal, and most importantly, no questions asked. Luke saw Bob pull a fistful of lobsters from his wallet and slip them into a wooden donation box.

"This was once a monk's cell," Bob whispered.

Luke eyed the big crucifixes on the wall above both beds.

"That desk in the corner is where he'd study scripture," Bob added.

Since they were all men, the threesome was allowed to eat supper with the monks. Over their simple bowls of minestrone with sourdough bread and honeyed olive oil, there was no talking beneath the watchful gaze of Saint Benedict; only the gentle sound of cutlery clinking on crockery, of slow slurping in contemplation. Bob and Luke exchanged furtive glances and tried not to laugh; seeing them, the white-haired monk sitting at the head of the table frowned. Sparrow tried to ignore them, too busy savouring the simple soup and honest bread. Unable to stand the silence, Luke surreptitiously shoved in his earbuds, turned his music player to max, and covered his ears with his shaggy hair. He would later admit to Sparrow and Bob that he "would've rather serenaded the room with armpit farts".

In the morning, Bob and Sparrow woke just after dawn. They encountered each other on the heritage verandah to take in the new light.

"Luke's still asleep?" Sparrow asked.

"Catatonic," said Bob. "Like a fat log."

"I didn't sleep great, I had a dream about my old man. He's dead."

"Sorry to hear that, mate."

"Don't be, he wasn't much of a dad. Wasn't his fault though, no-one ever really showed him how. My ma and aunties and older cousins raised me instead."

Bob leaned his back against the wall, letting it take some of his weight.

"And you always wanted to be a cop?" he asked.

"Not always, I tried to be a tradie once," Sparrow replied. "But we had the cops raid our outback community so many times, I was on a first-name basis with most of 'em. We got to talkin', they showed me the ropes. I figured if you can't beat 'em, may as well fucken join 'em. Though my mob didn't think so – reckon I'm a traitor."

"You made the right decision. I only hope Luke might do the same one day, choose the righteous path."

"Personally, I have my doubts."

"I fear that Luke's generation knows nothing about loyalty and hard work. All I want him to appreciate is fraternity and camaraderie."

"The righteous path."

A troop of kangaroos loped their way onto the green lawn for a nourishing morning feed. Sparrow watched their innocent marsupial faces with suspicion, wondering how many recent car accidents their tiny brains and muscular bodies had caused.

"So, when did you move to the city?" Bob asked.

"Not long ago, a few months."

"How's it been?"

Sparrow took a moment to answer, considering his response. He'd been involved in the accidental killing of an innocent kid on his first assignment and was still coming to terms with it all, despite being cleared of all official wrongdoing. Bringing in Bob and solving a cold case murder was his chance at redemption, of reaffirming his abilities as a police officer, which he doubted more than anyone.

"Challenging," he said.

"Change usually is, but it always does you good, in my experience."

"I hope so . . ."

"Did you leave anyone special behind when you moved?"

"I've *never* left anyone special behind. As the little black poof in an outback town, it's never been easy to make relationships."

Bob snorted a laugh. "I know what you mean. Stay the course, son. There's someone out there for everyone. Being in the city should help there."

"I wanna believe you. What about you, any dreams last night?"

"Just one, of the Pilbara."

Bob recounted a recurring vision of digging a hole under a blood-red moon the size of Jupiter. What the hell was he looking for . . .? He said he didn't know. All he knew was that he had to keep digging. The old shovel ripped at his fingers with barbed splinters, his knuckles torn and bloodied. He described burrowing into the earth like an animal, both fists hurling soil left and right. The hole was so deep it enveloped him.

"Then the earth returned and began backfilling the hole, covering me like rising flood water. As the last flicker of moonlight vanished, I opened my eyes and gasped for breath. It's always the same ending."

"Being buried alive. Sounds bloody horrible."

"It is . . ."

The wreckage that was Luke's face finally emerged from bed at eight o'clock. He said he felt terrible. Bob told him it must've been all that healthy food they ate for dinner, which his body wasn't used to. Sparrow chuckled.

Returning to his carer duties, Sparrow carefully massaged Luke's arms and legs for forty minutes; ten per limb, as Bob had instructed.

Sparrow thought he was almost convincing as a male masseuse; after all, he'd received enough massages in his time, and also given a few. Taking Luke's feet in his hands, Sparrow slipped on his long black compression stockings to prevent deep-vein thrombosis, pulling them tight around each fleshy thigh.

Bob went and showered, long and hot, checking his body for new purple marks. Then, coming back, he sat on the edge of the nearby bed wearing only a towel, watching it all.

"You'd look nice in some matching garter belts," he said.

Luke glared at him with wide eyes. He looked like he didn't know whether to laugh or whack Bob hard across the chops. But Sparrow snorted uncontrollably and nodded his head in furious agreement. Luke looked confused and in the end, he playfully clipped Bob around the ear.

"Friggin' smart arse," Luke smirked.

"C'mon, fellas," said Sparrow. "Time to hit the road."

For the first hour of driving, Bob dodged lumps of flyblown roadkill with the deftness of a slalom skier. His arms were getting a real workout, which he said felt good. The traffic was thinning with each kilometre, small sedans replaced by double and triple road trains.

"Notice how you never see any crows as roadkill?" Bob asked.

"No," Sparrow replied. "I mean, now that you mention it . . ."

"Why's that?" Luke asked.

"They're too smart," said Bob. "They're the only birds that seem to have worked out how roads work and know to cross onto the other side to avoid oncoming traffic, even when they're pecking at a carcass."

Bob rubbed his facial growth with a leathery hand, making a raspy sound. "The Pilbara's still a thousand kilometres away but I can already feel a familiar burning in my throat," he said. "Soon, my snot will turn orange."

"Gross," said Luke. "Just gross, dude."

The van's three-litre diesel engine laboured under the increasing pressure that Bob was applying with his Blundstone boot. He gestured to the glovebox.

"Sparrow, mate, give us a couple of pills from the container in there, please."

Sparrow passed him two pills and then a bottle of water from which Bob took a big swig.

"See, the thing is, I've actually never *driven* to the Pilbara," Bob said. "Back when I was workin' there, in the seventies, they always flew us up from Perth. What a bloody trip that was."

"Is your mob from up there, Sparrow?" Luke asked.

Sparrow bit his lip and considered how to reply. Eventually, he said, "No. My *family* is from somewhere else."

"Whereabouts exactly?" Bob asked.

Out of nowhere, a loud police siren beeped and booped. Everything went blue. Luke swore. Sparrow froze. Was the game up, would he finally need to identify himself . . .? What if he was somehow recognised? An alarmed flock of crested pigeons flew overhead, their wings beating a metallic whistling – *whip! whip! whip!* Bob felt his face drain of blood and his foot turn to solid tungsten. Then his grip on the steering wheel loosened and his calf muscles relaxed.

"Shit, what are you doing?" Luke's voice echoed through the cabin. "Don't stop, step on it!"

Bob waited a beat before replying. "Be cool," he said. "Everybody cool. Let me take care of this."

"Hey, Bob," Sparrow said. "You okay?"

"Perfectly fine, mate," said Bob. "Just follow my lead."

"I'm here if you need me. Just don't do anything stupid."

"Wouldn't dream of it."

The two cars rolled to a gentle stop beside a fluorescent yellow sea of flowering canola. Sparrow reached up and adjusted his new sunglasses. Bob looked out the windscreen to the horizon before checking both the rear-view and side mirrors. The highway was reassuringly empty in both directions.

A car door clicked open, slammed closed. From behind, they heard a pair of hard rubber-soled boots approach the van, crunching the rocks and dirt. Luke swore again and craned his neck right to get a look at the cop. Sparrow looked sideways and readied his fingers. He watched Bob roll down his window with one hand as the other reached between his legs and under the car seat.

5

Perth & Pilbara / Whadjuk Noongar & Yindjibarndi Country, 1969–1975

Bob

I woke up in the back of the police van with my jeans still around my ankles and my hair still wet. They started yelling obscenities at me. I was photographed and fingerprinted at the station. A few discreet blows to the solar plexus and they called me names even I hadn't heard before. Pillow biter, arse bandit, fudge packer. I couldn't lift my head, my neck was badly bruised. My eye was almost completely swollen closed, the lump above it the size of an egg. Blurry vision, left ear ringing. One of the cops said simply, "Write in the report he was resisting arrest."

They took my battered body home. Cliff answered the door and immediately knew what had happened. His eyes grew wild and he swung a heavy hand to my battered face. Norma intervened, copped it. Cliff then slumped to the floor and wept as he prayed and cursed God at the same time. My name appeared in the newspaper next morning. It was the same edition that I used as a blanket later that night in a storm-water drain. Cliff had kicked me out of the house at dawn, and I spent the day wandering. Lying on the cold concrete under the full moon, I considered my immediate options. Unfortunately, there were no high bridges nearby. I had no access to a firearm and was too adept an ocean swimmer. So instead, I kept my head low and knuckled down.

Three years of grime and sweat and I was fortified. My first job was as a murderous cog in a grisly machine at the local abattoir. My arms were soon thicker than my thighs. My next job as a garbologist thickened my mind when I saw a colleague lose an arm in the jaws of the truck's continuous compactor. It was more blood than I had seen pour out of any cow. To hide my face and conceal my identity, I grew a beard, long and black and thick.

And then, when a colleague mentioned an opportunity to share a taxi licence with an ageing war veteran, I jumped at the chance. The career change saved my spine, but the sedentary existence and a discovery of convenience food redistributed all the weight from my arms and shoulders to my midriff. For three years, drunks filled my cab with vomit. Hippies did runners or tried to pay with the holes in their pockets. Gone were the days when a thin, athletic version of me might have caught them, and they knew it. Couples bickered, husbands beat wives, adulterers saw the back seat as an inexpensive hotel room. Once around the block, Jeeves, and take it slow.

The holiday season always brought out the worst in mankind. I occasionally received a big tip thanks to end-of-year work bonuses, but those were outweighed by roads awash with drunk drivers and upholstery awash with festive spirit that I could only remove with bleach.

Boxing Day 1974, and my first fare of the evening took me to a two-storey mansion in the swanky waterfront suburb of Peppermint Grove. It was the whitest, cleanest building I had ever seen. A short, stout specimen shot out the front door and ran down the long paved driveway to the road. He wore a taupe-brown shirt, white suspenders, powder-blue pants and white shoes. He put his suitcase on the back seat and sat in the front. The cabin filled with the punch of Brut cologne, which struggled to mask the smell of peroxide. A set of strikingly white teeth smiled at me under a trimmed black moustache. I drove him to the airport and was tipped more than I would earn in a month. It left me speechless. His pearly whites smiled at me again. The man said he owned a mine.

"Wow," I said. "How is that?"

"It's fantastic, but I always have trouble retaining workers."

"Shame I'm not a miner."

"Actually . . . my company needs dumper drivers. If you can drive a cab, you can drive a dump truck."

"Seriously?"

"I reckon. And there's enough ore in the north to last a hundred years. If you're interested in making some good money, here's my card. Call me."

The checkerboard fields of crops and multicoloured wildflowers around Perth soon gave way to salt pans and rocky outcrops that stretched to every horizon. Eventually, the earth was nothing more than a noise of dirt – grey dirt, orange dirt, red dirt – and a spattering of hardy trees, lonely white ghost gums that defiantly challenged the sun and wind. Trees of iron.

I squirmed in my seat, a sick bag clenched between my fingers. It was my first time aboard a plane. I had expected something with big jet engines that left thick vapour trails. A thin metal bird powered by propellers seemed positively prehistoric; a pterodactyl.

They called it "the milk run", the three-hour flight between Western Australia's cloistered capital in the south and its wasteland in the north. The propeller-powered flea touched down at least a half dozen times at small airstrips to offload goods and swap passengers. An infrequent silver cluster of tin roofs was the only thing signifying a township or outback station. There were so many stops, I soon found the take-offs and landings indistinguishable. The further north the six-seat Cessna flew, the more like a sauna it became. I felt nauseous and dizzy. The cabin smelled of hot seat leather copulating with body odour. The barley sugar I'd been given to suck had lasted less than a minute, ending up in the sick bag alongside my breakfast. Soft-boiled eggs for breakfast was a bad choice.

Hidden beneath a vast emptiness once regarded by eighteenth century Dutch sailors as useless, an enormous mineral wealth now fuelled an almighty financial boom. As millions of tonnes of earth were moved to generate billions of dollars of revenue, an expanse that once supported a few Indigenous nomads now bolstered hundreds of thousands of people's livelihoods. Off the coast, metal leviathans tapped the oil that fuelled all these industries as fire-breathing steel dragon towers announced the arrival of a burgeoning gas industry. Viewed from above, the giant trucks and earthmovers looked like mere children's toys.

Hitting another pocket of turbulence, the plane rocked sideways. My head rocked with it as I briefly contemplated my mortality. The organs in my chest swapped places with those in my abdomen. Crammed into the seat next to me, the burly man spilled his morning beer everywhere. He didn't apologise and merely sought to save what was left of the precious amber fluid. He was one of several new arrivals who started panicking on the plane's final descent into nothingness. Having decided they were no longer interested in a northern adventure, the men refused to give up their seats when the plane landed. Meanwhile, those locals who had served their Nor'west sentence and were waiting to fly out tried in vain to physically remove them. The plane eventually returned to the skies with every seat occupied. I had made a spectacular entrance myself, stepping from the door, catching my foot, and flopping face first onto the dirt tarmac.

"Welcome to the bloody Pilbara," grumbled one of the grounded men as he chucked his bag down. "And good bloody luck to ya tryin' to get out."

I wiped the dirt from my lips and stood. The midday sun felt closer than I had ever known it. My lungs were hit by searing hot, dry air. Only the tin shed serving as a makeshift terminal disfigured the otherwise virginal landscape. The roof sent ripples of heat back into the sky, visible, destabilising. One of the three stranded miners said a bus was on its way.

I shielded my eyes from the blinding sun and looked around. Boundless horizons stretched in every direction, an infinity like I'd never before seen. Not a single living thing was moving. Grassy tussocks of spinifex with their spiky antennae littered the earth like landmines. The red dust hung in the air like pollen, quickly forming a thick layer of discomfort over everything. In the distance, an almighty detonation sent shock waves through my calves. An amber mushroom cloud metastasised into the blue yonder.

"Hey, sport," said someone. "Where yew bloody from, eh?"

A voice behind me said, "Perth."

"City slicker, eh?" came the response. "Just like every second bastard up here these days. Come to make yer quick fortune?"

"That's the plan."

This elicited an uproar of laughter from the peanut gallery. Crooked grins became shit-eating snarls that revealed inhuman canines. If I hadn't been thinking exactly the same thing, I might've joined in.

"No flies on you, eh, sport," the stranded man said. "But at least yer Westralian and not some Easternstater blow-in."

His beer-bellied colleague guffawed. "Or some greasy-haired wog or slanty-eyed gook."

An old yellow school bus with left-hand drive and no suspension arrived. I took a seat near the back. The land was dotted with anthills taller than the bus, clumps of termite-ridden timber, asbestos sheeting, car bodies, old tyres. We chugged through a town where the swimming pool was encircled with barbed wire.

It was a twenty-minute ride to our new home. I was to be housed in the single men's compound outside of town. Only married couples and families were allowed to live in the newly constructed oasis of furnished, prefabricated houses. Arranged in neat vanilla rows with lawns and gardens, their blocks were bordered by kerbs and bitumen. The companies built schools, shopping centres, hospitals, drive-in theatres, even a telephone exchange and TV station.

"Gudday."

A passenger leaned across the aisle and offered me his hand. I recognised the voice from earlier.

"Name's Lenny."

Lenny's ferret moustache was in dire need of a trim. It curled into his crooked mouth as he smiled. His football shorts and singlet were faded and his sweaty long hair hung where it pleased. His young, unweathered face mirrored my own mug even though his taut body was only half the size of my taxi-driver frame.

"Hi," I said. "Bob."

A set of tawny fingers extended another familiar greeting.

"Cheers," I said, helping myself to a smoke.

Lenny's introduction was completed by his Zippo lighter, which he snapped open with slender fingers in a single movement.

"Cool trick," I said.

"Thanks, man."

Lenny spent the rest of the journey trying to teach me the manoeuvre. I kept dropping the Zippo onto the floor with a hefty clank. Lenny would be living in the same compound as me but in another unit owned by another company. He had no idea what work awaited him but "was happy to do anything".

The work camp was a jumble of dilapidated asbestos buildings on stilts. We were shown to our huts by the bus driver, who doubled up as accommodation manager.

"Is there a key?" I asked.

"Nup," he replied. "No lock. Lock's stuffed. Been jimmied too many times with screwdrivers."

My donga was like a shipping container on concrete foundations. I had never seen a more perfect rectangular prism, a firm geometric shape reinforced by the rugged terrain around it. The collections of grubby clothes strewn through the portable building spoke volumes about its three current occupants. The fourth bunk was obviously mine. Closest to the entrance, it was buried under a mountain of empty beer bottles.

"Yip," said the manager.

He told me I had five minutes to unpack. I was due at work that afternoon to earn my heavy-vehicle licence.

The donga's walls were asbestos. It smelt of linseed oil from the bulky brown linoleum tiles curling up on the floor. Dirty yellow newspapers were laid between the lino and the pine floorboards underneath. Cigarette butts and boot marks covered the floor. The blanket on my bed was cigarette paper thin and bore dehydrated alcohol crystals and charred holes. Behind me, the donga's longest wall showcased a mosaic of carefully scissored naked female forms extracted from hundreds of under-the-counter magazines. Even my untrained eyes had to stop and marvel at the impressive collection of hips, thighs and breasts normally reserved for the inside of a brown paper bag. I'd never seen such a public expression of lust. Nailed to the furthest wall was a crooked bookshelf housing a number of tattered paperbacks and a dusty cassette player. Two electric fans in the corners circulated the tang of nicotine and old socks. Ashtrays overflowed beside the bunks and toilets overflowed in the latrines. It was all exactly as I had imagined. In fact, it had a certain mannish charm at a caveman level. I instantly and utterly loved everything about it.

Back aboard the yellow bus, I headed deeper into the red unknown. Disembarking at the other end of the line, I approached the first demountable building I saw and knocked hard on the metal door. From the window, I saw the site manager begrudgingly put down his tattered *Playboy* magazine, remove his feet from the desk and waddle over.

"Ah, yew must be Bob," he said. "I'm Nils. Clive told me we had a new man flyin' in today. Said yew were a driver. Zat right?"

"Yeah," I said.

"Well, c'mon then. Let's go see what yew can dew."

Nils was a retired Scandinavian bus conductor with thinning shoulder-length grey hair ending in a wiry mess of split ends. On his egg-carton chest, a fraying T-shirt served the remains of last night's dinner. Nils wasn't exactly what I had imagined, an outback buccaneer in a flowing cotton shirt, not some balding clippie from Copenhagen.

I hadn't stopped perspiring all day, but as we walked to the monstrous yellow truck, I was suddenly overcome by the sweat of apprehension. I'd never driven any kind of truck before, let alone an iron ore dumper that weighed hundreds of tonnes.

"Here," said Nils, thrusting forth a loose-leaf page. "Yer trainin'."

It was a single sheet of paper with driving instructions scrawled by hand, barely decipherable. I studied them carefully, the words and diagrams, but still proceeded to stall the great beast a dozen times and forget which button did what. I could hardly see where I was going from the driver's seat in the sky. But none of that mattered. The only competency my instructor wanted to see was that the company's newest man could reverse the dump truck in between two white tyres positioned so wide apart that a jumbo jet could have parked comfortably.

Back at the demountable, Nils stamped my new licence with an inky square the colour of dried blood. I was now on my way to earning my first million.

"Another pass!" he beamed. "I've got a one hundred per cent record. I'm teacher of the year, yew know. Right, that's knock-off time. Let's go get trolleyed."

With the dropping of the sun, the earth turned a vibrant umber and the chocolate ranges became deep purple. I sat and watched the cosmic palette change through the grubby window of the bus, which was now full of thirsty, sun-baked men. Driving home, we passed a band of gypsies camped on the edge of town. Someone said they were from Romania. The gypsies had no air conditioning and no refrigeration. Further along what seemed to be the only road in the area, a group of Aboriginal Elders trudged west into the setting sun. They carried nothing other than a quiet confidence about where they had come from and where they were heading.

Back at the donga, I stripped off my clothes. They were heavy with sweat and looked like they'd been pounded with a meat tenderiser. I carried them to the shower block to rinse off the day's filth but found the water in the cold taps emerging only as steam. The shower block had no tiles, doors, curtains, or even dividers. They might as well have lined us up and sprayed us with a fireman's hose. The towel the company provided smelled stale and made me feel dirty. I changed into what fresh clothes I had and went for dinner.

In the mess, the men wore the day's grime like a full-body medal of honour. They had earned the cold grog to wash the dry dust down their throats. Their clothes were rough, covered in salt stains and assorted mineral crud. Their bearded faces had orange dust traced into each furrow. I felt decidedly overdressed.

Someone on my left thrust a fat joint under my nose. I sucked on it till it glowed like molten ore, then handed it to whoever was on my right. Every second word of the group conversation had four letters. I struggled to keep up. I wanted to fit in, but my profanity quotient was dangerously low. The cook's sulphur-crested cockatoo, its snow-white feathers dirty with brown dust, repeated the same obscene phrases. Weak with hunger, I caught my gaze lingering on a sea of bulging pectorals and sun-faded tattoos. I had to look away before anyone noticed.

Naturally, this being the canteen of an iron ore mine, the announcement that dinner was served was made with a cast-iron bell.

"Come 'n git it, you caahhnts!" bellowed the cook.

"Come and get it," screeched his cockie. "Cunts!"

The mess shook with laughter.

I had never seen such gargantuan T-bone steaks, as expansive as the land on which they were reared, dished up in aluminium trays as long as canoes. The cook had grilled them on a barbeque cocooned in a fly-wire tent to protect the meat from airborne cockroaches the size of small birds. Thick-cut chips as long as timber planks, boiled vegetables as big as fists. Horizontal food, sprawling cuisine, not petite morsels and porcini mushrooms stacked atop tiny medallions of veal. Puddles of gravy, not drizzles of jus. Big food, real food, man's grub. I inhaled it all and went back for seconds.

Obscenity-riddled conversations continued long into the evening, and so did the drinking. There was no thought for tomorrow. A few men painted the red earth with their black innards; the guilty party was invariably "sunstroke". The longest bench in the mess sprouted a proud pyramid of used beer cans, formally a "beeramid". I eventually grew tired of listening to drunks talking about drinking and getting drunk and sought sleep in my shipping container just as things got ugly. Punches were thrown, few hit their mark, men were separated until an added word or gesture set them off again. The ultimate victim was all that spilled beer, needlessly sacrificed at the altar of male pride. It was just another day among Australia's drinking towns that had a mining problem.

Blundering back to what I thought were my sleeping quarters, I came across two men wrestling in the jibber. The night was dark, the moon a fingernail in the sky. One of the men was cursing a blue streak as the other complained of his fingers being bitten. With no-one else around to police, I reluctantly assumed the role of peacemaker. My approaching footsteps were enough of a deterrent as one of the brawlers fled into the inky blackness. The other writhed in the dirt, in apparent agony, which was a better sign than him not moving at all.

"Hey, mate, you okay?" I asked. "Take it easy, I'm not gonna—"

But the shadow had somehow found its feet and made off into the night.

I stepped forward and heard my Blundstone crunch on a stray piece of metal. I had to fish around amid the loose rocks and clay to find the relevant item. I picked it up, dusted it off, and saw it was a Zippo lighter.

My horsehair mattress was sunken in the middle and searing hot. But sleep came instantly, even with the lullaby of four-letter words and smashing bottles that echoed through the night. A solid, ten-hour hibernation was only interrupted when I woke to find a strange man sitting on the edge of my bed, mumbling about how he'd killed his wife.

Even as I put my Blundstones on for the day, I was pouring with sweat, my beard dripping like a watering can. With the first glimpse of sun, the blowfly bastards enshrouded me. I sat back on the step and spun

Lenny's Zippo through my slippery fingers, trying to replicate his trick and failing miserably. I wanted to find the young bloke and return it to him and ask about the night before. If only my head wasn't so dangerously close to shattering into a thousand pieces.

Breakfast was back in the mess, the same aluminium trays as the previous night, this time laden with scrambled eggs, short-cut bacon, burst sausages, fried kidneys, grilled tomatoes, baked beans and thick slabs of white toast. I slurped my mug of builder's tea noisily and overheard two men discussing what they called the "fresh meat" who had skipped camp that morning.

"Who's this?" I asked.

"That young prick, the jaffa, long hair, arrived only yesterdee," came the reply. "Someone broke into his donga round midnight. But the kid couldn't hack the attention so he packed his bag and marched out, first light. Whoever saw the dumb prick go reckoned he was still shaking. Jesus Christ, I mean, what did he expect happened round 'ere . . ."

6

Mid West / Yamatji Country, 2017

"Morning, officer. Sorry, I didn't realise my speed. I hope I wasn't over the limit."

The cop's mirrored shades stared back at Bob, expressionless. Bob struggled to maintain an innocent smile, his face cracking. Luke froze altogether; he'd stopped blinking, stared straight ahead like a stoned mannequin. The sunglasses turned in Luke's direction, paused, tracked over to Sparrow, paused again, before finally returning to Bob.

"Sir. Please switch off your ignition."

"Certainly," Bob said, turning the key left. The cop waited until Bob applied the handbrake before he spoke again.

"Just the three of you, is it?"

"Yep," Bob replied. "Just the three of us."

"Is this your son in the back, then?"

"That's right. My boy."

"And you?" He gestured at Sparrow.

"He's our carer," Bob said quickly. "He's looking after us, making sure we don't get into any trouble." He smiled.

The policeman eyeballed Luke a second time, checking for signs of life. Luke finally obliged with a crooked grin that looked more like an angry sneer. Sparrow nodded a polite g'day and wondered if he had been recognised.

"Can I see your licence, sir?"

"Absolutely," Bob said, thrusting forth his right hand. He had the licence at the ready.

Two long fingers snatched at the plastic card like a pair of chopsticks and held it up close to the sunglasses. The image of Bob's grizzled mug reflected in duplicate.

"Are you from New South Wales, sir?"

"Sorry?"

"Are you from New South Wales?"

"No. We've only just travelled up from Perth."

"But your licence here says New South Wales, Sydney."

Sparrow's heart skipped a beat. How was it that Bob was from New South Wales? He'd never mentioned that.

"Oh yes, that's right," Bob said. "Sorry! I only moved here from the east not long ago and still need to update my licence."

The cop examined the licence again. "Be sure you do. Can I ask where you're heading?"

Bob took a few quiet breaths to steady his voice before responding. "Wiluna. We got a family farm up there."

Another look at the licence. "Just a moment."

The boots crunched away, back to the patrol car. The highway remained empty, quiet. Bob's left hand stayed hidden between his legs while Sparrow's eyes remained on the rear-view mirror. Luke turned his thick neck as far as it could rotate to catch a better view.

"What's the fuck's he doing back there?" Luke asked.

"Oi!" Bob said.

"Steady on, sport. He's not gonna arrest us for swearing."

"He's probably running a check to see if you have any unpaid parking tickets or speeding fines," Sparrow replied.

"Well?" Luke said. "Do you?"

Bob paused, casting his eyes to the infinite blue sky. "Don't . . . think so. But I could be wrong. I hope not."

The longer the policeman took, the more anxious Luke appeared. An ever-growing ring of sweat pooled around the collar of his T-shirt. What if he blabbed and gave the game away? Bob remained calm, lightly tapping his fingers on the steering wheel to release his tension. The rows of canola swayed in the breeze.

"Bob," Sparrow said, eyeing the position of Bob's left hand. "Mate, I say again, just don't do anything stupid."

"Like I said, wouldn't dream of it."

"What's in Wiluna?" Luke asked.

"Nothing's in Wiluna," Bob replied. "But it's at one end of the Gunbarrel Highway so heaps of people end up there. It was the best thing to say. I was hardly gonna tell him where we're *actually* headed."

"Yeah, but a *farm* in Wiluna? The hell do they farm in Wiluna?"

"Emus," Bob said quickly. "It's an emu farm."

A pair of Torresian crows the colour of sump oil called overhead – *uk uk uk* – and disappeared into the distance, black dots above the highway.

"Whoa!" said Luke. "What about the number plate? We're screwed now."

"Stay calm," Bob said. "Wait . . ."

Bob maintained a veneer of cucumber cool. Sparrow was equally measured. Luke's forehead ran slick with sweat. Finally, after what seemed an eternity, they heard the sound of heavy boots on rocky soil.

A white plastic tube was thrust before Bob's face. "Sir, have you consumed any alcohol today?"

"Me?" Bob asked. "Today? No, sir! Not me. Not today, sir. Far too early for that. And I barely drink as is."

"I'll ask you to please blow into this tube until you hear three loud beeps."

"Certainly . . ."

Bob took the unit, wrapped his lips around the cylinder, and made his cheeks bulge. He wheezed a large lungful of air into the computer nose until it beeped him to stop. The policeman removed the tube, handed it to Bob, and waited for the digital reading. He removed his sunglasses, wiped his eyes, and looked back to the car. His eyes were powder blue and matched his shirt. They were strikingly beautiful.

"Thank you for cooperating, sir," the highway cop said. "Just to inform you, in case you didn't already know, there's a cyclone approaching from the north. It might not get as far south as Wiluna, but rain brews pretty quickly out here and the roads can flash flood."

"I understand," Bob said. "Always best to be cautious."

"That's why we're stopping motorists. To advise them to stick to the main roads and stay with their vehicle should it break down. Whatever you do, please don't leave your vehicle. People die when they do that."

He handed Bob three bottles of water, wished them all a safe journey, crunched his way back to his car, and accelerated into the distance.

Luke's jaw dropped. Sparrow exhaled and ran his hands through his hair. Bob smiled and handed them each a bottle as he slurped thirstily on his own. He drained it with two cocks of the elbow and burped his satisfaction.

Sparrow could tell that Luke was disappointed. He'd probably pictured Bob pulling out a .44 Magnum and spilling the cop's brains across on the highway in a show of gory defiance. By the time reinforcements arrived, the policeman would've been no more than a red smear, pecked to pieces by hungry wedge-tailed eagles. By then, they would all be in a hot tub somewhere with a blonde under each arm, smoking stogies and laughing at the world as they passed around a pair of mirror sunglasses claimed as a keepsake.

"Shame," Luke muttered as they pulled slowly away.

The van was soon driving through the Mid West region. Arid and empty, it was Western Australia's transition zone where the earth's treasures retreated from above ground to subterranean. The only things left behind on the surface were dashed dreams and sick livestock. Dead trees with bare frames and crooked branches extended fuck-you fingers to jeer at the cloudless sky.

Now far enough from Perth, the trio changed into their mining shirts, and Sparrow resumed the wheel. Luke was now even more bored, more vocal, more provocative and inflammatory. He needed stimulation, action, not emptiness. Sparrow held his tongue. He wanted to tell the little turd off for regurgitating the soundtrack of his wretched small-town life, but knew he couldn't. For Bob's sake, and in the name of the case, Sparrow had to keep him on side.

Bob shoved a dirty index finger up his right nostril and started digging. "Colonial Australia," he said.

Luke's sweaty moon face tightened. "Huh?" he grunted.

Crumbling facades and yellow rubble rolled past the window, once elaborately decorated banks and office blocks. Abandoned hotels with wide, shaded verandahs, curved stairways and spacious rooms sat silent and solemn. The string of ghost towns stretched north along Highway 95 like pearls on a necklace. A testament to great riches and the impermanence of a rush era, now shrouded in immense sadness.

"Didn't these all used to be gold towns?" Sparrow asked.

Bob swapped nostrils. "That's right," he said. "A hundred years ago. Nearly half the State's population lived out here. Almost as many people were trying to strike it rich as were living in Perth."

He pointed a crusty finger at the windscreen. "What happened out here was the very first mining boom. It shaped our national identity," Bob added.

"It still bloody does," said Sparrow flippantly.

"Huh?" said Luke.

"Mate, are you even listening?" Bob asked.

Luke sighed. "Yeah . . ."

But he clearly wasn't. Bob turned to face him and tried again.

"Mate, life in the goldfields was all about brotherhood. Mining men, gamblers, bound to a common life of toil and disappointment.

Cooperation was essential for survival. The goldfields were where the idea of 'Aussie mateship' was born. It saw us through wars, through places like Gallipoli and Kokoda. Mateship all started out here."

Luke stared out the window. "Uh huh," he mumbled.

The highway ahead was a straight black line to infinity. Sparrow barely had to move his arms to steer, only needing to tweak the wheel to avoid the odd flat roo. A chalkboard sign by the roadside warned of the "last petrol for 200 kms". Sparrow consulted his gauge, the needle sitting just below the red full line. The roadhouse flashed past the passenger side window.

The van was getting hotter the further north they drove. Bob kept reminding the others to make sure they were "always sweating. Sweating's good. It's only dangerous if you stop."

"Why?" Luke asked.

"Greater risk of hyperthermia if you don't sweat," Sparrow said. "You overheat and die."

"Like a car with a busted radiator," Bob added. "But if you feel a chill, that could be fungal pneumonia. I saw it happen to blokes in the mines who breathed in the outback dust. The dust carries spores. A white wedge of pneumonia lodges in their lungs."

Luke paused in thought. "Jesus Christ," he breathed. "Is there anything out here that won't goddamn kill me?"

"Well, mate, I think you're gonna die for a sight of this," Bob said. "Check it out. On the left."

Luke glanced up from his bumbag. Sparrow looked across as well.

It was a truck parked by the roadside. An eighteen-wheeler, and the hood ornament was a real-life woman. She was lying on a towel, stretched out across the bonnet, absorbing the sun like a weekend at the beach. Luke looked confused. For a moment, he thought someone must be filming a music video, but saw no cameras, no poodle-haired metal band lip-synching on a nearby cliff. As they passed, the woman took on exaggerated motions. She arched her back and sat up in her black bikini, presenting them with a balcony of breasts. Luke nearly dislocated a vertebra in his neck trying to identify the black object tattooed on her right ribs. She raised a slender arm in the air, smiled and waved.

"Holy shit!" Luke said. "Whatthefuckareyoudoin? Are you crazy? Go back!"

"Language!" said Bob.

"Back!"

"Back?" Sparrow asked. "What for?"

"Well, gee, I wonder . . ."

Bob waited a few seconds to respond. "Oh, you mean that girl we just passed?"

"Bloody oath, yes! Christ, I'm about to shit my balls back here . . ."

Bob shook his head lightly. "No, son," he said. "That's no girl. That's just our brains playin' tricks. The heat up here causes all kinds of mirages. The light gets bent, causes a false image to form in your mind. Happens all the time."

Sparrow smiled to himself. Cheeky old bugger, he thought.

"Mirages, piss off!" said Luke. "How could all our brains see the exact same thing?"

"It happens," Sparrow lied. "Not sure how but it's true."

"Look, mate," Bob said. "She's probably some prostitute headin' north to cut a swathe through the mines."

"Or maybe some trucker's wife," Sparrow added. "Or sellin' the latest energy drink. Or from the flamin' West Australian Tourist Bureau."

"Too right," said Bob. "Whatever she is, that's trouble right there. Capital T. And we got bigger fish to fry."

"But what if her rig's broken down and she needs help?" Luke asked.

"I'm no diesel mechanic. What about you, Sparrow?"

"Not me. I care for sick people, not sick vehicles."

"It's not that," Luke said. "She might need water or food."

"Nice try," said Bob. "Playing the humanitarian card. Good effort, son."

Luke had been begging to pick up a wayfarer but this one seemed too good to be true. Sparrow wondered if she had a refrigerated trailer full of bodies.

"Mate," Bob said, "the only thing that girl looked in danger of needing was more fifty-plus sunscreen."

Luke huffed his frustration. "Eff you," he said.

"Lukas," Bob said. "Listen, mate. I know where you're going with this. I'm not buying it. If she's broken down, she'll be fine. She'll have a CB radio in her cabin. If she really needs help, she can call the professionals. Like the cop said, don't leave your vehicle. And besides, where we're headed, there's much greater treasures that await us than a pair of fake tits."

Sparrow was relieved – this trip was about solving a murder, not some childish preoccupation with getting laid. The van kept rolling, with Luke's outback adventure soon growing increasingly smaller in its side mirror.

Three hours later, Sparrow was sitting in an air-conditioned corner of the world's most isolated roadhouse. His coffee was bitter. So was his mood.

"Great," Bob said. "Bloody great. Now what do we do?"

He was flipping a set of useless car keys between his fingers. The Hiace van sat dead outside. It wouldn't start. The likely diagnosis was something electrical.

"Probably the battery," said Luke, tucking into his second meat pie. "Summer's the worst time for batteries."

"Battery, eh . . ." Bob said.

"Yeah. Or the alternator. That charges the battery." Luke's teeth were covered in a mixture of gristle and gravy.

"Shit," said Bob. "Shit shit shit. Jesus."

Bob was taking the breakdown hard. Sparrow was too, but he was at least grateful to be stranded at a cool roadhouse and not frying beside a major highway with rain approaching. The silver-grey sky hung overhead like a reaper's hand as clouds with charcoal underbellies conspired in the distance.

"Could even be the ignition module," Luke added.

With that, Bob stopped flipping the keys and dropped them on the table with a sharp clink.

"You know," he said, "for someone who seems to know a bit about cars, you're not being very helpful."

Luke stopped chewing. He spoke through a mouth of gooey meat, spitting oily fragments into the air.

"Steady on, old man. Whatdyawant me to do? I can hardly bloody fix it with one friggin' arm, can I?"

"I'm not saying that—'

"I'm not the goddamn RAC."

"That's not—'

"And anyway, I don't see *you* doing anything to help with your four effing limbs. Nor our carer, Sparrow here, or whatever his *real* name is. That's eight perfectly able limbs and you can't fix one broken van."

"Go easy, mate," said Sparrow.

"Pathetic," Luke said.

He scowled with a dirty sauce moustache. Instinctively, Bob's fingers curled inwards, tucked in, his hand forming a fist. Sparrow watched his face tighten. Bob had to wait a while until his muscles relaxed before he could speak again.

"Well I don't know a thing about cars," he admitted. "And I can hardly push us to the next town. Nor can young Sparrow. But what I do know is that I didn't go to all this effort and come all this way to end up with nothing."

They were the only patrons in the roadhouse. An old proprietor leaning on the counter was asleep in his own hands. He'd woken long enough to tell them there was no mechanic on duty "'cos it's Sundee". The nearest garage was "four hundred clicks". A swarm of blowflies courted the empty, deep-fried nutrients in the fryer. A radio in the back room played an old Rod Stewart ballad that made Bob feel nauseous. Luke tucked his snout back into the miscellaneous meat.

"Going to the loo," Bob said.

He shambled away, a sad old man wearied by time.

"So, Bird Man. What's your game, eh, sport?"

Luke's query of Sparrow seemed to come out of nowhere. The young cop didn't have a clue what he meant.

"I mean, are you married or single?" Luke went on. "You got kids, want kids, what . . .?"

Sparrow didn't want to discuss his personal life with someone like Luke. He decided to paint things with a broad brush.

"I'm single," he replied.

"Why's that?"

"Dunno. Guess I haven't met that special someone yet."

"Makes you a bit of a failure then, eh?"

Sparrow wanted to say he'd rather be a failure than a bigot any day of the week, but in the end, he swallowed his words.

"Think I'll go check on Bob," he said instead. "I'm worried about him."

Sparrow headed for the bathroom. He missed seeing the bird that Luke flicked him with his middle finger.

Sparrow found Bob staring at himself in the mirror. Underneath the sickly fluorescent light, everything appeared washed out and harshly angular. Capillaries bursting under the skin around his eyes, razorback ridges in his face. He looked like a living corpse.

"Hey," Sparrow said. "Are you alright, mate?"

Bob forced a smile. "I'm fine," he said. "Perfectly fine. It's just the heat and humidity, I forgot how tired it makes me feel. It's like my lungs are stuffed with cotton wool, my head packed with gunpowder."

The novelty of being on the run had swiftly been replaced by its reality.

"Gotta admit, my batteries are feelin' pretty drained too," Sparrow said. "And now we're stuck. I can always call for some backup? My commanding officer would understand."

"No," Bob said firmly. "That'll give the game away. We'll find a way."

Sparrow paused, considered his response. "If we go on, if we somehow get out of here, at least consider getting a real nurse to accompany us. There's only so much I can pretend to do. And if you're really so unwell . . ."

"Nonsense," Bob said. "I'm fine, and so are you, you're doing just fine."

"I don't think Luke's at all convinced."

"Pah. He's young, he thinks he knows it all, but doesn't know his arse from his elbow. Leave him to me."

Bob ran the cold tap full bore and doused his head with tepid water.

"There," he said. "Right as rain."

They returned from the men's room to find Luke smiling unnervingly. And Bob's seat at the table was now occupied.

"There ya friggin' are," Luke beamed. "Thought youse blokes had fallen in! Guys, meet our new friend. She's agreed to take us to the next town and can tow the van on her flatbed trailer. Shit . . . sorry, Miss. I didn't ask your name?"

"Mouse," said the woman.

Sparrow immediately recognised the woman's face from above the black bikini. Mouse had straight raven hair shaped in a bob that brushed her smooth shoulders. Her fingernails were jet black and her lips hell red. Her fingers and thumbs were heavy with rings, she had a nose ring, a pierced eyebrow, and was covered in tattoos: barbed wire around both biceps, a life-size redback spider crawling up her neck, matching roses with thorns on both wrists. Braless under her dark-blue shearer's singlet, she was sipping a cold Coke through a red straw. Luke's black cap had been respectfully removed and his sauce moustache wiped clean.

"Shit, cool name," said Luke. "How'd you get it?"

"Bar bet," Mouse said. "I ate one. It was dead. So I ate it. Won a grand."

"Cool."

"Yep. Didn't get crook or nuthin'."

"Awesome. So, I'm Luke. This is Bob, and that's Andrew."

Jesus Christ, Sparrow thought. Did you have to use our real names . . .? She was smart enough to not use hers.

"Gudday," Bob said, extending his arm. "Nice to meet you."

Mouse shook his hand and smiled through moist sugary lips, lighting up a pair of perfectly chiselled dimples in her cheeks. Moistening a finger on his tongue, Luke ran a thin film of saliva over his eyebrows, reining in any recalcitrant strands.

Sparrow pointed at the rig parked outside. "Zat your truck?" he asked. A pair of shiny mudflaps bore the silver silhouettes of two reclining men.

"Yip," said Mouse. "Me truck and me house, when I'm on the road."

"Trucker, eh?" Sparrow said.

"Yip. Ain't many of us gals out there. But me mum always said I was special."

"Got a flatbed trailer?"

"Empty. Hauled some mining equipment down to Perth for repair. Now I gotta return the trailer."

"You headin' north too?" Bob asked.

"Perth to Darwin," said Mouse. "Then Darwin to Perth. Rinse and repeat. It's no biggie to drop you boys off. And besides, I like having company."

Sparrow paused in thought. Mouse seemed too good to be true. As soon as they broke down, she turned up. Too good. Was she in cahoots with Bob somehow? Was this some conspiracy that would soon blow up in his naive face? His career would be over, ruined on a hunch, odds that proved too long. Porter would have his balls and his badge. Then again, Sparrow couldn't see any other travel option north. Thumbing a ride was possible, but who knew who they'd end up with then? It was entirely possible that Sparrow was being taken for the wildest ride, metaphorically as well as literally. Bob and Mouse and Luke could be in on it together, and Sparrow would soon be down in the dirt, made to dig his own grave. What started off as an even contest – he and Bob heading north – was now mismatched, three against one, the odds stacked against him.

"Well," Bob said to Mouse, "that's very much appreciated. Thank you."

His face softened. Luke popped his preened eyebrows and fired Sparrow a look of optimism. All Sparrow could do was run a hopeful hand through his dusty hair and return a look of gratitude.

"Lemme take a quick slash and we'll hit the road," Mouse said. "Back in a tick." She sashayed away in her wheat-yellow Caterpillar boots and cut-off denim shorts.

Sparrow glanced over at Luke who looked like he'd seen the lights of heaven.

"Impressive," Sparrow said.

"Fucken aye," said Luke breathlessly.

7

Pilbara / Yindjibarndi Country, 1976

Bob

"Gudday, sweet'eart. What's your name, big boy?"

I didn't recognise her voice. She was probably new. Must be my lucky day, I thought. The new girl was always prized. If you were the first to have her, you had a bloody great yarn to tell the other blokes later to get their motors running.

This was a regular hoop I had to jump through, something essential to remaining inconspicuous. Every time a new cohort of men arrived in the north, they descended on the local cathouse not long after. Often in groups, usually at the end of a long shift working and a longer shift drinking. Same with the tattoo parlour, otherwise known as donga fifteen and the old Dutch bastard. The entire workforce turned over every few months, with my ink accumulating accordingly. The inability to retain workers was a headache for all the mine owners and made genuine friendships impossible. And besides, at the end of a shift, I had nothing better to do.

She showed me into her room. The blinds were drawn, the bedside lava lamp switched off. Only the new dawn light illuminated the edges of the window frame, creating the illusion of a floating white square. Swirls of dust rode the few beams of wan light which broke across the small space. The room smelt of cinnamon incense masking stale sweat.

"Name's Richard."

I never used my real name. Most blokes didn't, so I thought it best I did the same. The vastness of the north was a favourite hiding place for husbands who had deserted their families and were being sought for unpaid maintenance. Meanwhile, the blokes who were still with their wives feared them finding out what they were paying by the hour for.

"Richard," I repeated. "That's my name. Richard. Got it?" I needed her to remember it to retain the pretence.

"Sure thing, Richie," the girl cooed. "What turns you on?"

But what turned me on was nothing this tired girl could possibly offer. A spear of light fell crookedly across her face as she stepped forward to meet me. She let her silky slip fall to the floor and pushed me onto the bed, then forced herself upon me, arching her back like a desert cat. I calmly removed the teardrop breast from my mouth and my hand from her pubic bush.

"Nup," I said. "Not that, sorry."

I kicked off my dirt-encrusted work boots and sat on the bed, prematurely igniting a post-coital cigarette with my Zippo. I eased my body back onto the bed, feeling the warmth of the man who had come before me. The girl covered herself and flicked on the lava lamp, revealing an immoral glow and an assortment of items on the bedside table. Magazines, used tissues, baby oil, an enema kit, a wine cask. I wanted her to switch off the light but then I saw her eyes – they were large and eager to please, if a little uncertain. Pilbara guys were vanilla: a blowjob, missionary, frills and lace, and that was it. Anything else – tickle this, whip that, can I wear your French knickers? – and they risked the other men finding out, and earning their unending ridicule.

"Smoke?" I asked.

She nodded. I offered. She took. I ignited. We inhaled.

"What's your name?" I asked her.

The girl was all but ready to utter a standard response – "Bambi" or "Trixie" or "Ginger" – but then found herself saying "Hannah". Her turquoise eyes returned to their normal size under her orange ringlets and freckles. It was a complexion that made me fear for her safety under the harsh Nor'west sun. I had to look away.

"Hi, Hannah," I said. "New up here? Like it so far?"

Hannah exhaled a lungful of silvery smoke. She told me she'd worked all different parts of the Nor'west, hopping between townships. The police knew all about it; they were, after all, regular clients themselves. They turned a blind eye unless complaints were made, usually by the wives in town who saw it as evidence of civilised society crumbling. But that still didn't stop a local politician calling for supervised brothels in the Pilbara, like they had down south in the Kalgoorlie goldfields. The next morning, the local newspaper ran the headline: MAKE LOVE – NOT ORE.

"At least this gig runs out of a nice motel," Hannah told me. "Normally, I gotta ply my trade in dingy caravans on the outskirts of town."

"That must be crap," I said, peeling away my sticky shirt. I had given up on trying to wash my work shirts and simply hung them on the clothesline outside the donga, spraying them "clean" with a hose. As they dripped dry of red-dirt water, it was as if they were crying blood.

"Jesus, Richie. As God is my witness, I swear you miners have the best bodies."

My transformation hadn't taken long. A year working the Pilbara had fortified my legs and arms into steel girders. Inches had been stripped from my waist. Muscles rippled the surface of my arms, my neck a fence of tendons. Piloting a slow-moving dump truck weighing a million pounds was a whole-body workout light years ahead of any taxi shift, particularly when it was laden with three hundred tonnes of earth. It was twelve hours of constant motion, endless gear changes, wrestling with a steering wheel the size of a bass drum. When I got back to camp, I ate more food than I ever thought possible, heaping my plate high until I struggled to carry it from the mess, then went back for seconds, thirds. I drank enough water to float a battleship, which continually erupted as bubbles through pores in my now butterscotch skin. Every cell in my body was at optimal performance. I felt bloody fantastic.

"Cheers," I said. "But I'm no miner. I'm just a dumper driver."

"Well, whatever you are, I'm jealous of your girlfriend."

Hannah brushed at her downy thighs. She told me she was seeing a lot more clients like me who didn't want sex. All they wanted was to be held and they often fell asleep in her arms. Intimacy cost more, and they paid handsomely for the whole night.

All hopped up on frontier juice, the men flocked to the Pilbara from across the continent and seas. Global banks held top-level talks with multinational companies. The result was dump trucks full of money offered by international consortia to the best foreign geologists and engineers. With each week came an even bigger business deal. Companies held lavish opening ceremonies with oversized plastic scissors.

The most obvious new presence in the area was the Japanese. Their small archipelago was the biggest buyer of our ore. The men wore browline glasses and smart business suits. I saw them from my dumper, standing on site in tight groups holding a map the size of a bed sheet between them, pointing towards every horizon, then smiling broadly and shaking hands. Their shiny black hair gleamed in the hot sun while their wives' painted white faces shimmered frozen like snow.

The old Pilbara prospectors still remembered fighting in the jungles of New Guinea and the Solomons. They often cornered me in the mess and told me in no uncertain terms that "the little Nips weren't to be trusted", and that they could be "blindfolded with dental floss". The next generation – my generation – had worked hard to forget the past and move on. There was too much at stake. In the newspapers, local journalists ran out of superlatives to describe what was happening in their backyard. Stuff like: "Nature has piled the ore in a neatly accessible way – like bundles of rolls of $1,000,000 notes, waiting to be peeled away."

I went to Port Hedland once, to see the Indian Ocean again. Purple dust rose from Giza-sized pyramids of ore waiting on the wharves. On the deep-blue horizon, bulk carriers – five or six at a time – waited in an orderly queue like jumbo jets on a runway. They took an entire day to dock and take their load from a dirty great stockpile. Mountains of crisp white salt stored nearby were capped with violet peaks. Men poured into town and then dispersed south and east, inland into spinifex country. What was once a sleepy little outpost surrounded by curling fronds of mangrove swamps fast became the mining boom's ground zero. I saw people sleeping on verandahs, in crowded caravan parks, in the backs of cars, along the roadside, wherever. Cash registers rang day and night. The Pier and Esplanade hotels smashed world records for beer consumption.

The first weekend of every month, carloads of blackfellas descended on my compound to play cards. Their stakes were the clothes the Native Welfare Department had supplied, blankets and such. It was only when they lost their bundle that I heard them talk of a curse on the white man for what they were doing to their land. By that time, everyone was too drunk to take them seriously. But what they said stayed with me.

So, I spent my hour talking to Hannah or Debra, or Emma, Sharon or Beth. The girls didn't understand. Hannah didn't understand. And I didn't care – it was my money, my hour, I could say whatever the hell I wanted. I could even talk about my bloody parents if I wanted to. Just so long as I stayed in the room for the entire hour. Then I could return to my crew of men and regale them with stories of my performance. Of how "I gave her the big one", of how "she was begging for more", and of how "she'll be walking funny till Tuesday". We would all laugh heartily and they would slap my back hard.

8

Pilbara / Yindjibarndi Country, 2017

A storm was brewing on the horizon, clouds sweeping across the sky, heaping into something atomic.

"Crap," Mouse said. "That ain't gunna be good for business."

Sparrow didn't know what to make of her remark; it made her sound more like a taxi driver than a trucker. Riding behind them in the spacious sleeper cab, Bob and Luke looked unperturbed. Sparrow suspected they were simply thankful for the truck's modern air conditioning.

"I meant the roads," Mouse added quickly. "They flood fast during the wet season."

Little Mouse was stronger than she looked. She had single-handedly hoisted Luke into the high truck cabin using a makeshift block and tackle. She tied the van with steel rope and winched it onto the trailer, then secured it in place with ratchet straps. The muscles in her arms were so tense they could've supported a troupe of acrobats. Sparrow went to help but she shooed him away, cords showing in her neck. She was now working the red-hot CB radio like a livestock auctioneer. A garbled response crackled through the speaker seconds later.

"Gina," Mouse translated. "Now been upgraded to a category-three tropical cyclone. The oil rigs offshore and all of Port Hedland including the airport have been shut down as a precaution, which means the bulk carriers will be backed up. Non-essential port and construction workers have moved out and mines on the coast have closed. But the mines inland are still operational, which is bloody great news."

Luke was convinced Mouse was turning tricks. She'd already asked Sparrow on more than one occasion "how much fruit" he had in his wallet.

Conversation was instead left to the muscular pull of a deep-throated, six-hundred-horsepower Caterpillar engine. The brown draughty tufts of Australia blurred by, spindly trees and snappy gums like skeletal claws reaching out of the earth, bent and twisted into mangled abstraction. In the distance, mountains loomed out of the sky, while the rumble of machines shattered the silence of spinifex country. With each new explosion, each plundered truckload of dirt, somebody in a glassy boardroom made another million. A red haze of dust filled the air and covered everything in its path, penetrating closed windows and children's lungs.

"I love this smell," Bob said. "It's bitter but familiar."

They overtook a puttering Kombi camper. The long-haired driver was shirtless, in a pair of Y-fronts. He had his seat reclined so far back that he was steering with the dirty sole of his right foot.

"See that?" said Mouse. "Cowboys like that make my job deadly. Still, it's not all bad . . ."

Mouse rolled down her window and eased out a coffee-coloured forearm. She inhaled an invisible cigarette and sipped from an unseen tumbler of Scotch.

"Every six weeks, I clock enough miles to circle the globe. I've seen more sunrises and sunsets than you blokes have had hot dinners. I've driven under a moon so big and bright that I didn't need headlights. Evening's the best time of day. The temperature drops. There's less stress on the engine. The world takes on this golden glow. Hard to describe really. I used to envy all those people in their sleepy little outback towns I drove past. Their routines and interconnectedness. But not anymore. That ain't me. I'm a drifter."

Sparrow glanced back at Luke who wore a look of shock. Much to Luke's disappointment, Mouse was sounding more like a bona fide truck driver and less like a bona fide sex worker.

"Do you drive for a company?" Bob asked.

"Nah," Mouse replied. "I'm an owner-operator. This truck's mine. I pay me own insurance, me petrol, me parts and repairs. I go out and find me own jobs. Some jobs I get paid, some jobs I don't. The industry's like me – a bitch."

"How many hours a day do you drive?" Sparrow asked.

"We're allowed to do seventeen hours, six days a week," Mouse said. "Legally, that is. In the east, they can only do fourteen. The West Australian regime is at the extreme, and the eastern states are jealous of us. Drivers hate being told when to rest and when to drive. I like night shifts best of all."

"How so?" Sparrow asked.

Mouse smiled knowingly. "It's a time of possibilities," she said. "The squares recede, all the roadtrippin' families and grey nomads in their oversized campervans. And then, all the wild animals come out to play. You'll see what I mean soon enough."

Sparrow felt sleepy with the dropping of the sun. His shoulders relaxed, his eyelids half-closed As if on cue, a conspicuous blood-red Hummer roared up alongside Mouse's window. It was covered in halogen spot-lights and had a roo bar the size of Sydney Harbour Bridge. The windows were down, the men inside yelling incomprehensibly, hurling glass bottles into the night, their horn tooting like a car alarm. The end of the working day was reason to celebrate, a chance to switch off their brains and drown their neurons and synapses in booze and vomit. Sparrow was startled back into alertness.

"What's going on?" Bob asked from the sleeper.

"Hey cool," Luke said. "You got groupies."

Sparrow could see the attraction. A truck driver taking to the road was like a lead actor mounting the stage.

"It's the rig," Mouse said. "People are dumb. Like little kids, they're drawn to big, shiny things."

The two men inside the Hummer wore hi-vis shirts with big company logos. An Australian flag sticker on the rear side window proudly proclaimed "FOWF: Fuck Off We're Full".

"Here we go," Mouse muttered, moistening her lips. "About time you knuckleheads showed up."

From their seat in the back, Bob and Luke couldn't see everything that was going on. But Sparrow could. He leaned over and looked down. Both men – including the driver – had their flies undone, fists stroking away in synchrony. Sparrow's eyes grew large with renewed interest.

"See what I mean . . . ?" Mouse said. "Animals. This kinda thing ain't new out 'ere."

Mouse said it was usually women who pulled up beside her rig, their clothes to one side, fingers everywhere. When they got a better look at the truck driver and realised their identity, they sped off. Occasionally, it was a woman and a man out to spice things up, her dress exposed, his hand disappearing between her legs. But men came too, and that was precisely what she wanted.

"Who are they? You know 'em?" Sparrow asked.

"Not yet," Mouse replied. "But I will shortly."

Sparrow glanced back at Luke who wore an I-knew-it smile as wide as the Pilbara horizon.

"Some blokes even come prepared, their cars equipped with a light under the dash that shows off their laps," Mouse said. "Or they carry torches. All very sophisticated and highly twisted."

She rolled down her window. After a series of hand signals, the Hummer sped off ahead, indicated left, and turned off the road into a makeshift rest bay. Mouse eased her foot off the accelerator and went down in the gears. The Hummer parked in a discreet spot, as far away from the road as possible without risking the truck getting bogged. Mouse eased up nearby. The way she parked was so the cabin faced away from the Hummer, back towards the highway, which prevented her travel companions from seeing what was happening. She then reached behind her seat and grabbed a big black gym bag.

"Whoa, wait, where the hell are you going?" Sparrow's voice was urgent. "I thought you were taking us north."

"I am," she said. "This is just a pit stop. You boys wait here a tick. Twenty minutes, thirty tops."

She hopped down the cab's steps and was gone. The first droplets of Cyclone Gina started to splash on the windscreen, obscuring visibility.

By the time the sound of her footsteps on the scratchy dirt had faded, Luke found his voice.

"No," Sparrow replied. "No way."

"Aw, go on!"

"Mate, it's none of our business," Bob added.

"She's doing us a favour here," said Sparrow. "We should respect her privacy, whatever she's doing. Do you want her to dump us in the middle of nowhere?"

"Privacy?" Luke said. "You see that whopping great bonnet out there in front of us? It didn't look like she gave a flying frig about privacy when she was spread out on top of that! Christ, I'd go sneak a peek myself if I wasn't such a cripple."

Sparrow had hoped Mouse would return by the time Luke's debating skills ran dry. But she didn't. And Luke, eventually, wore him down.

"One look," Bob said. "Sparrow is going to take one *quick* look, then he's coming straight back."

Sparrow made it clear that it was just to be on the safe side after Luke suggested she might be stabbing the poor miners to death.

"What if we're next?" he argued.

Sharp drops of rain stabbed the top of Sparrow's head as he exited the cabin. Skulking across to the Hummer, he crouched to conceal his final approach. He had to tread carefully, this was big snake country.

They could be curled up like landmines and were filled with neurotoxins and blood coagulants.

To Sparrow's surprise, the van wasn't rockin'. Nor were the windows splashed red with fresh blood. What he really needed was a periscope to see without being seen.

Poking the top half of his head above the window line, Sparrow was blinded by the flash of a camera. And then another. As his retinas blinked away the flood of white light, the interior of the car came clear. Sparrow wiped away the rain from the window and peered in. The interior light was on.

Mouse was in a sheer negligee. A tattoo of an enormous hand grenade was on her right ribs, a rodent on the inside of her left calf. She was on her knees. The two men were lying in the vehicle's rear section in minimal dress. Sparrow looked closer at the immobile miners, lipstick and blusher on their faces, frilly women's briefs with matching garter belts and stockings on their legs.

Mouse was rummaging through a dirty pair of jeans.

Just as she found a thick wallet and began emptying it of its contents, she looked up to see Sparrow staring back.

9

Pilbara / Yindjibarndi Country, 1977

Bob

It was the first weekend at the pit lake that really kicked things off. I'd fallen in with a veteran crew who'd been sneaking off to an undisclosed location for months. They finally invited me along but swore me to secrecy. You'll see what I mean soon enough.

The workday couldn't go fast enough, and I was in no mood for slowing things up. Saturday's shift began at six a.m. with me hanging one arm out the window of my monolithic dumper and yelling at the prick in front.

"What are ya bloody doin', ya dumb bastard? This'll cost the company a thousand bucks a minute! And yer lucky it didn't cost some poor sod his life."

I had no patience for new drivers, especially those who spilled half their craggy load all over the road. No-one ever gave me a break when I was a rookie, so I figured this was simple payback. One day, they could break someone else's balls.

At my suggestion, the company had left the wreckage of a mangled Jeep Safari by the roadside. It was meant to be an ominous reminder, a warning of a regular car's mortality when faced with a dumper whose driver had only limited vision. From the very top of the mine, at the earth's surface, the vehicles' choreography looked so simple and elegant.

Trucks and shovels and dozers moved in intricate, prescribed patterns. An industrial ballet on a scale visible from space.

A siren sounded, lasting a full minute. They were about to blast, everyone had to clear the area. Dynamite was the scientifically proven most effective shovel. Dragline excavators then scooped up the ore with their long brontosaurus snouts, taking a hundred tonnes with each bite and loading it into an orderly queue of waiting dumpers. Twenty minutes later, having inched their way to the top of the mine, the tricera-tops dumpers arched their backs and tipped their loads, which were transported to crushers via an intricate web of conveyors. The primary crusher broke down the boulders into football-sized lumps before the secondary crusher moulded the misshapen footballs into smaller grape-fruits. More conveyors then carried the rocks to stockpiles, each of which had a load-out tunnel underneath. Gravity-fed chutes dropped the ore into a millipede of train wagons a mile long, which then whisked it off to the port. So simple, yet one wrong move could cost millions.

It was a rare occasion – such as a spilled load of ore – when I actually laid eyes on the miners. The metal animals went about their work like intelligent life forms on another planet, their diesel nostrils belching a continuous stream of tar-black smoke as they clanked out a working tune of metallic music. It was only when they ceased their labours and lined up to rest that their organic brains emerged from their dim cabins, themselves expelling great plumes of tobacco smoke from their head holes.

Quitting time at six p.m. finally arrived. My shift had been hellish. I'd had a shit truck that day, the pig of the fleet. The slopes had appeared steeper and the ledges more precarious. I shook the last petrous load off my back with a press of a big red hydraulic button and parked my Haulpak next to the other yellow monsters. I killed the ignition, opened the door, descended the ladder, and promptly fell flat onto the red earth. Twelve hours in the saddle can contort a man's hamstrings into forkfuls of spaghetti and turn his superheated brain to bolognese sauce.

The bus ride back to the compound was always an uncertain time of day that stirred mixed feelings in me. On the one hand, there was the relief of another dismal day over. But on the other, it was the first chance for news to spread of the shift's casualties – the men who went to war with land and machine and returned with parts missing, or not at all.

I looked for Rocky first, my big dumb Maori roommate with the truthful brown eyes. I pensively tugged at my beard when I couldn't find him. Then I saw him smiling at me from the back of the bus, raising his burly right arm and waggling all two of his fingers. It was a sign that all was well, or at least as well as it could have been ever since the day Rocky had hurried while unloading the dynamite they used to unblock an ore pass. Clumsy bastard. Along with half his digits, a similar proportion of Rocky's hearing had ended up strewn across the Pilbara dirt.

"Shortcuts are like that," Rocky had told me on his return from the hospital. "They got a habit of reminding you why they're called short-cuts."

"Yep," I said. "But at least yer alive, mate."

"Huh?"

They only managed to find Rocky's little finger, and they couldn't save it anyway. He kept it in a jar of brine beside his bunk as a memento, showing it off at every opportunity. Rocky kept telling me he was lucky, which I already knew. A month earlier, I'd seen a worker get his head crushed like a walnut in between a building and a cherry picker. He got wedged in and pinned over the lift controls, and the other men in the picker couldn't reach them to take it down. There was an override switch on the ground but the three blokes down there were fresh off the boat from Yugoslavia and couldn't speak English nor operate the controls. I'd been around the mines long enough to know the operators offered the drones extra cash in hand to do the most dangerous jobs, which was still cheaper than ensuring all the safety requirements were in place. The foreigners were also willing to do the most hazardous jobs and didn't understand what a union was. I felt for the poor, desperate bastards – they knew no better.

There were always rumours circulating around the camp that I couldn't help but hear and be tempted by. Of what other mines were paying or what food they served or which ones had concrete paths. I saw blokes spit the dummy in the middle of their shift and walk off on a whim. The latest whisperings that I'd heard were a little more disconcerting, of robots replacing humans in the Pilbara. It seemed far-fetched but would apparently start with fully automated trucks navigating around pre-defined courses from stockpiles to crushers to waste dumps. Driverless tunnelling machines and trains would soon follow. I didn't want to be made redundant so soon. All I knew how to do in this world was drive.

Back at camp, relieved to be alive and with livers intact, we drank the world dry. Great lakes of alcohol meant to replenish our dehydrated bodies. Since it was the end of the working week, the camp cook presented his special Saturday dessert, rich and moist and laced with homegrown ingredients. All it took was a mouthful of that loopy space cake and I would stumble back to my donga via the orbit of Saturn . . .

Hangover Sunday always arrived too soon, and with a fury that while not unexpected was always unwelcome. I was grateful for the little white coin in the silver foil, Alka-Seltzer, distributed freely in the mess from first light.

As with most places, Sunday was a day of worship in the Pilbara, and so it was spent in the region's only recognised cathedral – the pub. It was also a day of rest and recreation that entailed an element of creativity.

Like all the other men, I wasn't hungry and skipped breakfast. By lunchtime, our appetites had returned, along with the blowflies. Platters of corned beef and cabbage were dished up and devoured; a large intestine's wet dream. I pulled an incisor out of my stew that was not my own and kept eating. As usual, the plumbing in the toilets blocked, overflowed.

We were in a hurry. Our ears were pricked, waiting, listening out for an agonised sound at the gates of the compound. A hard-revving Volkswagen Type II bus converted to a flatbed pickup truck, and it would mean our departure time was nigh. I had my swag all ready by my side. When I heard the VW's anguished whir, I sprinted, leading the pack. I hurled my bedroll in the tray and jumped into the front seat. Ten more bedrolls followed in quick succession to complete the quota. Laden with over one tonne of man meat, the truck's muffler scraped the dirt all the way into town. Sparks flew from the car's underside until the town's asphalt road again became rough red earth.

As the vehicle skimmed across the scratchy orange clay, an expectant grin spread across my face. I had known for some time that there were abandoned mining pits dotted across the Pilbara. I had even seen them when I first flew in. The companies didn't bother backfilling them with dirt; it was cheaper that way. They just walked away, leaving a gaping sore in the face of the earth.

"It's called a mine void," Bandit, the powder monkey, told me.

The voids were below the natural groundwater table, so water seeped in over time, topped off during the wet season with fresh rainwater. The result was a pit lake, and a bathing spot for gritty landlubbers.

"And youse blokes swim in it?" I asked.

"Flamin' oath we do," Bandit replied.

"First I've heard of it," I said. "And besides, I thought those lakes were two feet of water and six of mud."

"They can be," said Bandit. "But not the one we go to. Took me yonks to find it. It's bloody paradise. Just don't dive to the bottom and don't swallow the water."

"Why? What'll happen?"

No day at the beach was without its casualties. Those who bared the contents of their guts to the world were quick to blame "the bloody lake water" with its high levels of acid, sulfate, and dissolved metals. Never mind the eighteen cans of lager they'd consumed in the baking sun beforehand. Bloody lake water!

All my life I'd felt like an outsider, but it still took me some time to realise that we were outsiders even to the outsiders. There was a newly minted swimming pool in the town, surrounded by barbed-wire fencing to keep out the wildlife and Aboriginal communities, but that wasn't what kept us away. What kept us away were the shiny, happy families that had flocked to the area. They'd been lured by mining companies who understood that a family-oriented workforce was the key to a successful Nor'west enterprise. When the small township of Wittenoom was built, the Australian Blue Asbestos Company constructed roads, sidewalks, an airport, racecourse, and even playgrounds, all of which they paved or lined with locally mined asbestos tailings. It was their generous way of giving something back. The ultramarine particles were also sprinkled liberally to reduce dust around houses and in children's sandpits. The kids greeted mum for tea every night with smiling faces covered in a fine blue residue. Social clubs and Australian Rules football teams were formed. Men took their wives for dinner and dancing at motels – the companies even flew up live entertainment from Perth.

We single men had none of that. This was the era for nuclear families, and each of us outsiders had something that excluded us. It was, after all, why we were in the Nor'west in the first place. We were scum. Mothers steered their children away from us for fear of assault, rape or murder. I was the stranger in the park and at the pool, the bogeyman under their beds, the vampire who drank their blood at night. But screw them. Like third-class passengers aboard the *Titanic*, the Pilbara's bachelors had decided to make their own fun. And that meant improvising.

I rode to the pit lake in the shade of the cabin, sitting between Bandit and Rocky on the bench seat of grey vinyl and duct tape. I was happy to avoid the sizzling skillet of the aluminium tray. The grog had a quick effect on those baking in the back. I watched as they peeled off their sodden blue shearer's singlets and passed the time Greco-Roman wrestling. Bandit drove, gently rolling the steering wheel from left to right, making the rear wheels slip and the truck fishtail on the dusty road and laughing along. The eight occupants in the back nearly kissed the dirt on multiple occasions, which only made Bandit chortle louder. Bandit had eyes that disappeared when he laughed. I liked that, although as a passenger, I preferred a driver who kept sight of the road. But Bandit just kept laughing and sucking on the tinnie resting between his sweaty thighs. I noticed a quincunx tattoo of five dots near the base of his thumb. It represented time in prison.

"Isn't there a national park round here?" I asked. "That'd have gorges, rock pools. Maybe even waterfalls."

"That's another four hours away," said Bandit. "And full of bloody squares anyway. Nup. Trust me, mate. This is *our* spot where we do *our* thing."

It was a three-hour drive. When we arrived, I thought the mine void looked more like a Swiss mountain lake, and just as cool and inviting, the cliff face on all four sides like cuts of fresh steak. There was an ancient boab tree, its trunk fat and twisted like a question mark, perched on the pit's southern edge, hanging on for grim death. It was a race to the water, sunburnt blokes leaping off the tray while Bandit was still applying the brakes. They stripped off their remaining layers and dived in head-first to wash away the dry sweat and dust suffocating their skin. Having grown up so close to the Indian Ocean, I was a strong swimmer and fancied my chances in the water. But I was warned by Bandit to "be careful 'cos this lake's much deeper than a normal lake".

"After all," Bandit added with a yeasty burp, "it's a pit."

Not that that concerned the drunks who staggered towards the water like newborn turtles, some of them falling over en route and mortally wounding their cans of beer.

But it was worth all the effort. I leaped and dived through the calm waters all afternoon, frolicking in the mineral tonic until the light began to fade. Unseen fish and eels tickled my toes; I nearly soiled myself on first touch, amazed that aquatic life could survive in such an industrial cocktail. They probably had extra eyes or had grown new fins. The men continued their splashing, grappling, holding each other's heads under the surface, doling out brandings with wet tennis balls. A makeshift diving platform constructed from stray boulders launched all manner of world-class bombs and belly flops. All the pit needed to be absolutely perfect was an old tyre swing.

The afternoon was everything for us condemned men, it was the essence of living for today, of freedom, of the times. So much of what I did in the Pilbara was with tomorrow in mind, whether it was twelve hours in the saddle or two years in the Nor'west. The less time I spent in the moment, in my own battered body and embittered thoughts, the better. But not on this day, at the pit lake, which ended all too soon. I emerged from the water years younger. All the men did.

"How good was that, eh, bro?" grinned Rocky.

I beamed straight back at him.

With our bellies full of sun and grog and devoid of food, the only thing left to do was collapse and sleep. There would be no driving back to camp tonight; that would have ruined the ecstasy of the day and also ruled out a second swim in the morning. Someone threw me my swag which I unfurled and eased onto. The lingering warmth in the earth against my back dissolved my aches and dried my skin like an electric blanket on low setting.

A chance to sleep under the stars was also simply a chance to sleep. In all my years at camp, I could count the number of uninterrupted nights on one finger, and that had been thanks to a debilitating head cold with the force of a coma. It was usually the sound of breaking glass or men fighting or yelling or an unexpected visitor in my donga. The previous week, a resident in the next donga had tried to kill a spider crawling across the ceiling with his shotgun and only succeeded in constructing his own skylight. But things were looking up. At least I no longer slept with a knife in my hand.

At the pit lake, the men lay like fallen sticks around an invisible campfire. As the last skerrick of daylight disappeared, a zillion twinkling stars took its place; nature's mobile serenading me into a newborn's slumber. I thought everyone was asleep until I heard the man behind me stand up, roll up his swag, and stagger up the road, out of the pit and off into the desert.

I found it strange but thought no more of it until a second silent man did the same thing about a minute later, following the trail of the first. I looked up to see the dark figure tiptoeing away wearing only a pair of desert boots.

When two more pairs of feet repeated the same routine a few minutes later, and again two more five minutes after that, I knew it was no coincidence. I lay there, listening, fascinated. But all I heard was the silent desert whispering through the chirruping of crickets and the fluted, languid call of a lone pied butcherbird. Peaceful and haunting, rolling over granite and sandstone, the resting bird's delicate whistle was the last thing I heard before the blackness enveloped me.

At first light, the blowflies assembled in squadrons to feast on my face. I sat up, rubbed my crusty eyes, swatted away the dive bombers from my mouth and nostrils, and counted the number of men lying by the water's edge. Eleven, all present and accounted for.

Had I dreamed the phantom footsteps the previous night? There was no mention of any nocturnal manoeuvres that morning while we swam.

But then I saw the fresh sets of footprints leading out of the pit.

The ride back to camp in Bandit's flatbed was decidedly less boisterous than the drive out to the lake. Perhaps it was the prospect of returning to the Monday grind, or a second collective hangover in two mornings. Or something else. Like those fresh black eyes that I saw two of the men now had.

The Pilbara's unwritten law had left me wanting.

10

Pilbara / Yindjibarndi Country, 2017

Mouse saw Sparrow staring at her semi-naked body through the Hummer's window. She immediately snatched and collected everything on the floor – sheer lingerie, a whiskey bottle, a dildo – and hurled them into her gym bag. The door flung open and she bolted for the prime mover in bare feet. Sparrow followed as fast as he could. He was gasping for oxygen by the time he fell into the cabin. Mouse stalled the engine. The diesel eventually roared to life sending a hot plume of orange dust out of its exhaust stack.

The truck flew north. The speedometer shot through the hundred kilometres per hour mark. It was soon nudging one thirty.

"Thought you said this thing was limited to a hundred," Sparrow panted.

"It was," Mouse smiled. "Till I disabled the speed limiter."

She had a look of drag-strip determination in her eyes. She popped two indistinct white pills into her mouth and washed them down with a mouthful of whiskey from a hip flask. The highway unwound before them like an endless roll of black wallpaper. Sparrow couldn't decide if he was shit-scared or relieved to be back on the road. After all, she could very easily have left him in the badlands with two motionless bodies. Luke looked like he'd creamed his pants, seeing an alluring young woman in a sheer negligee behind the wheel of a barrelling road train. He kept stretching and craning his fat neck in the hope of improving his frontal angle. Bob looked tired and appeared to be struggling to keep up with all that was happening.

"What's going on?" he whispered to Luke. "Are they dead, did she kill them?"

"Listen," Sparrow said to Mouse, "we mean you no harm. The boy, he's young, spare him. And the old man couldn't hurt a fly. If you're gonna hurt anyone, then take me—"

"Oh shut the hell up," Mouse huffed. "Can youse all just shut your gobs for one bloody minute and let me get us outta 'ere? Right now is the most important time, I gotta make the most of it."

Speeding is a helluva way to get yourself noticed, was what Sparrow wanted to say, among other things. The back of his skull burned hot with all the blood being dragged into it. Bob complained, said he felt nauseous. Luke said the road's rapid corrugations were sending shock waves up his "fucked spine".

A sharp rise in the road ahead threatened to rob the truck of all its momentum and traction. They were off the map now, Christ knows where, headed deeper into the red void of Australia's vast interior where others were less likely to find them. Mouse dropped a gear and pushed her orange-soled foot to the floor. The dashboard needles shot up into the red zone. The road was slicked with a wet membrane. Sparrow felt the wheels slipping, the cabin floor burning, and the unpleasant taste of stomach acid at the back of his throat.

"These bits are the worst," Mouse grumbled. "Turbo charger shoots up over six hundred degrees. All the gearboxes break a hundred. And now we're towing your bloody jalopy as well, extra weight."

The engine roared, the cabin shuddered, and the trailers threatened to break free. On the horizon, dark mountains beckoned. A lightning bolt fractured the sky like it was a pane of glass. As if willing the truck forward, Mouse let out a primal scream. Luke joined in. Sparrow tried to scream but nothing came out.

Just as the earth's angle evened off and gravity plopped Sparrow's heart back into his chest, nature's next obstacle appeared – a hundred-metre stretch of flooded road. There was no consultation; nor, at that speed, any other choice. Mouse slammed her rig headlong into the drink, sending two great arcs of water flying into the air like she was parting the Red Sea. Bob was howling, Luke was squealing. Mouse was laughing maniacally, devil horns sprouting from her head. And Sparrow was left wondering whether he might've been better off staying with her two victims in the middle of bloody nowhere, or even back in a quiet cop station in Perth.

"Just a big puddle!" shrieked Mouse with glee.

Another crack of electricity lacerated the sky, illuminating the heavens and sending flickers of light rippling through the cloud ceiling. In the distance, the Hamersley Ranges appeared, bruised, menacing. A thick curtain of rain raced towards the highway. A large, battered road sign flashed past. It was then that Sparrow realised that they had entered the infamous Westralian valley of death.

Wittenoom was a town of hovering threads and a cancerous breeze. It had been erased from all road maps so that visitors could no longer find it. The site of Australia's worst industrial disaster, which was still being played out in the country's nursing homes.

"Should we really be here?" Bob asked.

"Why, what's wrong?" Luke said.

"All the blue asbestos they mined here until the 1960s – big mistake. Malignant mesothelioma. I saw it first hand in elderly residents at the nursing home. Started with a cough. Then the fluid around their lungs gradually stole their breath away. There's still a risk from the tiny fibres left behind on the ground and in the air."

"Even without power, there's still six diehards livin' here in Wittenoom," said Mouse. "And a shitload more squatters."

"No power?" said Luke. "So how do they get by? Are they Abos or something?"

Sparrow scowled.

"No," said Mouse. "They're not *First Nations Australians.* They got backyard generators. There's no amenities either. Heck, even the cops stopped patrolling the area."

It was Mouse's last remark that Sparrow heard above all others. His mission was swiftly unravelling.

Mouse finally applied the brakes outside Doc Holiday's derelict American-style café. As she reached for her gym bag, another thunderbolt reached for the earth, and Sparrow reached for the door handle. He swore he'd spotted a solar-powered phone box a few kilometres back up the road that he could probably die trying to reach on foot and holding his breath. Mobile phone coverage had been poor to non-existent ever since they left the outskirts of Perth; mainly the latter. Luke gratefully received an eyeful until Mouse covered her dignity with a tight blue shearer's singlet. She flicked on an interior light and jumped into the sleeper cab, nestling down beside Luke.

"Now," said Mouse, "let's see what we have here . . ."

There were more dirty wads of cash than Sparrow could have ever imagined. Mouse licked her dark cherry lips and let rip a loud laugh.

"These mining morons who work Fly-In Fly-Out are always bloody loaded," she said. "They do jobs on the side and get paid in cold hard cash."

Luke's eyes grew large. "Holy shit!" he said. "Did you just make all that money?"

Sparrow, sneering inwardly, filled with an unexpected confidence. Something in him had stirred. It was the realisation that if Mouse was going to do anything to them involving either a shallow grave or a refrigerated trailer full of body parts, she already would have. No, this young hellcat was up to something else. Something unconventional.

"Hmm, yes," Sparrow said. "Tell us, sweet rodent . . . *How* in the world did you *make* all this money?" He smiled knowingly.

Mouse looked up from her accounting. Her eyes were puffy, cheerless, tired. Sparrow assessed it as a look of apprehension mixed with a tinge of trust. It was a look that mirrored his own.

Mouse swallowed the lump crowding her throat. Her gaze drifted to the windscreen, then outside. Savaged for decades by the scourge of blue asbestos, the town was now being smashed by the fringes of a cyclone. Perhaps this would finally be its merciful end. Bullet rain pounded the roof of the prime mover, amplifying the intimacy of an already confined space.

"Well, mister," she said. "You saw. I drugged 'em, dressed 'em, and robbed 'em. And just in case they decided to ark up and complain, I took a few photos as insurance to upload to social media or mail to their home addresses for their wives and girlfriends to see."

She took a moment to check she had ticked all her mental boxes, then re-moistened her thumb and returned to flicking through her piles of bills. Sparrow lost count after the first thousand. Putting the money to one side, Mouse reached back into her gym bag and pulled out a handful of silver sachets bearing the design of a red cobra poised to strike.

"Ha!" She laughed. "Synthetic dope. Fly-In Fly-Out workers love this shit 'cos it's not picked up by company drug tests. This is like gold for FIFOs."

"So, lemme get this straight," Sparrow said. "You're a prostitute who doesn't believe in customer service?"

Mouse shot him daggers. "*I'm no whore*," she said coolly. "I don't screw for money and I never will."

Luke pulled a face. "So," he said, "if you're not a hooker, what are ya?"

Mouse sat back in the sleeper, flicked her black hair and smiled slyly. "I'm a modern-day siren," she said. "Men find *me*."

"Yeah, but it helps if you wave a big friggin' flag!" Luke said. "You sound like a slut to me."

"Lukas!" said Bob.

Luke grunted a laugh. Mouse fired him a deathly stare that made him shrink an inch. She ran soft fingers through her sweaty hair, exhaled. Sparrow sensed there was more to the story. Bob shook his head, appearing overwhelmed and tired.

"Drivin' the outback for so long has shown me the absolute worst of men." Mouse sighed. "And when they work Fly-In Fly-Out, it turns ugly. They live far away and have no connection to where they work so they'll happily shit in someone else's yard. No-one's safe. Not locals. Not women. Not other men. And not even the FIFOs themselves. After a certain point, life's not worth living anymore."

Sparrow thought a while about what she'd said. Bob eventually spoke.

"Suicides, eh?" he said. "Happened in my day too. It's the isolation, the loneliness. Men slowly go mad out here. The only cost for mining the Pilbara is a shovel and your soul."

"I keep finding unopened packs of antidepressants," Mouse said. "FIFOs get them prescribed but they're too scared to take them. They fear it'll be picked up in urine tests and they'll lose their jobs."

"Jesus," said Sparrow.

"But it's not just the suicides," Mouse continued. "It's the accidents, beatings, rapes, murders. And it doesn't help if you go round shoving ice into your head every night."

Sparrow was especially familiar with the scourge of ice in his own community. It had transformed his home town into something unrecognisable. Leaving Cobb had been an easy decision.

"Back in my day, people had a few joints and mellowed out," Bob said.

"There's much better drugs now," Mouse said sarcastically. "Stronger chemicals, improved hallucinations. Times have changed."

"And how," Bob lamented.

"Look, let's not fuck about," Mouse said. "Out here, it's man's country. Always was, still is, and likely always will be. Mining towns have fifteen times more men, mining sites have fifty. Topless women are still paraded through pubs on skimpy nights for blokes to come ogle. As if we're fucking meat trays at a pub raffle. Fuck that. I needed to turn that shit on its head."

Sparrow couldn't help but offer a small mental round of applause. Mouse was a criminal, that was for sure. But she was having fun with it, being creative.

"I see myself as restoring their deeply suppressed feminine sides," she said coolly.

Sparrow nodded. Luke stayed silent.

"And those two shitheads today – Tweedledum and Tweedledumber – wanted to spit roast me!" She let rip a loud snort of contempt.

"So, the evidence you collect, the photos and whatnot," Sparrow said. "Does it work?"

"Has so far," said Mouse. "But just to make sure, I nick their driver's licences as well, so they know I'm not messing about. The shame's too much for most blokes. They know that things can spread like wildfire these days. Good ol' internet. One click and half the Pilbara can see 'em in drag. They'd never live that down. So they'd sooner just forget what happened with me, write it off like a car round a light pole, and just walk away. And anyway, they know what I take is chicken feed compared to what they earn."

Sparrow felt a faint smile creep across his face. The lawman in him was making careful cognitive notes of all he was seeing and hearing, storing it on file for later. This wasn't his jurisdiction, but he would look into contacting the local police at a later juncture. For the time being, he had other things on his mind. A murder investigation, which he was struggling to keep any kind of rein on. What started out simple and effortless was fast becoming complicated and arduous.

"Those blokes'll be okay?" he asked Mouse.

She nodded. "Bit groggy, but the Rohypnol will be outta their systems in a few hours. Tell ya what though, some of the bastards are big. I need a double dose to bring 'em down. The Islanders especially."

"But why?" Bob asked. "It can't just be the money. Is it the rush? The power?"

Outside the cabin, the violent rain eased and the wind dissolved into the night. The edges of Mouse's eyes glistened under the dim interior light.

"Look, I don't wanna rabbit on about it . . . But let's just say, I'm on a personal crusade after what two drunk bastards did to me last summer."

A prolonged silence engulfed the night. Then, with one almighty snort, Mouse reeled in both her mucus and her soul. Her dark face reappeared in the cabin, her cheeks sunken, moist, her eyes calm.

"So now that you blokes know all about me, it's my turn to ask you," she said. "You three bastards look *nothin'* like miners. At least no miners I've ever seen. First of all, and no disrespect, but you look about a hundred years old. Second, you're disabled. And third, mining companies rarely employ blackfellas and only ever 'cos they have to."

Bob, Luke and Sparrow all exchanged crafty glances. Their gazes bounced back and forth like three mirrors facing each other.

"Don't sweat it, fellas," Mouse added. "I already heard on the CB. The cops are after an old man and a bloke in a wheelchair who escaped from a nursing home in a stolen vehicle that looks a helluva lot like the one we're towing, if I'm not mistaken. So, I guess we're all up to no good, eh. Now, you wanna tell me what you did . . . ?"

11

Perth / Whadjuk Noongar Country, 2016

Bob

The day I met Luke, I woke suffocating in a quicksand of red earth. The more the years passed, the more the Pilbara came to me whenever I closed my eyes. A nurse entered my room and flicked the vertical blinds open with a swift hand. The morning sunlight spewed in. I winced and snapped my eyelids shut and lifted the jaundiced bed sheets above my head.

"Everything hurts," I whimpered. "I need more drugs. I'm sure I'm dying."

With every breath, I felt a chill in my lungs. My cells cried out for the sweet syrup of morphine.

"Mr Cooper, I refuse to speak to a blanket," the nurse said. "Come out and stop being such a baby."

There was a moment of silence.

"I'm dying," the blanket said.

"Fine," the nurse said, readying herself to leave. "Stay there and rot – die! It's less work for me. But so long as you're alive, the director wants to see you in his office."

I waited until I heard her footsteps on the corridor's vinyl flooring. And then another five minutes, just to be sure. I downed the glass of fluorescent red water sitting next to my digital clock with three gulps, sat up, and stumbled to the bathroom. Carefully, I lathered my jaw with a badger-hair brush and soap and shaved using my straight razor. Gone were the days of a heavy beard that doubled the size of my face. I missed it.

"Hmm," I said, examining a thin slice of my reflection in the long silver blade. "She's pretty blunt. I better strop her soon."

I stood before the mirror and examined my bare chest. A mosaic of faded and sagging tattoos swam through the networks of lines on my arms and shoulders. Every morning, I saw subtle changes in my shape as my meds redistributed the fat around my body. My arse had almost completely flattened. And I loathed my new beer belly even more than my buffalo hump. Both were side effects from years of heavy pharmaceuticals.

I applied the final touches. Musky aftershave, burning the fresh red spots pooling on my face, teeth flossed to a minty freshness, and a light moisturiser, a blend of coconut, vanilla and avocado oil.

Wearing a crisp new check shirt buttoned to the collar, tan trousers, and my trusty Blundstones, I stood by my door. I inhaled one last breath of fortitude and stepped outside my room, striding to the director's office as quickly as possible.

Blackford kept me waiting. The arsehole knew what he was doing. His time was more valuable than mine.

It was my third summons in a month. As usual, I knew what it would be about: another resident would've complained about me and "my kind". I thought at their age they would've had better things to do – dying, for example. But they didn't.

Blackford finally entered. He plopped into his weathered office chair and shifted his frame. The chair creaked and strained. He cracked the tab on a can of diet cola with cigarette-stained fingers. Although he tried to keep them out of view, I could see a carton of each in arm's reach beneath his desk. I watched him take a slurp and wince at the bitter aftertaste, letting the artificial sweeteners wash away the saturated fats into his bottomless gut.

He looked at me with eyes the colour of milk stout and started talking. It was white noise. After some time, the words got louder and more repetitive.

"Robert? Robert . . . ?"

"Hmm? What?"

"Did you hear me?"

"Yes, but if you can please just repeat what you said."

"Did you spit in the soup?"

"The soup? What soup?"

"In the dining room," said Blackford. "The tureen we have in there. Where everyone can go and help themselves."

I held up an index finger. "Ah. Ah yes. Lovely soup the other day, I think potato and leek, with a hint of chives. My compliments to the chef."

"And?"

"And what? You mean, it wasn't potato and leek?"

"For Chrissakes, man!" Blackford was in no mood. "Did you *spit* in it?"

"*Spit in the soup?*" I shifted on my flattened non-buttocks. "Why would I possibly spit in the soup if I ate two bowls' worth? Delicious."

Blackford was getting nowhere, his jaw audibly grinding. I flashed him my best smile. I was enjoying this. I considered it sport. It got me nowhere, but at least it deflected focus from my plight. My time was measured and I was fighting a losing battle.

"It could have done with a few croutons," I added. "But it didn't want for mucus, mine or anyone else's."

"Look—'

"You should join us for soup someday, Geoffrey, instead of going out and buying those greasy hamburgers and fried chicken you insist on eating. Good food comes in tureens, not buckets."

"Now just a—'

"It's a subtle difference but one that'll mean I'll no longer have to sit here and listen to your arteries hardening."

"Look, enough!" Blackford said. "Can it! I have it on good authority you spat in the soup."

I stayed silent, my mouth clamped shut with invisible stitches. Finally, I said, "Good authority, eh?"

"Yes."

"And what authority is that? Can I guess? Was it the same authority who claimed that I bled in the tomato sauce?"

Blackford massaged a thick violet vein in his right temple. He swallowed two ibuprofens with the remaining drops of his cola and poured himself a watery mug of black coffee from a carafe.

"No, thanks," I said, preempting any offer of a cup.

"Robert, I'm just trying to do a job here," Blackford said, scratching his hot eyes. "It's not easy being director of nursing. Budgets, inspections, staff. It's not just a headache, it's a throbbing migraine that never stops. Most days I feel like a school principal trying to keep the peace between unruly children. It's bad enough you have your own room. You know we're funded by the number of beds we fill."

I leaned back in my chair as if on summer holiday. "So you keep reminding me," I said. "And that's not my fault. I don't mind if you move someone in beside me. In fact, I'd prefer it. I like the company."

"You know we've tried that." Blackford blew out a deep plume of brown air from his black lungs. "You know I want nothing more than to see every bed in this facility filled."

"I do. I know."

"Robert, some of the people in here are very sick, much sicker than you."

"They're *sick* alright."

"I can't control what they think, nor can I control what they say or do. But I need to treat all accusations of food tampering seriously."

"Geoffrey," I said calmly. "I can assure you. If I ever have dark thoughts of spitting in the soup or bleeding in the sauce or pissing in the coffee pot, you'll be the absolute first person to know."

Blackford froze, his cheeks swollen with a large mouthful of luke-warm brew. I flashed him a smug grin. With some uncertainty, he gulped.

"Okay, Robert. I think we're done for today."

I left the office and strode past the lounge where the other children were just as I had left them, sitting, waiting. Occasionally, one poor thing cried for attention. At the beginning of life or its end, days are defined by waiting and accompanied by howls of disapproval. Mum's coffee date with her gossipy friends always took forever. So did the drive to the beach in a hot car, or the time it took the teacher to call on you in class when you knew the answer. When that blur otherwise known as "life" was over, the waiting returned. But now it was waiting for someone to help you out of bed, to dress you, to feed you, morning, noon and night. Waiting for the lights to go out, for the day, and forever. For the first time in decades, I had nothing *but* time. Only it was junk time, useless, spent waiting for the end.

The other residents had cleverly adapted to my unnerving presence. Children they might have been, but ingenious children knew how to keep the school principal on side. It wasn't for them to say anything to me about my issues, nor to confront me with theirs. At least, not to my face. They were much more comfortable sitting in arthritic clumps, watching everything I did, whispering . . .

Ooh look, he's picked up a book to read. Ooh, did you see that, he just poured milk on his breakfast cereal.

Like I was some freak show.

By the time I was ready to eat, what spare seats there had been at the dining table a minute earlier were gone. It was musical chairs and I lost every time.

I didn't say anything. I didn't need to. I went and ate by myself on the wonky table in the corner. It was the same when I went to the lounge to watch TV, except there they all slowly shuffled back to their rooms with their walkers and canes. I was left with my recliner of choice in which to watch a soap opera I could neither follow nor care about. Grudges were healthy, I told myself. Hate was the only thing keeping some people alive.

In my six months at Leafy Gums, I'd had five different roommates. Soon after they moved in, they all moved out again. Apparently, I had "driven them out". My nearest neighbours petitioned Blackford to lock their doors at night for fear I "might enter".

Of course, none of this came as a surprise to me. My whole life, I was used to being a pariah. But harder to stomach were the nursing aides who wore rubber gloves – sometimes two pairs – when opening the door to my room or changing my linen. They might as well have worn bright-yellow biohazard suits and brandished Geiger counters. Or the nurses themselves, particularly those from Africa, often from countries that were deeply religious. Perth was their first stop after crossing the Indian Ocean. Blackford liked them because they worked for nix, did the jobs no-one else wanted, and didn't talk back. Just like the migrant workers on the mines once did. But that didn't stop them from refusing to take my temperature or check my blood pressure for fear of an impossible infection. Some nurses even considered themselves literary critics and confiscated my magazines, or I'd find them ripped and strewn around my room. That was the worst.

I returned to my quarters, to wait for dusk, for night. To wait. Lying on my bed, my pre-coffin, listening to the birds on the roof, watching the fading sunlight on the new leaves. Clouds hung like smoke in the tangerine sky.

Nightfall meant the explosions would be starting soon. Meth-amphetamine labs blowing up in suburban backyards, followed by emergency sirens, helicopters whupping up the air. On other nights, it was cars burning rubber, raised voices, gunshots. I looked up at the wooden crucifix on my wall and wished that the cross I had to bear could've been that small. At least the sisters had stopped forcing me to pray and ask God for forgiveness, though they still said they would pray for me.

"Must you?" I had asked.

"We must," they replied. "We pray for all sinners."

12

Pilbara / Yindjibarndi Country, 2017

Without fully realising it, Bob, Luke and Sparrow had teamed up with Mouse and become highway robbers. Luke's thirst for danger and bigoted mouthing off were now part of the act, while Bob and Sparrow could only sit in the corner and watch, heads in hands, insisting that it wouldn't work and that sooner or later they'd all get their heads punched in.

The first time was at a roadhouse next to an outback zoo, a minor tourist attraction where people stopped to stretch their legs and look at the flyblown camels, emus and dingoes. Luke sat in his chair as planned, screaming at every FIFO in the place, calling them every hue of faggot and cocksucker in the thesaurus. At first, the miners were reluctant to act, stunned by what they were witnessing. Was this real . . .? Surely some kind of hidden-camera practical joke; a set-up. They milled around their table of empty food wrappers and aluminium cans, speaking in low, grumbling voices. One of them even glanced over at Sparrow questioningly. It was only when Luke brought up the men's mothers and claimed they performed poorly in bed that the FIFOs finally mobilised. Bob whispered to Sparrow that he'd "seen men in the Pilbara be obliterated for less". What few other patrons there were in the roadhouse quickly made themselves scarce.

Luke's body was lifted out of its chair by two meaty fists scrunching the front of his T-shirt. Bob lurched forward instinctively, protectively, but Sparrow touched his arm lightly to restore his composure. Luke momentarily dangled like a marionette until two separate pairs of thick arms steadied him from behind. It was a punishment to be delivered standing up. The sudden increase in altitude and drop in blood pressure made Luke's eyes roll back into his head. His cheeks pooled with blood, his brow glistening with the release of tense sweat.

The miners cracked their knuckles, loosened their shoulders and moistened their lips. Luke harnessed what little saliva he had and spat it in the face of his executioners. Jesus Christ, thought Sparrow. The kid never said he was going to do that. This was crossing a line and the miners didn't seem to care about Luke's condition – a dickhead in a wheelchair was still a dickhead. As a precaution, Sparrow reached into the pocket of his shorts, fingers at the ready. The unfortunate FIFO wiped his sticky face with an unwashed forearm and exhaled a noxious stench of alcohol and petrol station pie. Luke closed his eyes.

Right on cue, Mouse appeared at the door of the roadhouse, hands buried in her hair. The miners stopped what they were doing and returned Luke to his chair with a whump. Mouse stormed over and shoved him in the chest, jolting his chair back half a metre. They argued, pretending to be brother and sister. She was rooting half the Pilbara and he wasn't happy about it. Eventually, Mouse ran out of expletives and ordered Luke to go wait in the truck. Luke departed with an upturned middle finger. He fired Sparrow a smile and a wink as he rolled away.

Mouse apologised to the men. Their clenched fists unfurled like corpse flowers to reveal creased palms of grubby flesh. They stared at each other, at her. Sparrow loosened his grip. The danger had passed.

The sharp-tongued soubrette looked the three sweaty male specimens up and down, and thrust her plunging cleavage under their ruby-red, sunburnt noses. She made them an offer, a way for her to get back at her annoying little brother. They couldn't refuse. They all left together, heading for the car park. Last out the door, Mouse turned and blew Sparrow a kiss.

"Jesus Christ," Sparrow said, shaking his head.

"They pulled it off," said Bob. "Unbelievable."

Sparrow leaned back in his seat and stared up at the rotating ceiling fan. It made him dizzy. His head was throbbing, a feeling of detachment in his limbs, his chest heavy. He longed to keep moving.

And so it went. Luke as bait, the argument as distraction, Mouse as pharmacist, Bob as spectator, and Sparrow with his head elsewhere, thinking about the deep north and the prospect of an undiscovered murder victim. In their wake, a contrail of Rohypnol, a desert's worth of groggy transvestites, and more empty wallets than a Vegas casino. Luke and Mouse's plan was working. They reminded Bob and Sparrow of this fact with every successful haul.

Sparrow was shocked by how quickly he'd abandoned his policeman's sensibilities. It came from getting caught up in the pace of things, in the juvenile recklessness of the moment, and his own background as a wild youth. He pulled himself up from time to time to wrestle with his conscience, reminding himself that it was all an act for the greater good and trying to not think about what Detective Inspector Porter would make of it all.

But Sparrow also noticed a strange interaction between Mouse and Luke. She would hand him something with a closed fist that he accepted with a goofy grin and proceeded to swallow. Sparrow assumed it wasn't breath mints or roofies. Likely some kind of amphetamine.

"I just hope it's something pharmaceutical grade and not concocted in a dirty backyard shed," Sparrow told Bob. "Truckers live on that shit."

Luke's and Mouse's energy levels soared while Sparrow's flatlined. Old Bob was even less energised, fading faster and earlier in the day.

"Hey, Luke. Check this out."

Mouse threw a mustard-yellow bottle into his lap after their latest conquest.

"What is it?" he asked.

"Fake piss."

"Yuck!"

"Miners use it to beat workplace drug tests," Mouse said. "That is, the ones who can't get their hands on synthetic dope."

"I reckon the bloke you nicked that from will miss it more than the cash from his wallet," Sparrow said.

"Yep," said Bob. "Without that bit of kit, he might lose his job."

"Serves him bloody right then," Mouse said. "The dumb prick's over-paid as is."

She fired the ignition and wheeled her rig back onto the highway, leaving behind another clutch of comatose victims sound asleep in their car. A re-sealable bag containing a new assortment of coloured pills sat safely in the glovebox. In the back next to Luke and Bob rode a booty of stolen DVDs, their slick, flesh-toned covers pressed sensually against each other.

Dusk fell. Drawn by glowing headlights, honour guards of kangaroos lined the road. Pythons shimmered across the warm tarmac in elegant loops. The chatter on the CB radio went from a PG-classification to an R-rating. These occurrences washed over Sparrow nightly, an outback lullaby that made his eyelids heavy.

And then, Mouse thought she spotted one of her recent victims drive past in the opposite direction. They decided to get the truck off the road, to lie low for a night in an L-shaped motel.

"That's not the first time I've had to dodge my past," Mouse said. "The Pilbara is as small as it is vast."

She parked the truck behind the motel, out of sight. A toothless, atrophied old man of indeterminate age, all bones and grey beard, sat behind the office counter. Bob said hello but his glazed expression didn't change. He paid for the room with two avocados and received no change. The old proprietor received no relief from his boredom.

Mouse slipped him an extra pineapple from her own roll of cash. "And you didn't see us," she said. "We were never here."

Sparrow figured the lone battered Ford truck outside belonged to the proprietor. The roof was the colour of rust.

"Get much business here?" Sparrow asked.

"I'm turnin' people away," the proprietor yawned. "Checkout time's whenever ya feel like it."

Entering the room, Bob's feeble lungs breathed a long sigh of relief.

"A proper night's rest in a cool bed with fresh sheets," he said. "It's the only thing I miss about that goddamn nursing home."

Every day, it seemed Bob was feeling tired more quickly. Even with the small shots of adrenaline that accompanied the highway excitement, he quietly complained to Sparrow of all-over body aches. His head was stuffed with mucus, his thin face rough with thick stubble. Sparrow could tell that his soul was willing and implored him to keep going, but his body was weak.

Deep down, Bob knew what was happening, and Sparrow sensed it, too. Bob's meds were no longer working.

And now they'd been kidnapped by a highwaywoman.

13

Pilbara / Yindjibarndi Country, 1977

Bob

It was Saturday night. Sipping at my can of lager, I brushed the thin film of oily perspiration from my brow. I was lying on my bunk, trying to block out the usual mayhem raging in the world beyond my donga. Sunday's excursion to the pit lake couldn't come quickly enough. One beer for me was medicinal, a sleeping aid. I exhaled a week's worth of exhaustion and shoved two wads of wet toilet paper deep into my ear canals. The makeshift plugs stayed there till morning, emerging dry and encrusted in brown wax and assorted detritus. I flicked them against the wall opposite, watching them stick and momentarily defy gravity before dropping into the beer can graveyard below.

I now made sure I ate a full breakfast – bacon, eggs, sausages, plenty of coffee. Made from dried egg powder, the scrambled eggs tasted of the fish fried in the same aluminium pan the night before. Most men skipped breakfast altogether, their guts still straining with Saturday liquor. They didn't want to fill their insides with unnecessary nutrients – that space was better saved for more grog. But I, on the other hand, wanted to savour the trip to the pit lake and all the little sensations that came with it.

With my appetite sated, I headed for the camp gates to wait. Bandit soon emerged in the Volkswagen flatbed. He revved its whiny two-litre engine hard on approach before slamming a clumsy foot on the brakes and enshrouding me in an orange nebula of dust.

"Bloody 'ell," Bandit said, leaning out the window. "You're keen, ain't ya?"

I looked away to hide my guilt. "Beach Sunday is the highlight of my bloody week," I muttered.

Once nine other keen men had piled into the truck, there was just one quick stop at the pub for libations before the games got underway. I now refused to be chauffeured in the cabin. Riding in the tray, although it resembled tap dancing on a frying pan, meant I could participate in the wrestling.

I came to realise why such hand-to-hand combat was an essential part of the ritual. It was the men's first opportunity to size each other up and find a worthy partner for what was to come later that night. Naturally, as came with a culture of men, of animals, the alpha male was determined by a feat of strength. A battle of brawn, a reflection of work ethic, fought for under a man's terms. The new arrivals were young and chiselled and firm. But they were still no match for me. My three-year head start in the Pilbara had acclimatised my body to both the heat and the work and infused my veins with pure iron, carving my frame from the very land on which I toiled. My opponents were as malleable as clay in my oversized mitts, their warm flesh melting into nothing against my thick bronzed skin and shredded muscle. I laughed in their faces after every conquest. By the time we arrived at the pit lake, sweaty and sore, drunk and giggling, it was clear to everyone who was king of the jungle and would have first choice that evening.

The pit lake was the same oasis as always. Cool, refreshing, invigorating, the water glowing like polished glass. I just saw the scene through a different lens now. The men splashing about in the water and wrestling and pouring beer down each other's throats and laughing like hyenas was no longer the main event. It was simply the prelude.

Bandit reclined on a big smooth rock and cracked open a fresh one.

He emptied half the can's contents down his throat with minimal effort and scanned the elevated horizon under the vast blue sky.

"Well, pickle me grandmother," he said. "If we ain't the goddamn luckiest pack of bastards under the sun."

He talked of a future when the rest of the world discovered their secret watering hole. When the squares grew tired of their square world and decided to invade the fringes.

"There'll be towering hotels built round this lake one day, a luxury resort," he said. "A real fucking monstrosity."

Bandit drained the can's remaining half, erasing his apocalyptic vision in the process. He belched the air black and suggested he might bring out a tinny next time for a spot of fishing. His sentiments were echoed by those in earshot on the proviso the boat had an outboard motor for water skiing. I closed my eyes and pictured a skiing pyramid, matching costumes, flags waving. When I reopened them, I noticed Stretch's enormous penis had made its first appearance of the day.

Stretch was new to the Pilbara, but his legend had formed fast. Nearing seven feet in height, the aptly named individual was understandably proud of his gift from God and showed it off at every opportunity. He couldn't hide it under his tight footy shorts so it was often seen hanging free down the inside of his leg when he failed to wear jocks. Each time, I was left slightly breathless. I had to be careful to not let my gaze linger.

This was Stretch's first trip to the pit lake. From our earlier wrestling, he had proven to be my closest match. He had a cumbersome, baby giraffe frame, and the softest parts of him were his teeth. The wrestling had also allowed me to notice the tattoo on his right shoulder up close. It was a love heart. I couldn't make out the name written across it.

I fixed my eyes on Stretch, not far from where I was sitting by the water. He had somehow tucked his elongated middle leg between and behind the other two and begun strutting around, impersonating a woman and making the other drunks vomit with stupid laughter. Looking up, he fixed my glare; we both instantly looked away, as if we'd been caught doing something we shouldn't. I moistened my lips and subconsciously grabbed at my own crotch as the sun commenced its final descent towards the horizon.

Sunstruck and weary, their brains pickled in ethanol and cannabinoids, the men lay down to sleep. Some like me only pretended to rest, the earth a fiery bed of nails as we waited for the right moment to make our move.

It was no coincidence that I lay down with Stretch's yeti-sized feet beside my head.

It didn't take long.

After two minutes, my ears pricked at the crunching of boots on loose gravel. A pebble plopped straight into my ear and temporarily deafened me. I dislodged it using a stubby finger with an uncut nail.

That was my cue to start counting in my head.

When I'd reached sixty, it was my turn to stand and walk. There was a single road out of the pit. After that, I knew he could head in almost any direction. Straight ahead was the best bet, but there was never a guarantee that two men's minds worked the same. Stretch didn't come across as the sort to make it easy, dawdling along and going to ground the second I caught up with him. He would want me to earn it, probably weaving his way through plains of spinifex and leading me on a merry dance. I relished the prospect.

Five minutes passed. I was growing tired of my own footsteps keeping me company. In a fit of paranoia, I turned around. But all I saw was the empty blackness I had just traversed. The gibbous three-quarter moon was a cold white. It illuminated small unidentifiable rodents and marsupials that scurried out of sight into rock piles and samphire bushes as quickly as they appeared.

Jesus Christ. Where the hell was he . . .? Surely a beanstalk like that would stick out in this terrain and this light. My head spinning, I walked faster. I was turning circles in the scrub, tripping and skinning my knees. I didn't want to lose the lanky bastard. I couldn't call out – half the world would hear me, recognise me. Instead, from on top of the highest vantage point, a pied butcherbird chimed. Its liquid notes echoed among the bare red hills, drifting out across the pindan savannah. What was it trying to say . . . ?

Look behind you, you dumb prick.

The footsteps were ninja silent, the rugby tackle unseen. It rattled my brain about in my skull as my unprepared body went sprawling on the tundra.

We rolled for an eternity, tearing what little clothes we were wearing and leaving a shallow trench in our dusty wake. I used the momentum to ensure I ended up on top, pinning my assailant, who thrashed his legs like a frenzied bullfrog.

He wrestled like he had in the back of the truck and was some match for me as I rained down blows with alternating fists. My knuckles reverberated with the crack of bone on bone as they became coated with the warm splash of new blood. But he'd learned from his earlier defeat and flailed his mantis arms into the sides of my head, boxing my ears and momentarily disrupting my balance. As I toppled sideways, he seized his opportunity to lay a quick succession of body blows. My insides ignited. We remained careful to avoid the other's crotch, but faces were another matter. He nearly pulled the beard clean off my chin.

I was in heaven. The bloke was scrapping like he was in a coliseum, not a pillow fight. Not that I expected any less from him. A contest got my juices flowing.

Bloodied and bruised, we crawled to our respective corners for a moment of self-examination and lungful of oxygen. We were soon grappling again, with less intensity and coordination, a scene replete with air swings and stumbles that would have appeared comical to the watching butcherbird. I could no longer hear its dewy lullaby, its sweet melody replaced with a dull ringing in my pounding ears.

Injured, sweaty, dishevelled and spent, there was soon nothing more we could do than bump chests like two duelling elephant seals, our lips dangerously close to touching. Neither of us could give any more to the contest but we both refused to go down. We had earned the other's respect. It was an unfamiliar feeling to me, and it only made me savour what was to come even more.

Throwing punches and smashing chests soon gave way to inter-locking arms. It prevented further forceful contact and also kept us upright. We were breathing into each other's mouths. I could smell yeast and pot and salt. I clawed at his sweaty back, feeling the ridges of his spine through what was left of his shirt.

I couldn't discern whose knees buckled first. We collapsed into each other, to the earth, our limbs a tangle, hands everywhere.

There was no talking. There was never any talking.

Even out here, with only the gentle midnight butcherbird bearing witness, lips remained sealed with shame.

Riding out next morning in Bandit's tray, one of my ears was still ringing. From the corner of my swollen eye, I watched a broken-nosed Stretch avoid my gaze. So I shunned the bastard right back by staring over his shoulder at the flat plains of brave vegetation. And we weren't the only pair of men in the truck silently ignoring each other as its undercarriage scratched the earth.

A day on the grog, the rhythmic vibrations of the rough road, and the relentless sun proved tranquillising, lulling the men to sleep. I couldn't sleep in a moving vehicle – a byproduct of working as both an all-night cabbie and an all-day dumper driver. I was left to jealously watch those more fortunate, their heads seesawing, their necks rubber. The warm drool dribbling from their mouths was sugar water for blowflies. It was only when the smallest bloke in the tray accidentally leaned his snoring head on the shoulder of the larger man next to him that the spell was broken. Feeling the feather-light touch on his shoulder, the larger bloke woke and immediately croaked in protest.

"Hey! Watch it, ya bloody poofter."

It was the conversational equivalent of a blown tyre, sending the men skidding off the road. The comment was accompanied with a whack to the face so hard it seemed to reverberate on the Hamersley Ranges.

"Who yew flamin' callin' a poofter?"

In a flash, the wrestling was on again, and this time the stakes were higher. Startled by the sudden flurry of activity, Bandit tooted his horn with delight and wrenched the steering wheel left and right. The truck rocked from side to side, sending us all toppling. I managed to stay on my feet but couldn't discern between the original two wrestlers and the felled spectators, everyone had a hold of someone as fists and epithets flew. The action finally came to an end when the truck's front left wheel ran off the road, sank into a pothole and sent two men vaulting from the tray.

Half the Pilbara heard the crack. I had never seen an elbow jut out at such an obtuse angle. Meanwhile, the other bloke lost a lot of bark and was soon standing in a pool of his own blood.

"You'll be fine," Bandit summarily told the skinned bastard. He then turned to the other man. "But that there elbow's dislocated. C'mere, son. Bite down hard on this stick."

Outback surgery was just as gruesome as it sounded. Bandit pushed the elbow back in on the third attempt. The stick fell to the ground, snapped in two under the strain.

"Give 'im a beer if there's any left," Dr Bandit said, dusting his palms. "Ride up front with me, son. The rest o' you blokes, right, just calm yerselves down. We got a long drive ahead."

But the truck was dry. The men settled down in the tray again as Bandit floored it to the hospital (pub) for a drip (shot) of pain relief (whiskey).

The mine's prison-camp conditions had created a prison-camp mentality. Men in isolation are no different to those in a war zone or those stuck at sea for a long time.

*

Back in my bunk that evening, I closed my eyes and tried not to think of the previous night, of Stretch. "Any port in a storm," I reminded myself. And yet, there was something compelling about him . . .

I opened my eyes and sat up suddenly. I ran a hand through my dirty hair, watching a shower of dust fall. My breath momentarily escaped me as the realisation dawned.

Outwardly, I was like everyone else – pretending to enjoy it, acting ashamed.

But inwardly, I *was* enjoying it.

14

Pilbara / Yindjibarndi Country, 2017

Sliding the brass key into the lock, Mouse swung open the motel room door, flicked on the light switch, and lit up the room.

"Wonderful," Luke said.

It was filthy. Dead insects littered the windowsill, dry blood stained the yellow pillows. An old football sock lay on the faded coral-pink bedspread, and the brown carpet looked like melted chocolate. Luke's wheels got stuck in the shag. Sparrow tried to not breathe in.

"Two hundred bucks a night for this?" Luke said. "No fucken way! We could've rented an entire house for a month with that money."

Mouse snorted cynically. "No chance," she said. "A standard weatherboard in the Pilbara costs two, maybe three grand a week. Buying one costs over a mill."

"Fuck," Luke said. "Really?"

"In Sydney, that kind of money would get you harbour views," Bob said.

"Up here you get industrial glimpses," said Mouse. "I've heard about shared houses in the Pilbara where fifteen people cram in to cut costs. They're just fibro shacks but they're snapped up minutes after being advertised. The agents don't give a toss. Money money money. And in

Port Hedland, the companies bought the local pubs and turned them into accommodation for their workers."

"Sacrilege," said Sparrow.

Mouse tiptoed to the bathroom, carefully shunting the door open with a creak and sticking a cautious head inside. Even with her foolproof scheme, she knew she was collecting enemies left and right. She flicked on the switch, illuminating the naked bulb dangling in the room's centre. A swarm of dozy moths were sent into a fluttering frenzy.

"Wow," she said, returning to the bedroom. "Never seen a bathroom with shag carpeting before."

Mouse's training regime of manipulating brawny miners had toughened her up. She moved Luke's doughy body from his chair to the bed with minimal effort, again refusing Sparrow's offers of help. Bob flopped onto the room's second bed, sighing with relief. Mouse hit the floor, unzipping her gym bag to appraise her latest haul. Luke started tossing his new toy – the bottle of fake piss – up in the air, catching it, tossing it again.

"So what's the weirdest thing you've ever come across?" he asked.

Mouse thought a moment. "This one bloke had three pythons and a bright red skink," she said. "Found 'em in a sack in the back of his ute. Prob'ly took 'em from his workplace, gonna sell 'em on the black market when he got back to Perth."

"So you sold 'em instead?" Luke winked. "Pocketed the cash?"

Mouse's jaw hung loose, her pupils wide. Luke grinned in anticipation.

"I let 'em go," she said in a curt tone. "Back into the wild."

"Oh," said Luke. "Right . . ."

"What that bastard did was low," Mouse said. "Innocent animals, for fuck's sake. This may all be a game, but the game's still got rules."

Sparrow smiled to himself. The groups that Mouse was targeting had not escaped his attention. Grey nomads in campervans and vacationing families in four-wheel drives were off limits. So were lonely backpackers with erect thumbs. Her approach was systematic and tailored to her nouveau riche clientele.

Mouse's fist emerged from her black bag triumphant. She held up a gold chain crucifix that suddenly made the rest of the room appear darker than it was. Luke wolf-whistled his approval.

"The bastard started bragging, said it was worth ten grand," Mouse said. "He admitted he wasn't even religious."

Bob sat up, cleared his throat. "Mouse, with all due respect, just one question," he said carefully. "Does any part of you at all feel sorry for all these blokes you rip off?"

Mouse stopped admiring the crucifix and put it down with a hefty clank. She fixed her eyes on Bob, then on the wall behind him. She squinted, either in contemplation of his question or the lattice of brown brickwork immediately over his left shoulder. Sparrow felt the sweat on his cheeks prickle into ice. Luke stared, said nothing.

"Honestly? After what I went through?" Mouse said. "Nup. I don't feel sorry for 'em. No way in hell."

Bob wiped his brow with the back of his hand. "Don't get me wrong," he said. "What you went through must've been absolutely horrific, I can't even imagine. But returning here makes me remember who I once was – just another poor bastard, sweating in the sun, saving my pennies, hoping for a better future. For me, the Nor'west was a means to an end. It's probably the same for all the blokes working here, too. No-one *chooses* to come up here."

Mouse rocked forward onto the balls of her feet, then stood and walked to the grimy window pockmarked with orange dust. She peered through the metal blinds at the old plateau. The wretched plain bore the scars from eons of meteorology and decades of man.

"This place," she said. "This way of working, fly in, fly out. Companies love it, but it changes people, and not for the better. It's a blessing to many, sure. But also a curse. If you ask me, I reckon the way the men carry on now is *an insult* to blokes like you."

Bob nodded. Luke studied the floor. Sparrow studied Mouse. She turned back to face the room, to face Bob squarely. She looked at him with hunted eyes.

"Go to Port Hedland," she said. "See all the bulk carriers floating off to sea, at least thirty a week. Every single one of those freighters carries enough bloody iron in its gut to build four Harbour Bridges. Every single car on the road has Pilbara iron in it. Most of the men are rapists before they come north anyway, and they reckon this is a safe place. The companies count on hiring those kinds of bastards 'cos they use the Pilbara as a bolthole. At the end of the day, the owners know what's at stake. They don't give a fuck. And, when all's said and done, neither does the bloody country."

Bob shrugged his shoulders in resignation. "We dig holes in Australia," he said. "It's what we do. It's all we've ever done, we're just the world's quarry, an enormous pit, ever since we struck gold a hundred and fifty years ago. The early colonies would've gone bankrupt without it."

Mouse dangled the chain again, letting the bright-yellow crucifix spin slowly in the muggy motel room air.

"We run to isolated places like the Pilbara and dress ourselves up with shiny things," she said. "But we can't hide." Her lips curled, forming a half-smile.

"There's a new mining tax on the cards," Bob said. "Bet you a million bucks it doesn't get passed."

"A snowflake's chance," Mouse said. "As for the FIFOs, if they left me alone, I'd leave them alone. Ya can't blame 'em, they're just opportunists. But so am I. At the end of the day, it's all you can do. Make the best of a bad situation. Play the game. Try to win. And, if you have to, cheat."

The gold crucifix continued to rotate. Sparrow stared at it, hypnotised. He shook his head, as if to clear it. Mouse was right, of course. He knew of blokes who'd gone to work FIFO. He'd either never heard from them again or heard stories of their deaths.

Mouse slipped the gold chain crucifix elegantly around her neck, admiring it against her brown skin. Sparrow watched but felt his eyes closing, his brain shutting down for the day. The efforts of the ceiling fan rotating overhead were futile.

Bob also lay back on his bed, his speech and consciousness fading. His pupils were soon darting about beneath his shuttered eyelids.

"What do ya s'pose he's dreaming about?" Mouse asked. She was on her knees, her forearms on the bed.

"Dunno," said Luke. "He does it all the time. Maybe he's dreaming about teenage girls and perky tits."

Mouse threw something across the room that missed Luke and hit the far wall. "You're cruel," she said.

"I know," Luke said. "Sorry."

"Shh," said Sparrow. "You'll wake him up. Let him rest. He needs it."

"Nah," said Luke. "He'll be out for effing hours, sleeps like a log. Old prick doesn't like it when I swear, you know."

"I noticed," said Sparrow. "I think that's sweet."

"If you say so," said Luke. "I mean, I guess it is."

"It shows he cares about you."

"Maybe. But jeez, he pisses me off big time. The old bastard may have got me outta that nursing home, but he's a drag, a square, a loser."

Luke paused, then added, "Mouse, take me with you. Let's dump him here, leave him the van. Sparrow can look after him. Right, mate?"

Sparrow grunted his disapproval.

"What?" said Luke. "You're his carer, aren't you?"

"Well, yair," said Sparrow. "But I'm your carer too. That's why Bob hired me. Did you forget that?"

"I've got Mouse now," Luke said. "And we're doing fine on our own. We can split the profits fifty-fifty. Then I'll call the cops and say the old bastard abducted me, dumped me by the roadside. I'll tell them he took you hostage, that you're innocent and didn't have a clue what was happening."

The mention of official police involvement made Sparrow shake his head with some conviction. "Mate," he said. "I don't think that's a good idea. Bob's done a lot for you, he got you out of the nursing home and brought you on this trip. To now go behind his back and dob him in to the police is a bit bloody rich."

"Yeah, well where the hell are we going, do you even know? He hasn't ever said. For all I know, he's bloody abducted me. And maybe you too."

Sparrow stopped for a second. Was there any truth in what the kid was saying . . .? The possible charges ran through his mind: deprivation of liberty, endangering life, or the lesser offence of unlawful detention. They all paled alongside the most serious crime of all – murder.

Mouse stayed quiet. Sparrow imagined she was probably wondering if she was in too deep, if she should quietly back out now. Luke continued.

"I swear, if I hadn't come off my bloody motorbike, I'd be more of a man than he ever was . . . Always going on about what a tough bastard he was back in the day."

"You can't turn back time," Sparrow said.

"I wish I could. Every single day," Luke said.

"How old were you?"

"Eighteen."

"How long were you out?"

"Coupla weeks. Waking up was the worst feeling. I'll never forget it."

"What happened?"

Luke took a moment to gather his thoughts. "I remember looking down," he said. "It was dark, but I could see I was strapped to a bed. This chick's voice, the nurse, real soft, kept asking me if I knew where I was."

"And what did you say?"

"I didn't answer," Luke said. "I just tried to wake up."

He took a moment to compose himself.

"Broke both my legs and an arm, cracked my pelvis and ribs, punctured a lung, fractured my skull," he boasted. "But it was the C7 vertebrae that crushed my spinal cord. I had four ops, big ones. Now I'm Iron Man, held together with titanium plates and pins. But not the cord. The cord's fucked."

No-one said anything for some time. The only noise in the room was Bob's heavy snoring.

"Wait," Mouse finally said. "You were eighteen years old when all this happened?"

"Yeah."

She moved her body snake-like across the floor until she was leaning against the far wall.

"Well, well," Mouse said. "Ladies and gents, I do believe we are in the presence of the rarest of species – the adult virgin."

The room went quiet. Bob stopped snoring. Sparrow wondered if he'd actually been awake the whole time.

"Piss off," Luke said. "What, so now you get your kicks picking on fucking disableds as well? That's pretty low. Either do something about it or get stuffed."

15

Pilbara / Yindjibarndi Country, 1979

Bob

The Pilbara's unspoken rule was a double-edged sword. It was my friend when it kept others from knowing me, but my foe when it came to knowing others.

From a strictly animal standpoint, I thought the connection was clear. Stretch and I had locked horns almost every weekend, pushing each other to the very brink. The lanky prick was the only man who had ever matched me physically. He was also the only bastard who didn't refuse to look me in the eye during the moment. There was still no talking, but there was no need. The respect for the physical was obvious from the moment one nocturnal pair of boots followed the other out of the pit lake.

But there was one problem. I saw other things in him, things beyond the physical, things that I wanted to believe were real. It was the gradual avoidance of other men at the pit lake, the lingering glances, and a certain indefinable tension in the air before the explosive release. Drunk on the corporeal act, I got greedy. I wanted to know more. I wanted more.

But Stretch had proved elusive. His job was white collar, a geologist, which meant that I rarely saw him outside the pit lake. It also took away the main pathway to the male psyche – alcohol. The men let their guards down at the mess and pub, bonding over grog and steaks and fantasies of faraway women, whether real or imagined. I kept up as best I could, usually rehashing a story someone else had told, but changing the names. When I did see Stretch in the mess, those rare occasions, he was hunched over his food, hoovering it all before I'd even salted my chips. He then returned his plate and vanished.

"What's with yer roommate there, Bandit?" I asked. "Can't stay fer a chat?"

Bandit looked up from the T-shaped bone he was gnawing. Beside him, a dog of doubtful parentage performed tricks, hopeful for food. Bandit paid him no attention. He swallowed the artery of gristle in his mouth and flicked his oily fingers in dismissal.

"Pah," he said. "You know those shiny-bums, can't get enough of their flamin' books."

I needed two shots of whiskey after dinner the next night before I could knock on the door of Stretch's donga. The big man's bare feet were hanging off the end of his bed as he lay under a naked bulb reading a battered hardback. The cover was red, blank, the book unidentifiable.

"Oh," I said. "Ah . . . g'day."

It felt like I was greeting him for the very first time.

To my surprise, Stretch didn't run a mile. He didn't even bat an eyelid. In fact, his grubby feet seemed to wave a hello. His mouth added a literal salutation – "Gudday" – and curled into the shape of a smile.

I felt my shoulders relax. It was time to deliver the line I had so carefully prepared that morning.

"I, ah, hear you might have a copy of Shakespeare's complete works?"

Stretch put down his volume, dog-eared the page, closed it. His face contorted in confusion.

It was the solitary book I remembered from high school. Even then, I'd only flipped through it. It had certainly made a handy doorstop and window propper-upper.

"Who told you that?" Stretch asked. "But yeah, as it turns out, I do have a copy. Pull up a pew."

I looked down at the floor, covered with heavy tar-smeared malthoid matting that made me want to sneeze. I sat on the nearest bunk and rubbed my nose.

For the next hour, I feigned interest in Stretch's mobile library, contained in a large duffle bag stashed under his bunk. Tolstoy, Kafka, Nietzsche, Dostoyevsky, Solzhenitsyn, and a dozen other authors whose names I couldn't recognise, let alone pronounce. Stretch began reviewing them all, bouncing between volumes, what he liked and disliked, comparing philosophies and writing styles. I sat silently and nodded numbly. When it seemed appropriate, I asked a question that prompted another monologue. It was the same poker face I had mastered from my taxi cab confessionals. I could keep conversations going like that for hours, often securing a bigger tip.

"If you like, I can lend you some of these other books as well," Stretch said.

"No," I said. "Er, I mean, no thanks. The Shakespeare's fine."

"No worries."

I gauged the air in the room. Stretch's eyes suddenly appeared wide and dilated even if they were not. Outside the donga, the nightly mayhem of the camp reigned, the world coming to an end. Inside, all I could hear was waves lapping against a shore, an orchestra playing a symphony.

Bandit soon brought a tinny to the lake, and was able to combine his two loves – fishing and explosives.

Rowing out to the middle of the lake, he cracked a can of lager with one hand, lit a stick of dynamite with the other and hurled it into the water. He then sat back and waited for the *ka-boom!* before collecting his floating aquatic bounty with a scoop net. I considered Bandit's unorthodox methods against the true spirit of angling, but I was in no position to judge when a plentiful fish banquet was hauled in for barbequeing to the adulation of the hungry beach bums.

I lay down on a large smooth boulder, warmed by the afternoon sun. My belly was full of fish, my mind calm after an afternoon spent swimming. All I needed now was a nap to re-energise my body before the nocturnal activities got underway. Life was good.

Bandit kicked back in his small aluminium boat, reprising his tried and tested routine. One can, one stick, one down the hatch, one in the drink, and scoop . . . Can, stick, hatch, drink, scoop . . .

But then, an anguished wail echoed off the walls of the pit lake. A split second later, a loud, unexpected thump next to my ear made my head reverberate like a crash cymbal. The entire left side of my face felt suddenly hot, sticky. I sat up and opened my eyes. Feeling my head, I saw my palm had turned chili-pepper red.

I looked down at the boulder. My focus came slowly. At first I thought it was a dirty great lace monitor, its skin black and scaly, which had come to share my warm rock.

But then I saw it properly. It was no reptile. It was a human arm, missing most of its skin. I swear I saw it twitch.

Peering down into the pit lake, I searched for the source of the racket. I saw men swimming in the water and Bandit sitting in his tinny, flailing around the squirting stump.

"Jesus Christ," I muttered.

Stretch was frantically freestyling towards the boat with a shirt stuffed in his mouth. The water surrounding it had turned a deep purple. Blood spurted in a thick even jet from Bandit's shoulder, forming an elegant parabola. His body was reaching for things automatically as if it still had two arms. He rowed around in circles before passing out.

Stretch stemmed the bleeding with a makeshift tourniquet. The arm socket gushing thick red ropes was soon a dark stain growing ever larger.

I looked down at the arm, served up in its own blood. Much like its former owner, it was dying. I approached it cautiously, inspecting it with a sense of fear and dread. There was no hand attached, it had been shot off elsewhere into the outback. The skinny dingoes would feast that night.

My outstretched fingers trembled towards the blackened limb. It was all too human, with its bent elbow joint and hair. The sleeve tattoos added unwanted personality. I picked up the meat, watching the juice drain from both previously capped ends. I quickly corrected the angle at the elbow joint to counter gravity and retain the vital fluid. The arm was lighter than I envisaged, only a few kilos. It did not attack me.

Ice. The precious white crystals for which we worked so hard were stored in two eskies by the water's edge. I bolted for the lake, hoping I wouldn't have to dislocate the arm to squeeze it in. Fortunately, the eskies were big enough. But there was one other problem.

"Shit," Stretch said. "The beer . . ."

Had Bandit's injury occurred later in the day – problem solved.

In the end, the answer was obvious. Particularly after Bandit came to and said he could do with a drink. There was no point wasting the cold beer by letting it turn to warm piss in the afternoon sun, especially after such lengthy efforts in freight and refrigeration. Any excuse to drink faster was welcomed. And those who were already drunk couldn't get any drunker anyway.

I abstained. An intoxicated driver swerving all over the road would kill Bandit for sure, and I was the last remaining sober candidate to take the wheel. Stretch volunteered as navigator; he was Bandit's roommate after all. The rest of the bastards would have to stay at the pit lake or the truck would never get there. We considered driving Bandit the three hours back to camp, but all they had there was a first-aid kit with a half-empty packet of Band-Aids and a torch with no batteries. Typical mining companies. They would've then radioed the flying doctor, which would've taken even more time to get Bandit to hospital, pick-up and delivery. By road, the hospital was a mere four hours away. Between us, five hundred kilometres of the earth's oldest, roughest landscape.

We bound up Bandit tighter than an Egyptian mummy in whatever ripped clothes we could muster. He was loaded into the truck's tray, complaining of a cold feeling in his bones. Stretch rode in the back, doubling as a human seat belt and impromptu paramedic delivering the alcohol anaesthetic. I gunned the accelerator with the precious esky on the seat beside me. The primordial boab tree perched on the edge of the pit lake grew smaller in the rear-view mirror before vanishing altogether. I mouthed a silent prayer to an unseen god, acutely aware that our journey might amount to no more than corpse transportation.

"It was always gonna happen," Stretch said. "The more the dumb bastard drank, the less he could tell his left hand from his right and his brain from his arse."

Stretch sat opposite me in the empty waiting room, his face caked in dry red dust, his hair a shade of lilac. I felt like I had sweated away half my body weight. The hospital was small, remote, basic. It had been a rough, frenetic drive, but we now sat in private, in a white room, grateful for air conditioning and stillness after hours of bad roads and intense heat. The last hundred kilometres was the worst – with one headlight after collecting a towering western grey roo. It hopped away, though roos often did that only to later die in the scrub. Up to that point, I had minimised the truck's damage to minor dings and fresh smears of wild blood.

It was nearing midnight. The last fluorescent tube overhead flickered like a movie projector. My eyes continued to pound with blood. Bandit had been taken in on arrival, unconscious. Stretch kept pointing out to the medical staff that he was a universal donor with O-negative blood and thrusting forth his plank-like arm. I handed over the sloshing esky and slab to a triage nurse who looked less than impressed.

"Then again, even if Bandit hadn't been holding the stick of dynamite, it would've blown a hole in the hull," I said. "The drunk drongo would've flamin' drowned."

"At least we wouldn't be waiting here now," Stretch said. "We'd have gone straight to the morgue." He exhaled a large lungful of tight air, a distinct cloud seemed to form before his eyes. "This could take a while. Wish I'd brought a book with me."

"Youse two blokes the blokes who brought in the bloke who blew his fucken arm orff?"

A country matron, more bulldozer than woman. Almost as wide as Stretch was tall, her boxy figure blocked out most of the white light shining in from the corridor. Engulfed in shadow, I struggled to focus on the cinder block that was her face.

"Um, yeah," I said.

"Gunna be a while," she said. "We're prepping him fer surgery now. Doc's been summoned, he's awake, now on his way. Youse blokes can probably head home, come back in the mornin'."

I explained our circumstances, the journey, the roo, the one working headlight.

"Oh. Right, well in that case, there's a coupla spare cots in the empty ward down the hall there. Have a kip before you head back in the mornin'."

I watched her waddle ahead, her ankles showing the way under the hem of her pinafore. The hospital seemed deserted.

"So," said Stretch, "what are his chances?"

The gruff matron didn't hesitate. "Somewhere between jack shit and fuck all," she said. "But hey, I been wrong before. Just a tick, I got somethin' fer youse . . ."

She disappeared for a moment before returning to thrust forward her arms and present our esky. Her underarm fat wobbled.

"Hosed it out fer youse."

"Cheers," I said.

"There's a toilet down the corridor, to yer left there."

"Okay."

"I knock orff at six so make yerselves scarce by then."

"Gotcha."

"No-one should bother youse till then."

I took the bed nearest the wall, Stretch the one nearest the door, which he closed with a metallic click. There was no lock.

We sat listening to each other breathing for a while, each waiting for the other to say something.

130

"Well . . ." I said slowly. "This is a nice little break."

"Yip," said Stretch, with even less effort.

We sat on our respective beds, facing one another. A small lamp next to each bed painted the sparse room in a dim honey glow. Other than a few reminders of the clinical setting – the clipboard at the end of the bed, the vinyl flooring, the call button – it could just as well have been our own private motel room. The world around us seemed to melt away in silence. Instead of speaking normally, I felt the strange need to whisper.

"I reckon I'll sleep like a baby," I said.

"Me too," said Stretch.

I ran my hand along the bed, feeling the inviting crispness of the cotton sheets. Stretch did the same and bit his lip.

"Whatdya reckon?" Stretch asked.

I stopped in my tracks. My eyes opened wide and my brain went to forbidden places. Swallowing hard, I momentarily forgot the purpose of my lungs.

"About . . . about what?" I squeaked.

"You know," said Stretch. "Bandit."

A suppressed gasp announced the return of my breath.

"Oh," I said. "What the nurse said. Lap of the gods now."

I wanted to say more but found I couldn't. Deep down, I was quite distressed by what had happened to poor dumb Bandit. But life on the mines had hardened me externally, and emotions remained signs of weakness.

Stretch nodded lightly. "Yeah . . ."

I peeled off my sweat-stained shirt. My silvery torso caught what little light there was in the room.

"Look," I said, "nuthin' more we can do. Let's just get some shut-eye and hope for good news in the mornin'."

More clothes hit the floor, beside both beds. Only jocks remained in their place.

"Yeah," said Stretch, yawning. "Stuff it."

The feeling of fresh sheets on desiccated skin was like drops of cool, refreshing rain. Every pore tingled. My spine shivered like a plucked guitar string.

"Well . . . g'night."

"Night."

We extinguished our bedside lamps in unison. I turned away from the door, lay back onto my feather pillow, and sighed deeply.

The swooshing of a curtain track was the final insult. My neighbour preferred privacy.

I blinked in the darkness and sighed.

A second later, the curtain track swooshed again, louder than before, closer.

My bed springs compressed. A warm body nestled in beside me to spoon, as a heavy arm fell across my chest.

I closed my eyes and relaxed my neck, feeling the warmth trickle down my spine to my toes like some kind of reverse stroke.

In the morning, we drove in silence with the eastern sun in our eyes, the same salt-encrusted clothes on our backs. A squinting Stretch was now behind the wheel, his long legs working the pedals on autopilot. The procession of wild beasts had retreated with the new light, searching for relief under whatever cast a shadow. From the passenger seat, I watched a swirling willy-willy a hundred metres high form on the horizon. When I could, I stole sideways glances at my chauffeur.

The esky bounced about at my grubby feet. The tray was empty. The matron had gone by the time Stretch and I emerged from our room. We departed without an update on Bandit's condition, other than being told by the next shift nurse that "a transfer" had been made. It wasn't specified to where – another hospital, the city, the morgue.

I flipped my Zippo, welcomed my first cigarette. I dragged on it before stretching across the cabin and passing it on. Stretch sucked in his own lungful and returned the favour. The to and fro continued until there was only a wet nub left in my tawny fingers. I sneered and flicked it out the window like a ball of rolled snot.

The volley of nicotine exchanges took place using solely our roadside hands: my left and Stretch's right. Our inner hands had gone walkabout and found each other in the middle of the truck's vinyl bench seat. The connection was broken on arrival at the pit lake when the other men piled in, full of questions about their absent colleague. They feared the worst. I nodded as Stretch explained what we'd been told, my right hand still tingling with residual electricity. Did he feel it too?

16

Pilbara / Yindjibarndi Country, 2017

There had been no more talk that night, of betrayal or otherwise; everyone slept. In the morning, the truck set off as usual, but Mouse insisted they make an unexpected detour. Sparrow pictured her faking a flat tyre and asking him and Bob if they could very kindly go out and check like they knew what they were doing. She'd keep the engine running of course and then floor it, leaving them both stranded. They'd be picked up by the police within the hour, who would at least save them from a torturous death by heatstroke. Their van would be found a few miles away, and Luke would claim Mouse saved him from his kidnapper Bob, while Sparrow would have some serious explaining to do.

Mouse pulled up outside the arrangement of identical blue shipping containers. The four of them sat in silence a moment, the engine ticking. Sparrow glanced back at Luke, who looked sly and mean. Mouse was smirking. Bob looked clueless.

"Okay," Luke said. "So come on then. Let me out."

"Righto," said Mouse. "Keep ya bloody pants on."

Sparrow and Bob exchanged perplexed glances. What in the world was going on?

Mouse escorted Luke across the road and into the nearest container, slamming the heavy metal door behind her. Bob and Sparrow sat watching, brains in overdrive. The horizon shimmered, the wind picked up, the sun beat down. Sparrow couldn't make out the identity of the faded logo on the side of the shipping container, worn away by the elements.

"What do you suppose they're doing in there?" he asked.

Bob shrugged. "Endless lines of cocaine," he replied. "How the hell should I know?"

"As a cop – *and as his carer* – I should probably go investigate."

"What? And give the game away?"

"Hmm, yair . . . 'the game'. Mate, can I ask, how far away are we from wherever the hell you've been leading me?"

Bob chewed his lip in contemplation. "Could be a day's drive, maybe two," he said. "Hard to tell. But definitely no more than two."

"No more than two, eh?"

"Maybe three."

"Three now. Are you sure?"

"It's not my fault Australia's a bloody big country, and that the Kimberley's a bloody long way from everything."

Sparrow gave up watching the windowless box after five minutes. There was nothing happening anyway; no-one coming or going, only waves of dust washing up against the containers like an outback tide. He considered crossing the road and investigating in the same way he'd once crept up to a blood-red Hummer. Open the door, peer inside. But he wasn't going to stoop to that level again.

"I had another dream last night," said Bob.

"Same one as before?" Sparrow asked.

"Yep."

Bob described his endless visions of red dirt, of the atoms comprising the Pilbara's DNA. It was as if they had burrowed deep inside his neural crevices and permanently skewed his unconscious brainwaves.

"I was digging at my eternal hole, burying myself again. I only stepped out when I heard the call of a pied butcherbird. It was watching me from the fork of a tree, dressed in its black executioner's hood. Then

I saw my mother standing with a tall glass of beer, my dad was boxing a kangaroo, and there were two full moons in the sky."

"Whoa. Trippy."

"Tell me about it. The bird then spoke to me. It said, 'I know what you did.'"

"A talking bird, double trippy. Sounds like your conscience, mate."

"Maybe."

"Hopefully this trip and what we're doing brings an end to those dreams."

"Hope so."

"The butcherbird's actually really significant for blackfellas, its song helped structure our language."

"You don't say . . ."

After about five uneasy minutes, Sparrow had a wild idea: they should steal the truck.

"Mouse is young and fit," he said. "And Luke would be safe in the container until they were rescued."

"How do we steal the truck?" Bob said. "Mouse has the keys. Can you hot-wire it? You'll probably just electrocute yourself."

Sparrow's next suggestion was that they snatch the booty and take off on foot, hitch a ride and make their way north.

"But how are we going to carry it all?" Bob said. The loot was now spread across two big gym bags. "We'd die trying, most likely. Besides, my stomach hurts."

Sparrow eased up, let his crazy ideas pass.

After another five minutes, the container door finally swung open and was nearly blown off its hinges by a sudden gust of hot air. Mouse appeared, forcing the door closed with both muscular arms. She clomped across the road in her yellow Caterpillars and returned to her position behind the wheel.

"No Luke?" Sparrow asked anxiously. "Did you leave his body inside?"

"Kind of . . ." Mouse flicked on the radio, soft country music. "He's got an hour. Sit back, relax. He's with a professional."

Bob said it was the first time he'd let Luke out of his sight for longer than ten minutes since they'd scaled their prison walls together. He seemed antsy. Separation anxiety, which Sparrow found rather sweet.

"This place popular?" Sparrow asked.

"Always busy," Mouse replied. "When the mining scum aren't in Asia blowing their pay packets, they're out here blowing them on exactly the same thing. The bosses go, too."

"Of course, to enjoy the spoils."

"The problem is they're all stupid morons who reckon they're bullet-proof. Doesn't matter if they're a dumper driver or a boardroom exec, a prick is a prick, and they return to the Pilbara with all manner of nasties stowed away inside them. And not just shit that makes your piss burn. Stuff that can kill ya."

"And how'd you come across this place?" Bob asked.

"I picked up Mummy on the road a few times," said Mouse. "Or dropped her off, right here."

"Mummy . . . ?" Sparrow asked.

"Yeah," said Mouse. "The madam. It's what she likes being called."

They sat quietly for a while, listening to the blustering wind outside. The radio played ballads about stockmen and drovers, drought and dust and dire pubs with no beer. The skies were clear, the sun high, menacing.

"I feel cold," said Bob.

Mouse reached for the air con but it was already off.

"So, what do ya s'pose they're doin' in there?" Sparrow asked.

"Prob'ly the usual stuff," Mouse replied, looking straight ahead and nodding.

"Usual stuff?"

Mouse groaned lightly, tired of the conversation. "Well, toned down, of course. A head massage, maybe a striptease, or motorboatin'. Nuthin' hardcore. Like I said, she's a pro, she knows her stuff, she'll tailor it."

Bob admitted that getting Luke laid had crossed his mind. "Sex and disabilities is like sex and old farts," he said. "People prefer to imagine it doesn't happen."

Mouse snorted.

"I saw times in the nursing home when Luke was treated like a kid, the nurses talked to him like he was five years old," Bob said. "His folks probably did it too, out of love. There's no way he could've asked them for something like this. Or me."

"I'm annoyed this didn't occur to me earlier," Mouse agreed. "I reckon an hour with Mummy will be the same as a month with a physical therapist."

"Me too," Bob said, his breath heavy. "Hopefully it calms him down. Less swearing, less angst, less hate." He paused, then added, "Now you mention it, I'm surprised he didn't have a crack at you."

"Who said he didn't?"

He fired Mouse a look with white eyes.

"Don't worry," she said. "It was never gonna happen, he's not my type."

Sparrow checked the dashboard clock. Luke still had nearly an hour.

Without warning, Bob turned his head, rolled down the window, and spat a thick gob onto the earth. Something was brewing, and at the worst possible time.

Sparrow looked at Bob. His gaze was suddenly distant, watching the heat flickering on the sunbaked earth.

"Hey, mate, you okay?" Sparrow asked.

Bob raised his bushy eyebrows. "Actually, no. I'm crampy and my mouth's full of saliva."

Sparrow could see that Bob's face was drained of all desirable colour, with grey-white appearing around his sunken eyes. A purplish blue had taken up residence in his blotchy cheeks and around his mouth, and he was shaking like a wooden house by the sea.

"Is there a loo in there?" Bob asked meekly.

"Several," Mouse replied. "Outback plumbing though."

"That's fine," Bob said in a careful tone. "Back soon."

"Here," said Sparrow. "Lemme walk you over."

As though dragging a wounded soldier from the battlefield, Sparrow hooked Bob's arm around his neck and helped him cross the dusty front. Bob was limping, lugging his left foot like it was shackled to the earth. The wind whipped up in every direction as they walked, pelting their faces with dry grit and almost shoving them through the door of the shipping container. With some reluctance, Sparrow handed over Bob's rubbery body to a young Asian girl. Tottering clumsily on hovercraft heels, she showed him to a plastic bucket, which he immediately took to the nearest toilet.

Sparrow ran into a big woman as he headed back. She was moving at pace and with purpose and barged straight into his chest like a rugby front-rower. Sparrow's spindly body was limp and offered no resistance, causing him to fall flat on his arse. When his head stopped spinning, he looked up and saw two enormous bags of cement. She was topless and proceeded to swear at Sparrow through a red-lipped mouth.

"Jesus Christ. Where the fuck's Mouse? Where the hell is she, is she here? She needs to come and get this evil little shit outta here!"

"Is Luke okay?" Sparrow asked, getting to his feet. He didn't need to ask who she was referring to.

"No, in fact he's pretty fucken far from okay," she spat. "He's one sick, twisted individual."

Her big pink bosoms shook as she yelled and pointed, causing her stomach to ripple. She had a tattoo of a faded red rose on her shoulder.

"Very sorry to hear that," Sparrow said diplomatically. "Mummy, is it?"

"Yeah. Who the hell are you?"

"Name's Sparrow, I'm with Mouse."

"Sparrow? Mouse? What is this, a zoo?"

The young cop smiled. "Sorry, I'm Andrew. I just came in for my friend, he needed to use the loo. Sorry, I know what Luke's like – a little shit. What did he do?"

She pinned Sparrow against the wall with two brawny fists. He couldn't move. The tang emanating from her armpits was almost as powerful as her grip.

"Get him the fuck out of here. *Now*."

Two young girls stumbled past Mummy and disappeared into a room at the far end of the narrow hallway. They were whining loudly in a language Sparrow didn't understand, seemingly complaining and protesting. From behind a closed door, he heard more yelling.

Mummy let Sparrow go. His bony shoulders felt bruised. Sparrow followed her up the hall. He noticed her bottom half was a tartan skirt, several sizes too small. She headed straight for a whiskey bottle under the front counter and skolled from the neck. Sparrow slumped in a plastic chair in the corner of the waiting room, illuminated by two halogen work lights in opposite corners. Its walls bore the pink hue of excited flesh. Death metal music loaded with deep growling vocals and drumming blast beats was being summoned from an unseen source. A revolving portable fan interrupted the lethargy of the hot air molecules and recirculated the smell of burnt toast, cigarettes and bad breath.

Bob appeared, looking drained, and fell into the chair alongside Sparrow with a long groan.

"Thanks, mate," he breathed. "And thank Christ it's all out of me."

"How you feelin'?"

"Much better now. But I'm tired of seeing my insides."

"I can imagine. He's been making trouble, you know . . ."

"Who? Not Luke . . ."

Sparrow nodded. "Surprised much?" he asked dryly. "Remind me again why you brought him along." He was starting to genuinely wonder. Was the kid some kind of collateral? What lay ahead?

Taking advantage of a moment alone with Bob, Sparrow pressed him for information – locations, events, times. Bob had remained elusive with details, blaming a sketchy memory and weak constitution. He claimed to not even remember how he'd killed the man, if it was a gunshot or a stabbing or a blow.

"What's that? I can barely hear you above this bloody music," he yelled at Sparrow.

Sparrow approached Mummy, who was still holding the whiskey bottle. "Again, so sorry."

"Sick little bastard . . ."

She told them that Luke had called her all manner of names and demanded she object to sex. He then became more aggressive when she refused to play the part. He said it was his hour and he could do whatever he wanted, even if it was a rape fantasy.

"I may be a whore but I'm a whore because I say I'm a whore and not 'cos some paralysed shithead in a wheelchair wants a power trip," Mummy said. "I've put up with a lot of crap in this game, but that's rule number one – I'm in control, no-one else."

Luke appeared in the doorway, wheeled out by the two Asian workers. Their faces looked tired, their thin bodies weary of all that life had thrown at them. He wore a scowl and cursed a blue streak. His face looked slightly bruised. He looked up at Mummy as she walked past and blew her a kiss. She slapped his flabby cheek with all her might.

"Get him the fuck out of here right now or I'm calling the police," she said.

"No, please," Sparrow said quickly. "There's no need to do that. We're going, right away, right now."

"And if you ever fucken return, I'll call the cops then, too." She disappeared down the hallway, the two girls in tow.

"Jesus Christ, Luke," Bob said. "What the hell were you thinking?"

"Piss off, Bob," he replied. "What are you two doing in here anyway? Checking up on me? This was supposed to be *my* time. Can't I get a moment's peace?"

"Bob had to use the loo," said Sparrow. "He couldn't help it, he was feeling sick."

Luke grunted.

"I feel better now, but we really gotta go," said Bob. "Mouse is outside."

But Sparrow already knew she wasn't. Bob exited first, then his carer, with Luke following close behind. The door locked behind them with a loud click. The first thing they saw sitting outside was their van positioned at a crooked angle, with deep tyre tracks alongside it. A red Hummer was parked at the other end of the shipping container. It was covered in big halogens and had a roo bar the size of a farm gate. Sparrow found it strangely familiar, particularly the Australian flag sticker on the side window that proudly declared "Fuck Off We're Full".

"Hang on a sec," he said. "This wasn't here when we went inside . . ."

The eighteen-wheel automotive brown snake that was Mouse's truck was now gone, replaced by the vast nothingness of the unrelenting Nor'west.

17

Kimberley / Wilinggin Country, 1980

Bob

The pit lake didn't feel the same without Bandit. The refreshing sip he took from a fizzing fistful of nitroglycerin turned out to be his last. Out of respect, we stopped going. Some of the men left the Pilbara altogether, their eyes scarred by Bandit's horrific final hours. Stretch claimed the Volkswagen truck, if only because the last set of fingerprints left on the keys belonged to him.

Bandit's untimely departure was not entirely in vain. His lessons in breaking up the monotony of camp life and embracing one's short time on earth were not lost on his disciples. With a sense of adventure our only compass, Stretch and I decided to disappear together.

Stretch steered the German jalopy even further north towards Western Australia's remaining frontier. The soft brown soil of the Kimberley was infused with fewer riches than the hard orange dirt of the Pilbara, though it was more inviting in appearance.

We found the Kimberley's lush green environs a far more agreeable setting to while away our weekends in exile. The First Australians had adopted the same thinking at least forty thousand years earlier, spreading their communities liberally across the width of the Kimberley and through to the Northern Territory's tip in Arnhem Land. Their imprint was obvious as we drove deeper north and then east. Through my passenger window, I began to see black faces huddled under hooded sweatshirts and blankets, walking slowly by the roadside dragging a dead kangaroo or sitting around a nightly fire burning in an old oil barrel.

We slept in the truck's tray, huddled together under the stars. I fell asleep with a smile.

In the morning, we stopped at the last roadhouse before we left the map. A crewman in mining fatigues sat at a nearby table. He was a skinny white rake of a bloke with thick furry worms for sideburns that intruded on his cauliflower ears. Over black coffee, he leaned in and asked Stretch for a light.

"We're just doin' maintenance at the moment, mate," the crewman said, blowing out a stream of smoke. "They sent us in to clear the area, to get it ready for drillin'. Then when that starts, we'll become the miners. Till then, we're just fillin' in time. No-one saw this bullshit comin', no-one. So now we're not even the bloody maintenance crew. All we are is statues till them coons get a bit o' sense and let us get on with the job."

"You don't say. . ."

Three slow words were all Stretch could muster by way of a response, and only after a long, thoughtful pause. I didn't even have three. Listening to the crewman's explanation had torn out my voice box.

"And don't think we're gettin' paid for sittin' round neither," the crewman spat. "Till the work starts again, them good-fer-nuthin' boongs is costin' me money."

Stretch's green eyes fired me a glance that told me how he really felt. It was a look I clung to the rest of the day.

We realised the crewman's story had something to do with the convoy of trucks and drilling rigs we'd seen the previous day. I'd lost count at forty vehicles. The police escort indicated it wasn't just another big mining project.

"Wait a minute," Stretch said. "I heard a couple of blokes on site mention this. Is this about the oil they apparently found up here?"

144

"That's it," the crewman replied. Letterboxing his eyes, he focused on the lengthy individual before him. "Hang on, did you say 'on site'...? Are youse blokes miners too?"

Stretch and I looked at one another before reluctantly nodding. The crewman smiled broadly, his brown teeth showing like rows of rotten peanuts. He thought he'd found his comrades, his people. Surely we'd want to hear the story from his perspective. His plight was our plight. He could spill his guts without censorship or restraint.

An American company claimed it had found major untapped oil reserves in the Nor'west. It was an unprecedented discovery. The Western Australian Premier loved what he was hearing. He had visions of thrusting pumpjacks and gushing black geysers, raining down showers of new money on his great, entrepreneurial state. It would become a global leader in both mining and drilling, a new Texas down under. There was just one problem. The remote Yungngora Indigenous community, which had occupied the land for tens of thousands of years, said they were there first.

"Flamin' coons reckon they own the joint," said the crewman.

"Too right," Stretch said through clenched teeth.

"Christ, it's not like they were even *doin'* anythin' with it. It was just sittin' there. What's next, they gonna claim rights over my backyard?"

My half decade of isolation in the Nor'west had rendered me impervious to the news of the day. For all I knew, the war in Vietnam might have still been raging. Aboriginals had been given the vote around the time I went to high school. A cab fare once mentioned they were finally being counted in the census, much to his chagrin. Other than that, all I knew of the world was what my eyes saw.

"Of course, all this trouble is cuz of what happened in the Northern Territory last year at Ranger mine," the crewman added. "Blackfellas didn't like how that deal went down, so this time, they arked up."

"Zat right?" I said.

"Yip. Problem is they picked the wrong goddamn State to mess with."

"Bloody oath," Stretch said. "This ain't the Northern Territory."

"It may be 1980 in the rest of the world, but this 'ere's West Australia, mate," the crewman said. "And *this* is how we bloody do business round 'ere."

"Oath," Stretch repeated.

"So where'd the convoy come from?" I asked.

"Down south," replied the crewman. "Perth."

"No way," I said. "They drove all the way up from the city?"

"Two thousand miles, mate," said the crewman. "Left under cover of dark with the Premier's blessing. They should barrel through the picket lines in a coupla hours and round up them coons in a few paddy wagons. Shit, I don't wanna miss seein' that, I better run. But hey, real good meetin' youse blokes."

And with that, he grabbed his silver keys and gold packet of Benson and Hedges and disappeared into the cloudless day.

"You too, brother," Stretch called after him. "Keep fightin' the good fight."

Stretch and I swam naked in the Kimberley's crystal-clear rock pools and gorges. The stale dust peeled from our brown skin. I squirted water from my mouth like a fountain, looking up and around at the towering gorge walls. Ancestors were all around us. The walls rose up in strips of varied colour that made them look like ancient temples built to worship the sun. Signatures driven into rock in natural amphitheatres commemorated the Dreamtime; drawings of kangaroos, turtles, emus, thylacines, crocodiles. Stories etched in stone that fascinated and inspired us.

At dusk, I often found Stretch reclining on a rock with blank notebook in hand, chewed pencil in mouth, staring into the middle distance.

"Writer's block again?" I asked.

The elongated bastard grunted. Flies wafted his hair like a gentle breeze.

146

"Wish you'd let me read some," I added.

One of the flies crawled down his face but he didn't move, didn't even blink. I had to admire his restraint, his concentration.

"So?" I said. "Can I?

"Can you what?"

"Read some?"

"No. I flamin' told you, not until the first draft is finished."

Having absorbed most of the world's eminent literature, Stretch aspired to pen his own contribution. He claimed it was one of the reasons why he'd gone north – the chance to write about a region that very few white folk had ever seen. The other reason was something I had yet to uncover. I didn't know whether Stretch retained an air of mystery to hide his past or to drive me crazy with desire. Either way, he succeeded on both counts.

"Stuff it," Stretch said, throwing his notebook and flies aside. "Come on, let's walk. I need to clear my head."

Dusk was the ideal time of day for a ramble in the bush, after the heat of day had faded and before the emergence of the wildlife of night. To watch the colours change before melting into nothing and listen for the first honeyed tones of the pied butcherbird. Now being on our own, there was nothing rushing us. We walked east at a meditative amble with the last rays of sun on our exposed backs. Stretch shuffled his feet, same old army boots coming apart at the seams. Every now and then our fingers intertwined.

It was a time for sharing, for stories. The time of day when my heartbeat turned erratic and uneven; a pleasant feeling, pain free. When I nearly uttered to Stretch the three words that I'd never dared to say.

Stretch told me the woman's name on his love heart tattoo was his mother's. I didn't ask why it didn't simply read "Mum". He talked literature and I pretended to listen but loved whatever I heard nonetheless.

"Did I ever mention my brother works at Ranger mine?" Stretch said. "He wrote me letters."

It turned out that Stretch's brother worked at the same uranium mine east of Darwin that had had its development disrupted by the local Aboriginal community the previous year. The Mirarr Traditional Owners claimed the area had spiritual significance and vetoed the mine's construction under laws designed to recognise native land rights in the Northern Territory. But then the federal politicians weighed in, overrode the same legislation they'd drawn up, and pushed the lucrative mine through.

The Aboriginal Australians felt let down by the very laws and people that claimed to protect them. And now, they were up against a State that had never even recognised native title. The time for talk was over. With rousing chants of "no mining on sacred site!", protestors descended on the disputed patch of dirt, a pastoral station known as Noonkanbah.

There was only one problem. This wasn't the Northern Territory. This was the richest mining State in the country. It was a State not used to letting anyone get in the way of what it wanted to do. As if a few nomadic tribes in flannelette shirts and torn football jumpers would be any match. The Western Australian Premier was no fan of discourse – he was a man of action. Little consultation was needed before he took the unprecedented step of sending in the state police to smash the blockade.

"This isn't the first time that mining interests have crept into the corridors of power," said Stretch. "And it won't be the last."

"Your brother still works at Ranger?" I asked.

"As far as I know," said Stretch. "He doesn't write much anymore. But that kind of shit's been going on for decades. In fact, my great-granddad once worked in the Kalgoorlie gold mines. He came from the east with thousands of other miners."

"Really? Your family's from the east?"

"As far as I know. The locals started calling the new arrivals 'the Othersiders'. They brought with 'em all these rebellious ideas and notions from the wider world. They eventually challenged the conservative Western Australian government when a mining tax was levied."

"So what happened?"

"Ten thousand Othersiders confronted the Premier when he got off the train in Kalgoorlie one day," Stretch said. He lit the joint he had rolled earlier, took a drag, passed it to me.

"Ta."

I curled up into its warm fuzz, space dust zapping inside my brain.

"There were cries of 'Eureka!' in the air, harking back to the rebellion in Victoria forty years earlier," Stretch said. "It was the same thing there, rebel miners pissed off about a mining tax. What started with protests ended with fifteen minutes of bloodshed and twenty-two dead. But the rebels got what they wanted – they got the chance to vote. It was the first political democracy in Australia's history."

"Wow," I said, exhaling a stream of cool smoke onto the hot earth. I passed the joint back. We kept walking.

"Luckily, it didn't quite come to that in Kalgoorlie," said Stretch. "The Premier was scared of what the Othersiders might do to him, but he was more scared of what they might do to *his State*. The rumour from the east was of the separate British colonies forming a federation, but the Premier didn't want Western Australia to be a part of it. The Othersiders had other ideas – namely, avoiding the mining tax. So they proposed to form a brand new State called Auralia that would then separate from the west and form part of the new federation, Australia."

"Jesus," I said.

"They were rich, so they felt they could make their own rules."

"So what happened?"

Stretch took a deep drag and picked a dry scab off his arm. He flicked it towards a long row of anthills we were approaching and passed me the dope.

"The Premier was scared shitless," he said. "He didn't want to lose his rich goldfields to the new federation. So he put the question to his people in a referendum. The final vote was in favour of joining, with city electorates overwhelmingly voting 'Yes'. Most country electorates voted 'No', but with one exception."

"Lemme guess," I said. "The Kalgoorlie goldfields?"

Stretch laughed. "It was basically the Othersiders who carried the vote. Without them, Australia would've split and become two separate countries, east and west."

I flicked the spent joint in the direction of the same anthills.

"Strewth," I said. "That's some story."

"And if you doubt me, go check the Constitution," Stretch said. "All the States are mentioned in the preamble except for one: Western Australia. That's 'cos its support for finally joining the Federation was given too late for the document to be redrafted."

"Amazing," I repeated. "It's like your great-granddad was one of the founding fathers."

Stretch hmmed. "Never thought it of it that way," he grinned. "Guess he was."

I thought a moment. "You reckon these blackfellas here got any chance?"

Stretch's craving for nicotine was not sated; he lit a cigarette for himself.

"They got about as much chance as Bandit did," he said. "Just like the miners at Eureka and my pop's dad, they'll lose the battle. But what they wanna win is the war."

The sun dipped another degree on its natural arc to the horizon. My eyes were distracted. We were walking towards the anthills, a row of rugged lumps lining a dry creek bed. One of them caught the light and sparkled like it was impregnated with sequins.

"What the f—"

I crouched for a closer look, walking towards the anthill with bent knees. Black bulldog ants continued their vertical commutes along well-worn avenues, stopping only momentarily to whisper a chemical secret to their co-workers. I wondered whether someone stumbling past had drunkenly thrown a beer bottle at their home as target practice, or in anger for simply being a bloody anthill.

"You see that?" I asked.

"See what?"

Just then, a second anthill, a metre behind the first, twinkled in my eye.

18

Perth / Whadjuk Noongar Country, 2016

Bob

When I first laid eyes on Luke, I wasn't impressed. I was in Leafy Gums' high-security dementia wing at the time. It was where I went to seek sanctuary. The dementia patients didn't judge me like the others. They just sat and listened as I talked about whatever pleased me, or whatever I felt they wanted to hear, or sometimes nothing at all. They reminded me words were not absolutely necessary for a relationship, and that sometimes they even ruined it.

The bug that I'd been fighting all week finally caught up with me, slapping me hard across the chops. I was weak all over, my body stiffening and shivering. My extremities felt like they were someone else's, the overhead lights burning my eyes. I popped a pale-blue oval-shaped pill and two circular paracetamols, which I swallowed with a slug of whiskey from my kidney-shaped hip flask. As I waited for the chemicals to dissolve in my blood, I lingered in the empty corridors, examining the corkboard displays of photos outside each resident's room. Weddings, holidays, children, grandchildren. All the so-called "normal things" that define a life. My corkboard was empty. It was one of the things that had made me so conspicuous. I regretted not cutting out a few colour photos from magazines and sticking them up just for show.

The newcomer in the lounge was young, black T-shirt, black cap, and a neatly trimmed black goatee beard to match. His dark eyes were glued to the blue glow of the flickering TV, and his arse glued to a motorised wheelchair.

The young man's eyes remained fixed on the TV, the daytime cavalcade of commercials for life insurance policies, circulation boosters and easy finance. But I knew he wasn't really watching. Instead, he was miles away, doing something impossibly carefree and fun with people his own age. Wherever that was, I felt an overwhelming longing to join him there.

I stood back against the door frame. Fidgeting with my nail-bitten fingers, I suddenly felt uncomfortable in my own clothes, sweat prickling at my thick neck. I wasn't often at a loss for words, but meeting this young man seemed to tear the tongue from my mouth. Not because of who he was but more because of how he appeared – handsome and youthful, yet fragile and scared. It had been a long time since I'd felt so taken by another person. I wasn't used to talking to anyone who I actually wanted to talk to in the home.

I finally cobbled together some words, hearing the false enthusiasm in my voice.

"Uh . . . hi," I said. "Welcome to Leafy Gums!"

The young man was unmoved, kept staring at the TV.

I was too old for this.

"So, what you watchin' there?" I asked.

The glacier remained firm. What the hell do you say to kids these days?

At last, I worked out what I wanted to say. *I look like them but feel like you.* But that's not what came out.

"You know," I said, "you remind me of someone I once used to know . . ."

The young man closed his eyes, swallowed, and finally spoke.

"Oh just fuck off and die, Quasimodo."

*

I didn't approach Luke again. Instead, I stalked him from a safe distance.

A motorbike accident had severed his spinal cord and paralysed him from the waist down. It had also caused permanent nerve damage to his right arm. His parents had both died within a month of each other of different cancers. With no-one else to look after him, he'd ended up in a nursing home. Lucky him. Lucky me.

Luke always wore the same black cap and rotated a small selection of black and sometimes dark-grey T-shirts. He sat either alone in his room or in the lounge as the pensioners all around him slipped easily between different states of consciousness. When he wasn't corroding his mind with talk shows or soap operas, he sat in the corner wearing his white in-ear headphones, lost in the angry voices of his generation. I could hear the savage buzzing from across the room amid the relentless waves of elderly snoring. Luke often sat with his eyes closed, cocooned in his own youthful world. When his eyes were open, his face wore no emotion, irrespective of what was going on around him. Which wasn't much.

Humming through the hallways, a battery-powered Luke exchanged muted hellos with his fellow residents. He didn't take to bingo, rolling out of the activities room within five minutes as the first game's numbers were still being called. He lasted even less time in the poetry circle or around the piano at group singalongs that belonged in an era before the guitar became electrified.

The old external stone walls of Leafy Gums blocked out mobile phone reception. I only ever saw Luke speak to ask a nurse to help him outside to light a smoke or check his phone for messages which never seemed to come.

At mealtimes, Luke barely ate. Instead, he whacked his blocky mobile phone against his wheelchair to check that it was still working. All the messages he expected from friends were not getting through. When he went outside, he held his phone high in the air, searching for life, for connection. Instead of boisterous youth during visiting hours, the double doors spewed forth only devoted elderly spouses or strung-out middle-aged children sandwiched between generations and with one eye on their wristwatches.

I thought the little prick's upstart attitude left a lot to be desired. But the young firebrand's moxie to say whatever the hell he was thinking was also to be admired. I wished I could do that too. Deep down, I had the same middle finger I wanted to give the world.

Luke was still brimming with life, not riddled with the stench of impending death like everyone else around me. It was only natural to want to tap such an energy source before it was too late. All I needed was a way for him to see the outsider in me, too.

A week had passed since Luke's arrival. I was standing with my back to the lounge, looking out the large window. I could see Luke in the small courtyard outside. He reached into his lap, the black leather bumbag where he kept his most valued possessions. Music player and charger, phone and charger, wallet, chewing gum, cigarettes, lighter, spare lighter fluid. All of life's essentials. Normally, the nurse who helped him outside waited until Luke had lit a fresh smoke before leaving him to quietly puff away, alone with his December thoughts. But on this day, a paroxysm of spluttering alerted her back to the lounge to assist a choking octogenarian gasping for air. The sudden alarm caused Luke's lighter to slip from his grasp and become wedged out of reach in the gap between two loose paving bricks.

I sensed my chance. I made a beeline for the courtyard door, shunting two plastic chairs aside and accidentally elbowing a dozing grandma in the head. Luke was still straining when I arrived. I felt every one of my six decades protest through ageing sinew in my back and knees as I bent down to pick up the brushed chrome Zippo. Noticing the Harley-Davidson logo, I flicked it closed and extended my arm.

"Here you go, son," I said. "May I?"

He looked up. Cigarette still drooping from the side of his mouth, he went to snatch the lighter from my hand. I pulled back and quickly flicked the Zippo open with one hand and rolled it around in my fingers like an illusionist. I stopped and held the lighter up and snapped my fingers to magically conjure a tall orange flame. I leant in and lit his cigarette, which by now was dangling straight down in sheer amazement.

Luke took a long drag as I presented him with the lighter. He grabbed it and shoved it deep into his bumbag. He took the cigarette from his mouth and expelled a long quill of smoke skyward.

"Cheers, old man," he puffed. "Nice trick."

"Nice lighter," I said, taking a step back. "Had one of these myself once. Ya can't break 'em."

"Yeah. Lifetime guarantee. Smoke?"

"Used to. Quit."

A thin tendril of smoke curled above Luke's head. "I should too," he said. "I'm cuttin' down though."

"So was I, for years." I paused. "What you listening to?"

Luke's eyebrows rose, then lowered dismissively. "Music."

"What? Who?"

"Ya wouldn't know 'em."

"Try me."

"Nah."

"Go on. Might surprise you. I know a few bands."

"I bet ya don't."

"One way to find out."

Luke rolled his eyes. "Rage Against the Machine."

I paused. "Is that the band or the album?"

"Both."

"Ha. Course it is."

I pretended to think, scanning a non-existent library of modern music.

"You're right," I said. "I don't know 'em."

Luke snorted his lack of surprise and dragged hard on his cigarette. He couldn't get the nicotine into his system quick enough.

156

"Are they a new band?" I asked.

"Nah. Broke up years ago."

"They sound angry."

"We're all angry."

I turned to face the nursing home. "Yeah," I exhaled. "I hear ya."

Luke let his ash fall where it may. "So how long have you been in 'ere?"

"Not long. Few months. It just *feels* like forever."

Luke nodded to himself, agreeing with something he already knew. I saw the young man only half-listening, still burdened with his thoughts.

"Hey," I said, "I got some music in my room. Wanna listen?"

"Listen to who, what albums, what bands?"

"Ya wouldn't know 'em . . ."

It was the first time I saw him smile. His teeth were yellow and positioned at all angles.

"Probably not but try me."

"Umm," I said. "Hmm, I dunno. What about something like *Highway to Hell*, heard of that?"

A spark ignited behind Luke's eyes. Between two fingers he held up the thin sliver of green metal that was his music player. "Nice try, old man, but I got AC/DC's entire discography right in 'ere."

Now it was my turn to smile. "That may be true, but I bet you've never heard them the way I'm talkin' about . . ."

Luke sat with his eyes closed, his head nodding rhythmically, hypnotically in time with the snare's backbeat as the music thumped from the big black speakers in my room. We had played my LP copy of *Highway to Hell* through twice.

"That is fan-fucking-tastic," Luke said with conviction. "There's, like, all these fucking notes I've never heard before."

The kid's colourful language was burning my ears. I swallowed my comment.

"That's 'cos you listen to digitally compressed music through tiny earbuds on a matchbox," I said. I was lying on my bed, my feet tapping to the beat, occasionally strumming a riff on air guitar. "If you want the real audio experience, you need something big, booming and vinyl."

Immersed in the adrenaline-charged embrace of hard rock, we hadn't uttered a single word about our respective frailties all afternoon. A new face to study and a new brain to share thoughts with meant we were no longer two sickies shackled in a nursing home. I kept telling myself that what I was experiencing was in no way anything more than friendship.

"You know," I said. "I once knew a girl in Fremantle who went out with that guy . . ."

"Who, which guy?" Luke asked.

I pointed to the right side of the glossy record cover encased in protective plastic.

"Him."

"Bon . . .?" Luke said. "You mean, Bon Scott?"

"Yep."

Luke's jaw fell. "Getthefuckouttahere!"

I clasped my hands behind my head and grinned. "It's true. He was a nobody then though, just some delinquent who'd dropped out of John Curtin High."

"Bon was the shit. A goddamn Aussie legend. Fuck yeah."

He raised his left hand. As we awkwardly high-fived, I noticed a dark blotch peek out from under the sleeve of his T-shirt.

"Is that a birthmark?" I asked, being polite.

Luke laughed. "Nah. Shoulda shown you this earlier. Gimme a hand and roll up my sleeve?"

I sat up, moistened my lips and swallowed hard. As I leaned in to tug at Luke's sleeve, I cautioned my bony fingers to not linger against the boy's supple skin for an inappropriate length of time. I again reminded myself that I wasn't experiencing what I thought I was experiencing. In a cold nursing home environment, there's a natural longing for touch and affection. Luke never apologised for what he'd said to me the day he arrived. I figured the kid was a tight ball of anger that day, trying to work out whatever level of Hell he'd landed in. He mightn't have even recognised me. All the old fogeys looked the same.

"Like it?" he asked.

I leaned back to focus my eyes on the mottled design adorning his flabby bicep.

"Recognise it?" Luke asked. "It's a parrot. Just like Bon had. I was pretty hammered when I got it but the way I look at it, he probably was too. And I got another one on my right arm."

Luke did the honours this time, reaching across with his left hand to reveal a five-starred crux that I instantly recognised as the Southern Cross asterism.

"My mates and me each got one when we finished high school."

I leaned in again to study each design assiduously, like a jeweller appraising a rough diamond with a loupe magnifier. The Southern Cross was satisfactory, but even a six-year-old can draw simple stars. I was more concerned with what I saw on Luke's left arm – the shaky lines and incongruous thickness that supposedly passed for a professional tattoo these days. The blotchy shading and poor colour blending made it look more like a stuffed parrot on the shoulder of a pantomime pirate than anything ever seen up a tree. The bird looked ill, aged before its time.

"They're both very nice," I lied.

"I want more," Luke said. "Someday."

"Someday I'll show you mine."

"Really? You've got ink?"

"Stuff from years ago."

"What you got? Show me. Show me now. And how'd you get that cool scar on your face?"

"Steady on, son. You kids only seem to care about the destination, you don't realise there's more memories in the journey. Life's journey *is* the destination."

Luke pulled a face, trying to process my philosophy. The look in his eyes remained vacant. I decided to change subject.

"I, ah, haven't noticed many of your mates visit yet."

"They're coming," Luke said quickly. "They are. They will." His voice was sour.

I fixed Luke with a stare, communicating only with flitting pupils. This time, he understood. He sighed.

"I know," the boy said. "And I can't blame them for not wanting to. It's like I'm dead."

I saw my cue. I reached behind my pillow. It took a moment for the identity of the silver glint I was proffering to register.

"Swig?"

Luke nodded almost violently, and the flask landed in his lap with a gentle thud. He positioned it between his thighs and expertly unscrewed the metal lid, letting it rest to one side on its captive top. He lifted the flask straight up and chugged, his Adam's apple bouncing like a ball on a bat.

"Whoa! Easy there, Bon," I said. "That stuff's meant to be savoured, not skolled."

He winced at the aftertaste as the fireball hit his mouth. "Shit," he said. "I probably shouldn't have done that. It'll mess with my meds."

"Ah, you'll be right, son," I said. "See it as self-medicating. I do. And besides, you're young, and this is rock 'n' roll."

"Fucken oath."

Luke made a sign of the horns with his left hand before hurling the flask back onto the bed. I drained what was left and we both sat back, letting the honeyed warmth wash through our veins.

19

Pilbara / Yindjibarndi Country, 2017

Their only vehicle that even merited the description was the broken-down Hiace jalopy. Sparrow tried the ignition in case by some miracle it was fixed. It wasn't. Bob looked up at the sky, the blue infinity, for a sign. Luke continued to spit venom at his curtailed session in the outback brothel. Sparrow and Bob ignored him – they were of the same mind. In front of them, their former victims. Behind them, an angry madam with an ultimatum. Luke seemed to overlook both and focus solely on himself. The sun and wind blasted into Sparrow, his face and arms prickling and burning.

In the end, he told Luke to "go and sit behind the van, out of sight". Luke went reluctantly and with an upturned finger. Sparrow crouched down low, began to walk with bent knees. He narrowly avoided a scorpion that appeared from under a rock to flick its venomous dagger tail. He first checked the Hummer in case someone was lying in wait or had left the keys in the ignition. But it was empty, its doors locked, and no keys.

Sparrow walked back over to Bob and Luke. "There's good news and bad news," he said.

The good news, they had time. The bad news, they didn't have much, and their final hope rested on Sparrow's homespun charm.

"Whatever you do," Sparrow told Luke, "don't make a sound and don't move from behind this van or we're screwed."

"I'll keep an eye on him," said Bob. "Just do what you have to do."

"Can I have your wallet?" Sparrow asked Bob.

"Sure."

The shipping container was the same featureless object that had teased Sparrow an hour earlier. Leaning in to listen, he burned his ear on its hot steel. He heard muffled sounds but nothing he could make out. The door handle didn't move, still locked. Sparrow took two deep breaths, ran a wet finger of saliva over his eyebrows, formed a fist, and pounded.

"Piss off," said a voice from inside.

Sparrow bashed again, harder, hurting his fist, and listened. This time, the sound of heavy footsteps, getting louder. He stepped back a metre, ruffled his shaggy hair with his fingers, and moistened his dry lips.

The door flung open. In a cloud of dust, Mummy greeted Sparrow with a sawn-off shotgun aimed squarely at his brown balls. Sparrow didn't move; instead, he talked fast, explaining what had happened with their car. Mummy said they got what they deserved and repeated her previous sentiment about calling the police. Sparrow said if she truly wanted to see the back of them, they needed one tiny favour. Slowly, he reached into his pocket, which only made Mummy cock her weapon. He told her that he was unarmed and proved it by throwing dirty fistfuls of cash at her feet. She kept the shottie pointed at him with one hand and bent down to pick up the money with the other. When all the grubby notes were collected, she backed away and went inside.

Sparrow stared at his feet. Had he done enough? The wind whipped sand into him, hard and coarse. He wondered whether he should've identified himself as a cop, but then figured it might have only inflamed the situation. He gritted his teeth, half-closed his eyes, and didn't move.

After about three minutes, the door swung open again with a pained creak. Mummy said she had radioed for a tow truck on the promise they never return. The door slammed shut and locked again. Sparrow trudged back to the van, saying nothing. Luke didn't even make eye contact; he merely extinguished one cigarette and lit another. It was Bob who spoke first.

"Well done, mate. There's no more you could've done. Now we wait. Lap of the gods."

With the adrenaline seeping from Sparrow's system, he knew that Bob was right. All that was left was to wait and hope.

The sound of a fast-revving engine punctured the silence. Sparrow blinked himself to alertness, his eyes having closed during the long wait. He watched the vehicle's final approach, counting down slowly in his head from ten to one.

"I'll handle this," Sparrow told his travel companions. He stepped down from the van and dusted his hands on his cargo shorts.

It was a skinny man with grease stains tattooed onto his cheeks. He spat black gobs of tobacco from the side of his mouth and hitched the Hiace's bumper with a hook and chain, all the while eyeing the three men crookedly. Sparrow made no small talk, smiled politely, and thanked him profusely. More than anything else, he was glad to be back on the road before Mummy's latest clients finished up. To give them extra time to escape, Sparrow had paid for their former victims to enjoy a second hour and told Mummy to say it was on the house.

The tow truck driver drove them to a garage on the outskirts of South Hedland. The resident mechanic was a grimier version of the driver, his twin brother. They talked in murmurs and stared and sniggered at the odd-looking trio who had appeared in the shade of their workshop. They turned out to be some of Mummy's regular clients. Sparrow was quoted an obscene sum to replace a dead battery with a reconditioned one that looked twice as old and decrepit. He paid it anyway and kept saying thank you, thank you. Luke's face was expressionless, his black sunglasses clamped over his eyes.

They were back on the road an hour later, driving in silence.

"Look on the bright side, son," Bob finally said. "We got our van back."

"And it's somehow runnin' better than before," said Sparrow, now driving. "Those inbred bastards knew what they were doin', even if they fleeced us on the battery."

Luke was staring sideways out the window, his face unflinching in the afternoon sun. The skies remained clear. The radio said the ports had reopened. Downgraded to a storm front, Cyclone Gina was now dumping billions of gallons of rain in the south. Its northern legacy remained in the large chunks of highway that had been washed away.

"I just hope the battery lasts," Sparrow added.

There was no response from the back half of the van. Luke was clearly moping, missing his partner-in-crime.

"C'mon, mate," Bob said. "Chin up. Focus on the positives. We aren't incarcerated or dead, and we're now back on the road heading north."

Sparrow glanced in the rear-view mirror to see the sides of Luke's mouth twinge upward before flatlining.

"Luke . . .?" Bob asked.

"Fuck off," he said.

"Steady on there, son. You make out like it's my fault she ditched us."

Luke didn't reply. Sparrow kept watching him in the mirror but there was nothing more. He thought the kid might have been experiencing withdrawal symptoms. Not from Mouse, but from whatever the hell she'd been feeding him twice a day. He'd seen it in many junkies. He didn't know how much she had Luke strung out on, or what the stuff even was.

"Look, mate, if it's any consolation, I miss her too," Bob said genuinely. "She was unique, a one-of-a-kind. But she's on her own quest and we're on ours. They're different journeys. The best we can hope for is to cross paths a while. You saw the Hummer – she's collecting enemies. Sooner or later, they're gonna catch up with her. And personally, I don't wanna be around when that happens."

Luke still didn't know what their quest was. Nor did Sparrow, for that matter.

Bob and Luke had heard their names over the radio again. The report no longer concerned "missing persons"; rather, it was a case of "suspected abduction". The police officer was not, however, prepared to say if there was a link between their case and a series of abductions of men in the northwest.

They drove past the battered wreck of an old hatchback by the roadside. Sparrow looked back at Luke, staring with big eyes at the metal corpse, and tried to imagine what he might be thinking. He'd heard the story from Bob, whom Luke had confided in at Leafy Gums. Sparrow tried to picture Luke as a tearaway waking up drunk in an underground sex club, stitched up by his young mates late one night. Panicked and disoriented, stumbling through darkened corridors before finally emerging in a shopfront to be handed his Superman underpants by a snickering clerk. Speeding off on his trail bike, an angry kid with a bed sheet recklessly flapping in the wind, trying to erase all he'd just seen. The sobering chill of the night air on his face, his back wheel aquaplaning across the soapy tarmac of the five-lane Perth freeway. He had been riding faster than a speeding bullet until he tried to overtake a sheep truck, and got dragged under when his cape was caught in the wheels. He was just a joke gone wrong now.

The increased frequency of ore trains at crossings slowed their journey north and ushered their arrival into the twin Hedland towns. Desperate to make up time, Sparrow turned right off the Great Northern Highway with two wheels off the ground. Ahead, the malignant mansions of South Hedland sprang from the red earth. Every single house had a fleet of four-wheel drives and flotilla of motorboats on trailers parked outside. Front lawns were piled high with fallen branches and uprooted trees – fallout from Gina – and the roads were littered with dead leaves. Damaged buildings and crooked fences, asbestos fibres, a rottenness in the air. A half-finished, multi-storey residential development dominated the town's low skyline promising "resort style" accoutrements. Luxury apartments with scenic views, gyms and timber saunas, barbeques and alfresco dining, pools and sunloungers. Open plan, three bedroom, three bathroom. Happy shiny people in functional modern spaces.

"I remember Mouse saying the new hospital's somewhere on this road," Bob said.

"Reckon that could be it up ahead," Sparrow replied.

A long silver building spread out before them in both directions. Slender white poles propped up sharp angular yellow and orange awnings that sliced into the sky. Black-tinted windows did their best to resist the dog days. The car park overflowed with off-roaders and utility trucks. Round the back, new asphalt and a helipad. And spread across the land, caravans of squalid tents, rows of improvised dwellings made out of corrugated aluminium, plastic sheeting and plywood. Between them wandered whitefellas, blackfellas, women and children and elderly, most of whom walked slowly and looked painfully thin. The car park hosted a clutter of camper trailers and motorhomes in one corner, no access to food, no sanitation. They kept driving.

"I saw a sign for a pharmacy earlier," Sparrow said, reefing the steering wheel.

"Much appreciated, mate," said Bob.

Sparrow parked two rows back. All three disabled spaces were occupied by cars with no permits. One was a lowered two-door coupé with shiny mag wheels and P-plates that indicated a provisional driver.

"Do you need a hand gettin' inside?" Sparrow asked.

"Be appreciated . . ."

They turned their faces away as they marched past the rectangular security guard on the door. Sparrow started browsing the shelves while Bob asked a young blonde pharmacist for the strongest non-prescription painkillers she had. She spun on her heels, selected a large plastic bottle off the shelf, and turned back to him.

"These co-codamols are pretty popular around here," she said. "They're a combination of codeine and paracetamol."

"Perfect," Bob exhaled. "That should do the trick."

"For severe pain, take two every four to six hours. But no more than eight tablets in twenty-four hours." She sounded like an advertisement.

"Eight's the magic number. Gotcha."

"So it's a bulk pack of one hundred co-codamol tablets," she smiled, scanning the item's barcode. "That comes to seventy-four dollars and ninety-five cents."

Bob paid with an avocado and then blew his change on a selection of chocolate bars and energy drinks for Luke. He couldn't stand seeing his sullen mug, uglier than usual.

Sparrow appeared. "Ready to go?"

"Yep," Bob replied, collecting his bounty. He turned back to the pharmacist. "One question, miss. We're not from around here. What's with all the tents and shacks out back?"

The pharmacist's cheery mood faded. Hard straight lines appeared across her face where there had been soft angular curves. She leaned in close and spoke in a hushed tone.

"It doesn't normally look as bad as it does now, after the cyclone."

"Who are all those people?" Bob asked.

The pharmacist sighed. "They're sick patients who come to town for things like dialysis and chemotherapy but can't afford to stay anywhere so are forced to sleep rough. Family members move in alongside them."

"That's awful," Bob said. "Now you mention it, I thought I saw a few people wearing hospital gowns."

"They wander in here sometimes. Asking for fresh water, among other things."

Sparrow's eyes opened wide. "Wait, they don't even have water?"

"Not out there, no," the pharmacist said. "Out there is desert. The nearest tap they can access is in a sobering-up centre a few miles away."

"I saw some units being built up the road there," Bob said. "Can't those be offered?"

"Most of the new apartments are already bought by the mining companies. FIFOs get their housing straight away. It's hard enough to get doctors to move up here."

"So, what brought you up here?" Sparrow asked.

"My boyfriend's an engineer at the port," she said. "Once we pay off our uni debts and save up enough for a deposit, we're heading straight back to Perth. I can't stand it up here."

Bob's body was soon numb from the hairline down while Luke's was surging with caffeine and sucrose, re-animated. After they rejoined the highway north, Luke said, "So, dude, remind me again . . . What *is* our quest?"

Sparrow wanted to know, too. Surely it wasn't far to go now. They would soon run out of continent on which to drive.

They had just passed a cemetery on the right side of the highway. On the left, a dirt-bike track roared with excitement and risk. Having driven past salt lakes and overtaken road trains transporting the unrefined crystals, the van was now passing the colossal pyramids where they stockpiled the white gold. They were on the outskirts of Port Hedland, a town where the only green was the glint of an empty Victoria Bitter can by the roadside.

"There," Bob said, pointing ahead. "That."

20

Kimberley & Pilbara / Wilinggin & Yindjibarndi Country, 1980

Bob

Beside the glittering anthills in the Kimberley, our lives changed in a moment.

I approached them first, leaning in with a sense of trepidation and one closed eye. The bull ants appeared angry at my incursion, swarming, protecting their territory and queen from the hovering alien eyeball. I wiped a sweaty finger against my snug football shorts and manoeuvered it between the freeway lanes of ants clogging the craggy dirt mound. My chewed fingernails offered no leverage whatsoever. In the end, Stretch used a sharp stick to dig around the area, sending the crawling insects into a frenzy of communication and activity.

"See, the key is to leave a gap," Stretch said. "So you don't damage whatever the hell this is."

I snapped my own wooden dagger from a nearby fallen branch and approached the second twinkling anthill with a matching glint in my eye. I hacked away at the earth with less finesse than Stretch but the end result was the same: a big brown clump of ant-riddled earth.

"If only I had my geological tools with me," Stretch said.

"What do you s'pose they are?" I asked.

"Dunno."

If Stretch knew, he didn't want to say. He didn't even want to speculate, which didn't cut it with me.

"Well, whatever they are," I said, "they gotta be worth somethin', surely . . ."

"Dunno," he repeated.

I racked my ore-riddled brain. My geological knowledge extended as far as the giant black lumps of rubble I had hauled for five years. Colour in rock was a strange luxury.

"Rubies . . . ?" I asked. "Rubies are pink, aren't they?"

"Corundum, you mean."

"Huh?"

"That's the name of the mineral. Red corundum is ruby. Blue corundum is sapphire. Rubies and sapphires are the same mineral."

"I didn't know that."

"Tourmaline is also pink. So is spinel. Pink beryl is morganite, although that's usually lighter in colour than this. This is more like a deep champagne."

"Yeah yeah, okay, Mister Doctor Scientist. I get it. Let's just get these back to the truck."

Stretch fished the crumpled T-shirt out of his shorts pocket. He wrapped his clod of earth in it to protect his hands from ant bites and our find from view. I did the same.

"I'll take them in to work when we get back," Stretch said. "And until I can identify what they are, we *never* found these, okay? If word gets out where we found whatever this is, and it really is something, this place'll be crawling with sappers before you can say Jack Robinson."

In my mind, I'd already cashed in my chips, told my site manager and the other camp troglodytes where to go, torn up my heavy vehicle licence, and was now driving east across the Great Sandy Desert in a rocket-powered convertible.

"Yeah," I said. "Gotcha."

Stretch spoke with the wisdom of a man with a mining heritage. I was just a bum who'd struck it lucky, but even I wasn't that stupid.

Two evenings later, Stretch knocked on the door of my donga. I was lying on my mattress, pretending to read a book and quietly hoping I had killed all the fleas this time.

The results were back from the lab. Stretch had brought the stones with him, roughly cut and polished, in an old tobacco tin, to show me his word was true.

"Holy shit," he stammered. The tin was shaking in his hands, the contents rattling like a maraca.

"Rubies . . .?" I said, standing up. "Are they rubies?"

"Fuck rubies," Stretch said. "Rubies are for lightweights."

I reeled back. I thought rubies were as good as it got.

"Look, I'm no expert," Stretch went on. "Well, actually *I am* . . . but anyway, I'm telling you, there's no-one more surprised by these results than me."

Feeling my knees turn to marshmallow, I was forced to sit down again. Stretch started on a slow pace inside the donga.

"Those babies we found aren't rubies," he said. "Their refractive index is too high. Same with their dispersion coefficient. I didn't want to do a hardness test, but in the end I did a small one. Again, clean off the charts."

I'd grasped almost none of what the scholarly geologist had said. As usual, I feigned a light nod of understanding.

"I couldn't work it out," Stretch continued. "But then I went back to my geology texts and did some reading. It was their bloody colour that threw me. I was thinking of something transparent, not coloured. Turns out that coloured examples exist. Blue and yellow, even green. It happens when underground pressures push the rock to the surface. Light becomes absorbed, the crystal structure gets altered and bingo, you get colour. Amazing when you think about it, the chemistry. No wonder we found these little beauties in the side of a goddamn anthill. Just sitting there, waving to the world."

My breath was quickening. "Well . . ." I said. "What the hell are they?"

Stretch stopped pacing and leaned against the nearest donga wall, making it crinkle under his weight. He looked down at the floor, strewn with red sand and scuffed with dirty boot marks, then straight up at me like a judge delivering a verdict to a condemned prisoner.

"Bob, old boy, I'm pretty sure what we've got here are diamonds," he said. "Diamonds that happen to be pink. That is to say, pink fucking diamonds."

My face turned crooked, then froze. I tried to coordinate my brain and vocal cords but the messages weren't getting through.

"Pink . . . die . . . die . . ."

"Diamonds," Stretch repeated. "Pink ones. Freaks of nature. As rare as a flying pig and at least a billion years old. These aren't just any old diamonds, they're the stuff of royalty."

"What royalty?"

"Back in the fifties, a Canadian geologist gave the Queen a pink diamond as a wedding present. It sat in the middle of a diamond encrusted brooch in the shape of a jonquil. The diamond was found by a group of kids playing under a tree outside the geologist's mine in Tanzania. The French Crown Jewels in the Louvre also have a pink diamond, a big bastard from the seventeenth century."

It was too much for my tiny brain to process, even given my pre-imagined visions of grandeur. The moment of discovery cut across my mind as it had done every hour since our return to camp. It was conceivable that I'd been the first person to stand in that exact position at that precise time of day in thousands of years. A chance encounter at the intersection of space and time and light. The stuff of royalty? All my life, I had been no more than the stuff of scum.

"Even the sun shines on a dog's arse some days," Stretch said. "And you, my friend, are that arse."

"The diamonds," I said instinctively, desperately. "Show them to me, let me see."

Stretch got down on one knee and held forth the tobacco tin in a customary action. I acknowledged the faux gesture, clasping my palms together and holding them up to my lips in wild anticipation. I then fanned my startled face to avoid fainting.

"Splinters of stars, fallen to earth," he whispered. "Tears of the gods."

I secretly wished the ritual was genuine.

"Pink diamonds are so bloody rare it took the world's biggest mining company fifteen years to dig up enough of the bastards to fill a single champagne flute," Stretch added.

Taking the tin, my arms were infused with a sudden surge of electricity. I prised the lid open gently as if fearing to disturb the precious contents. The container was half filled with red dirt, still shaking itself free from the nuggets of pink ice and insulating them from the tin's metal surface. The rough, uncut diamonds retained their earthly signature, making them look less like life-changing symbols and more like glassy pebbles. I examined them all, but my gaze lingered longest on the first of the stones I'd spotted in the anthill. It was so large that it seemed to have its own gravitational pull around which the six other rocks orbited. I picked it up between two stubby, dirt-encrusted fingertips, letting it fall into the broad grooves of my rough palm.

"What's she worth, you reckon?"

Stretch exhaled. "Dunno," he said.

Don't know or don't wanna say, I thought.

"But what I do know is this – we've now got some serious business that we need to take care of if we're gonna do this properly."

My ears liked what they were hearing. "What've you got in mind?" I asked.

I knew what I had in mind. A quick score, a quick sale, wads of cash, and a quick escape from this hell on earth with my accomplice alongside. We would only materialise on the other side of the country with new identities and a new outlook on an enlightened world, to start a new life together.

But Stretch had other ideas.

Over the course of the next hour, with the small tin on the donga floor between us, and the drunken revelry raging outside, Stretch sat with me and explained "serious business" as he saw it. A claim over the land was needed. It was otherwise Crown land.

"So, wait," I said. "You mean, all this technically isn't even ours?"

"Nope," Stretch replied.

"Whose is it?"

"The Queen's. More diamonds for her."

"Bullshit. That's not fair."

"That's how it is, I'm afraid. That's the law."

"Bugger the law."

"I'd rather not."

His reply came unnaturally quickly. I knew the bastard had a past he was hiding. But didn't we all, for one reason or another? Maybe he'd done this same thing before, ripping off some other poor sod in another State and then hightailing across the border.

"So how do we make it ours?" I asked.

"We apply for a mining lease."

"A lease . . . ? How they hell do we—"

"Don't worry, I can do it, I know how. It'll take time and money though."

I scratched the side of my head. "Money, eh," I said, my voice infused with suspicion. "Christ, I thought this was simple. Can't we just find a diamond dealer or a jeweller or a bloody pawnshop to buy what we got, no questions asked? There must be dozens of 'em in Perth."

"Well yeah, we can absolutely do that," Stretch replied. "But 'no questions asked' comes with a price tag – they'll want a big discount. People will think we nicked 'em. Which, technically, we have right now. I mean, why else would two jokers who look nothing like businessmen be wanting to part with them so quickly? If it was me, I'd be suss too. So what we gotta show 'em to get a fair price is something that proves we're legit. Paperwork."

I hung my head. He was right. Though of course, the way I felt about him, the lanky bastard could've been saying that black was white and I would've still believed him.

"And besides," Stretch continued, "don't you wanna go back up there and see if there's any more of these little beauties waitin' to be dug up? Why be measly millionaires when we can be bloody billionaires?"

Caught up in the moment, I had completely disregarded the notion that the well was not fully tapped.

I smiled. "So," I said, "when the hell can we go back?"

21

Perth / Whadjuk Noongar Country, 2016

Bob

By the end of our first week together, I'd discovered a dozen modern bands in Luke's music player. My old ears thought they all sounded identical, loud and atonal. At Luke's insistence, we'd also given every vinyl record in my collection a spin. At the end of each night, neither of us could work out how the hip flask came to be drained so repeatedly.

By day, the reality of institutional life remained. Bingo and poetry circles during the afternoons, puréed spinach and creamed corn for dinner, daily medications and health checks.

I sat on my bed. I rolled up my sleeve. Out came the nurse's sphygmomanometer. She wore a sad necklace of silver tinsel to commemorate the holiday season. I insisted she take off her rubber gloves. She refused. Fft fft fft.

"Hmm," she said. "Your blood pressure's worse today, 180 over 110."

"Sorry," I said. "I promise I'll do better next time."

She flipped through the pages on her clipboard. "Your INR is up as well, 2.9. And your bloods are down."

"Sorry," I repeated. "Next time. Better. Promise."

"I'm afraid I'll need to discuss these results with the doctor. He may change your meds or try a different combination of antiretrovirals."

"New flavours, delicious."

"Oh, and one more thing. The director wants to see you in his office."

"When?"

"Immediately."

"Shit. What about?"

There was no response. It didn't matter, I already knew what it was about. Play dumb, I reminded myself. Dumb and cute and charming. I felt my face, glad to have shaved that morning. I'd cut my face a few times with my straight razor, but there was no shave closer.

On my way to Blackford's office, I stopped by the lounge. It was empty and I was in no hurry. This was the sweetest time imaginable – keeping *him* waiting for *me*. I wanted it to last, to savour it. My eyes lingered on the ugly pile of daily newspapers, left haphazardly on a coffee table. Picking up *The West Australian*, I absently flicked through the pages. I saw drug raids, nightclub glassings, mining profits; the usual garbage. But then, I stopped on a photo that made my jaw drop. It was an outback landscape I instantly recognised, deep in the heart of the Kimberley. Plans had been drawn up by developers to build a luxury resort. Eighty individual studio villas, a tropical island swimming pool, gazebo, waterfalls, palm trees, golf course. International guests, helipad, glorious sunsets. Excavation on the site was about to begin.

I closed my eyes. Memories swirled and sluiced through my brain, snapshots and voices and events. The hairs on my neck bristled, a chill down my spine, goosebumps across my arms. I snapped my eyes open, checked to see if anyone was watching, and swiftly tore out the page. I folded it twice, shoved it in my back pocket, and walked to the director's office as fast as I could.

My hand slipped on the doorknob, freshly coated in the oily remnants of Blackford's lunch. I found Blackford in the process of trying to fix a jammed photocopier with the finesse of an automotive panel beater.

"Ah, Robert, good, the nurse must've told you," he said. "Sit."

Taking a seat on the edge of the chair, I admired a quivering pyramid of cola cans Blackford had clumsily engineered on his desk.

"Hello, Geoffrey," I said. "Good to see you. Is this going to take long?"

Blackford stopped his mechanical repairs and fixed eyes on me. "Why, you in a hurry, somewhere better to be?"

I relaxed my shoulders and sat back. "Not at all," I smiled, "I was just wondering what you had in mind. Say, have you lost weight?"

Blackford tossed his stapler to one side and sat down. He snapped the tab on a shiny silver can and drained the blackened water into his cavernous gullet. Arching his back with a spinal crack, he belched a cloud of chemicals that made my head swim.

"Yeah yeah," he said. His breath was heavy with caffeine and fatigue. "Don't blow smoke up my arse, Robert. I've no time for it today. Another nurse is threatening to quit after she was groped by one of the residents . . ."

"I swear, it wasn't me."

"Very funny. I'll cut to the chase. I understand you've been spending a lot of time with one of our new arrivals."

I pretended to think. "Ah yes. Mr Crosby. The retired pastry chef in room thirteen. Lovely chap, told me about his triple bypass. But I can assure you, it's not me who keeps helping him break into the kitchen at four a.m. to bake scones."

Blackford fisted the table, making the aluminium pyramid crinkle, then collapse. "Dammit, you know who I mean," he said. "The boy, whatshisname . . ."

"The boy? Oh, you must mean young Luke."

"That's him."

"Sure. I've seen him around. I said hello. Was that wrong, should I not have?"

"That's not all you've said, from what I've heard. I have it on good authority that you and the boy are thick as thieves, spend a lot of time together."

"You seem to have lots of things 'on good authority' these days."

"Now look . . ." Blackford said. "Frankly I don't give a toss if you two stay up all night listening to voodoo music and laughing like morons. But what I do care about, above all, is the boy's welfare."

Having been distracted by the newspaper article, I stopped in my tracks. Blackford now had my undivided attention. I sat for a moment, processing what he'd said. Was this an accusation or simply a statement? Unable to decide, I played it straight.

"And I *also* care about Luke's welfare," I said.

The room went quiet, both of us waiting for the other to speak, to play their hand. My tongue felt too big for my mouth. It was Blackford who finally blinked.

"Now obviously, I wouldn't want anything bad to happen to the boy," he said. "For example, I wouldn't want to imagine he was being, you know . . ." Blackford cleared his throat. "*Interfered with.*"

I looked at him from a great distance. "What are you saying, Geoffrey?" I asked, squinting. "Or, should I say, what has been said *to you*?"

He leaned back in his chair, making its inner workings scream in pain. "Nothing's been said to me," he said. "And nor am I saying anything. We're just, you know, talking, finding common ground."

I felt the application of a familiar blowtorch. I tugged at my collar and swallowed concrete. "Sure," I said. "Talking. Common ground." My cheeks flushed pink.

"Why, Robert. Are you sweating?"

I was. "It's a side effect from my meds," I said quickly. "I get hot flushes now and then. Today is one of those days."

Blackford's tiny pupils flicked from side to side like two fleas in empty fishbowls. He was assessing me, scrutinising. At last, his eyes stopped scanning and his face relaxed.

"Remember, Robert. I'm just trying to do my job here. It's nothing personal against you. But every one of our residents is an individual with their own unique needs. Your needs are somewhat more complicated given your medical condition. That's why I asked to talk to you, to ensure we have an understanding and make you aware of your responsibilities. Do we need to run through those again?"

"No," I said. "I know who I am. I know what I need to do and I know what not to do." I heard the steel in my own voice.

"We can't risk your condition spreading. If that should happen, it'll be my balls in a vice."

"Rest assured, Geoffrey. The risk is minimal given the biology of it all. You know that."

"I do. And yet . . ."

"Obviously, I can't offer what you want to hear – a one hundred per cent rock-solid guarantee," I said, crossing my arms. "Short of making me wear a space suit, you need to trust me."

"I *have* to trust you," Blackford said. "Having to take the boy in at the eleventh hour under such unfortunate circumstances has made a difficult situation near impossible. We're haemorrhaging staff, our budget is getting slashed next quarter, and my blood pressure's so high it's leaking out my nose."

I shunted my chair back and stood with purpose. "I empathise with all those things, Geoffrey, I really do. But just because Luke and I have been spending time together, doesn't mean it's anything more than that."

Blackford paused to massage the sore spot blossoming on his right temple. He exhaled. "I hope so, Robert," he said. "I hope so."

I was halfway back to my room before I even realised where I was. A red haze of fury had numbed my five senses leaving only an innate sense of orientation to steer me through the corridors. If there were other residents watching me stagger along – which there probably were – I failed to notice. And I certainly didn't remember making the hot cup of coffee that I was carrying.

I couldn't refute that Luke's youth was an allure. Nor could I deny it was the first thing I'd noticed. I wanted to be close to him, to feel younger, more energised. I was aware of how it looked – like some sleazy old fart with a supermodel. But more than anything, it was Luke's company that had enriched my cardboard existence. And I liked to think that I'd also shone a ray of light into his windowless heart.

I resented Blackford's accusations. Bastard. I knew they reflected both the other residents' fears and his need to find a scapegoat. It wasn't my fault he was under the pump. People aged. Society forgot about them. But there was still a mess that needed cleaning up. It was a situation that would only worsen with time.

Remembering the newspaper article in my pocket, I shook my head clear and started making a mental list. Backpack, meds, a cab fare, a plane ticket, a rental car, garden supplies. I would leave the very next day or the one after. Time was short – excavation was "about to begin". I thought about phoning the developer or even the journalist to ask for more precise timing or intel but was worried I might tip them off. The last thing I needed was to accelerate excavation or to unleash journos sniffing around for a story. And getting me out of the nursing home was what everyone wanted anyway.

But things would likely have changed by the time I made it north. The whole area could be cordoned off or marked up in some way. That would certainly make it easier to find the right spot. But if there was a ring of protective steel fencing, I'd be in real strife. And if a concrete slab had been thrown down, I was completely stuffed. There'd be no digging that up with a hand shovel.

Back at my room, the door was ajar.

On the other side of the bathroom door, I heard a dull scratching noise, the tap running at a frenetic pace.

Looking down, I saw two fresh tyre tracks on the floor. Their path led to the bathroom.

Poking the door open, the first thing I saw was the white porcelain sink stained a deep crimson. There were a million red specks around the basin and red spots on the mirror and tiles amid puddles of warm water and slippery soap. The floor was covered with stained towels and fallen bathroom items, as if a struggle had taken place. And in the mirror, pockmarked with steam, I made out Luke's hazy young reflection. As the door opened and steam dissipated, the boy's face became clear. It was covered in the same shade of red that seemed to coat every inch of the small bathroom.

"Dude!"

His long yellow canines beamed at me through a splotchy face of ruby red and milky white. There were tiny cuts everywhere.

"I had a go with your razor. It's a prick of a blade, harder to use than it looks. My goatee needed a trim, then I got a bit carried away trying to sculpt the rest. I wanted to surprise you with one of those cool pencil-thin chin-strap beards. How's it look? Bad ass?"

I put a hand to my brow as if I'd been shot in the head. In that moment, Luke's face resembled an abattoir floor. The sound of a coffee mug shattering on tiles caused a dozen call buttons to flash at the nurses' station.

"Shit!" I said, seizing the long straight razor from his left hand with a swift snatch.

I threw the blood-spattered blade in the sink and flung on the tap full bore, making the wall pipes rattle and no doubt bringing more unwanted attention. Water hit the silver slice and splashed red everywhere.

"Shit shit fucking shit," I said, looking over my shoulder.

"What's the matter, bro?" Luke said. "No worries, it's just a bit o' blood, I'll survive."

But I wasn't listening. I chucked the bloody towels in the shower recess and turned on both taps for maximum water. The towels were soon sodden, heavy, with a watery red river snaking its way down the plughole. I grabbed a fresh towel from the cupboard in my room, a navy blue one I had bought myself, and fell upon Luke as if suffocating him with a pillow. I dabbed and rubbed and smeared away all the blood on his face until he was clean, then drowned him in burning aftershave.

"Ow, dude!" Luke said. "Back off man, that bloody stings. Relax, I said I'm fine."

"Sorry," I said, panting. "It's the alcohol. It's antiseptic, kills germs. Now, hold still . . ."

To absorb the spots of fresh blood growing larger on Luke's cratered face, I applied half a box of Band-Aids from my bathroom cupboard. Then I poked my head into the corridor to make sure no-one was coming.

I wiped away the bathroom mess with a second dark towel; the tiles, the mirror, the sink. I picked up all the loose strips of non-adhesive plastic, the soggy towels, the broken mug, and finally my wet straight razor. I carried the wet bundle, dripping, to my room and wrapped them in a fresh bed sheet, which I pushed far under my bed. I would need to dispose of the moist sheet – the evidence – in the nursing home's dumpster late at night.

"Jesus Christ," I heard Luke call out. "All this fuss over a few little cuts. You'd think I had fucking Ebola or something."

I returned to the echoing, humid bathroom. "You okay, are you sure you're okay?" I asked.

"Yes. Christ, relax would ya?"

"Now, Luke, listen mate . . ."

I was out of breath. I crouched down to Luke's height, my knees cracking like gunshots. I looked at the boy with my biggest eyes.

"You gotta promise me one thing," I said. "And this is *really* important. This here, today . . . this *never* happened, okay? You can't tell anyone about this. Not the nurses or the director or anyone else."

Luke screwed up his plastered face. "Yeah, sure," he said flippantly. "But I don't get why it's such a big deal. I was only shaving. It's just—"

"It's this place," I said. "This place they all reckon is a 'home'. Bullshit. They're all goddamn crazy in here. You know they are. They steal my money and give me all these drugs to keep me permanently sedated. They're probably doing it to you too and you haven't even realised. You're the single best thing that's happened to me in here. You and me, we don't belong in here. You know that. So please, can you please, please promise me?"

Luke listened with his full attention. I spoke in short bursts, staccato, at the speed of thought. Luke agreed with everything I said. He absolutely didn't belong in a nursing home. Everyone he'd met was certifiably insane. He was certain he'd lost some money as well, and felt tired and depressed all the time.

He looked hard into my eyes. They were practically pleading. His eyes then softened.

"Yeah, yeah," he breathed. "Okay, I promise."

22

Pilbara & Kimberley / Yindjibarndi & Wilinggin Country, 2017

The rust-coloured port authority control tower in Port Hedland jutted skywards like a single dirty tooth.

"Without that grimy little tower, this whole country would be stuffed," Bob said. "It controls the movement of dozens of bulk carriers a week. They've even had to dredge the crap out of the port so it can now handle bigger boats."

Sparrow drove to the water's edge. Everywhere was industry, activity and dust. There was a backlog to be cleared following the forced cyclone shutdown. Bulk carriers hovered on the surface of the great ocean. Helicopters melted into the distance as they flew out to the carriers. They delivered local marine pilots who would work with Chinese ship captains to guide them into the narrow port. Tugboats skimming over the waves zeroed in on the carriers, easing them into berthing positions through the tight channel. Hatches opened, and a maze of conveyer belts ground into life. The dirty brown gold was loaded into steep mountains that were flattened by excavators and bulldozers to maintain the ship's floatation and stability. It was an air, sea and land operation choreographed with military precision, buzzing around the clock. One mistake in loading, in balancing the immense weight, and the bulk carrier could capsize or break in half.

"C'mon," Bob said. "Let's grab a room and a drink at one of the hotels. We got a lotta driving tomorrow."

"More driving?" Luke's voice sounded heavy, lethargic.

"Definitely more driving. The port's just a pit stop. I needed to show you what it's all about up here."

Sparrow reversed the van and headed for town. The disabled parking spaces in front of the two hotels on The Esplanade were all occupied. It was the same scene in every other nearby car park.

"Bloody hell," Luke said. "There can't be that many friggin' cripples in this town."

The trio parked outside a coffee shop further down the road. They then walked, hobbled or rolled the two hundred metres back to the hotel, dodging four lanes of traffic en route. In the distance, at the road's northern end, a floating skyscraper sailed by, headed for one of the fourteen berths in the inner harbour.

"Christ," Sparrow said instinctively. "It's beautiful."

As they approached the entrance to one of the hotels, they heard giggling on the sidewalk directly behind. Sparrow turned to see a man in sunglasses, much younger than him, hunched over, ambling with corkscrewed knees, using an invisible walking stick, imitating Bob's slow arthritic gait. Next to him, one of his oafish pals swilling from a black aluminium can pushed a third neanderthal in a shopping trolley laden with two slabs of bourbon and cola. The comedian in the trolley had his tongue pressed firmly against the inside of his lower lip, his eyes crossed, moaning incoherently. They were all trying to compose themselves so as to not arouse suspicion, but failing spectacularly.

"Oh right," Sparrow said. "You dumb bastards think that's funny, do you?"

All three men, weighed down with tattoos, broke into fits of drunken laughter, guts bursting out from beneath their hi-vis shirts. Tears rolled down their faces, whiskey and sugar out their noses.

"Ha bloody ha, you idiots," Bob added. "One day, you'll be old too. I guarantee you. That is, unless you die young. Which, in your case, I'd wager is an odds-on bet. My money's on a car accident or a mining disaster."

Imitation Bob slapped the real Bob on his back. "Don't have a heart attack, ol' man!" he crowed. "We were just 'avin' a laugh."

"Yeah, lighten up!" the trolley comedian squawked. He lumbered out of his carriage, unloaded both cartons of bourbon, and kung-fu kicked the trolley to one side.

The three youths crammed themselves and their haul of grog into a ute parked in a disabled space, the chassis bottoming out under their collective weight. The car bore an enormous silver Southern Cross sticker on the tinted back window in between a pair of gleaming "Love It or Leave It" and "I Grew Here, You Flew Here" stickers. It had a personalised "RUMITUP" number plate. The engine roared.

"Fucken hell, Keg," the middle passenger said. "The new donk's a bloody ripper."

"V8, mate," Keg smiled. "Can't beat 'em fer grunt."

They reversed, rolled down the windows, blasted a detonation of heavy metal music and brandished a series of upturned thumbs and moronic grins. Bob returned fire with an upturned middle finger. Luke sat silently, staring, seemingly conflicted, as if watching himself in a parallel universe where he still had legs and felt invincible.

Shiny black cans were handed around the car's interior; rings popped, arms raised, elbows bent, music cranked. The ute slipped into forward gear and accelerated away. Luke turned and rolled away as Sparrow watched them in the distance where they overtook a truck he thought looked distinctly like one in which he'd just ridden.

The next day, Bob made Sparrow drive more than even he thought possible. The blistering heat seemed to melt the dashboard instruments. Sparrow lost his bearings soon after they left the highway and all signs of civilisation. It was only the soaring reading on the van's thermometer that told him they had veered inland. The landscape changed: less orange, more brown. The van filled with the distinct smell of burning oil. Luke wouldn't shut up, blathering almost incoherently. Sparrow didn't blame him – Bob had made Sparrow take to the non-road like a man on a sketchy mission.

"If you guys are gonna kill me and dump my body out here, I think you've gone far enough," Luke joked nervously. "They'll never find me now."

Luke's fears were not unfounded – the only stop they'd made after leaving Port Hedland was a garden centre to buy a shiny new shovel, a sharp pitchfork, and some heavy-duty garbage bags.

Bob turned and glared at Luke. "Can't be too sure," he said with no emotion.

That'll make his colostomy bag swell, thought Sparrow.

Compared to Luke, Sparrow suddenly felt exhilarated, energised. At last, they were heading into the Kimberley and had all the implements for digging, excavating, exhuming. They must be closing in now. Bob was going to fulfil his promise and, in turn, Senior Constable Sparrow would clear the old man's conscience by delivering sweet justice.

Sparrow could tell that Luke sensed such behaviour was strangely out of character for Bob, who had always been their enthusiastic ring-leader on the great adventure to nowhere. By this stage, surely the kid knew there was more to it, something significant that Bob had been careful to not reveal. And yet, the sense of the unknown was clearly adding to Luke's excitement, even if it came with a little apprehension. It was like their time with Mouse, both exhilarating and risky. And Sparrow's foot was now heavy, stopping for no man or beast or law of physics. He was guided by Bob, and for all Luke knew he was in on it too.

Sparrow didn't know what to expect. Did Bob know where the hell he was going? What was he guided by? A hazy image in his mind's eye? As they drove, Bob looked in every direction but seemed to find nothing familiar in the great tracts of untouched land they were barrelling through. Sparrow quietly cursed his empty, oversized country.

Crackling along unsealed roads, the van was a comet with a tail of thick bulldust. The puddles and washouts from the cyclone had dried, leaving an uneven surface. The ruts and corrugations made Sparrow's arms and shoulders tighten and ache. Bob complained that his spine felt like a steel bar – this was young man's terrain. Were they in the wrong place altogether? Sparrow kept driving.

Luke closed his eyes and started humming to himself, presumably in the vain hope of maintaining both his composure and his half-digested breakfast. This was excitement again, but perhaps not quite the brand he craved. They were now well and truly out of mobile phone range.

"Mouse was pretty effing hot, wasn't she?"

The comment came out of nowhere. Luke clearly wanted to appeal to his captors, to steer the conversation in the direction of something lighter, a topic over which the three red-blooded men could bond. But his companions weren't biting.

"Man, I'm tellin' ya," he continued. "If my body had its effing shit together . . ."

The front half of the van remained silent, focused.

"The things I woulda done to her . . ."

Sparrow ignored him and concentrated on frantically turning the steering wheel to avoid hazards. Rocks slammed into the underside of the van, peppering the chassis like fired bullets. Bob kept scanning the horizon and mumbling to himself, then telling Sparrow to "keep going".

"Bob? Nurse?"

"Huh? What is it, Luke?" Sparrow asked. "I'm busy up here."

"And I'm trying to keep us on track," Bob added.

"Mouse, eh."

"What Mouse?" Bob said. "What about her? She's gone."

"Sure, but hot stuff, yeah? I mean, in a slutty kind of way."

Bob sighed. It seemed he'd decided to humour him.

"Sure, mate," he said. "I reckon you would've wooed her with all your charm, no worries."

"Shit yeah. No wonder all those mining blokes beat a path to her door."

Bob took a few seconds before he spoke again, and then with a wry grin. "To be honest with you, mate," he said, "I'd have sooner rooted the blokes."

"Ha!" Sparrow snorted a laugh.

Luke looked confused. It wasn't quite the response he was expecting. Given his experience with the fairer sex, it was clear he wanted to discuss the subtle intricacies of the female form, not have his mind sullied. Sparrow glanced in the rear-view mirror and saw Luke contort his fleshy face like he was trying to ignore what Bob had said. But he couldn't.

"Yeah, right," Luke said. "Me too."

"Me three!" smiled Sparrow.

"Very funny, Luke," said Bob.

"Mouse not your kind of girl?"

"Now you *are* being funny."

"What? You started it."

"Started what?"

"This conversation," Luke said.

"No I didn't," Bob said. "You did. You mentioned Mouse."

"Sure, I wanted to talk about her. Not the fat ugly bastards she robs."

"Oooh, I dunno," Bob said. "Some of them were actually pretty muscly. Manual labour and all that grime and sweat. I used to have a body like that. You may not believe it to look at me now. But now you mention it, I don't mind admitting it was hard *not* to get turned on. I may be old, son, but I ain't dead."

Silence now occupied the van's back half. Sparrow was quietly grateful for it. He was tired of hearing Luke's incessant little parrot voice when he was trying to drive a van and solve a murder. Good on ya, Bob, he thought. Maybe that'll shut the little turd up.

"Wait a minute, what the hell?" Luke eventually said. "Where'd all this shit come from all of sudden?"

"What?" Bob asked.

"This. This shit. About . . . blokes."

Bob turned and smiled innocently. "What about it?"

Luke let out a nervous laugh and chewed on his thumbnail. Sparrow glanced in the rear-view mirror. He could see the young man's reflection trying to conjure a response but no matter how much his lip quivered and his head shook, none came. Sparrow sensed he better stay out of it. Whatever was going down now didn't concern him.

"Oh wait," Bob said. "Holy smokes. You're kidding me. Tell me, please. Tell me you're kidding me."

Luke didn't answer. He was still trying to gnaw off his thumb, staring out the window into the middle distance.

"I thought you knew," Bob said.

"Knew? Knew what?" Luke asked. "You, little bird man, did you know about this?"

"About what?" asked Sparrow.

"Bob, are you fucking with me?" Luke said.

"No," Bob said. "I genuinely thought you knew. Everyone in the nursing home did. And who cares anyway, right? What year is this, 2017 or 1967?"

Luke's gaze remained fixed. The subtle flickering of his pupils hinted at a racing mind. But Sparrow knew what was going on. It was a realisation he recognised from many previous occasions in his own life. His own Indigenous community had never supported his choices and always viewed him as a second-class citizen. He'd been made an outcast, like Bob seemed to be in the home. Both environments were throwbacks, as if frozen in time. He and Bob were more alike than he'd realised.

"Didn't you ever wonder why I was always alone?" Bob asked Luke. "Why no-one visited me or even sat and ate lunch with me?"

There was no response.

"To be honest," Bob added, "I thought spending time with me was part of your therapy or something. Like exposure therapy, you know, to overcome your fears."

Luke's eyes flitted away from the window and settled accusingly on Bob.

"Therapy?" he spat. "The fuck does that fucken mean? You sayin' I'm fucked up? Are you callin' me crazy?"

"Oi! Language."

"Fuck your fucken language!"

"Luke!" Sparrow piped up. "Mate, not so loud. I don't want to get us killed here."

"I knew it!" Luke said. "You're in on this. You're like him, aren't you? Another bum bandit. I knew you weren't just his bloody carer!"

"Jesus Christ, mate," Bob said calmly. "Luke, listen. Slow down. I'm not saying you're crazy. Not at all. Everyone gets therapy. There's physical therapy, like visiting the shipping container yesterday or when we went to the beach in Perth. And then there's mental therapy, like chatting with a counsellor or this trip with me."

Luke's eyes narrowed. "This trip," he hissed. "*This trip was your bloody idea.*"

"Sure, mate. But that's 'cos I didn't think you were like all the fogeys in the nursing home with their old-fashioned values and intolerance."

The revelation appeared to hit Luke between the eyes. He looked confused, dizzy, the van's tight interior closing in on him, the air starved of oxygen. He appeared more conscious of his disability and isolation than ever before. He looked around but there wasn't a single other car or soul in sight, and there hadn't been for a good few hours. Maybe the radio bulletin had been right. Maybe he had been abducted.

"Stop the car."

Luke's words were heavy and definitive. Sparrow turned his head, glancing over his shoulder before swinging back to face the road. With its bald tyres skating across the serrated surface, the van was dangerously close to skidding off the road and somersaulting through the scrubland. And such a crash would surely kill them all.

"Mate, we're doing nearly a hundred here," said Sparrow. "I can't really slam on the—"

"You heard me, you goddamn dirty arse fuckers. Stop the fucking car!"

23

Perth / Whadjuk Noongar Country, 2016

Bob

We spent the next day in Luke's room. I hadn't seen it before. An empty cupboard and spare bed; a mirror image of my own, with one exception.

"Wow," I said. "Great pictures. Whose are they?"

The walls were covered with drawings of dirt bikes, demonic caricatures, venomous animals, the naked female form, dimensions exaggerated. All black ink on ordinary white office paper. I marvelled at the accuracy and creativity. Street art indoors.

"They're mine," Luke said, without batting an eyelid.

"You drew these?"

"Yeah."

"*You* drew these?"

"Are you deaf, old man? What is it that you're sayin' exactly?"

"Nuthin'. You just never mentioned them before."

"You never asked. Bloke's gotta do sumthin' with all his free time in here."

"They're fantastic."

"Pfft, if you say so."

"I know so. You got real talent."

"Whatever."

"So, there's something I wanna talk to you about," I said. "And it's not what happened yesterday . . ."

"Why, what happened yesterday?"

I smiled. He was a pretty good kid.

I sat down on the spare bed. I brushed invisible dust from my thighs and eyeballed the budding artist.

"It's time to go," I said.

"Huh?" Luke said, forehead creased. "Go? Go where? Is it dinner time?"

"Ha. No, I mean we go . . . get the hell out of here."

"Oh yeah, right. And how are we supposed to do that?"

"Got it all worked out," I said.

Luke rolled his eyes. "Go on then," he said. "What's your plan? I'm all ears. Legs, no. But ears, yes."

I watched Luke stretch his working arm across and pick up a juice box from his bedside table. He held the straw to his lips and took a sip. He reached again to replace the drink, but it slipped from his grasp and fell to the floor.

"We load up on meds, pack a bag, nick a car and go," I said as I stood up. "Easy peasy."

"Oh yeah, right, that simple." His fingers were scratching at the last remaining Band-Aid on his scarred face.

"Don't be like that," I said. "Trust me." I returned Luke's juice trapezoid to his bedside table.

"Ta."

I sat back down. "So, what do you say? You in?"

"Nah," he said.

"What? Why not?"

"'Cos I'm sick, dude. Sick. You are too."

"Sure," I said. "That's why we steal some drugs before we go. I'm sick, not stupid."

Luke looked down at his pudgy hands. "I dunno," he said. Then repeated, "Nah."

I hadn't expected such resistance. I thought the boy and I were on the same page. I was stumped with which lie to tell first, there were quite a few to choose from. But then I decided on something simpler and more classic: reverse psychology.

"Okay," I said. "Fine, mate. I'll do it without you. I'll go – you can stay here with all your new friends. Have a good time."

I wanted Luke to picture the lounge, the residents trembling, moaning, crying or snoring. Or wandering aimlessly and mumbling and hurling random abuse at unseen troublemakers. Their heads flopped, their skin sagged or covered in tears and bruises from hasty, grasping hands. The December humidity sedated everyone into a dull stupor. Under the gentle burble of the television's neon gaze, some residents slipped to the floor waiting for someone to help with feeding. Fat blow-flies hovered over cold food on plastic plates.

"Piss off," Luke snapped. "I trust you. As if I wanna stay here with the living dead. I'm in. If you can make it happen, hell, I'd be crazy not to join you."

I swung my legs up onto the bed and lay back flat. "Excellent," I breathed.

"So? When . . . ?"

I pretended to consider Luke's ceiling. After a moment, I snapped two fingers. "This Sunday," I said. "At night."

"Why Sunday night?"

"There's a staff party on," I said. "There'll only be two nurses here. Both Filipinas who can barely speak English. It'll be nice and quiet. Even Blackford's going out."

"Shit, Bob. What's the rush?"

I groaned. "I've just had it," I said. "I'm fed up. I've had enough of this place and the people and I'm sick of pissfarting around."

Luke fiddled nervously with the contents of his bumbag. My voice had a sudden urgency and seriousness he'd never heard from me before. Maybe he was still unsure of what I was proposing, maybe he didn't trust me after all. And yet he wanted precisely what I wanted – adventure, happiness, freedom.

Finally, he spoke. "Righto. Screw it. Sunday night."

"Excellent. Late."

"Okay."

Luke tore the last Band-Aid off his face in a single motion, a crusty crimson line visible in its place.

"Sunday's good actually, it gives me some time to get my hands on all the drugs we'll need," I said. "And I have to make a few phone calls to arrange a parting gift and for a carer to join us. Like I said, leave it with me."

24

Pilbara / Yindjibarndi Country, 1981

Bob

In over a year of searching, we found no more diamonds. Stretch hauled increasingly heavy-duty tools to the Kimberley site, which soon began to resemble an archaeological dig. My life had transformed, and not for the better. My weekdays were spent with lips clasped shut in a mind-numbing day job, saying nothing to no-one, thinking about and preparing for the weekend of prospecting ahead. My weekend, which was once a welcome break from mining, was now just goddamn more of the same at the whim of a different demanding boss. I was working an eternal double shift, running a double marathon, and not being paid a cent in overtime. Ants were everywhere, and so were the angry little welts from their bites. Come dusk, neither Stretch nor I had any energy left for anything else. It wasn't meant to be this way. We'd become slaves to our own ambition.

If this worked out, I wouldn't merely move east. I would buy half of Sydney Harbour.

My longing for the continent's far side stemmed from a news article I'd read years earlier when I was still in Perth. It wasn't something I'd ever spoken about to another soul. It was about a dead man. A man who had drowned in Adelaide's River Torrens under a new moon in May 1972.

His name was George Ian Ogilvie Duncan, and he was an English law professor. Tall and slim, with fair hair sitting high on his fore-head, Dr Duncan had blue eyes and wore thick-framed glasses. He was profoundly quiet and withdrawn, which caused him some difficulty in communicating with students and fellow academics. Duncan had few friends and always ate his lunch alone. He was a devout Anglican and regular churchgoer.

Duncan had been in Adelaide only six weeks when he ventured down to the banks of the Torrens on a cold Wednesday evening. For what, no-one was sure. The specific location was Grundy Gardens, adjacent to the university and near a footbridge, across a normally peaceful stretch of river with ducks and swans. While by the water, Duncan was attacked by a group of men and thrown into the Torrens just before midnight. A bout of tuberculosis as an Honours law student had left him with one lung; he was frail and couldn't swim. He didn't struggle. The only eyewit-ness who came forward said that "his hands grasped upwards once, then he just slipped away, swallowed by the depths. The water rippled back again like nothing had happened."

It was only then that the story had piqued my interest. I was merely scanning the article to that point, absently, a sad and unfortunate inci-dent but nothing exceptional. But then, I stopped dead in my tracks. I was sitting on a garbage bin in Subiaco at the time, taking a break halfway through my taxi shift, reading yesterday's newspaper. I felt a sharp electric spark through my fingers, my hands trembling. I checked no-one was watching, tore the page out, shoved it in my pocket, and threw the rest of the newspaper back in the bin.

As it turned out, the banks of the River Torrens were often patrolled by police, who colloquially referred to the area as the "Number One Beat". Duncan's suspected assailants were three senior Vice Squad detectives who'd been at a nearby hotel earlier in the night for a colleague's retire-ment party. Further details revealed that it was common practice for police patrolling the Torrens to throw those they found in the river "as a means of publicly shaming them". They would go home to their families sopping wet and have to explain themselves. It was the same story in

Sydney – police who patrolled the sandstone rock of Mrs Macquarie's Chair were known to offer men the unenviable choice of being arrested or tossed into the cold harbour. I remembered my fateful night on the banks of the Swan River and wondered why I was never offered the option of a swim. On other nights, police cars with blazing headlights and spotlights had sent men scattering like it was a kangaroo shoot. In police circles, late-night raids of toilet blocks and riverbanks were widely considered "sport". But to me, such beats reflected the indomitable spirit of our community.

The sole witness declined to identify Duncan's attackers, and other witnesses who may have been present were understandably reluctant to come forward. A coronial inquiry was called. The three detectives all refused to give evidence and were suspended from duty. The *Advertiser* in Adelaide ran an editorial stating that the Duncan case "had touched upon attitudes towards a much broader issue in our society".

Ready or not, the public was about to find itself in the middle of fierce debate over a taboo topic. It was an Australia poised between two distinct epochs: the post-war years of outward sexual and gender conformity, and an uncertain new world of shifting values and identities. The debate would be played out in the public eye, in the mainstream press and in parliament. Freed from the yoke of three decades of right-wing rule, the new South Australian Labor government had already implemented reforms on abortion, capital punishment, and equal opportunity. With the untimely death of Dr Duncan and intense media scrutiny in its wake, the closest State capital to Perth now had a new social issue in its sights.

Needless to say, I was engrossed in these events playing out across the border, even if they were taking place more than a thousand kilometres away.

Years later, at the end of my cab shift, I would often point my car east like I was facing my own personal Mecca, sit on the bonnet, and squint. I was looking for the bright lights of Adelaide on the other side of the shark-infested Great Australian Bight. I had seen the future and it was in the east. Much of the lobbying for reform was coming from activists in the biggest cities of Sydney and Melbourne who were now holding up the shy law professor as a martyr.

At school, my Grade Four teacher Mr Palfreman had once pointed to Perth's location on a blackboard-sized map of the world. The lesson soon moved on, to fractions or grammar or whatever, but I just sat there staring at that little black dot that was my everything. Just a dot, way out on its own. Desert to the north and east, ocean to the south and west. Just a dot. Life was so civilised yet that dot was so bloody far away from everything. I wondered how that was even possible. Mr Palfreman never explained that.

It took a few years for that dot's position to manifest itself in my psyche.

I wanted out of my isolation. In fact, I wanted more than that. I wanted out of my isolation *within* isolation. I would head east. But for that, I needed money. And to get that, I had to trust my new business partner.

But trust only went so far. Holding the tobacco tin within the camp, either in a breast pocket during the day or down the front of the jocks at night, had become a shared duty. I was a stomach sleeper and found it hard to adjust, with the obvious alternative hiding place undesirable for an object so unyielding. Paranoia soon crept in, both with others and each other. Stretch and I watched our rear-view mirror more than the road to the Kimberley itself to make sure our trail to the glistening anthills wasn't being followed. We now regarded those Indigenous nomads who stumbled across our excavation site with suspicion.

My only respite came when Stretch disappeared to Perth, taking the tobacco tin and all of my faint hopes with him. Being a privileged shiny-bum, Stretch was allowed time off work, while blue-collar schlubs like me stayed chained to our gear sticks. Stretch told me these were his "fact-finding missions", exploring the unseen worlds of the Perth black market and the West Australian bureaucracy. The physical exhaustion I would have otherwise endured digging up half the Kimberley was supplanted by mental anxiety as I waited for his return, wondering what the hell he'd achieved, or if I was ever going to see the bastard again. He invariably came back empty-handed, citing either "offers so low even a dog wouldn't accept" or "more red tape than a gift shop on Christmas Eve".

The other men in the camp soon got wind of our find. I knew that I had said nothing, while Stretch claimed likewise. But one of us obviously had. I felt all eyes on me and soon returned to sleeping with a knife blade in my hand. It was almost a relief when Stretch took the tin to Perth for a week and I could relax.

I had been right all along. Get in, get out, and get on with it.

Lang Hancock was revered as a god of mining in Western Australia after discovering the world's largest deposit of iron ore in 1952, the same year I was born. He had flown low through a Pilbara gorge to avoid a storm and noticed the walls' rusty colour. I had heard the story a thousand times since arriving in the Nor'west; it was every punter's wet dream. Everyone wanted to be Lang fucking Hancock, and everyone thought they could be. But Lang had mining in his veins, his family already owned half of Western Australia. He'd discovered blue asbestos at Wittenoom Gorge at the age of ten and founded a company to mine it at twenty-nine. He didn't reveal his discovery for ten years. It took him that long to lobby the government to lift bans over the pegging of claims for iron ore prospects.

That was Lang. And I was no Lang. I was just some mug.

Mugs got in and stayed in, long after they should've jumped ship. That's why they were mugs.

Get in, get out.

The longer Stretch took cashing in our find, the louder those words reverberated in my parasite-infested ears.

I was sitting on the metal steps of my sweatbox donga. I'd been watching the horizon for so long that it had disappeared before my squinted eyes. Waiting can do that to a person. So can the passage from day to night. I didn't even notice I was shivering, my day-long sweat having dried into a thin film of cold. At my grubby feet, a pyramid of murdered cigarettes.

Sundays used to be spent at the pit lake, cavorting and rejuvenating a body ageing before its time.

I rubbed my eyes. "Fuck," I grumbled. "Fuck it."

A pair of brawny brown legs appeared in my field of vision where I'd hoped to see a pair of car headlights. The muscular outline of tight calves and firm thighs beneath a pair of shorts that left little to the imagination momentarily erased my anxious thoughts.

"Hey, Bob."

It was Ricky, the younger brother of Rocky, my former roommate. With more stumps now than fingers, Rocky the untrained powder monkey had returned to his Waikato home. So the family sent over his younger brother – even larger, with a standard-issue number of digits that he'd so far retained. His party trick was to cool off his one-eyed monster in blokes' schooner glasses in the pub when their backs were turned, which never failed to elicit a chorus of uproarious laughter and ridicule.

"Hey, Rick," I said.

"He's not back yet, bro?"

"Nah."

"I'll let you know if I see 'um."

"Ta."

I cremated another filthy cigarette. Still no headlights. I'll be back Sunday night, Stretch had said. Like hell you fucking will. I desperately needed sleep, but I needed an answer more.

The decision to become mining magnates had changed everything. Over time, with added frustration, I had come to see it as a decision I'd been too gutless to resist. And for that, I blamed my ever-deepening feelings. Curse the saying about business and pleasure. Mining magnates? More like mining bums.

"Fuck's sake," I muttered to the empty night. "That goddamn worthless piece of—"

The appearance of a white dot in the eternal black distance interrupted my dark brew and meditation. I leaped to my feet like a sprinter out of the blocks, my eyes thin and focused. I watched as the dot split in two, then changed colour from white to yellow, then came accompanied with sound, a panting engine, squealing brakes. The billowing cloud of dust reached me before the driver did.

"Jesus Christ. Where the bloody hell have you been?"

Stretch said nothing, kept his head low.

"Hey. I'm torkin' to you, ya big streak of piss."

He paused and looked at me with cold, clear eyes. "Good to see you too," he said, and continued walking.

I followed him, my heart beating faster. "I've been waitin' for bloody hours."

"What are you, my wife or somethin'?"

"I'm your *partner.*"

"Some partner. Look, back orff, orright? I need a drink. I just drove twelve hours through a flamin' furnace."

I continued to follow in Stretch's yeti footsteps, struggling to keep up with his exaggerated stride. He broke into a jog as he approached the rusty water tap outside the toilet block. He peeled off his T-shirt and threw it to one side as he got down on all fours. Hearing the commotion near the wet mess, a group of drunken shadows emerged to watch the outcome. Stretch flicked on the nozzle full bore and plunged the top half of his body under it, shaking and slurping like a woolly dog under a summer hose. I stood a metre behind, my hot dry feet getting covered in cool spray.

"Well . . . ?"

I was up for it. I demanded satisfaction, one way or another.

Stretch didn't answer, kept running the tap and his cracked hands through his stale hair. He finally stood up, dripping like a fucked fridge, and wielding a look that could cut my throat.

"Well . . . what?" he spat.

"How'd you go?"

"Blew a tyre. The tools were so hot that I couldn't grip 'em to fix it. Took hours. I just sat there sweatin' and goin' mad. Then I got blisters on my hands and feet. The wheel and pedals were white hot."

I paused. "No. Not that."

"Oh. Then, what?"

"You know what."

Stretch exhaled. "Oh, that. More paperwork."

"You mean the mining lease."

"Yep."

"I didn't mean the lease."

"Oh."

"I meant a sale."

"Sale, eh?"

"Yeah. *A sale.*"

"Nup."

"What's that mean?"

"It means nup, nada, no dice. No sale."

I paused, sighed. "Jesus Christ, man. Did you even bother?"

At that, Stretch raised his boom-gate forearm and barged past. He pushed me aside like I wasn't even there. I shoved him in the back as hard as I could, shunting him forward a clumsy step. I wanted to do more with my hands but in the end opted for my acid tongue.

"You're as bad as the bloody companies," I called after him. "Once you see dollar signs, you don't give a flying fuck about anything else."

He kept walking, leaving a dark trail of long wet footprints in his wake.

The American exploration company never found oil at Noonkanbah station. It was all for nothing – mining bums.

25

Kimberley / Wilinggin Country, 2017

Sparrow eased off the accelerator. He didn't touch the brake. The van slowed to a less perilous speed that was also more conducive to conversation.

"From the look of the landscape, I reckon we're close now," Bob whispered to Sparrow. "Feels like we've travelled light years."

"Yep," Sparrow replied. There was no stopping now.

Bob turned back to Luke. "Look," he said carefully, "mate, we can't stop the car because we're nearly there. But can I say, if you think I deceived you, I'm sorry. It absolutely wasn't my intention."

Luke fired tracer bullets with his eyes. He wasn't buying it.

"You invited me to your room," he said. "Jesus Christ, we've been *sharing* a room ever since we left the nursing home!"

"And so what if I did? So what if we have? Your cherry's still intact."

Luke's jaw fell an inch. "Well, I gotta trust you on that one 'cos I've got no effing sensation down there anyway."

Bob couldn't help but laugh out loud. Sparrow smirked.

"Yeah, right," Bob said. "Funny. So, let me get this straight. Just, you know, for the official record. I groomed you back at the nursing home, kidnapped you, and then my lover and I drove you to the middle of nowhere where nobody can find you. During this entire time, I've been drugging you and having my way with you each night after you conked out. Sparrow has too. Oh, and Mouse? She was in on it all. She was our dealer. I mean hey, you saw the stuff she had. Pretty strong gear. Brought down blokes twice your size."

Luke paused. "Can I get that in writing, as evidence?" he asked.

"Don't be stupid. I was being facetious."

"The hell does that mean?"

"It means I was joking."

"Well, how the hell do I know? You could've done all that and more. Filmed it, like Mouse did. My fat hairy arse could be all over the net by now. Sickos everywhere could be jacking off to it."

Bob stared straight through the grubby, chipped windscreen, taking time to respond.

"As if."

The van hit a succession of fresh potholes, causing the left wheel axle to shudder. Sparrow's arms and shoulders bore the brunt of the aftershocks. A pair of dull knives was plunged into the base of his neck. He nearly blacked out.

They drove in silence for a while. Finally, Bob said, "And don't flatter yourself, Luke mate. You're not my type."

"Nor mine," Sparrow added. "No offence."

"Christ, I feel dirty," Luke said. "Being here. Being around *you two*."

"Right this second, mate, the way you're carrying on, the feeling's mutual," said Bob.

"Fuck you."

"Oh, frig you too."

"Dirty old bastard. I feel violated."

"Stop being such a drama queen, son. At the end of the day, does it really matter?"

"Course it bloody matters," Luke said, sending a stream of spit flying into the back of Sparrow's seat. "It's who you are."

"Who I am is inconsequential," said Bob calmly. "I'm nobody. Forget me. Forget Sparrow here. Forget everyone. All you need to care about in this world is who *you* are."

Sparrow bit his lip and pushed down hard on the vibrating steering wheel. Luke ran a clammy hand through his greasy hair and exhaled a lungful of tension. The horizon shimmered with white light under the relentless sun.

"And what the hell else haven't you told me?" Luke said. "Is your name even Bob? Is his name really Sparrow or Andrew or whatever it bloody is? Where in fuck's name are we fucking going? What's the fucking shovel for?"

"It's Robert, actually. And yes, this is Andrew. We're nearly there. And the shovel, unsurprisingly, is for digging."

"Digging?"

"That's usually what shovels do."

"Or whacking, concussing. And burying."

Bob didn't answer immediately. He was distracted.

"Actually . . ."

His utterance of this single word was enough to turn Luke's face green.

"Now you mention it . . ."

"Jesus Christ," said Luke. "What?"

"No, the timing is good, we've come this far," said Bob. "There is one thing I am guilty of and that I've been meaning to tell you. If you're gonna hold anything against me, hold this."

Luke clasped the hand grip on his wheelchair. He narrowed his eyes. Sparrow clenched the steering wheel.

"You remember the day you were shaving in my room?" Bob said.

Luke raised a crooked eyebrow. "What about it?"

"You cut yourself and you were bleeding."

"Yeah. You told me to keep it quiet."

"Yeah, and thanks for that. Remember you used my straight razor?"

Luke paused. "Lemme guess. You once cut a bloke's throat with that razor and the cops are now looking for it as the crucial piece of evidence in an unsolved murder case."

Sparrow's ears pricked. What the hell had taken place in the nursing home . . .? Was that what he should've been investigating, a resident's death? Was the razor the crucial piece of evidence he needed?

Bob chuckled. "You kids," he said. "Such vivid imaginations. No, nothing like that, as great a story as it would be. But I never told you why I was at Leafy Gums, did I?"

"No."

Bob sighed and went silent.

"Oh no, wait, wait," Luke said. "Don't tell me you've got the plague?"

Bob's eyes flicked to the rear-view mirror. Luke's glare was waiting.

"Oh, you murdering fucker. The razor, the blood, fuck . . ."

Bob explained. He said why he had returned to Perth, the town where he was born. He explained what the disease had already done to his body, and was still doing, decades later. The dozen or so medications he took every day to keep it at bay. Bob spoke like a doctor or lecturer, cold and detached. How long he'd had it and how people caught it.

"So you gotta realise the chances of you catching it from a razor blade are very, very, *very* remote," Bob said. "Almost zero. But not zero. So, when all this is over, I'd recommend you get a blood antibody test."

And then, to round it off, Bob mentioned the the lack of any known medical cure.

The world outside the van was deathly quiet, not even a breeze to disturb the heavy air molecules. Tufts of tussock grass and dead trees stretched to every horizon. Sparrow continued to pilot the van at a steady speed.

Luke had sat silently through Bob's explanation, his confession. The speech sounded rehearsed. At no point did Bob lose his place, stutter, or repeat himself. It was as if he'd been speaking to the endless road and the unchanging landscape. Sparrow stayed quiet, focused on his task, his priority, his mission. Bob waited for some time before speaking again.

"Luke? Mate, are you okay?"

"So, lemme get this straight," Luke replied. "First, you lie to me. And then, just for good measure, *you infect me* and lie to me?"

"Aw, hey," Bob said. "That's a bit rich."

"You fucking cunt."

"It's not like I lied to you about who I was. I just assumed you knew and didn't care."

"Cunt."

"And I was always going to tell you about the razor. Not that it's anything to worry about. You'll be right, I know it."

"Piss off."

"They can do two tests, one for antibodies, the other antigen. The antigen test is more specific because it detects the virus directly."

"Blow me."

Bob's neck swung back, his eyes bright.

"No!" said Luke. "You know what I mean."

"Okay, okay. That was meant to be a joke. You're upset and angry, I expected that. But if you take a step back and—"

"*Fuck you*. Stop the car, let me out here."

"Mate, you haven't thought this through . . ."

"Let me out."

"Come on, Luke," said Sparrow. "You know that's not possible."

"And why not?" Luke snapped. "The brakes work. And who the hell are you even anyway? Are you a cop? Can you arrest this bloke for murder? Why would I possibly want to spend another minute in the company of a lying prick who gave me a death sentence?"

Sparrow froze at the prospect of his cover being blown – an instinctive response – before realising that Luke was simply venting his anger. His face had gone a fiery red; he looked like he might spontaneously combust.

"Okay now, just steady on there, son," Bob said calmly.

"No wonder you dragged me outta the nursing home, brought me all the way out here," said Luke. "Out here, there's nothing. No witnesses, no help, no hope. Take me back to Perth where it's safe."

"I thought we were having fun," Bob said. "I was having fun. Weren't you having fun?"

Sparrow didn't quite like the sound of Bob's last question; it was leading, the tone somewhat sinister.

"And here's me thinking you were all upset because of the way that old codger died," Luke said.

Sparrow's ears pricked yet again. "Wait, what's this?" he asked.

Luke described one of the dementia patients that Bob regularly visited. When Alfred's lungs failed, his family kept him on life support against his wishes.

"He died horribly in hospital one night with a tube rammed down his throat," Luke said.

Bob shook his head. "The poor bloke never deserved to die like that. He didn't *want* to die like that. Those pricks killed him."

"You gonna now kill me?" Luke asked. "Is this your way of destroying the evidence?"

"Huh?" said Bob. "Kill you?"

"No wait, of course not," said Luke. "You've already *done that.*"

A sharp pain cut across Sparrow's forehead. The road bent in a gradual curve to the right, crossing a wide creek bed filled with fresh cyclone water. He alternated between the brake and accelerator pedals until the van was clear of the creek, then slammed his right foot to the floor. Bob's eyes flicked left and right, searching, scanning.

"Oi! Are you friggin' listening, old man?"

Bob acknowledged the voice from behind by raising his right hand.

"Luke, mate. Just relax." Bob spoke slowly in the hope his tone would permeate the car. "You're on the edge, mate. Paranoid. No-one's trying to kill you. Sparrow's harmless, I'm even more harmless. I didn't think I'd dragged you kicking and screaming out of Leafy Gums. Tell me right here and now that you would've rather stayed in that bloody place."

There was a long silence.

"See, you can't," Bob said. "But I can hardly let you out here, in the middle of nowhere, alone. That would be bloody irresponsible."

"You'll die," Sparrow added. "People die out here. It's why they tell travellers to never leave their cars if they break down. You've got no survival skills. Listen to us, to me. This is blackfella country, and you're no blackfella."

"And thank Christ for that," Luke said. "But I'll take my chances. Besides, someone will come along sooner or later and pick me up. Maybe your mob will help me."

Bob flicked his head back. "Don't be crazy. How are they going to carry your wheelchair?"

His question hung in the air.

"And besides, what if some of the blokes you robbed with Mouse recognise you and pick you up?" Sparrow added. "Then they *will* kill you."

Sparrow turned back to face the road. He kept driving while Bob continued to scan the horizon. A few seconds later, an empty plastic water bottle shot past Sparrow's right ear and bounced off the windscreen. He froze at first, blinking. The bottle dropped to the floor and rattled around his feet, coming close to interfering with the pedals. A gob of thick spit followed, sticking to the back of Sparrow's head. He turned slowly and with intent.

Luke's face was emotionless. "Let me out," he said.

Sparrow swallowed hard. He needed all his restraint to take Luke's crap.

"I'll forget you did that," he said.

Bob retrieved the crooked bottle from around Sparrow's feet and stowed it inside the door panel.

"We can't let you out here, mate, but I don't know what else I can say right now, I've told you absolutely everything I know," he said. "How about we just drive in silence for a while, give you a chance to think and cool down . . ."

But Luke wasn't having it. He continued making what he saw as reasonable complaints and rational demands. Sparrow pretended not to listen and continued driving, turning his focus back to the boundless landscape. After some time, Luke seemed to tire, his pronouncements coming at increasingly long intervals before drying up altogether. Bob and Sparrow breathed a collective sigh of relief.

They drove with only the sound of tyres on the rock-strewn road for a while. Sparrow welcomed the peace and quiet and the meditative thrum of the unsealed road. Suddenly, a rustling could be heard from the back of the van. Sparrow braced himself for the impact of another plastic bottle or scrunched cigarette packet or CD flung with a view to decapitation. Instead, he felt a hard object press firmly against the back of his head. As a cop, he instantly knew what it was – the cold steel barrel of a firearm.

"Have I got your attention now?" Luke sneered. "I said pull over and let me the fuck out."

26

Kimberley / Wilinggin Country, 1981

Bob

I placed my work boot on the broad blade of an overworked shovel and again plunged it into the dry earth. Removing my foot, I let the wooden handle stand erect in the dirt. It was a brief monument to my manual excavation of the bastard continent. Give me another ten thousand years and I still would've barely scratched the bloody surface of this interminable land.

The pied butcherbird was late in coming. Or so it felt. Every evening, it seemed to appear later and later, alighting in the fork of its tree and watching me work like some kind of sadistic pit foreman. Or so it seemed to the man who took its song as the signal to finally down tools.

Digging for buried treasure had creased my palms with splinters and blisters. My back was as jagged as the terrain and my spine felt like it had been replaced with a steel rod. I often woke in the middle of the night with numb hands, my forearms tingling with nervy electricity. The only aspects of my life that remained unaffected by the continued prospecting were the contents of an old tobacco tin and my bank balance. It was the same arrangement of stones in the tin – the big mother diamond and her six babies – and extensive array of zeroes in my account, but still with no proper numbers parked in front.

Gouging away at his own plot of dirt on the other side of the dry creek bed, the ultimate source of my scars stubbornly refused to give up the cause. Every anthill for five square miles lay in ruins. It was an insect apocalypse. Conversation with Stretch now extended to him giving daily orders and me grunting in acknowledgement. We were a two-man chain gang shackled by our own determination and greed. We had changed in a way that I recognised from others lured by the promise and desperation of the Nor'west.

Stretch remained a mystery to me. I wanted to say so much more to him but felt my mouth was muzzled. Not because of our continued disagreements over what to do with our find, but because of what my heart might say if I let it speak on my behalf. It was vulnerability like I'd never felt before.

Coo coo coooo . . . coo coo coo coooo . . . quo-orr quo-orr . . . chu-eep!

The slow, blue notes of the butcherbird rang out, spreading out across the Kimberley's open savanna. A sonic heirloom from a time before time.

There you bloody are. Thanks for finally showing up.

Sorry I'm so late, Bob. The missus. You know what it's like. Yak yak yak.

Not really. But I'll take your word for it.

I threw my last mound of clay for the day, flung my shovel in its wake, and headed for the embrace and comfort of the esky. The first bottle of beer didn't even touch the sides, and the accompanying burp echoed for miles. I collected kindling and sparked a small fire, tossing on two cans of baked beans. By the time I had polished off my second bottle, dinner was ready. With caveman hunger, I burned my tongue slurping at the beans backstroking in rich tomato sauce. After a day sweating in the sun, even cold beans were refreshingly satisfying, but campfire beans always tasted better. Stretch forged on ahead with his earthy rummaging until the rapidly fading light also brought his day to a close and his hopes, once again, to a bitter, inevitable end. I didn't feel the need to say anything to salt the wound. I took Stretch's beans off the fire and laid the can opener beside them as he shambled over. I then handed him an open beer, which he drained in a single motion.

"Cheers," he breathed.

Without the energy to so much as twist the can opener, Stretch stood for a moment staring at his hands before falling to the dirt in exhaustion, moaning and grasping at his gnarled spine. I waited a beat, chewing, uncertain in my thoughts, before I spoke.

"You okay?"

"Yeah," he said. "Christ. I'm not cut out for all this constant bending over. My back, my knees. At least you're built closer to the ground. You got less distance to travel."

I snorted a combination of contempt and laughter. Without warning, a gooey orange bean in my mouth got sucked up my nose and went cannonballing out my left nostril. Stretch laughed, which only made his body shudder in more pain. He sprawled in the dirt, sending small clouds of liberated dust into the air, wincing in both ecstasy and agony. The blurring of the thin line separating comedy and tragedy, humour and hurt, and the rush of alcohol to my starved brain soon had me laughing as well. The moment was infectious, an almighty release of tension that had Stretch finally pleading for mercy on account of his searing pain.

"Enough!" he panted. "Piss off . . . enough."

Calling on what little strength I had remaining in my shoulders, I punched the opener into the top of the tin can and twisted. Stretch sat watching the veins in my arms bulge and my face contort. With a dull, anti-climactic pop, I revealed the can's goopy contents and presented them under Stretch's prodigious nose. A shirt-polished spoon followed.

"Dinner is served, sir," I said in my most uppity inflection.

It was a simple, playful gesture of the kind that had been missing for too long. I thought it was worth a shot.

"Ta," Stretch smiled.

A warm feeling of nostalgia washed over us as we sat opposite each other, chewing our tinned fare and alternating swigs from a big Darwin stubby. Stretch inverted the aluminium can and held it up to his lips, desperately tapping on its base to drain the last thick droplets of sauce. I went one better and swished a slug of beer around in my can before drinking the tomatoey swill in a single gulp.

"Bloody Mary," I burped.

Stretch followed suit, drinking his canned cocktail dry.

"Shenshational," he said, his shiny lips slowly peeling into a contented smile.

Rolling out our swags, we bedded down on a smooth patch of dirt I had raked clean with one of Stretch's many mining implements. We hunkered down on the western side of our vehicle to protect our faces from becoming fly-blown and roasting in the morning sun. The final drops of Kimberley light soon fell away and I heard my butcherbird singing me a final lullaby goodnight.

Coo coo coooo . . . coo coo coo coooo.

Just as my eyelids began to close, a sound tickled my ears. Stretch's boots crunching on the ground, his feet departing the scene.

I knew what this was about. A week earlier, I'd found a yellow envelope in the truck's glovebox. Inside was a slip of paper. It was ticketing information, the travel one-way. Stretch was finally leaving and he wasn't coming back.

I'd decided to not say anything. There was no point. All I could do was put my shattered heart to one side and be ready, on guard. And start concocting my own escape plans.

I only half-believed the prick might do something like that. The other half of me had suspected it all along. And what better way to make a getaway than by leaving your gullible partner stranded in the middle of bloody nowhere in the middle of the fucking night. He probably didn't care if I lived or died.

I summoned my reserves of energy, thankful for the fuel provided by the feast of stout and seed.

But then I listened closer.

Stretch wasn't heading for the truck to make his escape. Instead, he was wandering off into the scrub with something else in mind. It seemed that revived sense of nostalgia had proven too powerful. We were revisiting an old ritual.

I rubbed my eyes and scratched at my stale, sweaty crotch. I moistened my chapped lips and started counting.

"One, two . . ."

27

Kimberley / Wilinggin Country, 1981

Bob

I took to the chase after thirty, the anticipation too great. I soon found myself running through the grassy clumps and ruined anthills, something I vowed I would never do. Hunters stalked. Only prey ran.

The action came quick tonight, the body slamming into me from behind like a battering ram going through a flyscreen door, causing my neck to whiplash. Stretch was the first to recover his bearings, towering over me with a sneer before leaning ever so slightly and falling into my ribs with a leading elbow. The sound of snapping bone told me this was no ordinary night; it was tinged with a veneer of frustration that came from months of empty prospecting and fruitless negotiating. To Stretch, I was an inexplicable part of both ventures. But it was the mirror opposite from my perspective. Blame was a two-way street.

Summoning my strength, I grabbed Stretch by the collar and heaved his gangly grasshopper frame sideways. I threw a flurry of swift punches that sent his solar plexus careering into his weathered spine. An alternating series of clumsy slashes across the chops followed, which was all I could muster on such a moonless night. It was brawling by gestalt.

"Yeah, that's it, that's it." He spat out a gob of blood. "More, more."

"More?"

"*More*, motherfucker! Or is that all ya got?"

I was out of shape and out of touch for hand-to-hand. What once came as second nature, honed with regular trips to the pit lake, was now buried deep in the recesses of my brain under a useless mound of amateur fossicking. Finding our feet, we struck unsteady fighting poses, our clenched fists shifting in mid-air. We listened for shuffling feet and laboured breathing so that we could launch a "surprise" attack. We threw punches, awkward and random, that left only invisible bruises in the night air. I was grateful for my low centre of gravity even though I knew another perfectly aimed running tackle would drop me like a sack of wet shit.

I winced at the pain exploding from my fractured ribs. His sense of hearing honed by the darkness, Stretch seized on the opportunity and threw a jab that clipped me across the ear. I backed away and felt something awkward behind me, then tripped and fell on a jagged rock. I heard Stretch launch himself and a second later felt his grand-piano frame crash on top of me. Compressed for space, my internal organs screamed for freedom. My chest felt like I was having a coronary. With my ribs giving way like rotten wood under the immense bulk, I had no choice but to relax and let Stretch manipulate me into a position of submission where I could, at least, breathe.

"C'mon, you crazy bastard," the human caber said. "You can do better than that."

Stretch knew what was coming. So did I. He wanted it. So I delivered.

It was an old trick of mine from my golden age of wrestling in the back of Bandit's truck. My signature move, fittingly called "the dump truck". I hoped I could remember it. Letting my muscles guide my brain, I slipped my arms under Stretch's body and used the top of my head as a pivot point. I then pushed up with both legs and thrust my groin into the air, replicating a dump truck lifting a load. I crab-walked in a semicircle and only needed to apply minimal force. That was the beauty of the dump truck; Stretch was flat on his back before he realised. Even though he'd seen the manoeuvre dozens of times, he was helpless against it. Everyone was.

I pinned him and leaned forward, pecking him on the tip of his wet nose. It was a gesture that normally signalled foreplay was over. But he had other ideas.

"Fuck you!" he spat. "You wanna fight, fight like a man."

Jesus Christ, I thought. I'd been weary before the skirmish began, and by that stage had tired of the contest. I wanted to either screw or sleep. But Stretch shoved me to one side, stood, and kicked me square in the kidneys with his giant, size-sixteen desert boots. Two further clips to the head split my lip open and caused my jaw to audibly dislocate. A third whack pulped my nose with a discernable crunch. Stretch had exerted such force that he lost his balance and ended up in the dust himself.

Writhing in pain, my insides aflame and spitting black blood, I was forced to reconsider what was happening. What we were doing was less out of frustration than pent-up rage, and signalled an intention for the future. This time, we weren't just playing around. We were playing for keeps. I suspected it was a game he'd contested before, and won.

Stretch knew what Stretch knew – his ticket was booked. That was enough for me. Whether Stretch knew that I knew was irrelevant. *I knew.* And now, the solution was simple. I needed to beat some fucking sense into him so that *he* knew he could shove his pink diamonds up his arse for all the hostility and angst finding them had caused.

I reared back onto my haunches and launched myself at him with a fury that surprised even me. He was no more than a pile of stringy mincemeat beneath my tenderiser fists. He tried to defend himself with his arms but I was purging myself of every ounce of resentment, betrayal and heartache with every punch I threw. Muscle, fat, bone, vital organs – I'd stopped being careful and no longer cared where my blows landed. Spring-loaded with emotion, my fists packed more punch. All the while, ribbons of blood and spit oozed from my cut mouth.

It wasn't my fists that gave out first; it was my lungs. My knuckles wanted more action, but my need for oxygen took precedence. I dismounted Stretch's crumpled frame and rolled onto my feet, feeling every damaged cell wail in agony as I stood tall. Before he could focus his swollen eyes on me, I made sure to wipe the trails of tears from my flushed cheeks.

"Ha!" Stretch gulped for his own lungful of air as he stood and backed away. "Ya still got it. I knew you would, you always had the better of it, always were top dog. But can you defend this?"

His war cry as he came hurtling in would've alerted someone in the next State. It was all too easy for me to step to one side like a lazy matador and let the lumbering bull canter through. And I did exactly that, but at the last moment decided to stick out a careless leg in the hope of grounding the bull and ending the human blood sport once and for all. Shins collided with the clack of bone on bone. Stretch stumbled, his knees buckled, his arms flailed, and he fell from his full height of seven feet with the force of a thunderbolt, head-first into the pindan.

Oh, thank Christ, I thought. He was down, done. Finally, we could get on with it.

Remoistening my lips, I moseyed over. It had certainly been a while, and such a prelude was unprecedented. This was going to be extra good. Who knew, maybe it would prove to be a turning point. A reminder of how it all began, the moment when our rudderless sloop was guided back to calmer waters. In the morning, when we opened our eyes to the new dawn light and felt a warm sleepy arm draped across our chests, our purpose would again be clear, all this madness over. As crazy as it sounds, my heart still held out an atom of hope.

Stretch stayed silent, coy, lying as flat as the expansive plain supporting him.

"Sho what, sho now yoo playin' hard ta get, eh?" I chuckled as I wandered over, grabbing at my groin. I squeezed the words from between swollen lips, my jaw refusing to cooperate.

I remained wary on final approach in case it was some kind of ploy. In case Stretch rolled over, laughed, and flung a surprise dagger into my arm.

But there was no dagger. No movement or sound. Not even when I shook him with all my might, groaned his name, and slapped his face red raw. Or when I poured water over his face or blew into his mouth or slammed my fist into his chest over and over and over.

There was only a great gash in Stretch's forehead that matched the sharp ridges of a long, barbed rock, and a pool of warm blood lapping at my bent knees and slowly unfurling itself across the continent.

28

Kimberley / Wilinggin Country, 2017

Sparrow didn't say a word. He simply removed his foot from the accelerator and let the car roll to a natural stop. He didn't even pull over to the side of the road. There was no point.

"Good," Luke said. "So you're not completely stupid." He pushed the muzzle deeper into Sparrow's hair. "Now, both of you, hands where I can see 'em. No funny business."

"What funny business?" asked Bob. "You think we're going to run off into the desert? Or maybe I'll wrestle you to the ground with my almighty strength?"

Luke grumbled and flicked the firearm from Sparrow's head to Bob's.

"You bloody know what I mean," he said. "Just remember, there's a gun pointed at your heads."

"That's absolutely fine, mate," Bob said. "I'm used to it. I've had a gun pointed at my head for thirty years now."

Sparrow applied the handbrake with a crunch and killed the ignition. His police training had prepared him for such scenarios. Delicate but firm negotiation skills were needed to talk the individual out of doing anything stupid. He didn't have any first-hand experience of hostage situations, but at that moment, there was little choice. And if all else failed, he had his own trusty piece on hand in the pocket of his cargo shorts. Using it would likely blow his cover, but it was still a better outcome than a dead man and a failed mission. But the challenge was clear: to talk Luke down *without* the aid of his firearm.

Sparrow opened his door and swung his legs out one at a time. As he walked to the back of the van, he considered his next move. Luke leaned over to tap on the glass and show him the view down the length of the barrel. Sparrow kept going and didn't flinch.

Opening the rear door and engaging the hydraulic lifter, Sparrow lowered Luke onto the road. The wheels of his chair sank into the soft clay. Bob got out of the car slowly, and took up position opposite Luke and next to Sparrow, a two-man line-up for a one-man firing squad.

Sparrow was pretty certain that Luke hadn't thought this through. The kid was dumb, short-sighted. But that was fine. He'd wing it, like he did most things. He was, after all, indestructible. What didn't kill him only made him stronger.

Luke sat with the firearm in his lap, his fat sweaty fingers clasped around the handle and trigger. His arm was relaxed, pointing the barrel at his quarry as a gentle but constant reminder. Sparrow noted the safety catch was off. His margin for error had narrowed considerably.

"Gimme one good reason why I shouldn't paint the desert floor with your fucking brains right now."

Luke was reliving his favourite action movie, or writing a modern-day Western. The scar-faced villains stood opposite him, unsure whether to hold up their hands in surrender or hang them by their sides. Luke had the drop on them and now he was calling the tune. As they faced off in the blazing noonday sun, an end-of-the-world feeling descended. Not a cloud in the unremitting sky or a shadow on the ground. Not even the ubiquitous Australian white noise of a buzzing blowfly.

They stared at each other for some time before Bob finally spoke.

"You know, mate, it's interesting you're doing this . . ."

Luke pulled a face and tipped his head slightly to one side. "That's not a reason," he said. "Stop screwing around."

Bob folded his arms and started on a slow walk to the opposite side of the road and back. Luke stared at Bob blankly and then at Sparrow as if the old man had forgotten who was in fucking charge. Sparrow stood motionless as Luke angled the barrel downwards as if he wanted to fire a shot at Bob's toes to regain his attention.

"Now come on, mate," Sparrow said to Luke. "Don't do somethin' you're gonna regret, yair? You got your whole life ahead of you."

The gun barrel swung around to face Sparrow. His turn to be in the crosshairs.

"Regret? Why would I regret it? I can kill you and Bob right now and tell 'em it was self defence. Say you two came at my arse or something. I'm the cripple, mate. The poor, vulnerable cripple. The handicap who was kidnapped. A sitting duck. You two are the able-bodied cocksuckers with all the power. It's you they're looking for. If I off you guys, I don't just win this. I become a bloody hero."

Sparrow stopped and scratched his rough chin. When the kid put it that way, he could almost pull it off. That was, at least, until he realised Sparrow's true identity.

"So no," Luke added. "No regrets. Mate."

"You know," Sparrow said after some time. "You're absolutely right. Well played."

Luke shot him a smug grin. "In fact, when you consider what Bob might've given me, arguing self defence is about right."

"So, what, you gonna shoot us dead in cold blood for fun?" Sparrow asked.

"Dunno. Maybe."

"No fun in that, mate."

"Sez you."

"We're not the enemy here."

"Yeah you are. He poisoned me, and you're trying to cover it up."

"You can't be sure about that," Bob interrupted. "You still need your test results."

"Fuck the results," said Luke. "And fuck you."

"And besides, there are better drugs these days," Bob went on. "I read the other week they're doing trials with gene therapy, using cells resistant to the virus, and also new transplants with umbilical cord blood."

"That sounds disgusting. Stuff that. I don't understand what you're saying. Stop talking shit. I don't give a rat's."

"Mate, even if you had the virus, as I see things right this second, you got two other concerns that are much more immediate," said Sparrow. "First of all, your overall health's not much chop. Christ, *you're in a wheelchair*."

It was the first time that Sparrow had ever pointed out the bloody obvious. Luke sneered. He did not like it.

"Some carer you are," he said. "And I may be in a chair, but I still have a working hand and it can shoot a gun."

"That you do," said Sparrow. "But I'd be more worried about your lungs packing it in out here or catching an infection than I would be about a virus which you may or may not have, and which may or may not kill you in a few decades' time. There's plenty of other things that could kill you before then. Trust the blackfella when he says this."

Sparrow spoke in a measured tone, dispassionate, with eyes like bullet holes.

"And your other problem is geography," he continued. "Look. Just take a look around."

Luke rotated his neck to properly take in his surroundings. Bob and Sparrow did the same, turning around on the spot. Luke's gaze lingered on the horizon for longer, scanning, hoping.

"You mightn't see another car out here for days," Sparrow said. "Maybe even weeks. You'll be dead long before anyone reaches you, with pieces pecked away by birds of prey. Again, trust the blackfella. Listen to the blackfella."

Luke kept looking. The earth lay silent. There was suddenly more space than ever before. The sky was so vast it was hard not to feel small, agoraphobic, dizzy. Giant termite mounds and anthills littered the arcane landscape. Desert bloodwood trees oozed dark-red sap from deep wounds in their bark. With their thick leathery leaves, the bloodwoods were all curves and muscle. Spinifex clung to the backs of sand dunes that stretched into bronze infinity. The arid plains offered nothing more than a story of survival.

Sparrow was on a roll. He sensed Luke finally coming to terms with his mortality. If only Porter could see this – the new recruit redeeming himself after blowing his first assignment. He went in for the kill.

"So, if you do shoot us dead, you'll probably have to eat our corpses to keep yourself from dying," Sparrow said. "You up for some cannibalism? I've heard stories of it happening. Blackfellas don't make good eatin', by the way. We're too stringy. But you better make it quick 'cos we won't last long in this heat."

Luke returned his glare to Sparrow, his pigeon.

"Or can you catch blowflies with your good hand?" Sparrow asked. "Mm, tasty fat blowflies. Rich source of protein."

"You dark black arsehole," Luke said.

"Charming," Sparrow replied.

"You're enjoying this."

"I'm not."

"You and Bob bloody planned this. I should off you both right now."

His left arm snapped forward, pointing the firearm squarely at Sparrow's forehead, the juicy spot before his brain.

Again, Sparrow didn't baulk. He barely blinked. He stood and stared. Not at Luke's outstretched arm but deep into his eyes.

Luke met his gaze. His eyes were erratic, blinking profusely, sweat pooling around the sockets and obscuring his vision. His breathing shallow, rapid, irregular.

Sparrow didn't move. He stayed perfectly still, eyes like marbles. It took every ounce of his resolve. He tried to somehow summon the land, its secrets and its energy – mysteries his People safeguarded with a proud and dignified air.

After a few seconds, Luke's arm began to weaken and tremble. Sparrow sensed his bicep was flabby, the muscles soft like caramel. The gun barrel flicked left and right, jumping all over Sparrow's unflinching face. He soon moved the sight down to his chest; just as deadly, but with more surface area.

"Fuck," Luke muttered.

The gun swung back to Bob. Luke was indecisive, confused, the world against him, spinning. Indecision was a sign of weakness. Sparrow's fingers twitched. If he was ever going to draw his firearm, it had to be now. But he fought his instincts and held back.

Bob's eyes half-closed. "Go right ahead, son," he said coolly. "Do it. Like I said, a trigger pointed at my head is old news."

A cold trickle of sweat erupted down the side of Luke's flush face. His cheeks glowed volcano red with new blood.

"Fuck!"

He lowered the firearm slowly, unsteadily, in defeat, and let it hang limply on the outside of his left wheel. The tip made a tinny noise as it scraped the road.

Sparrow's expression remained unchanged, but his entire body seemed to go numb with relief. "That firearm's not really much use to anyone out here," he said. "Not to me or to you."

Luke collapsed into his own chair. "So," he breathed. "Here we are. Three pathetic bastards. I can't kill you, but I also can't go on without you."

Bob moseyed over. He eased his weathered frame down slowly until he sat inside the shade of the van's rear door. The suspension buckled. "Seems to be the case," he exhaled.

The dawn of a light smile broke across Luke's face. "Jesus Christ," he said. "How can you be so relaxed?"

"I told you, I'm used to it," Bob replied. "I'm old, I've seen it all. And I used to live out here, remember."

"I forgot that."

"So did Sparrow."

"Mm."

"And while we're dicing with death, that's why I said it's interesting you were doing what you did," Bob said. "Look me in the eye and tell me you've not once thought about ending it all."

Luke paused. Bob seemed to already know the answer. Sparrow took a step back, let them have their moment.

"Course I have," Luke muttered.

Bob wanted details. "When?" he asked.

"Ever since I got to the nursing home, absolutely. And right after my accident, of course."

"Did you get so far as thinking how you'd do it?"

"Overdose," Luke said bluntly.

"That was a disturbingly quick response."

"Well, I told you, it crossed my mind, which included how I'd do it. My options are pretty limited in this goddamn chair. I can hardly jump under a bus or off a bridge."

Bob paused in thought. "Overdose on what?" he asked.

"Whatever I could find," Luke said. "Amphetamines, antidepressants, paracetamol, cough medicine, laxatives. If you were serious about it, you wouldn't give a fuck what you used. You'd just shovel it in until the world went black."

"So what happened? Why are you still here?"

Luke paused. "Hmm." He shrugged his millennial shoulders. "Guess I wasn't serious about it. What about you, you ever seriously think about it?"

"Twice," Bob replied. "Once during the sixties, then again in the eighties. I was a teenager the first time, angry, confused, upset. I didn't know any better. And in the eighties, no-one knew any better."

Luke unzipped his bumbag and lit his first cigarette for some time. Watching his face melt, Sparrow figured it was the sweetest, smoothest lungful of tar he'd ever tasted. It made him want one, too. Luke narrowed his eyes as the coolness infused his veins. The horizon shimmered like a sine wave.

"Christ," he said. "Where the hell are we going? Who even are you?

I barely know you." He spoke half to himself and half to the only other souls in a thousand-mile radius.

Bob looked across at Sparrow. They exchanged smiles.

"We're just two ordinary guys tryin' to do the right thing," Sparrow replied earnestly.

"Nurse knows best," said Bob. "C'mon, I'll drive."

29

Kimberley & Pilbara / Wilinggin & Yindjibarndi Country, 1981

Bob

It took time to bury the body. Fortunately, all the implements for digging a grave were on hand. Holes and trenches littered the terrain like craters on the moon – all I had to do was pick the longest, deepest one and fill it in. But I had to work quickly. Dawn came fast in that part of the country and the circling dingoes would not be denied.

Even laid out on his side, the bastard looked tall. A mess of legs and arms, a squashed praying mantis.

Jesus fucking Christ. What had I done . . .?

There was no time. Dirt. Dirt covers all. I started digging.

A sudden thunderstorm before midnight softened the clay and washed away the pools of clotted blood that had accumulated on the pindan. Removing my claret-stained shirt, I stood bare-chested, arms outstretched, feeling the cool rain. I looked down at the fresh grave, the misshapen mound of dirt. The body was now gone, hidden from all but the earthworms and maggots.

I scavenged the mining tools that remained, strewn across the newly moistened earth, and tossed them into the back of the truck. I dropped my strides, calmed my breathing, and relaxed my pelvis. For a long time, nothing happened. Then, I pissed blood, warm and thick. It was a sign of renal damage, the fallout from the duel. The night air had turned cold, it pierced my chest like a spear. I changed into a dry set of clothes from the car and was about to hop into the driver's seat and stomp the accelerator when I heard the murmurs.

They were coming from nearby, from underground. Or were they coming from the fork of a nearby tree?

Coo coo coooo . . . quo-orr quo-orr . . . chu-eep!

Well shit. It's just you. Hi.

Who did you expect?

Never mind. You scared me.

What are you doing, Robert?

Nothing.

I know what you did.

No, you don't.

I saw.

You saw nothing.

I did.

Well, I did nothing. Please. Please don't. I have to go now. Goodbye.

I slammed the car door shut. Fired the engine. Spun the wheels and reefed the steering wheel around. The butcherbird's whistle melted into the night, and the body disappeared into the distance. I thought about the parasites invading every orifice, feasting on decaying flesh, growing fat. I planted my foot and gunned the Volkswagen towards Mach 1.

I couldn't remember ever driving so fast – not even when we made the mercy dash for Bandit. I felt drunk. My face congested with blood, my vision blurred, eyelids swollen, eyes stinging. The truck rattled like an overloaded tumble dryer, the metal panels threatening to peel off. At that speed, luckless wildlife stood no chance, reduced to bloodied streaks on the highway.

The plan was simple. Get back to camp before shift changeover, pack as many worldly possessions as possible into a rucksack, and keep on driving. Simple plans are usually the best, particularly when you're staring down the barrel of a life sentence.

The vehicle's tyres slipped on the greasy tarmac, its trajectory resembling a drunk speed skater. What was done couldn't be undone, and now one mistake behind the wheel would mean certain death, or at the very least attract the attention of passing motorists or the authorities. Either way, it would derail my ingenious plan.

I was convinced no-one would believe me if I told them what had happened. By contrast, men often walked off mine sites without saying a word. It was only later that news got around of the better offer they had received elsewhere. Or the gutful they had had. Or the neglected wife who had threatened divorce. Others disappeared with no explanation or logic whatsoever. As per the Pilbara protocol, no further questions were asked. Who knew how many deaths – accidental or intentional – had precipitated a subsequent disappearance. Probably a lot. My situation was not unique. To dwell on it was only wasting energy.

But there was one big thing working against me. Our lucrative find and vocal disagreements were common knowledge in the camp. The stakes were high and the friction palpable. Blood had been spilled over less. Which was why I knew that the only true way to avoid all the accusatory fingers was to give them nothing at which to point.

Shit. The tobacco tin. I didn't know where the hell it was. Surely it had been moved from the truck's glovebox. Surely Stretch had been carrying it in his pocket. Surely it had remained in his pocket since. Surely I had buried *all* the evidence and the painful memories that went with it. Surely, surely . . .

I nearly snapped my ankle slamming the brake pedal. The screech of tyres was so loud it made my ears hurt. The truck fishtailed for a few heart-stopping seconds, threatening to tip and roll. Clamped to the steering wheel, my arms jolted from their sockets under the strain. A great cloud of burnt rubber mushroomed into the atmosphere.

My hand shaking, shoulder aching, I reached for the glovebox. My blistered fingers could barely twist the small latch. I snatched my hand away as if bitten. The lid fell with a light thud in the quiet night to reveal if I was or I wasn't the stupidest man alive.

The darkened clump of dilapidated asbestos buildings came into view. I smiled for the first time in a long time.

The camp was a ghost town before shift changeover. It was my best chance at going undetected. The key was to time my arrival for the moment before one shift of men got up for work and the other returned from their all-nighter at the mine. The clock on the dashboard read a quarter to five. I had fifteen sweet minutes.

I went to my donga covered in dry sweat. There were no roommates to startle awake as I flicked on the unit's single dull bulb; all three were still working the night shift. Grabbing the canvas rucksack out from under my bunk, I filled it with whatever I could find – clothes, maps, loose change, cigarettes. My jaw and cheek still felt sore from the brawl and I rubbed them with scratchy fingers to facilitate blood flow. I opened my palm, closed my eyes tight, and with a swift uppercut using the base of my palm, snapped my jaw back into place at the third agonising attempt.

I had entertained but eventually ruled out the idea of pillaging Stretch's donga. As unlikely as it might have been for Stretch to have left the camp without his belongings, especially his books, it would it look more dubious if I were caught rummaging through them. And while Stretch and I absconding from the camp at the same time looked suspicious, we could always have just left together. It was no coincidence. After all, we were sitting on a fortune, we had a bloody good reason. People would believe it. The next time we would be sighted would be on the front page of a major metropolitan newspaper, clinking champagne glasses as we announced our find and the start of a new business venture as mining magnates.

The Volkswagen's engine turned over at the second attempt and I bid the camp a final adieu with an upturned finger and a gob of dry spit. I squinted at the dashboard. In and out in nine minutes and with not a single soul being the wiser.

I watched the camp grow ever smaller in the rear-view mirror. I'd done it. I was free. A criminal mastermind.

I found myself smiling and reached for the radio to heighten my mood even more. I pushed whatever cassette had been rattling into the player and turned the dial as far right as it could go. The high-pitched screech and Lothario swagger of Bon Scott became my co-pilot over the next two hours, the AC/DC tape being turned over six times until it pleaded for mercy. I sang at the top of my lungs with the windows down. There was no law against that and my speed was no longer eye-catching or life-threatening. I was just some guy enjoying the road, the countryside, the music, a balladeer.

A second storm, this time electrical, rolled in around Wittenoom. I flicked on my windscreen wipers and reduced my speed. Lightning was always more intense in the desert and positively fearsome over a ghost town. Everything in the Pilbara was amplified – the drinking, the violence, money, risks. It was what had drawn me there in the first place. The rain rinsed away the red dirt from the windscreen. Only a year earlier, the West Australian government had announced it would be condemning Wittenoom in response to widespread contamination fears over blue asbestos. What was once sprinkled like fairy dust on gardens, playgrounds and footpaths now lodged in people's lungs, causing inflammation and shortness of breath. Most of the town's residents had ignored warnings and stayed in the area; hardy country folk were not easily scared off by a few measly coughs and wheezes. I wound my windows up and flew through the town without stopping.

With the first rays of the new day warming my now swollen jaw, and with Wittenoom in my wake, I knew I'd made it. I eased off the accelerator, applied the brake, and let the Volkswagen roll to a gentle stop by the roadside.

It was only then, as I stepped from the vehicle and inhaled the fresh morning air, that the little hydraulic valves inside my head released, and silver rivers of tears flowed freely down my cheeks.

30

Kimberley / Wilinggin Country, 2017

A flyspeck on the horizon. Bob had recognised something – a landmark, a tree. He stamped the accelerator to the floor. Luke's head flipped back. Sparrow gripped his seat. The front half of the van burned with the searing heat of acceleration, while the back half vibrated like a spin dryer. Bob hunched over the steering wheel, pressing down on it with his full weight to maintain the van's speed and course through the pindan. He hit the brakes late, almost throwing them out the windscreen. Seat belts were inconsequential. The skid lasted forever.

Sparrow slowly let his eyes flicker open. Was he dead? It was as hot as hell and the landscape littered with just as many dry skulls. The dust cloud encircling the van took a full minute to dissipate. Everyone coughed up a lung.

"Well," Bob said, baring his teeth. "That's it, we're here."

"We're here?" Sparrow said. "This is it?"

"I think so. I think we're here."

Luke looked at them all confused. "Where the fuck are we?"

Through the chipped windscreen, there was nothing of note. Tufts of grass, bent trees, a dry creek bed with small pools of water, some crumbling anthills.

"We're here?" he asked. "We're where?"

Bob wheeled the van around, parked it under the nearest shady tree, rolled down all the windows and turned up the air conditioner to max. Sparrow reached into the back seat and casually grabbed the gardening equipment. Bob started whistling a melodic tune.

"Alright, mate?" he said. "You okay here, got enough water and food? Does your bag need emptying?"

"Huh, what? Wait, where the hell are you guys going?"

"What's wrong?" Sparrow asked. "Earlier today all you wanted was for us to go our separate ways. So, Merry Christmas."

Luke said nothing. Earlier in the day had been on his terms.

"Relax, son," said Bob. "We'll be back. Unless, of course, we drop dead out there in the heat. Which is possible, even probable. If we're not back in an hour, just come find us."

"Out where? Huh? Come find you? How? Where the hell are you guys going?"

Bob raised a big plastic water bottle to his parched lips. It was warm, virtually boiling, but he sucked on it like mother's milk.

"Gotta ... run an ... errand," was the extent of his explanation between gulps. He re-inverted the bottle until it imploded with a crack.

The last thing Bob did was insert a fresh AC/DC album into the car stereo. He hit repeat and cranked the volume as far as it would go. It helped to drown out Luke's stream of four-letter words. Together with Sparrow, Bob lumbered into the distance with a second water bottle in one hand and tools in the other, using them as a trekking pole.

"I never thought we'd get here," said Sparrow. "I totally doubted you."

"That's understandable," Bob said. "And we're not there yet, we still need to find the spot he's buried."

"You didn't mark it?"

"The grave? No, no way."

"Christ ..."

They walked on the soft soil. Bob said he wanted to slip off his shoes and feel the once-familiar warmth of the desert earth between his old crooked toes.

"I feel strangely calm," he added. "Thank goodness for the recent rain, it'll make digging easier."

Bob approached the ground with caution at first. As if the body were still alive.

"Is this the spot?" Sparrow asked. "Should I dig here?"

Bob assessed the surroundings, the landscape, comparing what he saw to his mind's eye, and briefly checked the newspaper clipping, which he also showed to Sparrow. The young cop studied it and thought it looked right, or at least, didn't look wrong. The land that time forgot. The anthills had been gentrified, a new generation of insects having taken up residence, renovated, extended. The heat felt like there were six suns in the sky. No hint of a breeze.

"It's hardly changed in three decades," Bob said. "I think dig here."

Sparrow placed his boot over the pitchfork's tines and plunged them deep into the crumbly earth. As he extracted misshapen clumps of heavy dirt, placing them to one side, Bob's eyes grew teary.

"Hey, mate?" Sparrow said. "You okay?"

"I'm alright," Bob replied, wiping his face. "After so long, you'd think I'd be over it."

The first place that Sparrow dug proved to be wide of the mark. It took several cubic feet of excavated dirt and cost him a kilo of sweat before Bob realised. The second location, five metres north of the first, yielded the same result. The third, three metres east, and the fourth, two metres south, was just more goddamn dirt.

"I'm glad you're here, mate," Bob told Sparrow. "Physically, there's no way I could've done this much digging – especially in this heat."

Sparrow nodded numbly, didn't speak, saved his energy. He arched his back, making it crack, and squinted into the western sky. The afternoon sun burned like hellfire. Their water supplies were dwindling rapidly and soon the daylight would, too. And it was the light that was their biggest obstacle.

"There was no moon that night," Bob said. "My memory's cloudy."

Sparrow implored himself to keep going, to find the strength, but was fast running out of shoulders, arms and spine. In truth, he hadn't dug so much in his life, not even as a kid in the country.

Bob had started muttering to himself. "Fuck me," he said out loud. "You idiot. You come all this way, drag an innocent cop from the city, survive all manner of shit, nearly get your head blown off, and you forget to bring a fucking metal detector."

"Metal detector?" said Sparrow. "Jesus. Is that what we need? For a body?"

"It might've helped, yes. I'm no Lang Hancock, I don't know exactly where the treasure is."

Sparrow scoffed a laugh. "Lang fucking Hancock!" he said. "That prick once had the idea of herding my people into one area and doping the water with a chemical that made us sterile. A proud Australian, a national hero."

Sparrow threw down his pitchfork in disgust. It made a dull clank as it wobbled to rest. He sat down in the dirt, unsure if he would ever get up again. Caked with dirt, his boots were twice their normal weight. He raised his plastic bottle to the sky and poured the last of the water down his dry throat. He caught his reflection in the bottle and saw his face was the colour of concrete. This bloody pensioner would be the end of his police career, and potentially even his life.

Sparrow approached him, put a hand on his shoulder. "Mate," he said. "I dunno what else I can do, I can hardly dig up the entire State. It's down to you now. Shut your eyes, slow your breathing. See with your mind, listen for the land's secrets, talk to the spirit of mining . . . or some shit."

Bob stood perfectly still and closed his eyes.

"What do you see?" Sparrow asked.

"Nothing yet. I can feel the drops of sweat evaporating on my skin, the dull thump of blood in my veins."

"Give it a moment . . ."

Another minute passed, then two. Bob breathed. Sparrow crouched. The wind blew hot dirt into their faces.

And then Bob snapped his eyes open to reveal a determined gleam. Bending down, he retrieved the fork and strode ten paces left in a diagonal, paused, and then ten to the right in another. There, he made a small incision in the earth.

"Here," he said. "This is the spot. Right here."

Sparrow looked up. His eyes were weary, doubtful.

"There? Are you sure this time?"

"Definitely sure. Here, mate. Dig here."

Sparrow shambled over and dug. There was a sound at first. A thud, then a scrape. Sure enough, Sparrow felt resistance; he'd hit something. His eyes protruded from their sunken sockets, his fifth wind kicked in. He swapped his pitchfork for the shovel. And then he dug and dug until he too was just another molecule of outback dust.

Sparrow felt a fleeting ratchet of panic. If he hadn't been a policeman, what he was doing would be a crime centuries old, a dark practice that went against all righteous and religious codes. But this was also Western Australia. A man digging a hole in the earth was no cause for alarm. In fact, it was to be respected, even celebrated. It was practically on the flag – a shovel and a money bag. The entrepreneurial spirit was what had made the State powerful. Nothing to see here. Carry on. And good luck.

"We're doing the right thing, aren't we?" Bob asked. "It feels immoral, disrespectful, like a desecration."

"We're not disinterring a corpse," the policeman replied. "We're digging up an old skeleton as part of a murder investigation. Ultimately, we're doing what's right by the universe."

Sparrow was pretty sure he should be wearing some form of protective clothing. A respiratory face mask at least. After such a long time, the smell wasn't what it once would've been, but it still made him retch and feel light-headed. The Kimberley's extremes of intense heat and fierce rain had caused the decomposing body's fat and lipids to soak into the porous bones. Together, they conspired to unleash a pungency that was a cross between sharp cheese and sweet meat. What limited bacterial activity had remained, the elements had eaten away. Human jerky, preserved as sticky, waxy pillars of petrified calcium. There was no flesh to speak of. Sparrow had to remove his T-shirt and wrap it around his face like a bandit scarf to keep from passing out. His experience with dead bodies was limited. He was more used to dealing with the dead drunk.

Had the skeleton been buried in more fertile soil, the high acidic content would have likely resulted in its complete dissolution. But the barren clods of sand that Sparrow hurled to one side by the shovelful meant the bones had retained their shape. They were the same shade as the soil, the colour having seeped in, and had a rough consistency. It was as if they had been rubbed with sandpaper, which was essentially what had taken place over three decades.

"Christ," Bob said, taking in the sight. "He's enormous."

The skeleton had femurs like two wooden planks, ribs like hula hoops, feet like flippers. That Bob had shrunken with time and medication only underscored the skeleton's size.

"Hard to comprehend we were once a match," Bob said to the silent remains. "Sorry about all this, old mate."

Careful to not damage the disarticulated skeleton, Sparrow gently wrapped each of the major bones in separate garbage bags: femur, fibula, tibia, pelvis, spine, humerus, radius, ulna, skull. The ribcage had one of its own. He threw whatever small fragments remained into another. All fitted snugly into a large hessian sack. The preservation of evidence was crucial for a successful conviction.

Senior Constable Andrew Smith approached Bob directly. He stared into the old man's thin eyes and spoke to him as if for the first time.

"Mr Robert Cooper," he said firmly, "I'm placing you under arrest on suspicion of murder."

Bob nodded. He looked disappointed, which left Sparrow feeling puzzled.

"I thought you'd be happy," the young cop said. "Isn't this what you wanted?"

"It is, yes," said Bob. "I just never imagined this would be the moment. It's almost anticlimactic, bittersweet." He held up his wrists in mock surrender, waiting for the application of irons.

"That's not necessary," Sparrow said. "And I didn't bring any 'cuffs. But I don't think you're much of a flight risk."

"So then . . . what happens now?"

"We drive back to Perth. I admit to my boss what's been going on and hand over these bags to the forensics boys, who run their lab tests. You'll be held in custody until the results come through, and then we'll let the legal process run its course."

"Fair enough," Bob exhaled.

"I reckon my boss may also fly a more experienced copper up here to examine the site and see if we missed anything."

"Oh." Bob waited a beat before asking: "Do you mind if we keep all this from Luke until we get back? Hate to ruin our trip."

"Sure, no worries."

Bob raised a hand to his brow, wiped away the sweat that had pooled. He eyed the sky, clear and blue and burning.

"You know, mate, at times on this trip, I wanted to resent you," Bob said suddenly.

Sparrow made a face. "Really? How's that? What did I do?"

"Well personally, you did nothing," said Bob. "But maybe that's why. I just don't know if your generation is grateful for the world you now have. I see someone who is walking the same path as me, and it was a path that I helped lay. It's kind of annoying, I'm envious. But at the same time, it's also pleasing to see the change. You grew up in a part of the country that didn't accept people like me."

"Mate," Sparrow said. "You mightn't realise it, but they didn't accept me either."

"What . . .? Who didn't accept you?"

"My mob, my community. I kept who I was a secret for a long, long time. Did stuff on the sly. But a small town is a small town, you can only hide for so long. When it all blew up, I was treated like an animal, rejected, beaten and made an outcast."

Bob paused, then said, "That's pretty crap. I had no idea that still happened."

Sparrow let his eyelids droop as though he were sleepy, and his shoulders relaxed. "Yair," he sighed. "Things are better now, but there's still work to do. But that's also why I'm truly thankful for all you did, your sacrifices. Without blokes like you and what you went through, the fight you put up, I'd be totally fucked. You're like a bloody pioneer."

At that, Bob smiled his own gratitude.

"Hey, do you mind if I stay a moment, say a final goodbye?" he asked.

"Sure," Sparrow replied. "Just don't tamper with anything important."

"I won't."

"I'll take all this stuff back to the van and check on our cheery friend."

"Thanks, Sparrow mate. I couldn't have done this without you."

"Ha. Same to you."

They shook hands for the very first time.

"I'll bring the tools," Bob said. "You've got enough to carry."

"Ta."

Sparrow headed for the car. Even with a heavy ten-kilo sack tossed over his shoulder, he felt lighter than he had in days.

Bob

I made sure you had walked for the van and weren't looking back. Nothing personal, young Sparrow, but this one particular moment in our journey wasn't meant for your eyes. Not for Luke's, either.

By that stage, both my fear and excitement had passed. As the adrenaline left my body, I felt an almighty fatigue take hold, like a deep shiver. Through my actions, I knew I had deprived the world of a life, a great book, and who knows what else. This was now my chance to at least partly atone.

But my work wasn't yet done. I stood and prodded at the hole with the weariness of a man fighting an unending war.

Then I saw it. A dull metallic edge sticking up through the dirt, reflecting its first rays of light in thirty years.

Dropping to my knees, I began to tear away at the earth with my rheumatic hands, flinging dirt from side to side. I had another look into the distance, in the direction of the car, to make sure no-one was watching. Bending back down, I gripped the wedged tin and pulled. In the end, it came away easily, anti-climactically. I looked down at my grubby palms.

"Hello, old friend."

I held the tin up to my ear and rattled the contents. A familiar sound made me both smile and weep. I wiped my hands on my shirt and carefully prised the lid open. My smile grew.

Shoving the tin deep into my pants pocket, I found my feet, slowly, achingly. My legs screamed like molten metal was leaking into the knee joints.

Refilling the hole with dirt, I shovelled like a rotary plough, my adrenaline back and now drilling through my system. I patted the surface down flat with the curved side of the shovelhead and wiped my brow. Whistling again, I headed for the car with a spring in my step.

31

Goldfields-Esperance & Adelaide / Ngadjumaya & Kaurna Country, 1981

Bob

My truck idled on one cylinder by the roadside of the world's longest T-junction. After two days' belting through the red-hot guts of Western Australia on little sleep, I considered my options. The Nullarbor Plain stretching east across the continent lay to my left. To my right, the road back to the sleepy capital, and my former life.

It was a momentary hesitation. I yanked the steering wheel hard left and picked up speed to underscore my decision. It was only a spinning blue light on the outskirts of Norseman that finally froze me.

Shit. The bloodied clothes were still in my rucksack. If the cop decided to search the car . . .

Should I try to outrun him, was there any point? I doubted the old Volkswagen had it in her, and any attempt would only bring unwanted attention. Instead, I needed to rely on my powers of persuasion.

My forehead beaded with sweat as the copper approached. I placed my right hand on my left shoulder to conceal my heaving chest and wiped my brow with the back of my other hand. My jaw had ballooned in the preceding forty-eight hours, swelling and distorting my face to comical proportions. There was a fresh cut on my left cheek, thankfully away from the driver's side window. I was going to have to keep my head straight when talking. The heavy footsteps grew louder, closer. A face appeared. It had an angular jawline and a sharp haircut I could set my watch by.

"Good morning, sir."

I flicked my eyes right and turned my head only slightly. His slender waist suggested he was straight out of the academy.

"Mornin' officer!"

I heard my fake voice and reeled it back.

"Is, ah, there a problem?"

"You could say that . . ."

The constable let me go after a lecture on road safety and a warning to "slow down, cowboy. It may be a hundred kilometre straight stretch of asphalt but it still has speed limits."

"Yes, yes sir. Won't happen again."

The cop explained that his was the largest beat in the world. His days were spent trying to keep the peace between the blacks, the whites, the blacks and whites, the rival biker gangs, and between the bottle and all of the above. He admitted he "was losing all those battles".

"Got enough water?" he asked me.

"Yes, yes I do. Four gallons. This isn't my first time crossing the 'bor."

Crucially, there was no paperwork and no search of my vehicle.

"You have a good day, sir."

"You too, officer!" I said with genuine conviction.

I took no chances after that. As soon as the patrol was out of sight, I pulled the VW off the Eyre Highway, ripped off the number plates with a pair of pliers, dug a hole and buried them. I was certainly making the most of Australia's vast underground closet to house my skeletons. I then removed the truck's dipstick. Wrapping my bloodied clothes around it, I inserted the stick into the petrol tank and pulled it out again, halfway. I reached into my pocket and extracted a crumpled matchbook. Dragging a wooden sliver against the coarse striking surface, I leaned in, lighting the fuse that was the shirt's dripping, dangling sleeve. Backing away slowly before turning and sprinting, I dived for cover under the nearest dead tree.

Just another exploding fuel tank, passing motorists would say when they saw the ream of black smoke rising in the distance. In that part of the world, in such sun and heat, it wasn't out of the ordinary, no reason for concern. Carry on, nothing to see here.

Thumbing a ride was easy, even though I needed to wait a while. Outback custom did not leave travellers stranded, and truckers were always grateful for conversation. I had my line ready. I was "headin' back east, back home to the glorious City of Churches".

"Great, I'm headin' to Adelaide too," the truckie said from behind a thick black beard and dark sunglasses. "Hop in."

The cabin stank like Satan's armpit. The trucker's pasty white gut was the size of a small planet. It leaked out the bottom of his blue singlet and rested comfortably against the steering wheel. It was a look his new passenger and the former cab driver recognised all too well.

"Cheers, mate," I said.

"So where you bin, sport?"

"Kalgoorlie."

"Gold mines?"

"Yeah, workin' the Golden Mile."

"Ain't not much else in flamin' Kalgoorlie!"

"Too flamin' right!"

"And what's waitin' for you in Adelaide?"

"Me fiancée."

"Is that right?" the trucker said. He moistened his lips. "You got a photo of the little lady?"

My face went flush. "Not on me, mate. Sorry."

He paused. "Wanna see my girl?"

It was an invitation not to be declined.

"Sure," I said, hesitantly.

I expected the driver to call my attention to the photo of a young family on holiday taped to the dash, or perhaps hand me a wallet. Instead, the trucker pulled back the curtain to his sleeper cab to reveal a young Aboriginal girl unconscious on her side. I estimated she was barely in her teens.

"Not bad, eh?" the trucker smiled.

I nodded without speaking.

"Their wide eyes, their big honest smiles . . ."

"Where'd you lovebirds meet?" I asked.

"Picked her up at the truck stop last night," the trucker replied. "All you gotta do is flash your lights, the locals milling around know the signal. Offer 'em a soft drink or some takeaway food, and Bob's yer uncle."

"The evening edition's forty cents, mister."

I handed the boy two silver coins, helped myself to a tabloid newspaper from the adjacent bundle, and took a seat in the corner. The Greyhound bus station on Franklin Street was near empty. My overnight to Sydney was about to depart. I had just enough time to scan the headlines.

There was no mention of my name. And the only reference to the Kimberley was on page seventeen – advertising it as a new tourist destination. Relaxing my shoulders and stretching my neck, I performed a full body sigh of relief. I inhaled the cool, new South Australian air and exhaled the hot, tense Westralian air still clogging my system. I felt my head and face, freshly shorn of every last hair that morning. With so much of my skull now exposed, electricity erupted inside my head. My new look and new persona would take some getting used to. But it was also symbolic of a new life ahead.

On the university stretch of the River Torrens, near Grundy Gardens, I sat and ate lunch under a shady blue gum. Joggers and cyclists and dog walkers strolled past, bored undergraduates lay leafing through textbooks or napping in the sun, oblivious to the sacred ground supporting their weight. A gaggle of black swans spied my cheese and tomato sandwich. I shooed them away to no avail, tossing a half-eaten hunk of bread into the water. The swans leaped on it until they had torn it to shreds.

Their feasting over, they glided away in search of the next picnic basket or cloud of plump tadpoles.

I sat staring at the water where they had been, watching it ripple like nothing had happened.

Standing, I dusted the crumbs from my shirt and faced the river. I dipped the brim of an invisible hat with my thumb and forefinger, then turned on my heels and walked to the station to catch the overnight bus east to freedom.

32

Kimberley & Pilbara / Wilinggin & Yindjibarndi Country, 2017

Luke had smoked half a pack of cigarettes in the time that Bob and Sparrow were away. He asked no questions after they returned; not even when Sparrow tossed a heavy, nondescript sack onto the floor of the van. He clearly couldn't be bothered. After an afternoon spent roasting in the stationary vehicle, Luke said he was just glad to be on the move again and not left to expire in the desert. The sack's pungency had faded but a distinct smell remained. Both Sparrow and Bob reeked of the sour tang of sweat.

They eventually found the highway after much trial and error. Luke said he was unsure it was the same one they'd left however many hours earlier. Back again behind the wheel, Sparrow agreed. The inexorable stretches of road, the dark black ripples of tarmac, like the desolate backdrop, tended to blur over time. After spending so much time traversing an undefined region of map with minimal automotive suspension, the trio's weary eyes and battered arses were grateful to see smooth asphalt again.

The Hiace would usually have been off the road by that hour, safe and snug in a roadside motel around dusk. Instead, they were out in the open; as Mouse had foretold, at night all the animals came out to play.

They were soon exposed by the blinding halogen glare of spotlights that reared up from behind. The interior of their van was bleached a deathly white. A blaring car horn pierced the tranquillity of twilight.

"Shit," Luke spat. "The cops!"

Sparrow gripped the steering wheel with white-knuckle force and pressed his foot to the floor. His eyes narrowed.

"They ain't no police," Sparrow said.

"That's a novelty car horn," Bob added, turning around to face the glare. "And given the attention they're showing our bumper, it makes me think they know who *we* are."

The roo bar jabbed the van twice. It lurched forward, inflicting minor whiplash. Sparrow's heart banged like it was in the wrong body as sweat peeled down the groove of his back. He craned his neck for a better look but only saw the indistinct outline of a metal grille the size of the Sydney Harbour Bridge.

"Softening us up," Sparrow gritted through clenched teeth. "They'll come in for the kill shortly. Like sharks."

His grip grew tighter, his foot heavier, the slits of his eyes narrower. The dashed white lines on the road were disappearing so fast, they appeared solid. The van's labouring engine spewed an unholy roar. Its high roof shuddered. If the battery chose this moment to die, they were screwed.

A third jolt sent a shock wave up Sparrow's weary arms. His grip on the steering wheel momentarily loosened, sending the van into a minor fishtail. The wheels of Luke's chair rocked, their tie-down straps tensing, threatening to snap and send him rattling around the cabin. The hessian sack and its contents rattled around the floor.

"Hey! Hey, you fackin' cunts! Remember us?"

They had pulled up alongside. Luke said he didn't remember them, whoever they were. Bob and Sparrow were equally bewildered. Two bearded men in fluorescent vests. A heavily stickered four-wheel drive behemoth. That was like describing half of Western Australia.

"Ah shit," Luke muttered. "I reckon I can guess. I bet we met these guys with you-know-who."

"You sure?" Bob asked sarcastically.

"Not really," Luke said. "They all look the same to me."

"Me too," said Sparrow. "I can't tell any of you bloody whitefellas apart. But I dare say you're right."

"Cunts! Motherfuckers! Hey, remember, remember us?"

The abuse continued, barely audible above the hundred-kilometre-per-hour winds of acceleration. Both vehicles were neck and neck. The van was redlining, while the four-wheel drive still had gears in reserve. Sparrow rolled up his window just in time to stop a plastic soda bottle, which exploded on impact.

"What do you s'pose they want?" Bob asked, waving politely.

A sudden collision of the cars' side panels caused another fishtail, more perilous than the first. Sparrow's arms stiffened as he wrested the steering wheel back to its centre axis and their two left tyres back onto the road. Luke's wheelchair rocked again.

"Probably their money back," Sparrow replied.

"Not to mention our guts for garters!" said Luke.

A full can of beer hurtled into the van's side panel. Sparrow felt the Hiace tremble. Seconds later, a third missile smashed clean through the van's side window. The back of Sparrow's head bristled with shards of fresh glass.

"Jesus!" he said, trying to control the spinning wheel. "Holy shit. Luke, are you alright?"

Luke felt his face. It was intact. His lap and bumbag were littered with fragments of broken glass. A full can of Emu Bitter spun at his feet.

"Luke!"

"Y . . . yeah."

"Those bloody . . ."

For a split second, Sparrow considered slamming on the brakes and bringing the madness to a grinding halt. Surely, the two cars could just pull over. Discuss their differences calmly by the roadside like gentlemen. Come to some mutual agreement. Continue safely into the warm evening. There were rules against police pursuits that endangered public safety, but this was hardly a pursuit, nor was there any public around to endanger.

Sparrow checked the hessian sack, made sure it was still down by Bob's feet. Bob was now gripping his seat like a castaway in a life preserver.

The four-wheel drive detoured a sharp right through the dirt. In the distance, a road train hurtling towards them blasted an air horn and flashed its headlights. It was fast running out of tarmac and so were they. Sparrow eased off the accelerator as Bob eyed the highway and Luke fumbled through his bumbag. Together, they watched the red menace bounce through the scrub. Sparrow hoped it would blow a tyre or bog in a ditch or wrap itself around a dead tree. But it didn't. The speeding metal bastard kept pace with the van and soon rejoined the highway. It quickly returned to their side, bashing again into the bruised bodywork.

Bob looked across at the two men and again waved kindly. He knew it was pissing them off even more.

"These guys are certifiably crazy," Bob said. "They don't care who they kill tryin' to run us off the road – us or them."

"They're prob'ly high as kites," Sparrow added.

The road train blasted its horn again. It had even less room now and was not about to deviate from its lane.

The back of the van was unnervingly quiet. Sparrow was concerned. He turned his head.

"Luke? Luke? Luke, shit no!"

It was too late. Luke had pulled the trigger, firing a shot out the broken window, and then another. He would later swear that he saw the reflection of terror in the bearded men's pupils in the metal of his piece. The first shot ricocheted off the asphalt, disappeared. But the second found the mark, bursting the four-wheel drive's front left tyre and sending the vehicle into a tailspin. The Hiace puttered harmlessly away. Sparrow watched in the rear-view mirror as the four-wheel drive veered diagonally across the highway, its tyre shredded, thin black tendrils whipping the air. It skidded through the dirt and finally came to an easy rest in a plain of straw-coloured spinifex. The road train ploughed past, its horn still blaring as its thousand red tail lights receded into the night.

There was no fireball mushrooming dramatically into the darkening sky. Only an unheard tirade of cursing and a satisfied young man in the back seat blowing away the smoke from a steaming muzzle.

33

Sydney / Gadigal Country, 1981–1989

Bob

I was too excited to sleep aboard the Greyhound. The treeless Hay Plains halfway between Adelaide and Sydney appeared barren and blue. Every time I looked out the window, it felt like I was on the moon.

In Sydney, I stumbled off the bus onto a street called Eddy Avenue. I collected my rucksack from the baggage compartment and walked up the hill towards Oxford Street. I threw my empty cigarette packet in the first bin I came across and vowed to never buy another.

I felt like a hayseed, wandering the dirty streets, staring slack-jawed at the garish costumes, exposed skin, and high jinks on display. It wasn't even midday. The vast horizon that had towered above me for so long was gone, replaced with only a thin rectangle of sky. Now, it truly felt like I'd landed on another planet.

There were people everywhere, heading to work, going for lunch, shopping, sitting in cafés. I saw more souls in half an hour than I had in my entire five-year exile in the Nor'west. Every single thing in my vision was moving at light speed, people, cars, lamp posts, buildings. Or at least, that's how it seemed. It was tiring having people barging past me every few seconds or trying to fight my own way through them. I wasn't used to needing to fight for space, which I'd always seen as unlimited, not a luxury.

I sought respite in the first venue I found. Club 80 was a dimly lit establishment of meandering corridors, alcoves and rickety stairs, heaving with male bodies and laced with a stale, acrid odour like an old gymnasium. Minor earthquakes shook all around me. I was startled by the rampant promiscuity on show – to me, it had always been so hidden and shameful. Bars had replaced beats. Despite being a small molecule in the big scene, it was the first time in my life I had ever felt three-dimensional.

I quickly realised my muscular Pilbara body and shaved head didn't fit in. The trend was for waifs in tight singlets and even tighter jeans and lopsided hair don'ts. I looked like a piece of freshly quarried rock alongside exotic butterflies and tropical flowers. One of these meat market moths was a slim-hipped man with a fey, whimsical bent. He was the cheery towel boy who greeted patrons at the front counter.

"Hey, big boy, what's your name?" he asked me. "I love a uselessly bulky man and you're the most impressive slab of beef I've seen in months."

His name was Jose. I'd never met anyone with such an exotic name before. Or anyone like him. Jose had a roughly angular face the colour of caramel and deep-green eyes. My heart palpitated in tune with a hummingbird's wings. After a big night at the club culminating with the new dawn, I asked him out for a greasy breakfast.

"I used to be a radar operator in the navy," Jose said. His young face flickered to life with the flame of caffeine. "I'm from Santa Fe."

"In America?" I asked.

"New Mexico, which despite what people think, is actually in the USA," he said in a nasal tone. "I've, ahem, docked in Sydney many times."

"Is this another visit?" My tone was hopeful.

"No, I finally moved here a couple months ago," Jose said. "I'd had enough of going port to port. I wanted to settle down in a nice spot. The weather and lifestyle here were exactly what I was looking for. And the job at the club is great, I meet all sorts of interesting people. Like you."

I felt a sudden dizziness, my head filled with strange thoughts and emotions and visions.

Jose ordered a second fancy-sounding "cappuccino"; my coffee was "black". As he ate another mouthful of breakfast, I leaned forward and made a bold suggestion.

"Wanna go away next weekend?"

Jose stopped chewing.

"Where to?" he asked through a mouthful of crumbly yellow egg.

"Come on, hon. Do it for me?"

It was after dinner one night, in our tiny kitchen, that I politely made a small suggestion to Jose. Out of fear. Out of love.

"But I've never felt healthier in my life!" Jose said. "Nope. Not interested."

It wasn't a decision to be taken lightly. This was no blood pressure or blood sugar check. The test was still new and not always reliable, sometimes producing positive results that were erroneous. Such "false positives" were harmless, save for the people who later went and committed suicide. Those cases were the worst. But even seronegative results came with consequences – people failed to modify their behaviour, deciding that whatever they were doing was safe. Either way, the test was a Pandora's box.

"It's not just about feeling healthy," I said. "Even if you feel great, you can still have the virus and pass it on."

"You don't think I'm clean?"

"I think you're irresponsible."

"Or is it you don't trust me? I told you, I told that slut Adam to piss off back to Redfern."

Despite community voices that viewed Oxford Street and Kings Cross as a modern-day Sodom and Gomorrah, legislators had succumbed to overwhelming public pressure earlier that same year, 1984. Up to that point, you could've been sentenced to fourteen years' imprisonment. With the stroke of a pen, our underground lifestyle was decriminalised when it had once been marked for extermination. A decade earlier, it had been a clinically recognised mental health disorder.

The change, wildly celebrated, was like releasing the handbrake on a fast-revving vehicle. A continental drift quickly swept blokes from across the world to the lush decay of Sydney's eastern suburbs. My cab ploughed a furrow in the road between Kingsford-Smith Airport and Oxford Street, ferrying planeloads of holidaymakers and migrants arriving daily. With bathhouses, pubs, clubs, drag shows and dingy back rooms, the new enclave enveloped fresh arrivals in a fierce, hedonistic lifestyle that celebrated the dawn of our liberation. It was a way of finally demonstrating defiance to the mainstream, a one-finger salute to conventional morality. Starved of our yesterdays, there was now no tomorrow.

But I was concerned. I didn't know where Jose went on his nights off. At my insistence, he'd reluctantly given up the grimy club scene for a job as a snooty waiter in a swanky Double Bay restaurant. When I was out driving on shift, I sometimes called home from a public phone box and got no response. Jose later told me he was "in the shower" or "out buying takeaway". I saw increasingly weedy characters slinking around the streets or passing out on park benches. They included many locals we knew intimately – both acquaintances and friends – whose taut bodies had become thin and emaciated, with swollen eye sockets and hunched-over physiques. Afraid of breaking down and showing it, the gaunt masses withdrew, then vanished altogether. The community newspaper needed a whole extra section to accommodate all the obituaries.

But trusting Jose was only one issue. History was the other. Neither of us had ever discussed what brought us to Sydney. I was in no hurry to mention the outback circumstances that had driven me east, so thought it best not to probe him either. What if Jose had an equally wicked story he was hiding? And although I would never admit it, I lost sleep knowing my beloved had sailed the venereal seas for Uncle Sam. It was, after all, the woodwork out of which the bug had first crawled.

"It's not Adam at all," I told my lover. "I believe you when you say he's history. It's that I'd rather know where we stand. Wouldn't you?"

"Knowing didn't help that street kid when they found him swinging from a branch in Green Park," Jose said.

I blew out my frustration. "That kid had other problems. He was messed up on heroin. You know that."

Jose didn't reply.

"Look, this isn't really a decision we can make separately," I continued. "Either we both get tested or we both don't. And I want to."

Jose stopped what he was doing. He'd been absently drying the same plate with a floral tea towel for five minutes as I stood at the sink washing up in pink rubber gloves.

"No."

I took his hand. "Come on, babe," I said. "Please? For me?"

Jose exhaled. I leaned in and nibbled his ear until he started giggling. He was too ticklish. It was the cutest thing.

"Okay! Okay, Bobby, fine," he said, pushing me away. "But you first. You know I hate needles."

I hated needles, too.

It had sounded so easy in theory, as a couple. In practice, on my own, it was harder.

It took three false starts and three pints at a nearby pub before I walked into the clinic the following afternoon. The nurse who collected my blood caught a whiff of my breath.

"Fortunately, Mr Cooper, we're looking for antibodies, not alcohol," she said. She slapped a crooked Band-Aid on my forearm with a thwack. "There, all done. We'll call you with the results. If you don't hear from us in a month, call us."

That month seemed like a year.

Then my phone rang.

I sank to my knees holding a dead phone as a sudden and acute vertigo overwhelmed my senses.

Whatever had once propelled me forward in life had evaporated. I was suddenly mired in my own body. What was once the embodiment of health and vitality, of sun and fresh outback air, now repulsed me. My blood was a poison. All I could think of was a cold-blooded reptile full of deadly venom. Nothing Jose could say or do made me see otherwise. I thought he would be angry, but he showed me more love and attention than I could have ever imagined. A week later, his test returned the same result.

The scene replicated itself across Sydney. Fearful plumbers refused to fix pipes in restaurants where men like me had cooked and eaten. Dentists banned most of their clientele. Police halted random breath-testing from fear of motorists' saliva. Morticians stopped embalming certain bodies. Even in death, we were stigmatised.

I refused to point the finger in any one direction. It was futile. I might as well have blamed the screen door for letting in cold air.

The first doctor we consulted was stony and grim-faced. He told us, in no uncertain terms, to finalise our affairs. The second did the same, but in the meantime prescribed a tiny ray of hope: a drug called AZT.

Jose squeezed my hand as we left the surgery. "I've heard about AZT," he said. "Everyone I know who was on it is dead."

I heard theories about the bug's origins. That it came from sniffing too much amyl nitrate. That it escaped from a laboratory and was created by scientists to fund their research. That it was the Wrath of God, His punishment for acts of depravity. That it stemmed from some extreme new sexual practice concocted in America. But what was in no doubt was which corner of the community was harbouring the fugitive. A media firestorm engulfed the tabloids after three babies died from a contaminated blood transfusion. It brought about a modern-day witch-hunt. Vigilante gangs roamed Darlinghurst and Paddington the very next night, kicking in the doors of Oxford Street bars and bashing those inside. Rotten eggs were thrown at our front door, and a broken house brick through our front window. We were viewed as grim reapers harvesting innocent souls.

We started living differently, treading on eggshells, jumping at shadows. I was washing my hands and brushing my teeth every five minutes, scrubbing both like crazy, gargling hydrogen peroxide, couldn't stop feeling the glands in my throat. Worst of all was my relationship with Jose. We'd become consumed by the underlying threat from an as-yet asymptomatic infection. We hadn't touched each other in months.

The next night on Bondi Beach, Jose expressed his frustration. We were sitting around a crumpled sheet of newspaper laden with battered fish and chips smothered in lemon and salt. The paper's headline referred to our people as "diseased rats". It was Sunday, early summer, sunset.

"Jesus Christ, Bobby, I've bloody had enough," said Jose. "What's done is done. There may be a gun pointed at our heads, but I don't see anyone pulling the trigger."

I stopped chewing my deep-fried flathead and stared out to sea. It was still and calm; the antithesis of what was happening on shore, only a kilometre inland.

"The problem is the sight of the gun is *messing* with our heads," Jose continued. "Like I said to you ages ago, I feel fine. I think that's significant."

For the first time since the diagnosis, I muted my brain and listened to my body. It also felt good. No signs of nausea, night sweats, weight loss. Not even a sniffle. In fact, the only thing afflicting me was a lab result. A mark on a piece of paper, a tick in a box. I realised that I was the sea, not the city.

"To hell with what they say," said Jose. "Something's gonna take us all, one day or another. Whether it's a heart attack or cancer or this. As far as I'm concerned, nothing's changed, we move forward. We live."

Jose was sick of being a victim, mentally and physically. Like me, he'd seen too many friends wither into the shadows and then vanish altogether. His empowering stance brought us together again, our bond stronger than ever.

"You're right," I said. "Stuff 'em."

We chinked our beers and locked salty lips. We drove home from the beach in my cab.

Two days later, we found a pair of leather-bound men brandishing heavy implements in our living room. They went for Jose first, whacking him hard across the side of the head with a length of white PVC drain-pipe. His skull cracked like an eggshell, and he dropped like a stone.

I ran to his aid, but they were already upon me. My return to the taxi driver lifestyle had also returned me to my long-lost taxi driver frame. I was no match for the two cavemen and their Stone Age tools, which included a claw hammer and length of car bumper bar. But at least I got a good look at their faces before everything went black. When I came to, Jose remained motionless beside me on the living-room floor, a dark pool of blood next to his ear, his beautiful young face broken. The men were gone. Every wall in our house was covered in graffiti or smeared faeces, our furniture upturned or trashed. I called triple-zero. Blaring sirens raced us to St Vincent's. Jose remained in a coma in Intensive Care. I had a severe, grade three concussion that lingered, giving me headaches for weeks.

The police case fell apart. No surprise. I'd often had cops in my cab who told me about "the good ol' days" when pushing a bloke in the cold harbour late at night was considered a legitimate pastime. Young men were also found at the bottom of an infamous ocean cliff at The Gap in Watsons Bay. The police conveniently wrote up such cases as "suicides".

This was no isolated incident. The assailants were well known at street level. A few well-aimed questions was all that a groggy taxi driver needed to identify their likely drinking hole.

I pressed the tiny spark of a light on my digital watch and held it up to my face. Ten past midnight. It was unseasonably cold for March, a patina of frost dusting the grass, a silver drop of mucus on the tip of my nose. The mist of Bogong moths enshrouding the nearest street light made the night feel darker than it was. Claustrophobic Green Park sat directly opposite ground zero – St Vincent's – smack in the middle of the stressed city. When I wasn't driving my cab, I kept a bedside vigil in the ICU.

From where I stood, partially concealed by a large white eucalypt on the park's northern tip, I could already see the men shuttling between Oxford and Burton Streets. The quarter-mile strip of inner-city bitumen was bordered by a massive edifice of sandstone that gave the place its name. "The Wall" was the eastern side of the old Darlinghurst Gaol.

An hour passed. I felt the glands in my throat, tender and swollen, my immune system in overdrive. I blew into my cupped hands. A fenced-in mutt let out an anguished howl, followed by the noise of its owner ordering it to shut up.

It was peak hour at The Wall, which resembled an airport arrivals area. My eyes were weary from the constant glare of brake lights. Happy punters slammed their car doors shut and zoomed off into the night.

At that moment, and despite having quit, I would've killed for a cigarette. Well shit, I thought. I might just have to ask someone.

I heard a voice in the distance. The pub on the corner opposite Green Park's northern tip had called last drinks. More men soon appeared on the street, stumbling home for the evening, or into the park for a quick recreational detour.

I crouched behind the broad trunk of the eucalypt, waiting for my moment.

They were even bigger than I remembered.

"Hey, guys," I said. "Gotta smoke?"

The men were drunk, their reactions slow, uncoordinated. They had only a split second to turn before I was on them, bundling them to the wet grass like a rugby front-rower hitting a tackling bag. All my experiences rolling around in the Pilbara dirt were concentrated into that single tackle. And my fists channelled a night in a cold public toilet block that started it all.

34

Pilbara / Yindjibarndi Country, 2017

The men lay on their backs, three outlaws staring up at the twinkling constellations from a smooth patch of earth that Sparrow had swept clean with a handful of long grass. With only one functioning limb out of four, Luke admitted to being slightly worried about slithering snakes and scuttling scorpions. Meanwhile, the craggy lines on Bob's face were still beaming. He was trying to hide his joy, but his words betrayed him.

"They'll be fine, won't they? Someone will drive past and pick 'em up. You reckon? Yeah. They'll be fine."

"You can stop now, Bob," Sparrow said. "You're not foolin' anyone, we can tell you're proud as punch."

"They'll be fine, dude," Luke said. "But what I wanna know is why we didn't think of this before . . ."

With daylight fading and no sign of accommodation, they had decided to make themselves scarce from the road and camp out in the scrub. It was preferable to sleeping by the roadside where their past could again catch up with them, and it gave them a chance to properly experience the wonders of the Pilbara.

"Dunno," Bob replied. "But I'm glad we finally did."

"I used to sleep under the stars all the time as a kid in the country," Sparrow said.

"I gotta admit, it's been years since I have," said Bob. "And out here is quite possibly the best place on Earth to do it."

They were parked on the edge of a precipice. A curved red wall formed a natural amphitheatre, and after all the rain, an ice-blue waterfall plunged down its face forty metres into an emerald rock pool. Sparrow imagined himself being rocked into the gentlest sleep that night by an aquatic lullaby. Luke said they could drive over the edge in a Hollywood-style blaze of glory. That would certainly be spectacular, Bob conceded, but he'd had enough excitement for one day.

Bob reached over and grabbed his backpack, shoved in his hand, re-zipped it.

"Dinner is served, sirs," he said, handing Luke and Sparrow a can of chili beans. They had stocked up on supplies before leaving Port Hedland.

"Thank you, Jeeves," Luke said in an intentionally haughty accent. He added an exaggerated wink.

"Cool, ta," said Sparrow.

"Won't you join us for this sumptuous feast?" Luke asked.

"Don't mind if I do," Bob replied.

With a little strain, Bob opened the can and they passed it between them, the three runaways – the old rogue, the young pup, and the under-cover blackfella. They each took their own slurp of chunky hot sauce, which they alternated with smooth swigs from a communal bottle of Scotch. A real man's meal, alpha male grub.

Bob insisted they make camp on the van's western side, to watch the sun disappear over the gorge and protect their crusty faces from the swarms of dawn flies. His snubnosed revolver was positioned between them in case of a surprise attack from local wildlife, animal or redneck. Sparrow, quietly, would provide backup. The hessian sack of evidence sat comfortably on the floor of the locked van.

Bob curled his sticky lips and half-closed his semi-drunk eyes. He leaned in close towards Luke.

"So," Bob said, "come here often?"

Sparrow snorted a laugh. Luke was about to tell Bob to piss off when he was cut off by a sudden sound echoing up from inside the gorge.

Coo coo . . . coo coo . . .

"Holy shit." Bob sat bolt upright. "You hear that?"

"Hear what?" Luke said, tilting his neck.

Coo coo coooo . . . coo coo coo coooo . . .

"Listen. Down in the gorge."

"What?" asked Sparrow. "You mean that bird?"

"Not just any bird," Bob said. "I think it's a pied butcherbird."

"Are they rare?" Luke asked. "Bob?"

"Shh. Listen."

The slow birdsong nestled in Sparrow's ears, firing his synapses and transporting him to another time. Staccato songs under moonlight. But also the silence in between phrases, the shaped and beautiful waiting. It took a minute before the languid fluting again echoed up from the gorge, adding a reverberation to the still of night.

Peaceful and melodic, the butcherbird's distant call to prayer seemed to speak to them all. Sparrow smiled, as if his soul had somehow been touched by its lilting aria. Luke screwed up his pudgy face to decipher the unfamiliar language as the landscape continued its whispering. The bird's silvery tones spoke of the palpable sense of space, of quiet and calm. It told of an unhurried existence, of the intangible. On a rocky slope below, a mob of black-tailed wallabies fed, their movements dislodging small stones. A barn owl flew unseen overhead, its call echoing against the rocks. Seconds later, a bat made a chipping sound. Tree frogs croaked asynchronously, crickets chirruped incessantly. And then, without warning, everything fell silent. Even the waterfall seemed to stop trickling.

Luke confessed to feeling suddenly giddy, with no sound to stimulate him, to support him, the world spinning. He didn't quite know where his body was centred. Meanwhile, overcome with exhaustion, and with a full belly, Sparrow closed his eyes but kept listening, pretending to be asleep, leaving Bob and Luke to share a moment like old mates.

"Shit," Luke said. "You feel that?"

"Feel what?" Bob asked. "The whisky?"

"Nah, no way, I haven't had that much to drink."

Coo coo coooo . . . chu-eep! Chu-eep!

Sparrow breathed steadily, deeply, savouring the serenity. Time had slowed, perhaps even stopped.

"Lukas, mate," Bob said. "You know, we've been on the road a while now, seen nearly half the bloody country. But we can't do this forever."

Bob's voice came across an octave lower, huskier than it ever had. The temperature seemed to drop several degrees. It was a while before Luke replied.

"I know," he said. "I figured as much. You've obviously now done whatever the hell you came here to do."

"No, mate," Bob's raspy throat croaked. "I meant this isn't real life. Sooner or later, we'll run out of road, even out here. And that's if we're not hunted down first. I think we should head back to the city. It'll take a while anyway."

Luke breathed out. "Dad always promised he'd take me on a road trip," he said. "Even after my accident, he was still talking about it, planning for it. He was determined. My disability wasn't going to stop him."

Coo coo coooo . . . chu-eep!

Coo coo coooo . . . quo-orr quo-orr . . . chu-eep! Chu-eep!

The avian voices had doubled.

"Sounds like a pair," Luke said.

"A duet," Bob replied.

Luke snorted. "Like they're singers."

"They do covers too. As in, they mimic other birds."

"Really?"

"Listen."

But the birds had fallen silent. Sparrow breathed on.

"Dude," Luke began. "This trip. I'd forgotten what it meant to live. That bloody home crushed me. Things appear so different now."

Sparrow flashed an unseen smile.

"Is that right?" Bob asked.

"Shit yeah," said Luke. "Without you, I would never have experienced this magnificent bastard of a place

"I'll take that as a compliment."

"I've been thinkin', you know," said Luke. "Thinkin' about what you said."

"Mate, I said heaps."

"You remember, about my drawings . . ."

"What about them?"

"You told me you liked 'em."

"I did. I do. Swig?"

"Hit me."

Silence, but for the sound of Bob hoiking the bottle to Luke's lips.

"Like vanilla ice cream," Luke said.

"Until it hits your stomach and burns like hellfire."

Luke cleared his throat. "I had this careers adviser once, way back when I had legs. She told me about art school. That put me off at the time. It sounded fruity. But, like I said, that was way back when."

Bob exhaled an ancient breath. "I'm old enough to remember 'way back when'," he said. "But don't be put off, son. Times change. I've seen them. I've lived them."

"She was this real old bird too, the careers adviser. Had false teeth that kept slipping in her mouth. She smelled of fried onions and ex-husbands."

"Ha. Yeah, I know the kind."

"So nowadays there's all this other stuff, right? Not just art school, yeah?"

"Like what? What were you thinking?"

Luke didn't answer right away. Bob waited patiently; so did Sparrow.

"Shit, I dunno," Luke said at last. "Stuff like graphic design, logos, advertising. Or comic books, computer animation, video games . . ."

"Definitely," Bob said. "Where do you think all those awesome things come from? Someone has to draw them, create them."

"That's what I've been thinking."

"All they once had 'way back when' *was* art school, galleries, exhibitions."

"Comic books would be cool," Luke said hopefully.

"Got any ideas?"

"Not really."

Bob scratched his gravelly chin, making a sound like sandpaper across aged wood.

"What about a female outback trucker superhero?" Luke asked.

Bob's snort of laughter echoed against the walls of the gorge. Sparrow failed to stifle a giggle. He opened his eyes.

"And aren't there graphic novels these days as well?" Bob asked. "Someone else does the writing, and you do the art."

"Think so," Luke replied.

"Hell, even tattoo artists are—'

"Artists."

Bob turned to Luke, their eyes locking. They were sitting closer to each other than either of them had realised. Sparrow saw the younger man's pupils dilate so wide that his irises looked black, depthless. The blood in his face faded, as if equally terrified and excited by the prospect of what he'd outlined – a tangible future.

"Mate, you're all over it," Bob said. "You don't belong in a home with pensioners dying of dementia and cancer. Even with your chair, you're young. You got potential."

Luke turned away, stared back into the dark, silent abyss. "Ya reckon?"

Bob nodded and lightly tapped the young hand resting on his left shoulder.

"And I'll do whatever I can to help."

Luke went quiet again. Their ears attuned once more to the birds and insects and marsupials. It was as if the land was breathing. Long, slow breaths of the deepest relaxation.

35

Sydney / Gadigal Country, 1996–1999

Bob

"Hey, Bobby, check it out," a shirtless Jose jiggled in the bathroom. "I'm an A cup."

We laughed harder than we had for some time. I squeezed his man chest and tweaked his puffy nipples until he squealed with glee and pushed me away. Ticklish little bastard.

For a decade, we'd been treated like lab rats. The newest treatments slowed the replication of the virus but also came with a dark side. A new rash, a tightness, a pain. The cure made us sicker than the disease. My body bore the scars from a three-way war between organs, virus and chemicals. My cholesterol and blood pressure were through the roof, I was pre-diabetic, and all these new deposits of fat had found their way onto my neck, belly and chest. But what was less obvious than the pubescent girls' breasts Jose had sprouted was the chronic inflammation that had crossed the blood–brain barrier and begun wreaking havoc within his neural circuitry.

It started at a funeral for a fallen colleague. Jose couldn't stop laughing, and there was nothing even remotely funny about the eulogy. I was forced to drag him outside, send him home, and tell the other mourners he was running a fever. Later that same week, Jose was caught squeezing women's breasts on Oxford Street and saying, "Mine are bigger!", and laughing maniacally. I was forced to sweet-talk the local constabulary to prevent him being charged with indecent assault. A week later, he was caught loitering without trousers in a department store. But when Jose was found engaging in minor acts of indecency, flashing tourist groups and elderly excursions in Green Park, no amount of talking could keep the law at arm's length.

It wasn't so much a cognitive impairment as it was a complete personality transplant. Jose's frayed social filters were left flapping like a screen door in a hurricane. I was both perplexed and dismayed. I found myself questioning my feelings – he was no longer the man I'd fallen in love with. And when Jose finally turned on me, rejected me, told me to piss off, said he wanted to die alone, all I wanted to do was die right there beside him.

"Fuck you, you miserable whore!" Jose hissed. "Don't touch me ever again."

In the space of a month, our whole dynamic had changed. Our relationship went from being one of equals, peers with the same power, to one of accidental carer and begrudging dependent. Still in my thirties, I couldn't deal with a problem most people didn't face until their seventies or eighties. I made endless mistakes trying to appease someone who had become a complete stranger.

My doctor referred us to a neurologist. I made an appointment and tried to convince Jose to go but after being persistently told to go fuck myself, I went alone.

"It's just the way the disease works," the neurologist told me. "We're only now coming to realise it ourselves, we're learning about it all the time, it's still too new. When combined with the drugs given to control it, the virus accelerates the ageing process throughout the entire body. Your body literally ages faster, you might be thirty but feel sixty. We'd hoped the brain might be different, but sadly it's not."

"I see," I said, holding an uncertain hand to my temple. "And you're sure it's the disease? That it's got nothing to do with the day we were attacked?"

"Pretty sure," said the doctor. "I'm hearing similar patient reports from colleagues in America. Exactly the same thing you're describing in Jose has been happening across the Pacific."

"I see."

"The attack was some time ago, wasn't it?"

"Five years."

"So much time makes it even less likely," the neurologist said. "Of course, the disease will affect people differently. Some react mildly, some much worse. But I guess that's partly why you're still here today while so many others aren't."

The neurologist sat quietly, one set of fingers touching the other. He shook his head lightly, marvelling at Mother Nature's strange ways.

"Is Jose still behaving erratically in public?" he asked.

"Not so much these days," I replied.

"That's good," the neurologist said. "It's obviously a phase people go through. What about hallucinations?"

"None I can identify."

"More good news because we're starting to see that in some people, too. Anyway, all this means that you can probably look into finding a nursing care facility."

"What, for Jose? You mean, like an aged care home?"

"Exactly. Where he can get assistance. As time goes on, he's only going to need more and more help."

"But he's still so bloody young . . ."

"Look, no-one's really talking about this, perhaps because the prospect is too frightening. But there's a real concern in the medical community about the future fallout from this epidemic. The virus isn't killing everyone it infects, but it is impacting the body in invisible ways that may take decades to see. Gerontologists are worried about aged care facilities filling up with patients as it shifts to a chronic disease or exacerbates other medical conditions."

"I see . . ."

"But that's a worst-case scenario," the neurologist said cheerily. "For now, I have several brochures for good facilities you should consider for your partner right here in my drawer."

At precisely four a.m. every morning, my bladder sounded an alarm that caused my brain to kick me out of unconsciousness. It was a routine more accurate than any atomic clock. Tiptoeing barefoot across the cold kitchen floor, I stepped in a warm puddle. I sighed softly and found the light switch. An intrusion of cockroaches went scurrying for cover.

I stood before the puddle of urine. One of its dark-yellow edges had found the groove between the kitchen tiles and was now snaking its way under the fridge. I cringed at the sight of it, at the gall of the puddle, trying to escape on my watch. Next to the wet patch was a pair of slippers and a scrunched blanket that I recognised as a makeshift bed. In the living room, Jose was snoring, passed out on the couch in his moist pyjamas.

I fetched a mop and bucket and cleaned up. With a light kiss to Jose's forehead and the strategic positioning of an absorbent towel beneath his pyjama bottoms, I let the sleeping dog lie. Trying to move Jose had once led to a hard slap in the face, and another time to a sharp clip to the jaw. I stood, smiled at the sight of my dry tiled floor, switched off the kitchen light, and went back to bed.

My eyes flickered to life four hours later to the sounds of normality. The fluting of morning birds, the honking of traffic on the road outside. It wasn't the awakening I was used to, which only made me stress more. I forgot my slippers as I scampered down the stairs. The fact that I'd had another unsettling desert dream merely added to my anxiety.

The awakening to which I was more accustomed was the sound of someone wandering the house, opening doors, slamming cupboards, searching for something and preparing for somewhere he thought he needed to be. Sometimes it was the smell of burning toast, forgotten, or a kettle whistling, unwatched. Checking the deadbolt on the front door was still locked, I braced myself for whatever awaited me in the living room.

But it was just Jose again, standing dressed, watching the world through a crack in the curtains as was his wont. He was still in his wet pyjamas but he'd at least managed to put on a mismatched pair of sneakers. He looked over to me with the eyes of an infant.

"Can you take me to work today?" Jose asked. "I've got to go to work today, I can't be late."

"Good morning!" I said, my voice full of joy. "Yes, hon. Of course I can."

"I've got to . . . got to get to the restaurant early today 'cos . . . 'cos the boss wants me to clean out the kitchen area before . . . before the lunchtime rush."

"Of course. Let me just make us some breakfast first. Now let's take off your pyjamas so I can chuck them in the wash."

"Mm . . ."

I drew the curtains and removed Jose's pyjamas, then went to fetch a change of clothes. Jose stood motionless, silently waiting. His eyes ricocheted around the room, taking in the peeling wallpaper and piles of clothes and assortments of knick-knacks that crowded every dusty surface. I had stuck labels written in thick black marker pen under the photos on the walls. Jose studied the images as if they were abstract art. I returned with a clean T-shirt, jeans, underpants, and a warm damp towel. The curtains remained drawn.

"Where was that taken?" Jose asked, pointing.

"Which one?" I said, dabbing the towel across his torso.

"Over there, above the TV."

"That's from our holiday on the Gold Coast."

"When was that?"

"A few years ago."

Jose pointed at another photograph. "What about that one?"

"America. That's the Golden Gate Bridge in the background."

"Where's that?"

"San Francisco. The sun was out but the day was cold. We rode the cable car down to Fisherman's Wharf."

Jose looked blank, his mind a blizzard of white noise.

"We ate clam chowder in a bowl made of sourdough bread," I added. "It had celery and onions and even some bacon in it. You loved it, said it was delicious."

Jose continued staring. Trying to remember something he couldn't recall only made him glaze over. As I watched, I died another little death.

A black turtleneck sweater completed Jose's outfit, chosen to hide the inky blotches and swollen cervical lymph nodes. It was the terrifying signature of Kaposi's sarcoma, a weakness lurking in the waning immune system of ageing survivors. Every time I took a shower, I checked my own body for the deathly purple marks.

"There you go, all done." I thrust the curtains open for the world to behold a clean, dressed Jose. "Now, I'll make breakfast. Perhaps we could even fry up some bacon today, whatdya say? All nice and crispy and salty."

Jose stayed mute. He no longer had a favourite food or drink or TV show, but that was not the worst part. "Each new minute is as if the previous one never existed," is how the neurologist had explained it to me.

The vitriol had vanished. Jose now seemed happy to see me, even if he didn't recognise me anymore. At times, he called me Neil or Hugo or Philippe; former friends, or purely random names. But there was always that look in his eyes the instant he saw my face. It told me the embers were still glowing even though they would soon burn out.

I returned with the gooey scrambled eggs and crunchy bacon, which I cut into small pieces and fed to Jose one trembling mouthful at a time. I then held the back of his head and pushed three pills down his throat and force-fed him a glass of water, most of which ended up down his turtleneck. He squirmed under the weight of my plastic comb as I teased out the knots in his hair.

"Hurry up," he said. "I'll be late! I can't be late."

"Okay, calm down, you're ready," I said. I undid the deadbolt with the silver key that hung on a long string around my neck. "Let's go."

I left the dishes unwashed in the kitchen sink. The cockroaches re-emerged from their bunkers to reoccupy their playground.

Walking up Sodom's main street had been much less taxing with twenty fewer kilos and twenty fewer years. I was sweating and breathless by the time we reached Taylor Square. Jose's hand kept slipping from my grip. He'd recently lost a lot of weight and developed a subtle limp.

I was loath to admit that I'd seriously considered the neurologist's proposal for Jose. For about two seconds. Sticking Jose in a nursing home felt like throwing a Christian to the lions. Money was tight, and local charities were strained as the health crisis moved from an acute to a chronic phase. So the burden was left to Jose's family; in other words, to me. There was no-one else, or at least, no-one who seemed to care.

The few hours a day when I drove my taxi, a local sex worker sat with Jose. In return, she had unlimited access to the household pantry and laundry.

"I really like Jose," the girl told me. "He listens to all my stories and doesn't judge. It's like he's the only one who truly gets me."

I insisted on checking her forearms for puncture wounds, her eyes for cracks of crimson. The Sydney that I'd once known had changed and these were the most sensitive forms of detection at my disposal.

The fast-living, self-indulgent excesses of the eighties had collided with the rave scene of the nineties to spawn throbbing underground parties. To me, they appeared like nightmares come to life. The debauchery and creativity that came from being a marginalised subculture was gone. With liberation and the demands of the mainstream came a homogenised blandness.

My big brawny body had proved to be ahead of its time. The desire for slenderness, so desirable in the eighties, came to be associated with sickness; in the nineties, as a direct result, it was supplanted by raw masculinity. On our way up Oxford Street, Jose and I limped past a gym that, even at that early hour of the morning, was as crammed as the dimly lit nightclubs had once been. Men now strained every sinew to maximise their mass and transform their bodies into temples of brute muscle. Their oversized frames swallowed every poster plastered on every wall and lamp post, lumps of leather with steroid-plumped arms and barrel chests. This shallow obsession with appearance was Sydney all over. It had just taken its time to permeate into our world. And it bored me to death.

"Where are we going?" Jose asked innocently.

"Nearly there," I said. "Just past this next set of traffic lights."

On the street, perfect Botoxed complexions, tapered beards, and bodies with overwrought tattoos sauntered past us every few seconds. All of my old haunts had closed. Coffee chains had moved in, along with boutique stores and gyms and juice bars that sold sickly green shots of wheatgrass juice. Gone too was the sense of camaraderie that was once the eastern suburbs' heartbeat. And all around me, in every café and on every street corner, all I could hear was the hollow chatter of drug talk.

Jose was my last remaining connection to the past. The problem was the bug had robbed him of all his yesterdays and left him with no thoughts of tomorrow. I knew this would only get worse; the neurologist had told me so. In time, Jose's bowels would wave the same white flag that his bladder had already hoisted, and his voice box would close down. It was an orderly process, one organ at a time. And with the mind all but dissolved, the opportunistic infections would then arrive to take the body and complete the deathly procession. I would again be left alone. On the surface, Jose still looked young. That was nature's cruellest deception.

"Here we are," I said. "Are you tired?"

Jose nodded.

"Then let's sit down," I said. "Thirsty?"

More nodding.

"Don't get dehydrated again. Here, have some water."

I handed him a plastic bottle that he threw back. With my shoulders supporting his weight, I eased the younger man's brittle body onto the seat in the park like it was precious glass. The city's green lung was where I took Jose and sat for a while until he forgot whatever he was stressing about and I could walk him home again. It was also the site of my most inglorious hour when I had first stooped to the level of my aggressors. It hadn't ended there, I was forced to wield my battle-hardened fists two more times when my people came under threat. The anonymous vigilante enjoyed brief underground fame in Sydney's eastern suburbs.

Those days were long gone. There were no more familiar faces for Jose to not recognise. It was just me and him, the dotty old couple, sitting on a park bench holding hands, watching the outdoor Tae Bo classes and new mothers in tight gym gear pushing their jogging strollers in the mid-morning sun.

36

Pilbara / Yindjibarndi Country, 2017

The next morning, they all slept in. It was as if they had a collective hangover from the night before, the excitement and drinking. Luke claimed he had "an effing incredible night's sleep". Bob seemed less energised. Sparrow offered him the wheel, which Bob declined. He said the previous day's exertions were starting to catch up with him, which he'd expected might happen. Muscle pain was always worse the next day. He downed an entire litre of water with two co-codamols before they even set off, which wasn't until almost lunchtime.

Sparrow was worried; it would still be a few days before they reached the city. Bob's eyes were coal black and he was complaining of headaches. A giant vice clamped around his ears, was how he described it. His brain felt swollen and his mouth and jaw hurt from excessive yawning. Now that they had what they came for, Sparrow wondered whether to call for official backup, but worried he'd be betraying Bob's trust. He hoped Bob's malaise was only temporary.

"Bob, you okay?" he asked.

"My coffee is tired," Bob mumbled. "I should drink brain."

A whistle sounded in the distance.

"Aw, hell!" Sparrow said. Press any harder on the accelerator and he would be gunning his foot through the floor.

The van didn't make it; he was forced to hit the brakes. The ore train had beaten them to the crossing. There wasn't enough time to roll up windows; the cabin was filled with debris as the flying comet became engulfed in its own dirty tail.

"Whoa," Luke coughed. "Cool. About time we saw one of these."

Bob looked down at his palms, creased white. "Shit," he said. "Shit shit shit."

Sparrow craned his neck in the hope of seeing the end of the line. But he couldn't. He counted one, two, three locomotives. Not too bad, until halfway through the train he saw three more.

"Christ," Bob said. "It's a big one. We could be here a while. Kill the engine."

Sparrow turned the key. They were going nowhere fast. The train was descending a steep gradient, its dynamic brakes squealing and smoking the entire time, which meant even more of a delay. If anyone with bad intentions should pull up behind them, they were sitting ducks.

"Relax, dude," Luke said from behind. "I got our back."

Six million dollars' worth of loaded wagons later, the road was finally clear. Sparrow turned the ignition and they rolled gently forward.

The red sun was hovering low, threatening the red horizon. They'd not seen another motorist all day. Even the grey nomads had made themselves scarce. It was quiet, but an uneasy quiet. The local wildlife would soon be lining the roadside. And the local ferals would be out, too.

"Let's camp again," Luke insisted.

Bob adjusted the rear-view mirror and looked into the squinted eyes of their trusty tail gunner.

"Mate," he said through bloodless lips. "As great as last night was, after sitting in a hot car all day, tonight my old bones need a cool bed to lie in."

"But *the earth* is our bed, man."

The crags in Bob's dry face softened. A faint smile of satisfaction pulled at the shadowed corners of his mouth.

"Be that as it may, I propose we stop at the next motel we find." There was fatigue in his voice.

Luke took a moment to think before replying, "Yeah, okay, mate."

"I'll pull in as soon as I see something," Sparrow said.

A miscellaneous roadkill carcass was splayed out across the road. Crows were feasting. Seeing the Hiace approaching, they casually sauntered into the other lane until the vehicle passed, then returned to their banquet.

"Smart little buggers," Sparrow muttered to himself.

Luke was momentarily speechless when they arrived at their inn for the evening. As the van pulled into the L-shaped building, he started cursing his misfortune. He'd thought the odds of them "finding another half-star motel were effing zero". Running on empty and aching for a pillow, Bob mumbled that his "standards couldn't have been any lower".

The place looked abandoned. The car park was teeming with tumbleweed, while the office was unattended. In an unfamiliar cold wind, Luke's pale, adipose skin broke out in a rash of dark goosebumps.

Sparrow retrieved two paperclips from the glovebox and set about constructing a torsion wrench. He straightened out one of the clips, then bent it at right angles. He then straightened the second paperclip, but twisted it at one end to fashion a rudimentary hook pick. Approaching room number seven with trepidation, Sparrow applied light torque to the torsion wrench, which he scrubbed back and forth over the pins, pushing them upwards as he raked. It took five attempts before he heard a click.

"It's complete bullshit in the movies when you see people do it in one go," Sparrow told them. "It's a lock. And locks don't just give. It takes patience."

Bob stood before the first bed and let himself flop onto it with the lethargy of honey dripping from a spoon. A large ring of dust was liberated from the synthetic doona cover, falling to the floor in a perfect semicircle.

"Jesus Christ," he groaned. "I'm spent."

Luke crossed the splintered threshold and examined the latest flop-house he would have to endure. Dead bugs, soiled walls, an odour like swamp gas, carpet thickened with a decade's dirt and dust. He curled his lip at the expectedness of it all. Sparrow imagined he'd have preferred to have seen a decomposing human corpse on the bed – while inconvenient, it would have at least made the room vaguely interesting.

"Friggin hell," Luke said. "You sure we can't camp out again? Seems a step up in class from this."

But Bob was down. And he wasn't getting up any time soon. Except for one thing.

"Crap, I forgot," Bob slurred. "Sparrow mate, sorry to ask, mate, but can you please grab the stuff from the car?"

"Sure thing," said Sparrow.

He returned with their backpacks and the hessian sack, placing them all in a corner of the room. He then shifted Luke onto his bed while Bob helped himself to another two co-codamol tablets. They watched Bob, his Adam's apple bulging, trying to swallow the pills without water.

"Hey, dude, you feelin' okay?" Luke asked.

Bob's lips barely opened as he spoke, his pulse appearing in the jugular vein of his throat. His pallid skin was the colour of twilight.

"After yesterday and today," Bob said, "I can honestly say my shoulders have never felt lighter."

Luke scrunched up his face like a used tissue. Bob eased back on the mattress and the lines on his forehead disappeared like creases in an ironed sheet.

"What's the plan for tomorrow then?" Luke asked. "More of the same?"

"Tomorrow…"Bob said. "Hmm, dunno. I dunno about tomorrow."

"More drivin', I reckon," said Sparrow.

"Maybe we could go shootin' proper tomorrow, eh?" Luke asked. "Maybe go send some big reds up to roo heaven?"

Sparrow tried to picture roo heaven. He saw mobs roaming free across open hectares of lush grassland, and punching bags hanging from the branches of gum trees. By contrast, roo hell was a dry, fenced-in paddock with a crack sniper and unlimited ammo.

"Hmm, yeah, maybe tomorrow," Bob said. "Maybe."

"I reckon we've had enough gunplay for the time being," Sparrow said. He'd already confiscated Bob's firearm, much to Luke's chagrin.

They lay on their backs in their respective beds, staring at a ceiling with the consistency of stodgy porridge. Bob complained of rigors crawling through his limbs "like centipedes" and a head that felt like it was full of "sloshing oil".

Sparrow took a shower. He was in desperate need of a shave; his overgrown stubble made him look a decade older. It would be the first thing he did back in the city after stopping by the station. There, he would deliver the hessian sack to the evidence locker, and Bob to the attending guard on duty in the jail cells. Porter would have questions but Sparrow would have all the answers.

Bob and Luke were laughing by the time Sparrow returned. "What's so funny?" he asked.

"Bob was just telling me about the parting gift he organised for the director of our nursing home," Luke said.

"What?"

"A drag show!"

"Some old friends of mine," smiled Bob. "Owed me a favour."

"Blackford would've gone apeshit," said Luke. "I only wish I'd been there to see it."

Sparrow chuckled. It was fitting, that was for certain. He wandered into the bathroom to brush his teeth. He could barely hear Bob and Luke over the sound of rushing water.

"Argh, no," Bob said.

"What's up?" Luke asked.

"I remembered something."

"Remembered what?"

"It just occurred to me, in all the rush to get out of the nursing home, I never got you a Christmas present."

"Mate. You didn't need to get me a present. S'not like I got you anything."

"That's where you're dead wrong," Bob whispered. "Either way, do me a favour and look in your bumbag in the morning," he added.

"Sure, dude. Whatever blows your hair back."

"Whoa, not 'whatever' . . .!"

Bob threw a soft pillow that narrowly missed Luke's fat head. It tumbled onto the floor and landed with a light thud.

"I've organised something, some insurance for your future," Bob said. "To help you be the artist you wanna be. But you have to promise me. Just don't look in your bumbag until the morning."

"Yeah yeah, okay. I promise."

"Good."

Sparrow returned, his breath minty fresh, and lay in bed. Nobody said anything for some time. Bob's steady breathing hinted that he might have fallen asleep with the lights on.

"Bob," Luke said, "I reckon we could blast a hole in that wall over there and no-one would ever tell the difference."

The bed creaked as Bob shifted his weight. "You know," he said, "I reckon you're right. First thing tomorrow morning. C'mon now. Sleep. I'm tired."

Planting his feet on the floor, Bob groaned as he stood. He removed his shirt and let it fall where it may.

"Whoa," said Luke. "Cool."

"Yair," added Sparrow. "Very impressive."

It was the first time that Bob's travel companions had seen him shirtless, his colourful tattoo history finally exposed. On his left arm, the blonde: Marilyn Monroe in her white dress billowing up over a subway grate. The brunette was on his right: Liza Minnelli in her black bowler hat, stockings and eyelashes. Both captured in their heyday, now their shrivelled images looked as tired as the human canvas on which they were drawn.

"The poor girls are getting old," Bob said. "They used to look much better than this."

"I think they're beautiful," Luke said.

"They look like they've aged with you," Sparrow said.

"I never thought of it like that," Bob said. "It's a lovely way of putting it."

"You're beautiful," Luke added.

Bob looked up. Luke was grinning stupidly. Bob smiled back. Sparrow watched them like a proud parent.

"What's the goanna for?" Luke quickly asked.

He was pointing at the scaly reptile snaking its way down Bob's back. A big bear paw was stamped on his chest, marking the position of his heart.

"You know, mate, to be absolutely honest with you, I can't even remember," Bob said. "All I remember was it hurt like hell."

Bob chuckled and wrapped his two thin arms around the back of Luke's thick neck. He pulled up Luke's milk-jug head, smothering him in a warm embrace against his tracing-paper chest.

Bob eased him back onto the bed as gently as a butterfly on a flower. His calcified fingers took hold of the younger man's buttery hands and squeezed.

"You okay, mate?" Bob asked.

Luke squeezed half as many digits back. "I'm alright."

"G'night, mate."

"Night, Bob."

Sparrow shambled to the door. A single flick of the nub plunged the room into a profound darkness.

"Ah shit," Sparrow said. "Luke, how's your bag, does it need emptying?"

Bob

I knew you were asleep, young Sparrow. Luke as well. I could hear light snoring.

It'll be better this way, I told myself. Less traumatic. You won't see or hear a thing.

At first light, you'll wake and find a body in the tub. There'll be no sign of any blood.

You'll immediately attempt CPR but fail. An ambulance and police backup will arrive within the hour, but it'll be too late.

The emergency services will help Luke out of bed and wrap him in a silver Mylar blanket to protect him from the elements. Wheel him outside and strap him safely into the back of a police car. Offer him water and food and pain relief.

From the car window, Luke's big eyes won't deviate from the door to room seven. Eventually, he'll see a wheeled stretcher being pushed by a grim-faced paramedic. A crisp white sheet will cover the outstretched body. They'll take it away of course, far away, to a white room with cold tiles. What it deserved was to rest in the warm red soil.

The other paramedic will remain inside the room, rubber gloves on, searching, making notes. He'll see something on the floor in the bathroom, bend down, pick it up. The container will be empty. Reading the label, he'll shake his head lightly, regretfully.

You'll then curse my name and call me a coward. Hopefully you won't be in too much trouble for what you did; what we did. You're more than welcome to pin it all on me, and I hope you do. When the dust settles, I know you'll receive commendations for fine police work – maybe even a promotion – and also for bringing closure to a victim's family. I'll forever be the murderer who escaped prison, and don't mind being remembered that way. Ultimately, I did it all for a bigger cause. And perhaps I may have even taught you a little about what us old farts once went through, what we faced and what it took. I hope so.

Luke will look away as the cop car turns and heads west for Port Hedland. He'll tell them I was acting out of love, or words to that effect. Concealed by the silver blanket, his bumbag will sit heavy in his lap. He'll be in need of a cigarette. He'll pray his pack isn't empty.

With blood pounding through his stubby fingers, he'll reach out, clasp the slider and drag it across the two rows of sharp silver teeth. A hand will disappear inside the darkness of the bag, feeling its way past a mobile phone, wallet, chewing gum, lighter, looking for his pack, usually at the bottom. Instead, he'll feel a strange object, cold and hard. His hand will jerk back at first, uncertain, before clasping the unfamiliar item and retreating back to the light.

A dirty metal tin.

He'll study it for a moment, and then rest it in his lap. He'll struggle to open it with his single operational hand. But then he'll hear a light crack, and it will open, revealing its contents. His face will light up when he sees what's inside, shining back. And then he'll snap the tin closed just as his eyes begin to overflow with tears.

37

Pilbara / Yindjibarndi Country, 2017

Luke stared sideways out the window as the police car sped west towards Port Hedland. An ambulance followed close behind. In the city, an anxious and irate Porter had been informed of developments. Sparrow was now preparing his official story but personally, he felt grateful for the ride. It had opened his eyes to the injustices and sacrifices that had come before him and allowed him the freedoms he enjoyed today.

"Can I smoke?" Luke asked.

Sparrow flicked him a glance in the rear-view mirror. "Normally no," he said. "But given what you've been through, kid, yair, go on. Hell, I'm tempted to have one myself. Need a light?" He reached for the cigarette lighter on the dashboard.

"Nah. I got a Zippo."

Sparrow wound down the electric window. Luke's hair flapped in the hot wind. He smiled a thank you to Sparrow and reached into his bumbag. A look of confusion crossed his face. He withdrew his hand from the bag.

Luke held the unfamiliar tin before his eyes. He squinted in consideration, examining it for a long time, turning it at all angles. Was this another prank?

He sneered and extended his left arm. Flicking his wrist with a snap, he flung the tin out the window. Sparrow heard something crash onto the dry earth with a sharp ping, then heard Luke say to the empty plateau, "Fucken selfish prick."

The car drove on, leaving the dented tin behind. It had opened, spilling its contents across the dirt. The wind picked up, swirling the earth and sending the first few specks of red dust onto the tin and its contents, sticking to them, covering them, and slowly swallowing them.

Acknowledgements

Sincere thanks to Katharina Bielenberg and Paul Engles for incredible publishing, editing and support; to Martin Shaw for being an agent extraordinaire; to Kay Gale for copyediting; to Rachel Wright for proofreading; to Terri-ann White for insightful manuscript comments; to Maurits Zwankhuizen, Troy Hunter, Dexter Petley and Anthony Ferguson for careful reading and feedback; and to my family for their enduring love and belief in my books and writing.

As part of the writing of this novel, the author researched numerous primary sources – academic papers and published reports – concerning young people in aged care and also the framework for diversity in aged care given immense changes that have taken place in society over recent decades. The author acknowledges this is a complex issue, especially for dementia sufferers and their families, and has tried to convey these important themes with sensitivity and accuracy in this work of fiction.

The author has also used the place names of Australian Aboriginal origin as an approximation for the geography of the events in the story. Many Australian jurisdictions are adopting dual naming policies, which allow geographical features to be identified by both their traditional and colonial name. The author acknowledges the Traditional Owners and

Custodians of the lands, waters and skies where this story is set, and pays his respects to Elders past, present and future, and honours those who continue to share their wisdom and learning with new generations. He also acknowledges all Australian Aboriginal and Torres Strait Islander peoples as the first inhabitants of the nation of Australia and the traditional custodians of the lands where we live, learn and create. Sovereignty has never been ceded. This always was, and always will be, Aboriginal land.

PETER PAPATHANASIOU was born in northern Greece in 1974 and adopted as a baby to an Australian family. His first book, a memoir entitled *Son of Mine* (Salt), was published in 2019. Peter's writing has otherwise been published by *The New York Times, Chicago Tribune, The Seattle Times,* the *Guardian, The Sydney Morning Herald, The Age, Good Weekend, The Australian Financial Review,* ABC and SBS. He holds a Master of Arts in Creative Writing from City, University of London; a Doctor of Philosophy in Biomedical Sciences from the Australian National University (ANU); and a Bachelor of Laws from ANU specialising in criminal law. *The Pit* is the third novel in the series that began with *The Stoning* (2021) and *The Invisible* (2022).